A Girl
He...
In La-La Land

Whistler watched with the melancholy calm of a man who knew the worst would always happen. There were only two cars on the road, and they were going to have a smashup. That's the way things happen on a rainy night in La-La Land.

The BMW smashed into the side of the station wagon, bulldozing it across the boulevard and up onto the curb right outside Gentry's plate-glass window. The wagon slammed into a light pole, a fire hydrant, and a stack of newspaper vending machines, the doors flying open and the driver flying out.

By the time he finished bouncing, he was busted up like a porcelain doll. His blood was all over the place. But that wasn't the worst of it.

The worst of it was, another body came flying out of the back end of the wagon. It ended up sitting against the racks for *The Enquirer* and *The World*. A naked body. A woman's naked body. A woman's naked body without a head.

IN LA-LA LAND
WE TRUST

IN LA-LA LAND
WE TRUST

ROBERT CAMPBELL

THE MYSTERIOUS PRESS

New York • London

MYSTERIOUS PRESS EDITION

Cover design by George Corsillo

Mysterious Press books are published in association with
Warner Books, Inc.
666 Fifth Avenue
New York, N.Y. 10103

A Warner Communications Company

Printed in the United States of America

Originally published in hardcover by The Mysterious Press.
First Mysterious Press Paperback Printing: December, 1987

10 9 8 7 6 5 4 3 2 1

*In appreciation to R. R. Irvine,
who suggested the title . . .
for only ninety-seven percent
of the royalties.*

"When you got nothing to do, anything to do is something to do.
When you got nobody to love, anybody to love is somebody to love."

—Bosco Silverlake

One

CHIPPY BYRD was sitting in his lipstick-red 1976 Plymouth four-door with the vinyl top, showing his right hand full of ten-dollar bills while trying to get his left hand up Lacy Ohio's dress.

His real name was Chester Bucherleider. Her real name was Loretta Oskanowsky. Chippy fancied he looked a little like Fred Astaire and wore his hair combed slick and flat in the fashion of the thirties. Lacy believed she resembled, in a certain light, the younger Bette Davis. He was a petty grifter. She was an amateur doxy thinking about turning pro. Their courtship was a case of mutual and benign deception.

They were parked under the magnolia trees growing around the lot that serves the amusement pier jutting out into Lake Pontchartrain. Which everybody knows is in New Orleans. But which Chippy told Lacy would be in heaven if only she would unclamp her thighs.

Having counted ten Hamiltons out of the corner of her eye, and knowing what good times they would buy, Lacy was about to do as requested when another car, a white Cadillac convertible with a right front fender primed with gray Bondo, braked to a stop just short of the water, spraying rooster tails of gravel behind the rear wheels.

While Chippy and Lacy watched, two men—a big one and a little one—tumbled out of the car, laughing and scratching,

1

clearly drunk on something that made the night glitter and the world sing. One of them had something that looked like a soccer ball wrapped in newspaper tucked under his arm. First thing you know, they were tossing it back and forth. When one of them missed, it fell on the ground but didn't bounce. So they took to kicking it around, laughing like a couple of banshees baying at the moon.

Chippy was not surprised to find that his hands were wet. He sat there as still as a mouse, hoping the two drunks wouldn't happen to look his way. Hoping Lacy wouldn't honk the horn just for laughs. There was something about the two men that gave him warning. His instincts told him they were the sort who would kill him and rape Lacy just for the hell of it. Or maybe they'd do it the other way around. He didn't know how he knew it, but he knew it, and suddenly he realized that Lacy knew it too.

The little one gave the ball a hell of a boot. The big one made a dive at it and missed. The ball scooted into some reeds growing in and around the water. They went down on their hands and knees, hunting around for maybe five minutes. When they stood up, all they had was mud up to their knees and elbows.

"The hell with it," Chippy heard the little man say.

"For Christ's sake, it's gotta be around here somewheres," the big one said. "It couldn'ta grown itself legs and walked away."

"Well, I don't give a fuck. If we can't find it, nobody else is gonna find it. Barcaloo said lose it, so we lost it, right? Didn't we just goddamn lose it?"

The big man started to giggle and laugh and slap his thighs with his big, meaty hands. Then he got serious. "Barcaloo's gonna be mad as hell we don't tell him we buried it like he tole us."

"I'm gonna be mad as hell you don't shut your mouth. You're worse than a fuckin' cunt the way you harp on things. The damn thing sunk down to the bottom of the goddamn lake. What you want me to do, *dive* for it?"

"Fuck it," the big guy said.

"That's what I said," the little man said. "All I ask is just you should act a little reasonable."

"Well, I just said fuck it, didn't I?" the big guy said, getting into the car on the passenger side.

"That's all I ask," the little man said. He kicked the motor over, and the Cadillac squealed out of the lot.

Chippy and Lacy sat there wondering.

"What the hell was that all about?" Chippy said.

"I don't want to know," Lacy said.

"Where was we?"

"We was just about to drive me home."

"There's nothin' to worry about. They're long gone."

"They might get a notion to come back."

"Why the hell would they want to come back?"

"To look for whatever it was they was kickin' around."

"You heard 'em say screw it."

"I also heard one of 'em say Barcaloo would be mad if he found out they didn't bury it. If two people like that are afraid of this Barcaloo, I don't want to be here if Barcaloo decides to come around and see if they did what he told 'em to do.

"My God, what in the hell is that?" Lacy squealed.

Chippy looked where she was looking and saw the comical obscenity down at the water's edge.

"Nothin' but a possum."

"Yech. Ain't he the ugly thing? What's it doin'?"

"How the hell would I know?"

What it was doing was dragging the round thing wrapped in newspaper out of the water. The wet paper shredded away.

"Chase that thing away," Lacy said.

Chippy turned on his headlights. The slow-witted creature turned to the light, blinking rapidly, dazzled but unafraid. One paw remained on top of the object of its interest.

Chippy picked up the sawed-off baseball bat he kept on the floor of the car in back and opened his door.

"Where you goin'?" Lacy asked.

"Chase that goddamn possum the hell away," Chippy said, showing how brave, how manly, how fuckable he was.

He walked up to within ten feet of the possum. It looked at him like an old man without his specs. Chippy could see that the animal was trying to work it out if the thing he'd found was worth fighting for.

Chippy got a good look at the prize the possum held.

"Oh, dear fuckin' me," he yelled.

The possum took off at a shambling run.

"What is it? What is it?" Lacy shouted from the car.

It was a head. Mangled and swollen. Skin broken here and there. One eye opened, one eye closed. A head with shiny black hair. A human head.

Now, how the hell was he going to tell her *that* without queering his chances of getting into her pants anytime that night?

Two

I T WAS well after one A.M., and a party was still going strong at Walter Cape's house on top of Hollywood's highest hill. He wouldn't have it called a mansion. That smacked of privilege.

The entire hill had been chopped, channeled, and honeycombed to create ten thousand feet under roof that rivaled, if it did not surpass, the old Xanadus of the movie moguls whose lusts had been commonplace and acts of evil simple.

There were those who laughed and sneered at it, but no one he'd ever met, man or woman, would not have kissed his proverbial ass in MayCo's window to have a weekend in one of the incomparable bedroom suites or an invitation to one of his fabulous parties where deals were cut and fortunes made.

There were whispers about other, even more exclusive, evenings when actresses of considerable fame pranced around on stiletto heels wearing nothing but horsehair tails belted to their rumps and men of wealth and power rode them bare-assed. Talk of delicious crimes against nature committed with young actresses. Sins against God involving children.

Cape consumed high-concept but acted low-profile, in constant subtle conflict between his public and private lives.

There had been two hundred people at the party. There were still about a hundred left. The diehards. The greedy. The fearful ones who just knew something earthshaking would happen the minute they got in their automobiles and drove out of sight. Something spectacular. A ten-million-dollar movie deal; a cherry vintage Rolls-Royce put up for sale at a bargain price; a drunken actress upended bare-assed in the punch bowl, ready to be buggered by one and all.

Others who waited for a talk with Cape waited for a deal.

Cape had worked the crowd like a snake-oil salesman, touching flesh, bumping asses, laughing up a storm. Flashing, dashing, gliding across the costly carpets with the smooth assurance of a winning politician or a pope. Now, in the quieter shank of the evening, when many were drunk and most were winnable, he offered a quieter performance, a twinkling, slightly weary eye and the face of everyone's favorite uncle.

He tapped a woman wearing beaded turquoise satin on the rump. She turned around, smiled, and followed him down a long hall into a small office paneled in wood and furnished in leather. Butterflies, pinned to green felt and framed in walnut, hung on the walls.

He refreshed the glass she had in hand with three fingers of Scotch and asked her if she wanted ice. She shivered, bare-armed in the air-conditioned chill. He went over to the Adams mantel and touched a button. A fire flamed to life amid a pile of realistically sculpted logs.

"Ain't we excessive?" she said as she sat down in the chair closest to the hearth. "Chill the air and light the fire?"

He sat down in the facing chair.

"Atmosphere counts for plenty, May."

"I do better in a stable," she said.

May Tuckerman liked to say that she, like Otis and Dorothy Chandler, was in the communications business. They owned the *Los Angeles Times*. She owned the biggest string of shopping guides in the state, covering the territory from Monterey County in the north to San Diego and Imperial Counties in the south and out to the Nevada border to the east.

She liked to say that the Chandlers might influence more people when it came to national and international affairs than she did, but when it came to state and local issues, she was the one with the clout. Ask any sucker who ran for office without calling on old May for a cup of tea.

She was no Dorothy Chandler in other ways. Her interest in the pursuit of finer things was less than minimal. A rousing performance of *Oklahoma!*, a recording of Glenn Miller's "Chattanooga Choo-Choo," the tap-tap-tapping of a tap dancer's flying feet was her style. Steak and potatoes, whiskey and a beer chaser, straight fucking, nothing fancy, these were what suited her best. She had the typical American preference for an overloaded plate.

She dressed the part in jeans and flannel shirt. When events demanded she wear an evening dress, she was not one bit shy about squeezing into bugle beads and satin a size too small, even though she was the first to say that she had an ass six ax handles wide and tits like twin cannons.

Fifty, she looked forty, screwing no man over thirty-five. Preferably young gardeners or telephone linemen. Rich, she played poor, driving around in a much-used and battered pickup truck that reeked of the horse shit collected on her ranch in the Malibu foothills where she kept thoroughbreds and quarter horses side by side in equal-opportunity stalls.

She didn't have a husband and didn't want one. There were no men available who could offer her more money, more excitement, more security, or more power than she had already. Besides, she often said, she'd get a husband and all of a sudden some slick magazine would have him listed among the fifty most powerful people in the city and she'd be nothing but the little woman doing good works. She was self-made, she often said. For sure, no man had ever made her.

"Great party, as usual, Walter."

"Enjoying yourself?"

"I notice you got a lot of new waiters working it."

"If there's one you fancy, May. They're all aspiring for one thing or another."

"You know, Walter, you would have made a great pimp, you ever wanted to give up being a millionaire."

"It's not the money, it's the game. You know that, May."

"Why have you invited me into your inner sanctum, Walter?" she asked with a hint of uncharacteristic coyness. She glanced over at a huge American Wooten desk, the kind with thick doors that open like a clam shell to reveal a honeycomb of pigeonholes and little drawers for the filing of a hundred matters. It had been made sometime in the fifteen years between 1860 and 1875, a rare treasure of walnut worth its weight in gold. "You pick my file out of your collection for something special?"

"You think I have a dossier on you, May?"

"I think you had a dossier on your mother before you were born."

"I have a new venture in mind that might interest you."

"For the money or the game?"

"What do you know about home videocassettes?"

"You mean movies?" May asked.

"Motion pictures, music videos, instruction tapes, erotica . . ."

"Fuck flicks?"

"Got anything against them?"

"Depends who's on top. Who's getting double the pleasure, double the fun."

"As long as the principal parties are getting equal time?"

"I suppose. Frankly, Walter, most women don't get hot by looking, or haven't you heard?"

A tic quivered briefly beside his left eye.

"Maybe in the future," he said blandly. "Women are taking their place in the world. Their real preferences may soon be known."

"I'll have to watch out where I sit my ass on that issue. I wouldn't want to get stuck in a position I hadn't thought about. What's the proposition?"

"Erotica—"

"Pornography."

"—is a three-billion-dollar-a-year business."

"So is bagging horse shit, give or take a billion."

"Exactly my point. You don't take a moral position when it comes to horse shit, do you, May?"

"Just so long as nobody tracks it on my rugs."

"I'm not asking you to watch skin flicks instead of Johnny Carson, May. Just to make yourself a profit."

"How far do you mean to go?"

"I'm not interested in live sex acts, nightclubs, or any other aspect of the business that presents ongoing personnel problems. I mean to consolidate the production and retail distribution of printed matter, films, and home videocassettes under one management for the territory west of the Mississippi."

"Seems to me, even looking at what's on offer with half an eye, that there's more than enough of that crap to go around already."

"There's never enough, May. And rarely the right mix. Like every other market, the one for erotic entertainment is fragmented. Very handsome profits are being ignored because the mass-market producers won't tailor-make a product for some very small, but very rich, groups of specialty consumers."

"What will your start-up capitalization be?"

"Ten million. Four to product. Three to distribution. Two for litigation if needed."

"And the last million?"

"Contingencies."

"What's your management strategy?"

"I've already engaged the services of a firm with broad experience in the field."

"Where's it based?"

"New Orleans, but it will be here within the week."

"So, how long is this proposition on offer?"

"Three days?"

"That's not a lot of time to reconcile some deep feelings."

"If you have strong reservations about it, May, why don't you just pass this one up?" Cape said, standing up to splash another two fingers into May's glass. "There may be other venture opportunities in future."

May caught the implication very clearly. Turn your back on a Walter Cape enterprise and chances were very good you'd never be invited to join another. Paternal. You'd have to call Cape paternal. As long as you let him be big daddy, he'd make your life sweeter. Turn his little golden marks of affection down, and he'd give the chances to others.

"I'd just like a better idea about the kinds of films you're asking me to help finance. I'm running a series condemning kiddie pornography, and my conscience wouldn't allow me to support anything that even hinted at that."

"Oh?" Cape said, as though questioning her sincerity. He sat down again. May noticed, with a start at her own instincts, that his chair was disposed in such a way that no light fell on his eyes, though she was brightly lit, her expressions open to his scrutiny.

"I'd like to see the bastards who mess with children strung up by the you-know-what," she said vehemently, showing the measure of her condemnation.

"Well, May, I don't think anyone would say anything except amen to that," he said in the flattest kind of voice.

She knew she was being warned off the subject. For a moment she wondered if some of the tales told about Cape were true and not just the sort of shit balls thrown at the rich, the famous, and the successful by the viciously envious.

For instance, one story claimed that Cape kept a beautiful woman on hand in one wing of the house. Gossip from "reliable sources" had it that other young women, always generously endowed in the tit department, were stashed here and there in apartments and hotel suites throughout the city.

Another rumor said there was a chid, a little boy, maybe seven or eight, living in the house. The resident whore might even be as much companion for the child as Cape's in-house fuck. One version hinted at a cuckoo twist, like a tale from Grimm or Mother Goose. The boy, it was said, never aged, but always remained seven or eight.

"But you have to understand, May," he went on, "should you choose to join me in this enterprise, I'd expect you to consider our common interests concerning the series of articles."

"Not publish?"

"I didn't say not publish, did I? I'm talking about tone, emphasis, and fairness. The jury is still out on what pornography is. There's also the matter of first-amendment rights. I'm simply suggesting that you don't come down too hard on one side or the other but offer your readers a well-balanced argument for all sides of the issue."

"For Christ's sake, Walter, I can't go around pussyfooting on this. Unless a strong position is taken, there's no reason to even bring the subject up one more goddamn time."

"Well, of course, there's that. You don't have to publish. There's enough out there to make our lives unpleasant without stirring up matters that might well be considered deeply personal. But you know your business better than I do, May. Settling conflicting interests is what it's all about, isn't it? So why don't you think it over and see where your best interests lie?"

May mumbled and stroked her face with a scarred, rough hand.

"Horse shit is horse shit," Cape said. "Skin flicks are skin flicks. I'm sure you share my view that anything not specifically prohibited under law is open to enterprise. Cassettes have taken erotica—call it pornography if it suits your prejudices better—and packaged it for the eighties. The man in black socks doesn't chase the lady in rolled stockings around the horsehair sofa anymore.

"I'm bringing an executive in from New Orleans who knows the business. He has extensive experience and a working knowledge of the industry. The stockholders will simply be buying into an entertainment enterprise. They won't even have to look at the product if they don't want to."

"If you don't intend anything too outrageous, I'll consider the proposition," May said.

"I don't make promises about things that cannot be precisely described, May. You know that. You'll just have to trust me and the people I'm bringing in."

She was being dismissed. She stood up. Cape, as mannerly

as he usually was, didn't get up to show her to the door but just sat there in the red leather chair with the shadow falling across his eyes, making it so hard for her to read them.

When she reached the door, he said, "Would you ask Frank Menifee to come in for a minute, May?"

"Sure. Are you going to ask his people to invest?"

Cape didn't answer.

"Why do you do it, Walter?"

"Why do I do what, May?"

"You could retire with your money right now. You could buy up something else like a chain of retail stores or a small oil company. Why are you always out there on the fringe?"

"Because that's where the heavy action is, May. Out there on the barrens with the wolves."

Three

H E HAD a first name, but with a last name like Whistler, hardly anybody ever used it. He was sitting in a window booth at Gentry's, a fancy name for a seedy coffee bar run by a failed kazoo player named Bosco who'd lost an arm in an argument with a shotgun over a whore.

The rain had washed all the baby prostitutes and twangy boys, the chicken hawks and queer bashers, the gonifs and petty grifters off the four corners of Hollywood and Vine. The empty streets looked as quiet and innocent as they had in the fifties when Hollywood was still a small-town beauty and Whistler was just a youngster looking for a score.

The city and the man had grown old and run over at the heels together. Both a little fragile, their faces battered from the impact of too many closing windows and too many slamming doors.

There was only the two of them. There was no cook at two A.M.

Bosco was reading *The Lives of the Saints*. Whistler was reading *The Enquirer*.

"Whattaya read that crap for?" Bosco asked as he came over to refill Whistler's cup.

"Because I'm sick and tired of the true horror of the news," Whistler replied. "Along about now I want to read fairy tales about actresses strangled with feather boas and corpses rising up from graves all over La-La Land. A man's got to have some hope in miracles, and these pages are full of them."

"You should go home and get some sleep."

"I'm waiting for the rain to let up."

"It never will. This is July fifteenth, St. Swithen's day. When it rains on St. Swithen's day, that means it's gonna rain for forty days and forty nights," Bosco said. He went back to his book.

Whistler returned to his tabloid.

On the third page of the "Stinky Ink" there was an item datelined New Orleans, a few days before.

> Early this morning at the deserted amusement pier on the shores of Lake Pontchartrain, Mr. Chippy Byrd, 978 Bourbon Street, sitting in his automobile with a companion, Miss Lacy Ohio, saw two men apparently engaged in a game of football.
>
> "They was acting drunk," Mr. Byrd told this reporter. "They was kicking this here ball back and forth until it lands in the water, at which time they get in a white 1981 Cadillac convertible with one Bondoed fender and drive away. A possum comes along and drags the ball out of the reeds. My friend says there is something very funny about that there ball, and when I say, 'How, funny?' my friend says it don't look really round and was wrapped in newspaper, so I go to drag it out and have a look. It

like to scares the hell out of me when I see what I thought was a ball is a person's head."

The head, hacked off at the neck, was collected by members of the New Orleans police. Gross examination so far indicates that the badly decomposed head is that of an Oriental female approximately twenty-five years of age.

"A head without a body was found in a lake in New Orleans," Whistler said.

"It happens all the time down there," Bosco said. "Those witch queens do a thing where they cut off two heads and put them face-to-face alongside any body of water. Ask those heads any question you want and they got to answer."

"You know things unheard of by your average counterman, Bosco. You think we could set up something like that in MacArthur Park and see if a couple of heads could tell us which horses are going to win the quiniela at Santa Anita?"

A crippled station wagon came lugging along the boulevard.

From the crossroad by the movie house, a silver 635 CSi BMW chased down the tunnel made by its own headlamps.

Whistler watched with the melancholy calm of a man who knew the worst would always happen. There were only two cars on the road, and they were going to have a smashup. That's the way things happen on a rainy night in La-La Land.

When it came, Whistler was already on his feet.

"Is fifty bucks a fair price for an expert eyewitness?" he asked as he started for the door.

The BMW smashed into the side of the station wagon, bulldozing it across the boulevard and up onto the curb right outside Gentry's plate-glass window. The wagon slammed into a light pole, a fire hydrant, and a stack of newspaper vending machines, the doors flying open and the driver flying out.

By the time he finished bouncing, he was busted up like a porcelain doll. His blood was all over the place. But that wasn't the worst of it.

The worst of it was, another body came flying out of the

back end of the wagon. It ended up sitting against the racks for *The Enquirer* and *The World*. A naked body. A woman's naked body. A woman's naked body without a head.

The publishers of *The Enquirer* and *The World* couldn't have asked for a better tribute. Whistler couldn't have been more surprised, if he hadn't lived so long in La-La Land that he'd long since lost any sense of astonishment along with his innocence.

The BMW, and the people in it, had fared better than the station wagon. It was still on its feet, though its radiator was wrecked. Day-Glo coolant bled from it onto the curb. The front fenders looked like crumpled aluminum foil.

The blasted vehicles hissed like wounded beasts in the strange silence that always seems to follow a crash.

A high-pitched moan was coming from the passenger's seat.

Whistler stepped around and dragged the door open. A very pretty woman sat staring at the starred windshield. Her skirt was up and her pants were off. She was unaware of the picture she made. She didn't look injured. Her moan started to stretch out and run up the scale.

Whistler took a handful of her long blond hair and turned her head around so she had to look up into his face. Her eyes didn't change focus, and her safety valve was still threatening to pop. He slapped her twice, and she fell forward into his arms without another peep.

There was nothing else he could do but lift her out of the car. It was carry her and risk a hernia or lay her down in the filthy gutter. The driver got out of the car and stood spread-legged, his hands up on the roof of the car, steadying himself. Then his hands dropped out of sight. He was closing the zipper on his fly.

Whistler knew him. Well, he didn't *know* him, but he knew him. The sucker was on the tube every week on some police show. He played a white undercover cop. Some actor who looked like a Caucasian with a deep tan was the black cop. There was another show just like it. Except on *that* show the black cop wore the earring, and on this guy's show the white cop wore the earring.

He put his hand up to his ear to see that his earring hadn't been ripped out of the pierced lobe of his ear, looking at Whistler as though wondering if he meant to steal his girl-friend. Why else would a stranger be standing in the street holding her in his arms?

"Hey, you," he said, with more than a trace of belliger-ence.

"You mean me, my name is Whistler," Whistler said. "You're Emmet Tillman. I see you on the tube."

The actor grinned and brushed his hair back.

"Can you walk?" Whistler asked.

"What the hell's going on?"

"You drunk or on toot?" Whistler said.

"I had drinks with dinner. I don't do drugs," Tillman said with a careful show of dignity.

"Can you walk?"

"Of course I can walk."

Tillman came around the back of the BMW. Whistler could see that his boner hadn't died away completely.

"Well, follow me into the coffee bar before I drop your lady in the street."

Tillman did as he was told, just as though he were blocking out a scene under a director's orders.

Bosco pushed open the door for them.

As Tillman went through he spotted Bosco's empty sleeve.

"My God, were you in this goddamn accident too?" Tillman asked.

Frank Menifee, the labor lawyer, also managed the largest investment fund amassed by the reigning Mafia family in Los Angeles. He had the Irish gift of gab, though his silences were legendary. The tale was told of one negotiation during which he spoke not one word, except "Good morning" at the beginning and "Good evening" three weeks later at the end, getting up from the bargaining table with all he'd asked for in his written proposal and even a little more.

Before he sat down, he moved the big leather chair away from the fire and the light. Cape and he were both wearing masks of shadow when he sat down and looked at Cape with an expression of mild expectation on his rice-pudding face. It was all bumpy with little translucent specks like tiny sun blisters. They shone when the light struck a certain way. Shone like bits of wax. His eyebrows were pale and had an odd shine to them as well. If somebody told you Menifee was made of plastic, you'd think twice before calling him a liar.

"Well, Walter?" Menifee said.

"Well, Frank?" Cape said with the slightest of smiles. "Have you talked to your clients?"

"I did."

"And what do they have to say?"

"They mentioned the fact that they are already enjoying a piece of the action."

"Prostitution? Old-fashioned pornography?"

"Well, yes, Walter, is there any other kind?"

"It ain't what you do, it's the way that you do it, Frank," Cape said in the voice of a burlesque comic.

"What are you going to do that's different?"

"Better photography, better stories, better actors and actresses, new subject matter."

"Well, I wouldn't know about that, would I, Walter? You're talking about art, and I'm talking about money."

"You see all the movie and television stars taking off their clothes for *Playboy* and *Penthouse*, Frank?"

"I keep a Catholic house, Walter. I've got teenage daughters."

"But you've seen the magazines, haven't you? Like at the barbershop?"

"I've glanced through one or two. Yes, I have."

"Miss America gets printed up bare-assed, and they have a four-million-dollar issue. Does that tell you something, Frank?"

"Americans like brand names."

"That's one way of looking at it. Our films are going to have beauties in them. No sluts and whores, Frank."

"You know how to slice it that fine, Walter?"

"I expect to sign them up just before they're ripe."

"You've got a way to make them famous afterward?"

"I'm working on it. I'm making friends. The right opportunity will come my way."

"Oh, you're a collector, Walter. No doubt about that. But my people still don't know why they should even let you start doing business."

"Because I'll do it better than they've been doing it. They'll make more money with none of the bother. I've got a hundred ideas for profit where there was no profit before."

Menifee stared into the fire.

"Have you got a thought, Frank?"

"You know, Walter, the old struggle between the mustaches and the young turks came about over pushing hard drugs on the street to the school kids. Now, I'm not making a judgment, here—"

"I should hope not, Frank."

"—but it could be that the next generational struggle might be over certain aspects of the skin trade."

"Certain aspects?"

"S and M, Walter. Kiddie porn. Snuff films. New subject matter, what you call it. Am I right, Walter, when I make the prediction that these are some of the areas of greater opportunity you're talking about?"

"They're on the agenda."

"Some of the old men, the family men, don't like that sort of thing."

"Tell them to wash their hands, Frank. Like their fathers did about the drugs. The business needs organization. There are too many free-lance operators making costly competition."

"That came up. What do you mean to do about that?"

"Ask them to join my group."

"And if they don't, will you be needing the kind of persuasion I can offer?"

"I wouldn't want that sort of attention. I've got better ways. You notice the tall woman in the silver suit?"

"I noticed her, Walter. That's Janet Hyer, the assistant state's attorney, isn't it?"

"That's who it is, Frank. And we've been discussing the

possibility of bringing certain producers of pornography up before the grand jury."

"It's been tried. Nobody can agree on what constitutes obscenity anymore since the Supreme Court threw it over to prevailing community standards."

"But they do agree on what constitutes conspiracy to solicit an act of prostitution. What we're going to do, Frank, is bring these producers up for pimping, and their actors up for being whores."

"It could work." He looked at the Wooten. "That's a grand desk you've got over there, Walter."

"I'm glad you like it."

"A desk like that would have room for a thousand documents."

"Would you like to see?"

They got up and walked over to the massive piece of furniture. Cape opened it up, revealing the many drawers and compartments inside. Cape reached over and pulled out one drawer. Menifee took his billfold from the breast pocket of his dinner jacket and extracted a check. He placed it in the drawer. If asked, he could honestly say he'd never handed over money of any sort to Walter Cape for any purpose.

Menifee looked up at a butterfly with hot-blue and green wings.

"Butterflies," he said.

"I've been collecting them for years," Cape said.

"Drink some more coffee," Whistler said, leaning across the table toward Tillman. "Go ahead."

"I don't need any more. I told you I'm not drunk or high," Tillman said. "I've got a full bladder."

"Well, for Christ's sake, don't sit there suffering. Go use the john."

Tillman slid out of the booth. The girl's leg, resting against Whistler's thigh, jerked as though she wanted to run away too.

Whistler saw a look in Tillman's eye.

"Just take a leak, Mr. Tillman. Don't try coppin' a sneak. That's your car out there, and you can't hide it. You should know that it'll go a lot harder if you try to leave the scene of the crime."

Tillman tapped his forehead with his fingers as though saying he wasn't thinking straight. Then he said, "Crime? What the fuck you mean, crime?"

"Accident. Go take your leak, Mr. Tillman, and hurry back. The cops'll be here before you know it. And we should talk."

Whistler looked at the girl. She smiled back at him as though he were her big brother. She carefully kept her back to the plate glass and the carnage on the other side of it.

"I don't know your name," Whistler said.

"Well . . ." she said.

"You're an actress, right?"

"Trying to be."

"Whatever you call yourself will do."

"Shiela Andes."

"That's got a certain lift to it," Whistler said.

"The Andes are mountains in Peru."

"You feel all right now?"

"Well, no, I feel awful. I mean, those two people out there. They're dead, aren't they?"

Whistler almost said one was deader than the other, but he caught himself.

"Well, you saw, didn't you?" he asked instead.

"Not really. I mean, I couldn't see very good out of the windshield, and then I fainted. Did I faint?"

"Yes, you did."

"I'm almost glad. I don't like to look at dead people. Especially—"

Her pretty tongue curled up like a cat, and Whistler thought she was going to cry or be sick. But she grabbed hold of herself.

"There's a lot of blood, isn't there?" she said.

"Yes." Whistler looked out the window.

A lot of blood from the driver but not a drop from the headless body. The driver lay sprawled on his face in the rain. It pasted his shirt and slacks to his skinny body. His hair wavered like river weed in a puddle of water. Bosco appeared outside. He went to the body without a head and covered its nakedness with a blanket he took from the back of the wagon. Only the ankles and feet were exposed, nicely molded, as delicate as ivory carvings.

"So I must have seen something, but I don't remember. I'd rather not," she said, as though refusing a cup of coffee.

"Well, you don't have to," Whistler said, touching her hand.

It was trembling fiercely. She was strung tight and about to snap.

Tillman was coming back from the rest room. Whistler got up and met him halfway along the aisle.

"What did you mean, 'go harder'?" Tillman demanded.

Whistler, keeping his voice low, said, "You know and I know that you had half a load on when you hit that wagon. And you had your hand up Shiela's skirt mining for gold just before the crash. While driving in the rain. You're in for it if they question her."

"She wouldn't say."

"Think not? Take another look at her. She's scared to death. She'll answer any questions they put to her without a care in the world about you. She your woman?"

"Just a squeeze."

Oh, for Christ's sake, Whistler thought, this gazoony was going to talk like the character in the show.

"I wouldn't talk like that when the cops come. Nobody really talks like that. Something like that could make the cops take a dislike to you."

"Hell, I know most of them. I even carry a reserve badge."

"Don't let that turn your head. Five'll get you twenty they'll drop the book on you. Five'll get you fifty they'd like to bring you down. What are you making? Two million a year playing a cop? Well, they're making twenty thousand running through the shit and blood in the streets. Take my word. They get a chance to do you, they'll do you."

"That's bullshit," Tillman said, making a hard jaw.

"Tell me about it. Send me a letter from jail."

The jaw turned to pasta. "So what should I do?"

"You'll take a little advice?"

Tillman nodded.

"You'll let me represent your interests?"

"You're not an agent, are you?"

"No, and I'm not a lawyer, either."

"Then what the hell are you?"

"I'm a private investigator."

"An eye?"

"Nobody's said that since they buried Humphrey Bogart in his trench coat."

"What can you do for me?" Tillman said, rubbing his fingers and thumb together and looking wise.

"No, I can't pass a bribe," Whistler said. "What I can do is advise you to sit down and wait for the cops. Answer any questions they ask. Refuse a breathalyzer until your attorney can get here. You got lawyers?"

"I got lawyers, agents, managers . . ."

"Refuse to walk any lines or blow into any balloons, but do it like you'd like to cooperate. However, you're scared half to death and you don't want to do anything without your lawyers tell you it's okay. Understand me. Do *not* act like you're an honorary cop just because you pretend to be one every week on the tube. Do *not* get unduly familiar with the officers or detectives, even if you're acquainted with them. Do *not* talk like a goddamn script."

Out on the street a siren wailed, rushing toward Gentry's, and Bosco's summons.

Tillman jerked his head around.

"We got time. Sound carries on wet air," Whistler said.

"I'd better make a call," Tillman said.

"Make your call after some conversation with the police. Drink more coffee. Piss as much as you can. Take your time. Your lawyers got any brains, they'll take as long as they can getting here. What you want to do here is delay a blood test as long as you can, until its value as evidence can be put in doubt."

"What am I paying for this advice?" Tillman said.

"The advice is for free. What you'll pay me for is seeing

that Miss Andes gets home safe and sound. And maybe for what I can do for you after."

"I understand," Tillman said.

Whistler went back to Shiela and held out his hand.

"What?" she said, her mouth trembling.

"I'm taking you home," Whistler said.

"Is it all right?" she said, looking at Tillman and sliding out of the booth. "Are you sure it's all right?"

"I'll explain it to you on the way," Whistler said.

He walked over to Bosco while Tillman got up close to Shiela.

"I'm taking the lady home," Whistler told Bosco. "You understand?"

Bosco nodded. "What lady?"

Whistler looked at Tillman, holding Shiela's hands, playing the protector, reluctant to let her go, acting a part.

Shiela's eyes were shining as she looked up into the actor's face. There was a little smile on her lips.

Whistler had the notion that Shiela thought Tillman absurd. He had another notion that she knew she'd just been dealt the card that filled out an inside straight.

"I'll make him a dish of potatoes," Bosco said.

"What?" Whistler asked, not certain that he'd heard correctly.

"Confuses the breathalyzer."

"Who told you that?"

"I learned about it when I was in England."

"Does it work?"

"Who knows? But if somebody thinks it works, it makes for a better attitude under interrogation."

Whistler led Shiela through the kitchen and out the back door to the parking lot where he kept his Chevy.

Four

MONSIGNOR TERRENCE Aloysius Moynihan, chancellor to His Eminence Cardinal Eustice, chairman of the Financial Discovery Committee, keeper and wielder of the bank accounts of the richest archdiocese in the country next to those of New York City and Chicago, was wearing his purple sash and the outfit with the little cape and purple piping.

He was black-haired, white-skinned, red-cheeked, and blue-eyed, the greatest dissembler since Pontius Pilate washed his hands and gave the decision between Christ and Barabbas to the mob.

It is sometimes said by those in the know that if most cops were not allowed to carry a gun legally, they'd be on the other side of the law, carrying one illegally. It was said of Moynihan that if he'd not become a priest, he'd have become a loan shark, a Hollywood agent, or a pimp.

A Catholic buck, once in Moynihan's pocket, rarely left it. He had an ancient mind. And a powerful lust for women that he did not exercise but sublimated in his pursuit of power and money. Sometimes even Cardinal Eustice thought he went to too many parties and stayed at them far too late.

The young monsignor had stood in a well of serenity by the fireplace nearly all night, as the party swirled around him. His slender hands held a double old-fashioned as though it were a precious relic. For hours he'd been taking congratulations upon his latest appointment to the County Board of Adjustments—the civic body that passed on architectural design review—and was taking them still.

He'd soon be rubbing palms and asses with the contractors. Finding the corners that could be cut, discovering closets filled with old bones, accepting little contributions to the archdiocese, like parochial school buildings constructed at cost. There was money to be made by association with Monsignor Moynihan, and this was a crowd where a person's popularity was in direct proportion to the thickness of their fleece.

Frank Menifee joined Moynihan when the priest was otherwise unoccupied. Menifee wore his tuxedo as though it were made of black cardboard. The bow tie looked like it was pinned to his neck with a nail. Whenever he moved his head, the tie moved with him. Moynihan found the tie fascinating and could scarcely tear his eyes away.

"Congratulations, Monsignor," Menifee said, smiling like a winking shutter.

"Why, thank you, Frank."

"Is it true?"

"What would that be?"

"That you're going to run for county supervisor next?"

"It's a thought."

"I wouldn't."

"Why not?"

"There'd be no profit in it for you."

"I'm not looking for personal profit, Frank. You know that."

"Ah, well, Monsignor, that's what you say. But there's profit and then there's profit. You sit on enough boards right now to work any con you've got a mind to work. Go public and you open yourself up to a great deal of scrutiny. That wouldn't do you, the cardinal, the archdiocese, or the Church a bit of good."

"I'm sure His Eminence appreciates your concern and counsel, Frank."

Moynihan plucked a gold watch as small as a half dollar from his cummerbund and consulted it.

"I've left my good-byes much too late. I must go find our host."

"I just left him in his office."

"Oh? Business, Frank? Are you taking your people into

Walter's new enterprise?" Moynihan asked. "You didn't seem too eager about it when he first approached us."

"I'm like you, Monsignor, a man with many masters."

"But a good Catholic, Frank. Never forget that."

"'Give unto Caesar . . .'"

"To coin a useful phrase."

"I took the offer to my principals. They like it. They see a future in home entertainment. And you?"

"The Holy Father takes a dim view of such entertainments," Moynihan said.

"How many do you think he's seen?" Menifee asked with a curly twist to his mouth.

"I doubt he's ever seen any. But you don't have to stick your hand into the fire to know it burns."

"But you've got to bite the apple to know if it's sweet."

"Don't tease me, Frank. It's cruel to tease a man who's taken a vow of celibacy."

"If you ever decide to break your vow, I know a young woman."

"You'll be the first to know if I do, Frank."

"What does the Holy Father have to say on the subject?" Menifee said.

"I won't quote verbatim from his latest encyclical on pornography, but I can tell you he's definitely agin it."

"Sure of himself, isn't he?"

"Infallible."

"Does he threaten excommunication?"

"For the lookers or the makers, Frank?"

"Either. Both."

"Shouldn't you be more concerned about the souls of the venture capitalists?"

"I don't know that money carries sin with it, Monsignor. There's a debate there for your Jesuits about the moral neutrality of money."

"I often think about it, Frank."

"I mean, I was just wondering about those buildings the Church owns on Santa Monica and Western. I was just wondering if you knew that one small manufacturer renting space from you makes studded dog collars, whips, and punishment gags. Another prints a magazine called *Where the Boys Are*, a little directory for pedophiles. And, from what I've been told, there are three whores working out of a third-floor apartment."

"Well, no, Frank, I didn't know that," Moynihan said evenly. "I'll look into it."

"And raise their rents?"

"I expect, if what you say proves true, that we'll give them notice."

"Then you'll have some empty square footage."

"Considerable."

"You wouldn't want it left vacant too long."

"No, we wouldn't, Frank. Now, I'd better go say good night and thank you to Walter."

And have him sign a lease, you hypocritical, holier-than-thou son of a bitch, Menifee thought.

Shiela lay back against the worn seat of Whistler's old Chevy.

Whistler looked straight ahead, his hands on the wheel. Making like a chauffeur. Playing the game.

She was glancing at him from time to time, and Whistler knew it. He expected she looked at every man the same way. Weighing his balls. Estimating his power and clout.

"I want to thank you for this," she said.

"Just what do you think you've got to thank me for?" Whistler said.

"Removing me from the scene of the crime."

"No crime. Accident."

"That naked body had no head," Shiela said. "I thought I was going to toss my cookies."

"Oh, you saw that, did you?"

"There's not much I don't see, Whistler. And something like that is very hard to miss."

"You just take a miracle drug when I wasn't looking?"

"What?"

"I never saw anyone recover so fast. You act in front of the camera as good as you did on the street and in Gentry's, you'll be collecting a brass doll one of these days."

"Thanks."

"If you'd stayed at the scene, you'd have gotten your picture in the paper."

"I could use the exposure," Shiela agreed, "but I can use the leverage better."

"What leverage is that?"

"I just did Tillman a big favor. Leaving the scene. He was promising me a hand up. He meant up my skirt. And I meant a part on his show. It was going to take a long time before either of us really delivered, what with all the jockeying around we were doing. Now he owes me. It wouldn't have helped him any if I'd told the cops he was playing with my pussy and not minding the road."

"You've got a mouth."

"You men teach us how to talk dirty, then you flinch."

Whistler said nothing.

"I suppose I do sound as hard as nails. It bother you?"

"If you think that's what it takes."

"Turn here, first apartment house on the corner," she said.

Whistler turned off and parked at the curb. When the wipers stopped dancing, the rain, like a mist of gelatin, obscured the view of the pink-plaster court apartments.

"I'm not hard," Shiela said. "Really, Whistler. I'm butter and cream. But, Christ, they don't make it easy for you to be good."

"You don't have to explain yourself to me."

"Why not to you? You're the nearest thing to a knight in shining armor I've bumped into since I left the plains of Kansas for L.A."

Whistler shrugged and smiled.

"So, maybe if you take the time to look, Whistler, you'll see I'm a princess worth rescuing. Your good deed wasn't a waste of time," Shiela said.

"I'm not a Boy Scout."

"You should have a reward, anyway."

They stared at each other quietly, like enemies.

She moved in closer, her lips starting to part, the pink tip of her tongue already showing. He pushed her away.

"I think it's only fair you should know I wasn't saving you trouble. I was cutting myself a slice of the action."

"Sure. I understand. That's fair. If you can't get a meal off the fat cats, who can you get a meal off of?"

She opened the door and stuck one long leg out into the rain. She kept it there while she said, "I'm in the book, Whistler. I'd appreciate an invitation to whatever."

Whistler nodded. She stretched out and kissed him on the mouth, her lips still trembling from the strain of keeping her screams in check. This time he didn't push her away. Her leg was still out in the rain getting wet.

Five

RALPH PARKER was wearing maroon trousers with a black satin stripe down the sides and a forest-green dinner jacket. He had a beeper clipped to his cummerbund. People often mistook him for a doctor. He controlled the beeper from a battery in his pocket. It interrupted conversations he wanted interrupted and got him out of parties that were proving a waste of time.

Cape's parties were rarely a waste of time, but Parker wore the beeper because it was a habit and he was used to it.

The crowd was almost gone, the last of them moving toward the exit hall, round-eyed with fatigue and the effects of so much alcohol. Only a few were left, wandering around as though in a daze, like commuters in a train station early in the morning or very late at night. He made the beeper beep as though reminding himself that it was time to go.

Henry Warsaw came up to him and said, "Why don't you just suck your thumb when you're in need of comfort?" Warsaw was petroleum. Out of the most powerful fifty in Los

Angeles, featured in a recent slick that chronicles the shifting pecking order of La-La Land, eight were petroleum. Warsaw's name wasn't among them. He was into oil and natural gas the way you could say a pirate on the high seas was into cargo and transport. He was a raider. He ate oil companies for breakfast, but none of his corporations would ever show up in the Fortune 500.

Everybody but his victims liked him for his country ways and straightforward manner.

He had a taste for little boys between the ages of nine and ten, some of whom he got from Walter Cape when Cape was done with them.

He prided himself on being a good judge of men, but he didn't have a clue about who Ralph Parker really was, because he'd never bothered to find out. Parker said that he put deals together and sometimes called himself an investment banker.

Los Angeles is full of people putting deals together. Anybody with a tattered script in his pocket is packaging a film. Anybody patching roofs is into construction. Anybody with a five-dollar bag fancies himself a dealer.

Warsaw didn't have to be friendly to anybody he suspected was a con merchant, but you never knew when some asshole would prove useful, so he slapped Parker on the back and joshed him like they were both a couple of good old boys and grass-roots Democrats.

But Parker was really an investment banker. Not one of those who operated out of glass-and-marble buildings on Wilshire Boulevard in Los Angeles, or in New York, Paris, or Rome, but a banker who collected doctors, dentists, and lawyers with smooth salesmanship and invested millions out of an armored briefcase equipped with a mobile phone, a book of private numbers, and a .357 Magnum.

When Shirley Quon drifted over to join them, Warsaw put his arm around her waist and she didn't even flinch. Quon's fortune was based on restaurants and real estate. Properties purchased for a song in all the most strategic places along planned freeways and areas of future public condemnation. Buildings allowed to crumble around the ears of illegals from

every quarter of the world. Restaurants that had once had
plenty of trouble with the inspectors from the Health
Department until Quon had learned how to spread the grease.

Ordinarily she didn't like to be touched by white hands.
That was a well-known fact.

What was not a well-known fact was that Quon was a man
in Oriental drag. It was not a well-known fact because
anyone who found out and tried to use it disappeared. Quon
had a taste for little boys between the ages of ten and eleven.
That was why he allowed Warsaw the familiarity. Warsaw
passed the children he got from Cape on to Quon. And Quon
passed them on. Each pedophile had a taste for children of
the age they'd been when they'd had their innocence taken
from them. Now they traded in lost innocence, passing the
children from hand to hand as they grew older, until they
were so old that there was nothing left to them.

Parker was a gonif and a con and had been, more than
once, a killer, but in many ways he was among the best of
them.

He saw Monsignor Moynihan enter the room, which meant
that Cape was probably alone. He excused himself and went
down the corridor to the paneled door and knocked. Cape
called out, and Parker went in.

Cape looked small in the red leather chair. Small and
weary and melancholy.

"Hello, Ralph," he said without warmth or enthusiasm.

"You look worn-out, Walter."

"I am worn-out. How's the party going?"

"Winding down."

Cape made a movement, as though meaning to get up, but
settled back again. "I should be out there seeing my guests
off."

Parker made a question with his eyebrows. When Cape
nodded, he took the chair that so many people had occupied
that night. "Don't bother yourself, Walter. They'll never
know."

"Parties are bothersome things," Cape said. "But they can
be useful."

"Did you put your consortium together?"

Cape made a shape in the air like a ball and smiled. "There's still some thought to be given to casting and recruitment."

"Plenty of twat around," Parker said.

"I wish you'd clean up your language," Cape said mildly.

"Sorry."

The phone rang. Cape stared at Parker without moving to lift the receiver until Parker got up and started to go.

Tillman had gotten himself more than half sober. He'd counted up his options on his fingers as the siren died outside. He could call his agent and let her work the angles, but that would mean she'd have him by the shorts forever and ever. He could call his lawyers and let them put in a fix, but he couldn't be sure a lawyer's fix would stay nailed. Fixes worked out by lawyers were made of cardboard and were known to fall apart, causing complications that required another lawyer's fix—and another and another. Lawyers could get you hung for a ten-dollar parking ticket. He could call the producer of the series, but Manny Ostrava had said more than once that it wasn't the old days anymore, and thank God he didn't have to get his actors out of jail or find doctors to scrape out the pussies of his starlets. Besides, Ostrava was no friend and would use whatever he could get his hands on to sandbag Tillman come contract time.

The one-armed asshole behind the counter was looking at him with bland contempt, waiting to see if he'd just stand there doing nothing. Like he was no better than any other schmuck with no juice to call his own.

There was one person known to Tillman important enough maybe to put a lid on something like vehicular homicide and rich enough not to ask for payment.

Tillman dug for change and came up dry.

He took a hundred-dollar bill from a silver money clip. "Can you change this? I've got to use the telephone."

Bosco looked at the c-note and smiled but didn't touch it. He opened the register drawer and scooped out some dimes. He spilled a half dozen on the counter.

"You owe me."

Tillman gave him five bucks' worth of charming smile and went over to call his friend, Walter Cape.

It was a lousy hour, yet somehow he had an idea that Cape was the kind of man who never slept, or slept only when the rest of the world was awake.

He didn't know about the party. He'd never been invited to one. Friendship with Cape was like climbing a ladder. You had to wait awhile on each rung before he invited you to climb the next. Right now Tillman was at that stage where he'd been assured that he could call upon Cape as a friend in case of need.

Cape played the part of a simple man who would take the time and trouble to get a drunken brother-in-law out of jail or arrange for the friend of a friend to sit in the steward's box at any racetrack in the country. A man full of fatherly concern and advice, always ready to lend a hand. He'd been known to personally take charge of a birthday party for a child or spend half a day planting daffodils in a garden bed, kneeling right beside an old woman in Santa Monica who knew him only as a friend she'd met sitting on a bench facing out to sea. His life was filled with such simple acts. His pockets were full of favors, large and small. That's how the stories went.

What Tillman didn't know was that Cape, sooner or later, sent his bill the way great nations send bills to small client nations or Mafia *capos* finally ask favor for favor from those who have placed themselves in their debt.

In spite of the weather, nighthawks were finally gathering outside Gentry's, their images distorted by the console flasher on the black-and-white and the rain streaming down the plate-glass window. Two uniforms got out of the squad car, setting their caps and holstering their batons. Neither one wore the regulation yellow slickers against the rain. The black cop wore a leather flight jacket with a fur collar, the white one a hooded football jersey that zippered up the front.

The white cop made a half-assed attempt to move the crowd along. They eddied and flowed around his outstretched arms like sheep turning away from the dog that herded them. The black cop went to squat down beside the dead driver.

Tillman dialed Cape's private number, given, he believed, as a mark of special favor. The receiver was lifted after several rings.

"Yes, how can I help you?" Cape said before Tillman even had a chance to identify himself.

"It's me, Emmet," Tillman said. "I hate to bother you so late."

"You're not bothering me," Cape said in a voice of such kind patience that Tillman's own voice became choked with longing for the father he'd never really known. "I was having difficulty sleeping, anyway," he lied, taking the advantage.

"Well, thank God for that. I mean . . . look, Walter, whenever you can't sleep, all you've got to do is call me. It doesn't matter what time. Anytime you—"

"Thank you, Emmet. Where are you?"

"A coffee shop called Gentry's on the corner of Hollywood and Vine."

"Can you speak up? Are you in some kind of trouble?" Tillman raised his voice half a measure.

"Well, I got into a foolish accident in the middle of town."

"How foolish?"

"I was out with this woman, you know, and we were fooling around a little bit while I was driving."

"You were trying to take her temperature with your finger," Cape said without the slightest change of tone.

Tillman laughed.

"Oh, goddamn, leave it to you, Walter, to make a joke out of it and make me feel better."

"Does it make you feel better when I talk in the vernacular?"

"It always makes me feel better *anytime* I talk to you. I mean, you put things in focus. No fucking around. Right to the point. The cops just pulled up a minute ago."

"Take your time. No need to jump. Go on."

"It was raining, and I didn't see this station wagon speeding down Hollywood Boulevard. . . ."

"And it crashed into you."

"Well, no, I hit the wagon."

"Are you injured?"

"No."

"Are you drunk?"

"Well, I had a couple of drinks. . . ."

"Half drunk. Would it be fair to say that you were half drunk?"

"Okay," Tillman said.

He glanced out the window. The black cop had left the station wagon driver's body and was bending down beside the blanket-covered corpse. He was lifting the top edge of it. He half leapt up and stepped back so fast that he nearly fell down on the rain-slick road.

"Your companion? Is she injured?" Cape said.

"No."

"Drunk or high?"

"No."

"What's her name?"

"Shiela Andes."

"What does she do?"

"She's an actress."

"Tell your companion to be civil but not too friendly."

"I already sent her home."

"I see. What about the driver of the other car?"

"Dead."

"Not so good. Still. Rain. Poor visibility," Cape murmured as if instructing himself.

"Streets get like goddamn glass in L.A. when it rains," Tillman pitched in eagerly. "Sucks the grease up out of the pavement . . ."

"Just so. Were there any passengers in the station wagon?"

"Ahhh," Tillman said.

"Not a child, I hope. Not children?"

"I don't know what to call it."

"Are you talking about an animal?"

"There was a woman's body in the wagon. I mean, a woman's corpse fell out of the wagon right into the street."

"A corpse?" Cape exclaimed with the slightest rise of inflection.

"That ain't all," Tillman said, losing the last of the mid-

Atlantic accent that had been so carefully learned and nurtured back in drama school. "It didn't have no head."

"You're sure of that? You're sure you weren't just so drunk . . ."

"Who wouldn't be sure of a thing like that? I'll never forget it. It was a woman's body with little tits and no head. . . ."

There was a stretch of silence, and then Cape said, "Go talk to the police. Be polite and cooperative."

"Should I call Baggot and Barrow?"

"I don't think we need any lawyers yet. Perhaps we won't need them at all. I'm going to make a call or two. Remember, be polite, but don't try to be a pal. You're a toucher and a glad-hander, Emmet. That's good with your fans, but people in authority, or people who think they're in authority, don't like to be touched. Be polite and cooperative, but don't get pally with the police."

Son of a bitch, Tillman thought. *Here I am an actor making two hundred thousand dollars a fucking episode and everybody's telling me how to act.*

Cape rang off before Tillman could say anything, though all he would have said was "Thank you" in the nicest way.

"That was our casting director, I think," Cape said aloud, to himself.

Cape stared into the fire for a long time. After a while he stirred himself, reached for the phone, and tapped out a number without bothering to check the hour.

"This is Walter Cape. I regret the hour and the necessity, Bill," Cape said into the telephone.

A sleep-drugged voice assured him that William Burchard, Deputy Chief and Administrative Commander of Inspection and Control of the Los Angeles Police Department, was happy to be of service, no matter what the hour.

"This is police business. I may be doing you a favor."

"What is it?" Burchard asked clearly and alertly.

"A young friend of mine, Emmet Tillman . . . Do you know him?"

"The actor on the cop show?"

"That's him. He's been involved in a smashup at Hollywood and Vine. I should think that he's being interviewed by the uniforms right about now."

"How many vehicles involved?"

"Only two were mentioned."

"Who was responsible?"

"Who can say? Tillman hit the other car but claims that the other driver was speeding and the crash was unavoidable."

"What does the other driver say?"

"He's dead."

"Oh, for chrissake, Walter, that makes it tough."

"I wouldn't have called you otherwise. It gets tougher. There was a previously dead body in the station wagon."

"Previously dead?"

"I can't state it more accurately than that. The driver of the other vehicle was transporting a woman's corpse."

"Well, that gives me some reason to put a gag on it."

"The corpse is without a head. Are you there, William?"

"I'm here. You present me with the damnedest things at the damnedest hours. No head."

"You see why I called you? With a television star's involvement it's the kind of story the papers would find lip-smacking good."

"I appreciate the concern, Walter."

"Then you'll see to it that Tillman's part in this doesn't appear on the blotter or in any police officer's report?"

"I can promise that. At least until we find out if Tillman had any previous connection with either the driver or the corpse."

"I'd like to be informed of any progress you might make on this, Bill."

"No trouble about that."

"What story will you give the cops on the scene about the headless body?"

"I haven't had time to give that a lot of thought, Walter," Burchard said a bit sourly.

"Well, I have had a little time to think about a scenario. Maybe you could tell your police to say the driver worked for a company making special effects for the films. The headless body is a dummy."

"Any other place, who'd believe it?"

"Any other place, any other time," Cape said. "I'll expect to hear from you, Bill. Never mind the hour."

Six

AFTER THE white cop had gone over to see the curiosity for himself, both cops put their heads together. Tillman walked out of Gentry's and stood in the rain, catching snatches of their conversation like pieces of rag blown on the wind.

". . . see the fuckin' head anywheres around . . ."

". . . anywheres around where?"

". . . like in the fuckin' gutter . . . down the sewer . . ."

". . . could be Japanese."

". . . how the fuck you figure that?"

". . . cunt hair like black wire wool . . . that funny color skin . . ."

". . . sounds like a fucking ethnic slur . . ."

The black cop threw Tillman glances every now and then, but it wasn't until the white cop went to the radio car and the black cop came walking over that his eyes lit up with recognition.

"Sir? My name's Officer Auburn. My partner over there is Officer Schoonover. Were you a witness to this accident?"

"I was nosing out into the boulevard after making a stop. . . ."

"I asked, were you a witness or a participant?"

"I'm telling you that I was driving the BMW. I came out

into the intersection until I could see that nobody was coming
either way. Then I hit the gas. . . .''

"Your name, sir?"

"Emmet Tillman."

"Do we know each other, sir?"

"You may have seen me on television."

Auburn grinned whitely. "Oh, sure. You're on that funny
cop show."

"I don't know where the hell he came from, except he
must have been going like hell," Tillman said. "I didn't see
him when I started nosing out into the intersection and put my
foot down on the gas."

"Which one of these vehicles did you say was yours, sir?"

"The silver six thirty-five CSi BMW."

"I can see the color."

The white cop walked over.

"Ho, Schoonover," Auburn said. "You call the meat
wagon?"

"I called for some detectives and a supervisor. That's
really something, ain't it? Fuckin' awful." He looked at
Tillman. "You happen to know where the head went, sir?"

Tillman tried it again. Maybe it would be third-time lucky.
"The boulevard was clear when I started pulling out. . . ."

"When you stepped on the accelerator?" Auburn said.

"That's right. That wagon came out of nowhere."

"Well, no," Schoonover said. "It came along Hollywood
Boulevard going east to west."

"You know what I fuckin' mean!" Tillman said.

"There's no reason to use that kind of language, Mr.
Tillman. You might have servants. You got servants?"

"Yes, I've got some help."

"You might have servants you can crap on, but although
we're called public servants, we don't stand for being
crapped on."

"I'm sorry. This is all getting to me."

"Take it easy, Mr. Tillman," Auburn said, seeming to take
pity. "We're not out to get you. I watch you on the television
with my wife. She thinks you're very good-looking for a

honky." Then he added, "How many drinks would you say you had tonight?" like he was slipping in a knife.

Always the goddamn zinger, Tillman thought. Always the shit when they got you to open up your mouth because you thought they were going to give you candy.

The detectives arrived in a maroon sedan, looking pleased and mean. Pleased for something to do on a rainy night and mean because they meant to make somebody's life miserable for making them go out in the wet.

Tillman recognized them and felt much relieved.

They were detectives well-known to him. They'd even worked his show as technical advisers for a stretch a year or so before. Lubbock and Jackson. Tillman thought it was even fair to call them pals.

The rain had slowed to a drizzle. Maybe it would blow away. Maybe it was coming up sunshine. He stood on the sidewalk near the curb, waiting to be recognized as Lubbock squatted beside the driver's broken body, tucking the skirts of his raincoat under his knees to keep them from trailing in the dirty water. Jackson stood nearby. He glanced at Tillman and said nothing. Lubbock looked at him as though he were a creature made of glass. Auburn went to stand by Jackson, notebook in hand.

"Hi," Tillman said. "Ain't this the shits?"

"You say something?" Lubbock said.

"You addressing me?" Jackson said.

Tillman felt a sour bubble of fear rise in his throat.

"You probably don't recognize me. . . ."

"Oh, yes, Mr. Tillman, we know who you are," Jackson said, taking a step toward him. "What are you doing on the streets at this hour?"

Auburn murmured something into Jackson's ear, keeping his head averted from Tillman. Jackson listened carefully without the trace of a smile on his broad face, looking as serious as he knew how to look. Intimidating.

"Officer Auburn tells me you were driving the BMW."

"That's right."

"Looks like the BMW plowed right into that old station

wagon," Lubbock said. "Killed this poor fucker on the spot."

"Instantly," Jackson said.

Lubbock stood up and snapped his fingers, indicating how fast. "This is very bad." He went over to the other body under the blanket. Tillman began to follow. Jackson spun around on him.

"Where do you think you're going, Mr. Tillman?"

"I was just going to—"

"You just stay back there, Mr. Tillman. No reason for you to get your shoes dirty stepping in all this crap. You just stay out of the way until we get to you. Anybody get Mr. Tillman to blow into the bag yet?"

"Not yet," Auburn said.

"Walk the line, touch the nose?"

"Not yet."

"Shit, do your job, Officer."

Auburn nodded but didn't ask Tillman to go through the paces.

Lubbock looked under the blanket.

"Twat without a head, Jackson. What do you think about that?"

"I think it's very, very bad."

"Listen, for Christ's sake," Tillman said. "What the hell you talking to me like this for? I thought we were friends."

"Did you? Well, I don't know if we're friends. Acquaintances, maybe. But even if we was friends, this is a serious matter, and we have to go about it in a serious manner. No time to guzzle a couple beers, cut up any touches, tell each other any lies or dirty stories."

"I wasn't going to tell you any lies, for Christ's sake."

"I wish you'd stop taking the Lord's name in vain, Mr. Tillman. I'm a practicing Catholic," Jackson said.

A lieutenant in uniform, driving alone, rolled up. Lubbock, Jackson, Auburn, and Schoonover made a beeline to the supervisor like moths to the flame. They stood around talking in low voices for maybe three minutes. From time to time Lubbock, Jackson, and the lieutenant glanced over at Tillman.

The siren of an approaching ambulance sobbed five blocks away. Then, like a wolf answering a mating call, another siren wailed from the other direction.

Lubbock and Jackson walked over to Tillman, all smiles.

"Well, son of a bitch, ain't this the shits?" Lubbock said.

"That's what Emmet said just a little while ago," Jackson said, as though the coincidence was too amazing to go uncelebrated.

"Ain't this something? Had yourself a little spot of trouble here, did you, Emmet?"

"For Christ's sake, fellas, you had me worried there for a minute," Tillman said. He reached out a hand to grab Lubbock's arm, but Lubbock flinched away, and Tillman remembered what Cape and even Whistler had warned him about. "You acted like you didn't even goddamn know me."

"Well, look here, Emmet, we only got to work your show for eight weeks, then we were canned."

"I didn't know that."

"Oh, yes, we were fired," Lubbock said.

"What the hell for?"

"Well, we really don't know."

"What we was told," Jackson said, picking it up, "was that you put the knife in."

"Oh, for Christ's sake . . . I'm sorry. . . ."

"Go ahead. No offense."

"I mean, son of a bitch, what would I want to do that for? Just why would I want to have you fired off the show?"

"That's what we've been asking ourselves. You know what I mean? We always thought we was friends," Lubbock said.

"Yeah, you know. Guzzling a few beers, cutting a few touches, telling each other lies and dirty stories," Jackson said.

"Well, fuck yes, so did I. Who told you I put the knife in?"

"Nobody actually said so. Manny Ostrava hinted at it when he give us the air."

"He's a fucking liar."

Jackson looked at Lubbock. "Didn't I tell you our old buddy, Emmet, would never have done such a thing?"

"That's what you said. Now, Emmet, about this dead citizen and that cunt over there without no head."

"Jesus H. Christ."

Jackson smiled benignly. "You get a good look at that thing under the blanket?"

"I didn't want to look too close."

"Of course you didn't. Make you sick. Ain't it something?"

"It's awful."

"Fucking thing looks almost real."

"What do you mean?"

"Don't it look real? It's not real. Oh, no. That's just a dummy. That man laying there in the street used to make things like that for the movies. He's dead, that's for sure, but that other thing, that's just a dummy."

The first ambulance arrived. It was private, the establishment's name, Khymer Mortuary, discreetly printed in gold on the doors.

Auburn's eyebrows went up as he glanced at Schoonover, silently remarking on the private carrier as two men got out and put the headless body in the back, still wrapped in the same blanket Bosco had thrown over it. Not even bothering with a body bag.

Lubbock, Jackson, and Tillman waited.

The lieutenant, Auburn, and Schoonover watched as though picking up headless bodies were an everyday affair.

The junkies, whores, hustlers, gonifs, and homeless watched as though it were the next best thing to television.

From behind the window of Gentry's, Bosco watched and winced at the pain of a clenched fist that wasn't there.

A minute after the private carrier pulled away the wagon from the morgue pulled up. The female medical examiner got out and looked the dead driver's body over. It only took a minute before she was satisfied and stood up. They bagged the driver, piled back into the ambulance, and took off.

"Here's what we're going to do," Lubbock said. "We're going to get all the facts from Officer Auburn, here. We're going to call for the wrecker, get that sweet BMW out of the rain and over to the police impound. Save you the trouble, okay?"

Jackson leaned his mouth close to Lubbock's ear. "You're right," Lubbock said. "Look, Emmet, we're going to see what we can do about leaving your name out of the report. We want you to go home and put this out of your mind. Okay? You just forget all about it. We'll clean up the mess."

Walter Cape's mansion was empty except for the staff cleaning up and his own servants, most of whom had long since gone off to their beds in the farthest wing.

The phone rang not more than an hour after Burchard had first been awakened by Walter Cape. Nobody could say that Burchard didn't know the wires or wasn't a good man with a phone.

"Your actor friend should be home any minute now, if he isn't home already," Burchard said.

"I owe you one, Bill," Cape said.

"I'm not counting, Walter."

"Well, you know me, Bill. I like to pay my way."

"Forget about it."

"How did you dispose of the headless body?"

"Private carrier is taking it to a contract mortuary."

"Oh?"

"I don't want the press barking at my heels just yet. What's your interest, Walter?"

"I'm not without a certain natural curiosity, Bill."

"That body'll be kept at the private mortuary until I find out what the hell's going on."

"Have you found out anything so far?"

"Not much. It's the hour, Walter. Most people are in bed. I have found out that the driver killed at the scene was Willy Zabadno, a night attendant at the county morgue. I'd say it's a dead certainty the body came from county. Now all I have to do is find out who she was and what the hell Zabadno was doing taking her for a joyride on a rainy night. You know what, Walter?"

"What, Bill?"

"This is a very fucking funny town."

The first thing Tillman did when he got home was to be sick in the toilet. It sobered him up, so he went to the bar and made himself a drink. He opened up the blinds and looked out the window at the panoramic view of Hollywood. A plane with blinking rubies and emeralds on tail and wingtips came in from somewhere. He wanted to cry but was afraid that if he started, he'd never stop. He felt like he was waiting for the shit to hit the fan. The telephone chattered. There it was now, he thought.

"I've been calling every fifteen minutes," Shiela said. "I was just about to call the county jail."

"Now, why would you want to do that, sweetheart?"

"I was afraid they might have you in a cell for whatever they call what you did."

"You would've caused some confusion if you'd done that. The cops at the station wouldn't have known what the hell you were talking about. My friends told me to go home and not give it another thought."

"Just like that? Just like that they let you go?"

"Christ, Shiela, who the hell did you think you were out with? Some asshole featherweight?"

"No featherweight, you."

Well, if she was going to say "no featherweight," why didn't she say "no asshole," too? Did she mean she thought he *was* an asshole? Was she sticking it in and twisting it a little? Smart-ass cunt.

"So, that schmuck got you home okay?"

"If you thought he was a schmuck, why did you let him take me home? You didn't even know him. He could've raped me."

Well, thought Tillman, somebody would've gotten a little piece of ass, which was more than he'd ever got.

"I was saving you a lot of questions, a lot of trouble."

"You were saving yourself some embarrassment and maybe some jail time."

Oh, shit, Tillman thought, here it comes. He should have

checked her fucking teeth and claws before asking her out on a date that first time. Who the fuck did she think she was— giving him a sniff, then closing the gates?

"Say again."

"I have it on my conscience that you and I were doing things people shouldn't be doing in a moving car, on a wet street, in the middle of the night and, by so doing, caused an accident and the death of at least one fellow human being. I don't think I'm going to be able to get much sleep for a while. Maybe a long time."

"Take a Valium," Tillman said in his flattest voice.

"Drugs can get to be a habit. I've just got to find some way to occupy my mind and tire myself so I'll just fall into bed at night and conk right out."

"You have anything in mind?"

"When I'm working on a picture, I just work, eat, and sleep. I mean, I love it, but that's all I've got the energy to do. Just work, eat, and sleep. If I had a job—"

"On my show."

"It wouldn't be very hard to do. I mean, you're certainly no featherweight."

"Small part? Maybe a two-, three-day run?"

"That could do it. I don't know. We could try."

"Maybe if I had them write in a character that you could play for maybe four or five weeks."

"Wouldn't that be lovely? I mean, all that hard work and long hours on the set would surely make me so tired by the time night came, I'd just fall into bed and sleep. Every night for weeks."

"Because when you work on a picture, all you do is work, eat, and sleep."

"And maybe fuck a little."

"Well, you know what?"

"What?"

"You're just going to have to fuck yourself."

"My God, the picture of that headless woman laying naked in the gutter with the rain falling down on her just won't go away."

"That was no body, that was a dummy."

There was a hollow pause.

"You making one of those jokes? Like 'That was no woman, that was my wife'?"

"I'm telling you, you've got nothing to sell. You don't have to lose any sleep, I don't have to give you any job, and you can sew your twat up for all I give a fuck. Now, what do you say to that?"

"I say I'm going to have to think about it and maybe seek some advice."

She hung up and he hung up, and then he called Cape, as he'd been told to do.

"I'm still here at your service, Emmet. You're at home?"

"Yes, sir, I'm home," Tillman said.

"How did it go?"

"I couldn't believe it. I mean, there's these two bodies laying in the street. One without its head. The cops are there giving me the drill. You know. No smiles. No jokes. Just this chilly, polite way they have. Name, address, and telephone number. They know who I am, all right, but they don't even blink. Then the detectives arrive. They're not so sweet. They go shovin' at me with their eyes. You know what I mean? Like they warn me with their eyes that they know I'm a killer and a liar and I'd better watch myself or they'll hang me from the lamppost right then and there."

"Did they know you?"

"Oh, sure. Lubbock and Jackson. They were detectives I knew from the show. You know what I mean? They drew a paycheck for eight weeks. Technical advisers. They told me that, but I already knew it. I didn't know it was eight weeks, but I knew they were on the locations with the company. In the streets. Night and day. We split more than a couple of beers together. I thought we were friends. Lubbock and Jackson. Do you know Lubbock and Jackson?"

"Is there any reason why I should?" Cape said.

"Of course not. Am I crazy? Why should you know anybody like Lubbock and Jackson? Why should you want to know anybody like Lubbock and Jackson? I just figured you knew everybody."

"I know everybody I want to know. Everybody I've got

reason to know. I'll know Lubbock and Jackson. So. They gave you a difficult time and . . ." Cape said.

"At first. They went over and picked up the blanket the counterman from the coffee shop had thrown over the body without a head and looked at me like I'd done it. Then the uniformed superintendent drives up. They have a talk. All the cops have a talk. They come back all smiles. They tell me it isn't a body, it's a dummy. They tell me to go home and forget about it. I can't believe it. They tell me to go home and just forget about it. They'll file the reports. They'll clean up the mess. That's the way they said it. I wasn't to worry. Jesus."

"What is it?"

"I can't forget it. I can't forget that naked body falling out of the back end of the wagon. Her feet were sticking out from under the blanket. I was sick in the toilet when I got home."

"That was the drink. That other thing. The horror show. That was just a dummy. Didn't you just tell me that's what they told you?"

"That's right. I'm not to worry about it. They'll clean up the mess."

"Well, that seems to be that," Cape said. "You can go to bed and get a good night's sleep now."

Tillman cleared his throat. Cape waited. Finally he said, "Is there something else?"

"The woman I was with—Shiela Andes—she called me up."

"She got home safely?"

"Oh, she was just fine. I sent her home because I thought she couldn't make it. She thought I sent her home because I was afraid she'd tell the police what we were doing before we crashed."

"Before you killed the driver of the station wagon because you had your hand between her legs. No reason to kid ourselves, Emmet. What did she want from you?"

"Help with her career. A lot of help."

"What did you say?"

"I told her about the dummy."

"And what did she say?"

"She said she'd think about it and maybe get some advice."

"Don't concern yourself about her. She can be managed. Now, is that all you have to tell me?"

Somebody once told Tillman that the reason why Cape never lost out in business was because he could read a person's mind from the inflections and hesitations in that person's voice. He wondered if Cape knew he was leaving something out. He was leaving that son-of-a-bitch jackal, that night creeper, that Whistler out. He didn't want to tell Cape he turned the cunt over to a scavenger. He didn't want Cape to know he was dumber than he already looked.

"That's all," Tillman said.

"Then give me the Andes woman's address and telephone number and then go to bed and get a good night's sleep."

Seven

TILLMAN'S HOUSE was up Woodrow Wilson Drive in a neighborhood like country. One of those patches for people who'd come from the farms and small towns, learned to hate the city, but couldn't leave it because they were tied to it with chains of gold. So there were neighborhoods that pretended to be small towns or country. It cost a fortune to live in them.

The rich paid half a million for a fair reproduction of the house they could have had back home for sixty grand. The very rich lived in recycled history that cost even more.

Tillman's house had been built for a silent-movie star sixty years earlier. It had been enlarged and remodeled so many times, only a carved cornice here and a beautiful old copper drain spout there gave evidence of the graceful Mediterranean villa it once had been. It was, for all of that, about as big as the garages at Cape's mansion.

There were three signs, lit by baby spots, stuck in the flowering borders of the private access road, that read,
WARNING. ARMED RESPONSE.

The iron gates swung open as Whistler nosed the Chevy over the kick plate. Malibu lights went on all over the grounds. The rain had dwindled to a pretty mist. The sun was threatening to come up.

Tillman, dressed in white slacks, sandals, and an open-mesh shirt, came walking down the drive as though it were mid-afternoon. He had a tall drink in his hand. Whistler stopped the car.

"What do you do about the electric gate if the power fails?" Whistler asked Tillman as he stuck his hand through the window to shake. Tillman ignored the ritual courtesy.

"You've got to crank it open by hand," Tillman said.

"You got a coolie to do that?"

"I do it myself unless I got a broken arm," Tillman said evenly, staring at a spot between Whistler's eyes.

Actor's trick. Throw the other guy off his stride, Whistler thought. *Tillman doesn't like me and isn't going to make this meeting friendly.*

"I had a friend had electric gates," Whistler said. "A friend of his came to show off his new white Corniche Rolls-Royce—one hundred and twenty thousand bucks—and something fritzed the gates. Goddamn things closed on the Rolls before it was through. Opened and closed, opened and closed. Did twenty-two thousand dollars' worth of damage before they stuck."

"I know the feeling," Tillman said. "It's not the cost, it's the upkeep. I can't slip the kid in the parking lot a deuce, it's got to be a sawbuck." He was friendly all of a sudden. Chatting away, forgetting he didn't like Whistler.

"Everybody hates a winner," Whistler said.

"I thought it was supposed to be the other way around," Tillman said, frowning slightly. For a moment he looked wistful, like a kid who'd lost the magic penny.

"That's only one of the lies they tell you in school."

Whistler got out of the car so they could see eye to eye.

Tillman handed Whistler his drink. He dipped his hand into his pocket and pulled out a small fold of bills in a silver clip. It looked like they were all hundreds. He counted off two and handed them over between two fingers, tipping the boy at the parking lot.

"No thanks," Whistler said.

"Two bills. For driving Shiela home. Go ahead. Take it."

"No thanks."

"You earned it. She called me and said you did good."

"How is Miss Andes?" Whistler said, keeping his hands and eyes off the c-notes.

"On my shit list."

"Oh?"

"She said I owed her."

Whistler nodded as though that were a reasonable assumption, but didn't say anything.

"Gave me an idea of how I could repay the favor," Tillman went on.

"Greedy, was she?"

"Oh, no. She was ready to start small enough. Just a small role. Maybe a two-parter a while later. Next year maybe a running character for half a season."

"Well, why not? You must like her, and she's proved herself a friend," Whistler said.

"She's a user like everybody else."

"What the hell," Whistler said. "Some people couldn't find an apple in a stable full of horse shit."

"What's that supposed to mean?"

"It means that some people got no luck. No matter how good the cards look, the last one dealt leaves them with a busted flush. So they go broke and have to build a new stake wherever they can. However they can. From whoever they can."

They were hard-eyeing each other. Tillman had money and was actor-trained, so he was better at it.

For Christ's sake, Whistler thought, *something's happened to queer the pitch. This gazoony isn't scared and he isn't*

*needy. I should just pluck those two yards from his fingers
and run.*

"Well, somebody asks, maybe I'll give. But I don't share
because somebody sticks a gun in my face," Tillman said.

"I don't think Miss Andes got the part," Whistler said.

"She's lucky I don't have her ass kicked."

"Oh, you do that sort of thing, do you?"

"Take the two hundred bucks, Whistler."

"If all you think I did was cab a lady home, that's too
much."

"I'm a big tipper. I even tip people who give me lousy
service and bum steers." Tillman grinned, showing five
thousand dollars' worth of caps. He had that look poker
players get when the bets are doubling and doubling and
they're sitting there with a full house. Even players who think
they have no eyes give it away.

"You got it all wrong, Whistler. The detectives on the
scene—"

"Who was that?"

"Lubbock and Jackson. Hey, why should I tell you who
they were?"

"Who gives a rat's ass? Is it a secret?"

"Well, they did right by me," Tillman said, as though the
news were a triumph over Whistler. "They knew who I was.
We split a couple beers more than once. They treated me like
a friend. Like a fellow cop."

"They didn't book you on drunk driving?"

"They did better. . . ."

"What do you mean 'better'?"

Tillman clammed up. His mouth became a wire with an
insulting curl at one end and a sarcastic twist at the other. He
shoved out the two hundred-dollar bills again.

"What about the dead driver?" Whistler said. "What
about the body with no head?"

"That was nothing but a goddamn movie dummy, you
asshole. The driver was delivering it for a movie."

Whistler stood there doubting himself as the mist took the
crease out of his pants.

"Go on, take it," Tillman said, shoving out the bills again. "You did good. You got the bitch home safe."

Whistler stared at the money and then into Tillman's eyes. He felt like telling the actor to shove the two hundred up his ass. But that way, Whistler thought, you go home two hundred bucks short just for the satisfaction of making an asshole pucker.

He plucked the bills from Tillman's hand without touching his fingers or looking away from his eyes. He folded them up small and put them in his watch pocket. Small change. He got back into the Chevy.

"Hey. I hope your gates don't attack my car," he said.

Eight

THE RAIN hadn't really let up, after all. The four corners were deserted again. Gentry's was still empty except for Bosco, perched on his stool by the register, and a sad lump of a man wearing a wet felt hat slurping up a bowl of soup at the counter.

Isaac Canaan was a Detective Three working the Sexually Exploited Children Detail, Vice Unit, out of Hollywood Detective Division. His eyes were always red-rimmed, as if he'd just got over crying. He worked alone and was rumored never to sleep.

Bosco was reading Darwin's *On the Origin of Species by Means of Natural Selection, or the Preservation of Favored Species in the Struggle for Life*. Whistler came in and sat in the booth by the window. He stared out at the wreckage of the newspaper vending machines that still lay scattered in the gutter. All the rest had been swept away except for some glass and ugly stains.

Bosco came over, book tucked into the pit of his amputated arm, with a cup of coffee for Whistler.

"Sit down," Whistler said. "What did we see tonight?"

"A wreck in which one driver was killed and a body without a head was flung out the door of a wagon. A wreck because of which a television actor, half high on rum or toot, lost his chance to get some nooky."

"Is that what you'd say we saw in case anybody was ever to ask?"

"No, I'd say I saw some asshole slam his brakes on to avoid a pussycat, upon which his vehicle skidded and smashed into a light pole, killing said driver and tossing a special-effects prop that looked like a headless woman out into the gutter."

"Is that what you'd say?"

"I'd take my oath on it."

"How come is that?"

"Because the cops told me that's what I saw."

"You roll over easy."

"I never contradict a cop," Bosco said, rubbing the stump of his arm and looking content.

"They're making assholes out of us, Bosco."

"Nobody's keeping score. Nobody's going to ask the questions."

"That thing ever bother you?"

"All the time. Sometimes it itches, and sometimes it has a heartbeat, and sometimes it remembers my hand. Sometimes it even remembers the feel of the watch I used to wear on that wrist."

"What do you do about it?"

"I don't do nothing about things I can't do nothing about," Bosco said, answering any and all questions on any and all subjects.

"Is that what you learn, reading so much?" Whistler asked.

"I learn that the world ignores you when it ain't stickin' it up your ass," Bosco said. "I learn not to try to eat the holes in Swiss cheese. I learn that iron rusts."

He reached over and grabbed Whistler's wrist with a hand like a bear's paw.

"Hey, Whistler, can't you see the sun would be up if it wasn't rainin'? Go on home and go to bed. There's nothing you can do about fixing the world this morning."

"It don't bother you there's a head without a body in New Orleans and a body without a head here in Los Angeles?"

"Not as much as it bothers that dummy."

Whistler gestured with his head toward Canaan.

"He know about the accident?"

"I didn't ask, and he didn't say," Bosco said.

Whistler slid out of the booth and sat on the stool next to Canaan.

"I heard about the accident," Canaan said.

"When?"

"Just now."

"You got good ears."

Canaan crumpled a handful of crackers into the remains of his soup.

"Breakfast?" Whistler asked.

"Supper."

"What do you think about them letting Tillman take a walk in the rain without getting wet?"

"Who's Tillman?"

"The television actor. You know."

"No, I don't know. I don't have time to watch television. I wouldn't know what I was watching."

"Well, what do you think?"

"I think it's a matter for West Traffic Division. Maybe for Homicide."

"It was Lubbock and Jackson gave him permission."

"Maybe they got their reasons."

"Wouldn't you like to know what they could be?"

His elbow resting on the counter and showing three inches of dirty shirtsleeve, Canaan held up a hairy hand nearly as big as Bosco's. "What does that look like?"

"Your hand."

"Not a paw? I mean, you can see it's a hand and not a paw?"

"I can see it's not a paw."

"Not a cat's-paw?"

"What the fuck," Whistler said, looking at Bosco and asking him to witness the asshole conversation Canaan had drawn him into.

"The story about the cat's-paw—" Bosco started to say.

"I know what the fuck a cat's-paw is," Whistler said.

"Detective Canaan thinks you're going to try and use him for your own purposes again."

"I wasn't going to ask for a favor. I was just making conversation."

"The favor comes next. It always comes next with you, Whistler," Canaan said.

"Well, I mean, if you happened to hear anything here and there, I'd like to know about it. What's the big deal?"

"It's none of your goddamn business is what it is."

Whistler reached for his pocket.

"Don't do it, Whistler. Don't pay for my soup," Canaan said.

"For Christ's sake."

"Shitty, ain't it? A man can't even buy a bowl of soup for a friend anymore."

Whistler was weary but not sleepy. He walked down the boulevard. It started coming down cats and dogs. He saw himself in the dark mirror of a plate-glass window. Hair plastered across his forehead. Rain like tears racing along the streambeds and gullies of his face.

He turned into the shelter of an adult movie house. The lady in the ticket booth had a body like a stack of lumpy pillows. No longer meant for bed. While she took his money and tore a ticket she looked at Whistler as if she'd like to crush him with her thighs or smother him between her tits. She was in a sudden, desperate rage because she knew he wouldn't have her even if she told him it would save her life. She smiled like a shark and called him dearie.

What the hell was anybody doing in a ticket booth at six o'clock in the morning, anyway? Whistler wanted to know. It wasn't natural. It was something only a vampire would do.

The dark gray light inside the movie house was like the light of the rainy morning outside. The obligatory exit signs stole the privacy Whistler had come for. He could make out the faces of the other patrons without difficulty. There were not many. All older men. All waiting for a miracle to come down off the screen and make them young again. Hands in their laps. Hearts elsewhere.

Whistler's clothes gave off the odor of wet dog.

Up on the screen a very pretty girl and a young man were going at it as though it were a pleasure. Was it a pleasure? Whistler wondered. After all, her nipples were erect, and there was a flush on her bosom. The body did its tricks when buttons were pushed. Heartache and disgust notwithstanding.

The girl had the face of a precocious child. A spray of freckles across a snub-nose. As wholesome-looking as sweet cream. He'd known a hundred girls like her back in New York. Had seen a thousand more come to Hollywood just as sweet. Watched them bite the poisoned apple. Shrugged his shoulders and said what the hell. World going to ruin. Who cared about a few more virgin twats turned to stone?

He remembered a girl from a long time ago. Her name had been Suzy. She'd lived in an apartment in one of the fancy hotels along Sunset. Her bedroom was in a tower and it was round. The bed was round, too, and there was glass all around so you could make love to Suzy and later lay propped up against the pillows and count the cars down in the streets of Hollywood. She was the most beautiful whore in town. She was a legend.

They told the story of how an up-and-coming movie star came banging on her door the night before his wedding to another up-and-coming movie star. He wasn't looking for a good-bye fuck. He was begging Suzy to run away with him. She smiled and showed him her tongue and told him it would only cost him fifty bucks because she wanted to give him a wedding present. The story was true.

She gave it to Whistler for free because he was as skinny as a bird and had dark brown eyes that she said made her soft and weak. She called him the little prince.

They lost touch the way it happens in La-La Land. Twenty

years later Whistler bumped into Al Lister, an old extra who used to run errands for Suzy, like scoring hash or snort, for which Suzy also fucked him for free because she felt sorry for him and because she didn't like to pay out cash. Lister hadn't lost touch with Suzy. He knew where she lived out in the Valley.

He was going out to see her, he said, then he was free to have some dinner. He knew Whistler would duck his company unless there was something extra, so he offered him the chance to see Suzy again as an appetizer.

She lived in a ticky-tacky box on a patch of dying grass out in North Hollywood. When she came to the door, Whistler's heart nearly stopped. Her hair was still blond and her eyes still blue. She had a pretty face, with a mouth like the bow on a child's shoe bunched up below a nose like a candy chew. She must have weighed three hundred pounds.

When Lister said, "You remember Whistler, don't you, Suzy?" she said sure, she remembered Whistler, and kissed him on the cheek. Whistler could tell she wasn't glad to see him because she'd grown old and fat and Whistler was no little prince anymore. But still she asked him to come in and offered him a drink.

They sat in a living room full of auction furniture. They had nothing to say. In a corner of the room, in a sort of alcove, she'd hung an enormous photograph of herself when she'd been twenty and the most beautiful whore in La-La Land. It was on the wall behind a kind of altar with a dozen lighted candles lined up on a white linen runner. Whistler excused himself and finished his drink in two swallows. It's better to get some things over fast.

The past and the present did a lap dissolve.

Up on the movie screen two couples were doing it.

He realized he was getting an erection, and that made him sad. So he went back through the falling rain to Gentry's parking lot where he got his Chevy and went home and tried to get some sleep.

The drowned sun shone unseen high above the hills. Smoke the color of a tobacco chewer's spit climbed up to meet it. A single ray broke through a hole in the smog and rain, like a finger pointing the way to nowhere.

Cape picked up the phone when it hummed, just before it rang. It was Burchard back again.

"More news?" Cape asked after they'd exchanged hellos.

"More and less," Burchard said.

"Have you had a look at the woman's body?"

"It's without a head all right, all right."

Cape said nothing. He just let the silence sit there like a rock.

"It's the body of an Oriental woman between twenty and twenty-five years of age. Probably Vietnamese," Burchard said.

"What makes you say that?"

"Something you pick up. A Jap's skin is muddy. A Korean's legs is thick in the knees. A Chinese has broad feet and a big ass. This woman's skin was like pearl once upon a time."

It's not every man who can appreciate a corpse, Cape thought.

"She's been dead a long time."

A long-dead corpse.

"She was probably a Saigon whore. She's been tattooed on the hip."

"With what?"

"With a butterfly."

"You see many of those?"

"We see enough."

"Was she taken from the morgue?"

"Her toe was tagged. The mark shows, but it's not on her toe anymore."

"Have you looked into the files?"

"I'm down here at the county morgue right now," Burchard said. "There's no record fitting her description."

"Are there many Vietnamese in residence?"

"We got a few."

"Surely someone must know something about her."

"It's not the beginning of the business day yet. Give it some time. There anything you want to tell me, Walter?"

"About what?"

"*I'm* asking about what."

"I'm a fan, Bill. Sometimes I think I should have been a cop."

"It pays shit, Walter. You did better becoming a millionaire."

Nine

TEN O'CLOCK in the morning in New Orleans. You could grill saints on the pavement outside the iron lacework gate that guarded a tunnel made of shadows. Shadows that promised to be cool but were as smothering as yards of velvet. The courtyard and the house were walled around with stuccoed brick two feet thick, soldiers trying to keep the sun at bay.

The house on Ursuline Street, converted to apartments, was known as a haunted house. Singular horrors concerning slaves and the sadistic excesses of otherwise forgotten aristocrats were recited by tourist guides to busloads of visitors in the evening hours. On rainy or foggy nights, they declared, hoarse screams and the rattle of chains spilled out into the night from the old torture chambers now used as storage cellars.

Nonny Barcaloo enjoyed the illusion of celebrity. He often sat out on the gallery over the street in the afternoon or early evening, sipping a drink, aware of the visitors gawking at a man who dared to sit his ass among ancient ghosts.

The courtyard smelled of magnolia blossoms—big, white, fleshy flowers like baby's hands stained with nicotine. They couldn't hide the stink of death.

The inner gallery off the master bedroom overlooked the

fountain in the central court. Barcaloo sweated and tried to imagine cool.

Goddamn useless fountain. Put cakes of ice in it, he thought. Cool the water. The spray could maybe cool the air. Make the goddamn fountain—cost him four hundred fifty bucks just this one year in repairs—do some goddamn good. Everything you paid for should do you good. Otherwise trash it.

He caught himself up short. What the hell was he going on about? Fuck the fountain. Blow it up. Blow up the goddamn apartment and every stick of furniture in it. Blow up the building and collect the insurance. He wasn't going to need it anymore. Blow up the goddamn city! A few more arrangements and he was gone. A little housekeeping here and there and he was gone.

His coffee, heavy with chicory, pinched his tongue and gums. Flat, square doughnuts, ordered and delivered from a little shop in Cathedral Alley, left a cake of powdered sugar on his lips and chin. He paid attention to his chewing. He paid attention to the bitter coffee in his mouth. One thing at a time.

He wondered if he should rent out the maisonette or keep it for winter holidays. Come down around Mardi Gras every year. Arrange some filthy games for old times' sake. Maybe run some screen tests. Maybe just get away from being a California big shot for a week.

His brain went from thought to thought like it was sorting mail. A little box for each thought. All his energy focused on each one as his brain plucked it out of its cubbyhole.

Look at me, he thought. *Going west. Going big time. Going to be a prince of La-La Land.*

The phone on the wrought-iron table rang. It was hot to his touch as he cradled it under his ear.

Cape's cool voice came in from the Coast.

"Are you all packed and ready for your trip?"

"Got the sheets on the furniture, Mr. Cape."

"Your lady's excited about the move?"

"She don't get excited about much."

"Anything I can do to stir her up?"

"Get her a date with some movie star," Barcaloo said, laughing at the craziness of such a thing.

"I can certainly arrange an introduction," Cape said in his flattest executive voice.

"Jesus Christ, I was only kiddin' . . ."

"You just name the celebrity she'd like to meet."

"Christ. Any fuckin' one of 'em would make her pussy pucker . . . excuse my French."

"I've heard the expression. If meeting a film star will please her, consider it a favor done."

"I don't know how I can pay you back for something like that."

"There is a little something you can take care of for me if you will, Barcaloo. It shouldn't take but a day or two. I'd like to send a young woman down to you. She thinks she's replacing an actress in a motion picture shooting on location in your city. She threatens to be an embarrassment to a friend of mine."

"You want me to do for you like I done before? Consider your friend unembarrassed."

"No, no. Nothing that final this time, Nonny. Just a little photography. Just some footage that I can have in hand in case she persists in making demands and threats."

"Can it wait until I get to L.A.?"

"Well, no, it can't. I want her out of town right away." Barcaloo laughed. "I gotcha. How dumb can I get?"

"Name a fee."

"Nothing. It don't cost you nothing."

"I want you to name a fee."

"It's my gift to you," Barcaloo said. "A favor for a partner, a favor for a friend."

"You have good manners. I'll call you when I have it arranged."

"I'm always here when you need me, Mr. Cape."

"By the way," Cape said.

"Yes, sir?"

"This young woman I'll be sending to you. She was witness to an accident last night. A man named Willy Zabadno was killed in a car crash. Do you know him?"

"No, sir," Barcaloo said, hoping that he hadn't missed a beat. Cape had ears like a fucking fox. Maybe that was what gave him his edge.

"A body was flung out of the back of the station wagon. It was a naked woman's body. It had no head."

"I never heard of such a crazy thing."

"The body is that of a young Oriental woman. It has a butterfly tattoo on the hip."

"Lots of tattoos around."

"That other woman I sent you. She had a butterfly tattoo. Could this be her body? I told you when I offered you the position that I wanted assurance that you had nothing outstanding that could draw attention to you or me."

"For Christ's sake, Mr. Cape. You think she was the only slant-eyed cunt running around with a butterfly on her ass? I'm telling you, I been around a lot of women got no brains, but I don't fool around with any what got no head," Barcaloo said. He chuckled.

"You have an amusing way about you, Barcaloo," Cape said impassively. "I just ask the question. No offense intended."

Getting information from Motor Vehicles was a snap if you didn't mind standing on your hind legs and panting like a dog.

The lady with blue-rinsed hair and harlequin spectacles wouldn't think Whistler was cute even if he tap-danced and tilted his head to one side. She was hard because her life in the file cabinets was hard.

"What I've got here," Whistler said, "is a reason to ask about an accident what took place last night on the corner of Hollywood and Vine during which six of my vending machines got crushed like empty cans of Miller Lite. I make my living with those machines, and I got to see that someone pays to have them replaced."

"Go to the police. They'll have it on their night sheet."

"You'll also have it in your reports, and there's not a day in the week when I wouldn't rather do business with a pretty woman than some cop with indigestion and flat feet. If the cop has had a sleepless night, next thing you know he'll be asking me to show cause why I should not be sued by the driver of the offending vehicle for obstructing the roadway with a public nuisance. That could lead to litigation and a big fight over first-amendment rights. You know how things can start to happen if you go to a cop. Once I asked an officer how to get to the library. He sends me across the street. Then he gives me a ticket for jaywalking."

"Christ, you can really talk a mile a minute, can't you," the blue-haired lady said, and went to rob the data bank.

She was back faster than Whistler ever hoped, tapping a three-by-five card against her ruby fingernail. She had a little smile on her face.

"Report of accident called into Hollywood Division, two-twenty-one, by one Roscoe Silverlake . . ."

"Bosco?"

"Roscoe Silverlake . . . from Gentry's Coffee Shop and Snack Bar, corner of Hollywood and Vine."

The smile grew broader and richer.

"One-car collision with traffic-light stanchion. One death. William Zabadno, employed by the county, driver of said vehicle."

"Employed by the county?"

"He carried a license to operate municipal vehicles for the morgue," she said.

"No mention of my vending machines?"

"Not a word." Her smile streamed into her ears with the pleasure she was feeling about giving out bad news.

"No witnesses?"

"One Roscoe . . ."

"Bosco . . ."

"Silverlake."

She dealt him the file card like it was a deuce to an inside straight.

"What are you going to do now?" she asked.

"Talk to the cop on the desk," Whistler said.

Barcaloo picked a grape from a bunch in a bowl and turned his thoughts to grapes. Each one crunched audibly when he bit into it. Sometimes he threw a grape at a pigeon. When he scored, he laughed with real pleasure.

"Fachrissakes, leave them little birds alone," a voice like a parrot's scream—without real energy—speared out of the pool of gloom that lay like swamp water on the canopied bed inside the room.

There was a yellow-haired woman in it. She was naked, her breasts sagging with their weight on her rounded belly as she lay propped against a white mound of lacy pillows. Eyes as brightly blue as bits of glass, lying inside tiny puffs of flesh like sugared pastry. Tall glass in hand, tinged with green, slightly fluorescent.

"Drink your worms, Bouche, and let me do what I wanna do," Barcaloo replied.

"Ain't we nice this mornin'. No worms in absinthe."

"Why the hell they say they make it out of wormwood, then?"

"That's just a name for some herb. Like oregano," Bouche said.

"I don't know why you drink that crap, anyway," Barcaloo yelled, without turning around to look at the woman who made faces at his back. "The goddamn stuff's illegal. Don't you know that?"

She laughed, sounding like a small barking dog.

"Got to import the stuff all the way from Switzerland," he raved on. "Could get me busted anytime."

She laughed again, in one short burst, as though she measured out her laughter by the ounce.

"Make you crazy. Give you dee-lirium." He stood up, brushing crumbs of doughnut and specks of sugar from his naked chest and potbelly, where it glistened in a tangle of body hair. "Give you more hallucinations than you can handle. Shrivel your pussy." He stumbled into the bedroom, knees bent, arms dangling, absurdly but menacingly, nearly to the floor. The mane across the hump of his neck and shoulders gave him the look of a stalking beast. He bared his fangs. "Turn you into a goddamn idiot. Dry up your tits."

He leapt upon her.

"Watch out, you silly son of a bitch," she complained.

"You're gonna spill the goddamn drink. There, goddammit, you see there? You spilled my drink all over my tits."

He fixed his snout to her teat and sucked.

"Stop it, you loony son of a bitch, stop it," she screeched through her laughter in a voice like chalk on slate. "Don't you bite me."

He rooted at her breasts and belly, making animal noises as he worked his way down to her crotch. His furry arms and legs clasped her as she bucked and writhed away from him.

"You weigh a ton," she said. "You should be on a goddamn diet. You should be eatin' carrot sticks instead of doughnuts. You should be eatin' lettuce leaves instead of grapes."

"Lookayou talkin'. Lookayou fat ass. Lookayou fat gut." His words struggled up out of her flesh like bubbles bursting out of a mud hole. One hand was fumbling down in the fold of flesh at the bottom of his belly, trying to arouse himself. He fixed his teeth in her plump, white shoulder amid a lacework of tiny, shining scars.

"Oh, no, fachrissakes." She moaned, all laughter stopped off with a plug of pain. "You brush your teeth? You scrub your teeth? You gonna give me blood poisoning. Not this mornin', fachrissakes. I was goin' for a swim."

Real fear shaped her mouth and filled her eyes. She looked over his shoulder and down his back as he plowed her, her eyes fixed on the place above his kidney where she would place the knife if she ever got the nerve.

"My name's Polokowsky," the operations corporal said, "it ain't friend. Here's yesterday's book. It says here in black and white. One-vehicle collision with municipal property. One death. Just like you got it on that card. Where'd you get that card?"

"Motor Vehicles."

"They ain't supposed to intercourse with the citizens in matters of this kind. It's a police matter."

"That's what I say," Whistler said. "I want to talk to a cop."

"You're talking to a cop."

"I want to talk to a cop that was on the scene."

"Them cops was working last out. You know what last out is?"

"Sure. It's the midnight-to-eight shift."

"That's right. Which means they is in bed sleeping, I trust. You come right back here at midnight. That's when Officer Auburn and Officer Schoonover come on."

"You got a home address on whichever?"

"You intend to bother one or both of these officers at home while they're sleeping or recreating with their wives?"

"I got an urgency about my vending machines, and I'd like to talk to somebody who was there before the statute of limitations on my property runs out," Whistler said. "Besides, it's already past noon, and those policemen probably ain't even in bed yet, anyway."

"I need persuasion," Polokowsky said.

Whistler tapped the night book and, like magic, a folded twenty appeared between its pages.

Polokowsky closed the book and wrote down Officer Auburn's address on a piece of paper.

"Why'd you give me Auburn's address and not Schoonover's? Why not both?"

"Schoonover's got troubles. If he's in bed, he needs his sleep."

"What kind of troubles has he got?"

"He's got a hernia, five brats, and a wife he can't stomach what runs around on him every chance she gets. It makes him sad and it makes him mean."

Her name was Hanna Susan Cazebone. She'd been a whore since she was twelve. Barcaloo had called her Bouche from the minute she'd done him in the back room of Jimmy Flynn's four years before. *Bouche* means "mouth," in French. It could be he called her Bouche because her mouth was pretty, because she ran it all the time, or because it was her sexual specialty. He'd bought her for two liver-spotted hounds, three handguns, an ounce of China white, and two hundred bucks.

He screwed a hundred women a year, but he needed her.

She promised him her respect but never gave it. That was her edge.

She was alive with prickly heat. Fucking Barcaloo was like coupling with a shaggy dog.

He lay next to her, breathing and grunting like a pig, tossing his head from side to side, looking for breath, holding her hand.

"One of these days you'll blink out like a light, the way you go at it," she said. "Heart'll pop like a balloon in the middle of a stroke. Alive going up, and dead coming down."

"You'd like that, wouldn't you?"

Bouche laughed her short, demented laugh.

"You're a nut," Barcaloo said.

"Look what you did to my shoulder again, you fuckin' animal," she said, wiping the pale mix of blood and saliva from her shoulder with the palm of her hand. "You're going to give me a goddamn infection, for sure."

"Germs can't live in your blood," Barcaloo said. "Full of wormwood. Full of poison."

"I got to wash. I got to put on iodine. Oh, shit, it's gonna hurt."

She waited for him to let go of her hand. He still held on, measuring his breaths.

"I was born right out in those gutters," he said. "I was selling pipes of hash when I was seven. I was peddling my sister's ass when I was nine."

It was going to happen again. He was going to tell her his life story again. There was something about telling it that satisfied him. Some men fell asleep right after they came. Like horses dropped with the pipe gun at the slaughterhouse where Barcaloo sometimes took Bouche just to watch the killing. Some men liked a drink or a cigarette, but he liked to tell his life story. He told it in the dreamy voice of a kid reciting fairy tales.

She shrugged slightly, wanting to get up and wash herself.

"I got to take a pee," she said.

He held her hand tighter.

"Go ahead and do it," he said.

"For Christ's sake," Bouche mumbled, but stopped pulling away.

"My sister taught me how to fuck," he said. "You know that? That's supposed to be about the worst. I mean, a sister with a brother, like a father with his daughter, you know what I mean? They're crazy. What's wrong? Nothing's wrong."

His eyes blinked open and shut like a camera's shutter.

"I *own* this apartment house. I used to run errands for whores and painters who lived in this house, and now I own it."

Bouche wiggled her fingers inside his fist, trying to work some blood into them. She glanced down and saw that the tips were white. There was a drying snail track on her thigh.

"Sold playin' cards for a dollar a pack to assholes come down from New York, Chicago, Minneapolis. Cards with whores doin' tricks and capers on the backs. Fifty-two poses, plus two jokers and a title card. All different. I gave good value. I was twelve."

He took a long, shuddering breath and tossed his head back. He stared up at the reflections on the ceiling.

"My sister Ina's dead, you know. Her boyfriend cut her twat out of her in an alley off St. Ann Street. Oh, he shouldn'ta done that. He shouldn'ta put that big hole in her and let her bleed to death."

"But you did for that son of a bitch, didn't you?" Bouche whispered, hoping to deflect his growing agitation that could easily turn on her. "Even though you was only a kid?"

His grin gleamed whitely in the shadows. It was the most—maybe the only—attractive feature he had. White teeth like chips of porcelain, the canines small and pointed like a dog's.

"I done him. Oh, yes, I done him. I paid three cruel buggers a hundred bucks apiece, and they caught that rat for me. Very queer dudes they was. All big fuckers what liked to dress up like women and give it to men up the ass. How can you figure such a thing as that?"

Bouche felt her stomach roll. It frightened her. She knew the world was crazy, but she also knew, without being able to say so, that she was safe as long as she didn't lose her immunity to the insanity. If she saw it, felt it, let it touch her mind and heart and make her sick, she'd end up running naked down the street looking for someone to shoot her.

"Oh my, oh my, oh my," she whispered.

"Had my own goddamn playing cards printed when I was fourteen. I had ideas. I did pictures with black men doing white women and the other way around. I could read inside the heads of all those square johns. Oh, yeah, I could. Square janes too. I took pictures of women with dogs and ponies. . . ."

Bouche really did have to pee. She could feel her bladder filling up. She ought to give him a golden shower, she thought. Make him happy. She hadn't pissed on him in a long time. My God, the things some people did for kicks.

Ten

REGINALD AUBURN had skin like iron polished with stove black. He sat at his kitchen table in starched white shorts looking at Whistler with yellow eyes. The man looked so evil, it took your breath away. But when he spoke, his voice was as gentle as a dove's.

"Let me get you straight," he said. "Tell me again what it is you want."

"I distribute newspapers and tabloids to vending machines. . . ."

"You lying to me," Auburn said mildly.

Whistler grunted as though struck a blow.

"What makes you say that?" he asked.

"You haven't got the right kind of clothes for that hustle."

"I knew I was going to be talking to people, so I dressed up for the occasion."

"Shee-it," Auburn said. "You want coffee?"

"You having coffee?"

"If my wife made a pot before she left for school, I'm having coffee."

He waved his arm and gave Whistler the idea that he was meant to lift the pot. It was heavy. He set it back down on the burner and turned on the gas flame. Then he leaned against the counter between sink and stove.

"This going to be a good day," Auburn said, pleased that there was coffee in the pot. He peered one-eyed into the cream jug and grinned. "A gooood day."

"What time did you get to the scene of the accident at Hollywood and Vine?" Whistler said.

"I logged it at three thirty-five," Auburn said lazily, as though the information were of no account.

"A citizen reported the accident before two."

"You know one hell of a lot for a newspaper boy." Auburn grinned slowly and slickly as he drawled his words out, cruel cat playing with the mouse.

"I figure you reached the scene no later than two-twenty. Two-thirty on the outside."

"One hell of a lot."

"You mind telling me what you found when you got there?"

"You mind telling me what business it is of yours?"

Whistler tapped the bread box and the toaster.

"You want me to make you some toast?"

"You playing mother?"

"Just like to make myself useful. I find it pays off."

Their eyes explored the eyes of the other. Reading between the lines. Shorthand code of the streets and alleys. Saying one thing and meaning another. Saying nothing and telling all.

"Make me some toast," Auburn said.

Whistler took half a loaf of raisin bread out of the box. He popped two slices into the toaster and depressed the lever.

"You carryin' a private ticket?" Auburn said.

"Remind me never to try to shit you," Whistler said.

"When I arrived on the scene with my partner, we saw a

nineteen seventy-four Ford station wagon piled up against a hydrant and a rack of vendors. The driver—"

"How did you know it was the driver?"

"There was nobody else hurt or dead."

"Nobody else on the scene when the accident occurred?"

"Nobody except the counterman in the all-nighter."

Something flickered in Auburn's catlike eyes. Something that sparkled like sudden shame. Here was a man who didn't like to lie, Whistler thought.

"And that was all?"

"You telling me different?" Auburn said softly.

The toaster popped the slices up. The coffee steamed. Whistler poured the coffee while Auburn roused himself and got the butter out of the refrigerator.

The policeman sat down and saw the twenty under his cup. He sat there with the butter knife in his hand and stared at Whistler with his yellow eyes.

"What did I miss?" Auburn said. "You got a client? You on expenses?"

"I'm making an investment in the future. I figure there might have been somebody else injured in the accident. Somebody who was in the station wagon. I figure there might have been a witness besides the counterman."

"You better not tell me how you figure all this," Auburn said.

"So, there was nobody else there? Just you and your partner, Schoonover, and the counterman and the corpse of the driver?"

"And the plainclothes what came, and the team on the morgue wagon, and, later, the people what come out of the bricks when anybody dies in the street. Nobody else. That's official. You understand?"

Whistler glanced at the twenty and nodded, waiting for more.

"You better pick that money up," Auburn said, "or I'll start asking you some questions right now, right here, unofficially. You won't find it a comfort."

"I don't suppose your partner ever sees things different than you do?" Whistler asked, picking up the twenty.

"He sees the same as me. But maybe I see different anytime I know more than I know this minute."

Auburn stood up. He wasn't all that big, not as big as Whistler, but all the same, there was something intimidating about the simple move.

"You don't go botherin' Harry, you understand? Is that coffee you poured for yourself to go, or are you gonna drink it here?" Auburn said.

Whistler took three swallows and set the cup down half empty.

"Thank you for your hospitality."

"Anytime."

There was a knock on the door. Barcaloo yelled for whoever it was to come in without even asking who it was. The football players in the night game Chippy Byrd and Lacy Ohio had witnessed came through the door. The big one was Dom Pinole, the little one was Jickie Rojo. Pinole had a folded newspaper in his back pocket and was looking nervous, reaching back every ten seconds or so to make sure it hadn't caught fire.

Bouche grabbed the end of the sheet and drew it across her lap.

"What have you got in your pocket, Dom?" she asked.

"Nothin'."

"My God, it looks like something to me. If I didn't know you couldn't read, I'd swear it was a newspaper."

Barcaloo rolled out of bed and put on a bathrobe. "So, what the hell you doin' bustin' in here like this? Did I send for you?"

"Lemme see the newspaper," Bouche said, enjoying Pinole's agitation and curious about the cause of it. "You got the *Wall Street Journal* there? You got the *Christian Science Monitor*?"

"Please . . ." Pinole started to say, his heavy-featured face screwing up in anxiety. Barcaloo started to tell her to shut up, but Rojo showed his teeth to Bouche and said, "Lay the fuck off it."

It was like dropping cold water into a pot of hot iron.

Barcaloo's rage took about five seconds to boil up. It sizzled and flared.

"What I hear you just say? What gives you the right to use your mouth like you just used it on Bouche? Who the hell done that? Give you the fuckin' privilege? Give you the fuckin' permission? You come breakin' into my bedroom—"

"It just slipped out," Pinole said, making quick excuses. "Jickie don't mean nothin'."

"It's all right, Nonny," Bouche yelled above Barcaloo's shouting, half enjoying his anger when it wasn't directed at her.

". . . without even fuckin' knockin'," Barcaloo roared on.

"We knocked," Pinole said.

"Then you talk to Bouche like you done? Then you—"

"I was just teasing Dom," Bouche broke in. "No cause to get mad at me, Jickie. Dom's just a big kid and I like to tease him." She snatched the paper from Pinole's pocket.

". . . like she's some whore off the goddamn street!"

"See? It's just the *Enquirer*," Bouche said. "It's just nothing. . . ."

"I ought to leave you in this shithole of a city," Barcaloo mumbled.

". . . but that rag what writes about all sorts of crazy things. See? Here they got this story about some head these two people see somebody kicking around over to the lake."

"Lemme see that," Barcaloo yelled. He grabbed the newspaper out of her hand and started to read. All the blood drained out of his face. His cheeks and the end of his nose looked frostbitten. He read slowly, his lips making the words one by one as he plodded right on through to the end. He stared at the two cuts of Chippy Byrd and Lacy Ohio. His eyes came up and fixed on Pinole.

The buzzing of a single fly seemed loud as it closed in on Barcaloo, drawn by his odor. He waved his hand around his ear, but it came back. He watched it hover near his eye. His brain focused on the bug, as though it were the only thing of importance in his life. His hand flashed out and trapped the fly in his fist. He slapped his hands together, then wiped them off on his robe.

Pinole opened his mouth and looked at Rojo for support, but Rojo was staring at Bouche's heavy breasts.

"What the hell you doing, Bouche?" Barcaloo whispered fiercely, "runnin' a goddamn fruit stand, sittin' around with your melons hanging out like that? Get outta here."

"Oh, fachrissakes, you got these two assholes livin' in your pocket, right the fuck downstairs in the cellar flat. They walk in any goddamn time they want without even knockin', and you fuckin' yell at me," Bouche shrieked, wrapping the sheet around her and dragging it off the bed as she stood up. "Besides, these two assholes of yours has seen every inch of skin I got taking my picture for your goddamn dirty movies."

"That's different, that's in the line of business."

"Why'd they come back from L.A. in the first place? We're going to be there in a few days, but you send them out there and they come back here, and now they'll be going back there again. They're like a couple of goddamn businessmen takin' the shuttle flight. I don't know why you put up with two such assholes in the first place." She glared at Rojo. "I'm going to take a crap, dum-dum, you want to come in and watch?"

He raised his stare to her eyes. She ran into the bathroom with the sheet trailing behind her.

"I ought to kick your asses out, just like she says," Barcaloo raged. "I should leave you facedown in the bayou. One fuckup after a goddamn other. What the hell you think you was doing?"

"It starts out we have a couple of drinks and a toot, you know?" Pinole said.

"I *don't* know. It's why I'm asking."

"We was having a little fun. It got away from us," Rojo said.

"Here's your little fun," Barcaloo shouted, slapping the paper with the back of his hand, smashing a hole in the faces of Chippy Byrd and Lacy Ohio, who grinned out in black-and-white halftone from the newsprint. He lowered his voice with great effort. "I ask you to trash that head, and you play football with it. Which is goddamn weird. You play kickball with it and you don't get rid of it."

"We thought we got rid of it," Pinole said. "We dump it in the mud by the lake. How the hell are we supposed to figure this creature comes along and pulls it out for its dinner? How the hell we know that?"

"What makes you pick the goddamn lake in the first place? We got the city dump for things like arms, legs, and heads."

"So we'll know better next time."

"Just like that, you silly son of a bitch? This could maybe queer the biggest deal of my career. You unnerstan' that? I'm supposed to take over the porno trade for the entire fuckin' country west of the fuckin' Mississippi. You unnerstan' what I'm sayin'? I'm told to make sure there's nothin' outstanding could attract undue attention. I go to the trouble. Now I get word this morning that a body without a head turns up at the corner of Hollywood and Vine. Guess who's driving the car what it fell out of? Willy Zabadno."

"Jesus H. Christ."

Barcaloo's eyes flicked over to the bathroom door, as though making sure that Bouche wasn't on the eary.

"And right after that good news I got to read this crap. Suppose the man on the West Coast happens to read this goddamn scandal sheet? Suppose he just happens to read about this here head which you two kicked around? Suppose he puts two and two together and comes up with this head down here and a body without no head in L.A.?"

"Well, for Christ's sake," said Pinole, "why's this head here got to belong to that body back there?"

"Because it's a gook corpse and it's got a butterfly on its ass and I don't think the country's overstuffed with so many heads and bodies without heads that it don't merit some attention and maybe a remark or two. Now, you got any idea what I want you to do?"

"You want we should find those two assholes what run off at the mouth to the newspaper and see they don't run off at the mouth no more?" Rojo said.

"And we bury 'em in the city dump and not by the lake," Pinole added.

"Yeah," Barcaloo said. "Also you dump that goddamn Cadillac with the Bondoed fender in the bayou right away."

"We was gonna drive out to the Coast in it," Pinole complained.

"Dump it right the fuck now, I said."

"We could get it sprayed . . ." Pinole persisted.

Barcaloo stared at him, and Pinole looked away. "So, we'll bury them two assholes in it," he said.

"But first you bring 'em out to the studio. First we shoot a little footage. No sense lettin' them two go to waste altogether."

Whistler ran Harry Schoonover down in a little bar across the street from the apartment building on Western Avenue in which the cop and his family lived. He was seated by a window laced with yellow rain, a beer glass getting warm in his two hands, his eyes on the windows third-floor front. He had the sad eyes of a spaniel. His hair was red and combed across his forehead like a small boy whose mother got him ready for school.

Whistler introduced himself and asked Schoonover if he wanted a cold, fresh beer.

"It took me half an hour to warm this one," Schoonover said in flat accents, an immigrant from the East. "Who are you and what do you want?"

"My name's Whistler."

Schoonover took a second to flick a glance at Whistler, then turned his eyes back to the windows of his flat.

"Auburn told me about you."

"You see the same thing he saw at the corner of Hollywood and Vine?"

"The very same thing. Get the fuck out of here."

"You live up there?"

"Up where?"

"Up there behind the windows you're looking at."

"What do you know about where I live?"

"I don't. That's why I ask."

Schoonover gave Whistler his full attention.

"If you want to be a cop, if you want to do for law and

order," Schoonover said sarcastically, "why don't you put in your application? Be a blue?"

"I got a limp."

"You got a belly full of shit."

"You mad at me because you know I'm going to make you an offer and you probably aren't going to turn me down?"

Schoonover let his eyes go flatter than they already were. Flat and mean and filled with melancholy despair over a life that had become a tangle of old rubber bands and bent pins.

"What are you offering?"

"Twenty."

"I roll up twenty-dollar bills and use them for suppositories."

"I doubt it. Not with five kids and a complaining wife you don't. How about fifty?"

"What do you want?"

"Nothing much. Just what you saw at the corner of Hollywood and Vine last night."

"What's your interest?"

"I was there and I saw what I saw. Now everybody's telling me I didn't see it."

"Who gives a rat's ass?"

"I like to know I'm not going crazy."

"How you going to use it?"

"I'm no bird dog for a newspaper. I don't know how I'm going to use it. Maybe I just don't like to see shit covered up. Sooner or later I could step in it. Call me curious."

"Two-car smashup. A brand-new silver BMW and a seventy-four station wagon. The driver of the station wagon was killed. The driver of the BMW was waiting for us outside a coffee shop. We called for detectives because there was a fatality—"

"Excuse me for interrupting. Just one fatality?"

"There was another body under a blanket. A woman's. Strictly speaking, her death had not been caused by the accident."

"Can you describe that body for me?"

"It had no head. If it would've had a head, she would have been about five foot one, a hundred five pounds. Oriental.

Maybe Chinese. Probably Vietnamese. Her legs were a little bowed, and her tits were small. She was probably a Saigon whore."

Whistler almost said it was a wonder that Schoonover could tell that from looking at a bloodless corpse, but he didn't. "What makes you say that?"

"She was wearing a tattoo on the side of her belly by her hipbone. A butterfly. And that's the way a Saigon trader marks a Saigon whore."

"You try to look her up back in Records?"

"We were told not to browse. We were told she was the little woman who wasn't there."

Whistler handed over the fifty.

"Who asked you and Auburn to forget about her?"

"Lubbock and Jackson *told* us to forget about her."

"You do everything detectives tell you to do?"

"I do most everything my supervisor tells me to do."

"What was the supervisor's name?"

"Good night, asshole."

"You got my fifty."

Schoonover stared at the fifty-dollar bill spread out between his hands as though it were the first sign of his corruption. He looked up at the windows of the apartment house where he lived with a wife and five kids.

"Lieutenant Muncie."

He touched his hand to his groin and winced as he shifted his weight to his other hip.

"Get the fuck out of here," he said.

Eleven

WITH HER makeup off Lacy Ohio looked like a Loretta Oskanowsky. She looked like a Loretta Oskanowsky with sallow skin, small eyes, and crooked teeth, and that's what she intended to remain, even if that sweet-talking son of a bitch Chippy Byrd came around again trying to get into her pants. Asking her out to some bar or nightclub to listen to a little music, a little jazz. Have a little fun. Have a few drinks. Buttering her up. Oiling up her hip joints so he could push her knees apart.

Not that she wasn't ready. She was ready. But she was no pushover. Her heels weren't round. Man or boy wanted to fiddle with her treasure, he had to work for it. No quick-and-easy roll me over in the clover.

When he'd taken her home that night, after the fright of her life, the son of a bitch had tried to con her into fucking right there in her own parlor with her deaf old grandmother sleeping in the next room. Jesus Christ, did he have no shame? Did he have no fear? Fucking with her grandmother right in the next room and maybe having to get up to take a pee.

He'd had plenty of fear over to the lake. She'd smelled it on him when those two wackos were kicking the head around. Before they knew it was a head. When it could have been two drunks kicking a ball. But Chippy had known there was something not right. Something very wrong. He'd known it and sat there as still as a mouse, his lips moving, silently praying they wouldn't look his way. That's why she hadn't honked the horn like she was about to do. To try to scare the two drunks. To have a little fun with them.

Something about the way Chippy sat so still told her to be just as quiet as he was. Lucky for them.

By the night after, though, Chippy had forgotten the scare they'd had. Nothing front-page in the *Times–Picayune* about the head. Just an item on the fifth page. Nothing much on the television news. Just a wry item with a twisted grin at the end of the six o'clock, as if heads without bodies weren't horrible but merely odd. Remarkable but somehow funny. It was the head of a gook. Who gave a fuck about the head of a gook or a nigger?

"Small potatoes," Chippy'd said, "not worth worrying about. Come on out and play," he'd said, flashing a sheaf of tempting green.

So off she'd gone with him. Over to the French Quarter to Al Hirt's for a little trumpet, a little jazz. Over to Algiers and Manny the Mule's joint. Over to Jimmy Flynn's on St. Peter where Jimmy Flynn himself stood behind the bar telling stories and lending an ear.

And that fool, Chippy, couldn't resist showing off. Couldn't resist telling Jimmy Flynn and one and all that they'd actually been witness to the game of football played with a human head.

Instant celebrity. Free drinks. People smiling at them. Touching them. The character what put his hand on her sleeve and said he was a stringer for *The Enquirer,* the great national newspaper.

"Don't you know it? In every supermarket in the country. Right next to the registers. How'd you like to make a hundred? How about two? Just tell me your story. Give it to me exclusive. Do tell. Oh, do fucking tell. Is that what you sat there looking at? Go on, go on. Tell it in your own words. Let the little lady tell her story. Just a minute. Just hold it." And the flash of the camera. Once for Chippy and once for her.

The next day nothing happening. Those two crazies never showing as she'd feared they might, ready to do to her what they'd done to that head.

Next day after that, *The Enquirer* on the newsstands, in the supermarkets. Still nobody coming to do her harm. The terror

of the name Barcaloo—whoever that might be—starting to
fade away. The memory of all the smiling faces, admiring
eyes, free drinks, hundred-dollar bills, coming back as sweet
as wine.

When the telephone rang five minutes after she got home
from work, while she was cooking up sausages and sauerkraut for herself and her grandmother, she knew it was
Chippy again, ready to ask her to be Lacy Ohio for another
night.

"So what did I tell you?" Byrd said. "Nothing to worry
about. Nothing to be scared about. Just a couple of drunks."

"It was a head," she said. "We both read that in the
newspaper. We both saw it on the tube."

"Well, nobody seems to care. Nobody's doing anything
about it. So nobody's *going* to do anything about it. I want to
spend my hundred on you. I want to turn your belly into
whipped cream."

"Is that dirty? Are you talkin' dirty to me?"

"No, I'm talkin' love. Don't you think it's about time? I
been holdin' my own and dreamin' long enough, don't you
think?"

"I don't know."

"Come on out and play. If you don't want to love me when
the night's over, you can shoot me and put me out of my
misery."

He laughed and she laughed. She hung up after saying yes
and showered and put cake, rouge, and powder on her face.
Turned her cheeks into magnolia petals. Made her lips two
cherries. Made her eyes as big as pansies, all black and
purple. Put Loretta Oskanowsky in the closet with her flannel
nightgówn and sensible shoes.

Gave her grandmother supper and told her not to fall asleep
watching the television.

When Chippy Byrd pushed the bell in the lobby downstairs, Lacy Ohio, in tight black skirt and scarlet shoes, was
out the door and down the stairs like a sprinter.

Jimmy Flynn listened to the horror story about the head as
told by Chippy Byrd and Lacy Ohio as if he'd never heard it
before. In fact, he never had heard the version they now told,

in which Byrd scared the two killers away with fierce threats in defense of his lady love. Ohio stared starry-eyed at her boastful would-be, soon-to-be lover as though he spoke the gospel truth, much preferring to fuck a motion picture hero than a skinny asshole with a squint. She was too busy mooning, and Byrd was too busy lying to notice Jimmy Flynn when he tipped the wink to a big man and a little man who sat hunched on two stools in the gloom at the end of the bar, so they didn't look like a big one and a little one. Didn't see Rojo go to the wall phone and dial a number. Didn't know that the Barcaloo they once had feared, without even knowing more than the name, was telling Rojo that he was too tired and it was too late to lift Byrd and Ohio off the streets.

"Follow them two and find out where they hang their jocks and where they earn their bread. Tomorrow. Tomorrow you pick them up. They can wait until tomorrow."

Tillman, Lubbock, and Jackson each had a tall drink in hand. They were sitting in a booth in a bar on Hollywood Boulevard.

"We asked you to come meet with us because there's this thing about the car."

"My six thirty-five CSi BMW."

"With mag wheels," Jackson said.

"The silver one," Lubbock said. "What a son of a bitch of a machine." He held his arms out and pretended to be driving at speed down a long straight road. "A man wouldn't even need a cock to fuck the cunt, he owns a machine like that."

"It's a nice car, all right," Tillman said. "So what about it?"

"It's in the police impound in need of some repair."

"I was waiting for the word."

"The word? What word?"

"That it was all right to come and get it. I got the pink and registration with me, just like you said."

"Well, you'll just have to make up your mind about that."

"About what?"

"Coming to get the BMW out of impound."

"Something wrong?"

"Well, it's like this," Jackson said, the sober accountant of the team of Lubbock and Jackson. "We swept a few facts under the rug, so we don't have to take you downtown and book you on vehicular manslaughter."

"Which, under the law, we are sworn to do in the case of any such accident that causes injury, let alone death. You know what I'm saying?" Lubbock chimed in.

"Begging your pardon, Ernie, but I'm trying to apprise our friend, Emmet, here, about the facts. Which I cannot do if you interrupt."

"Sorry, Marty, I just wanted to emphasize the seriousness of the breech of procedure, if not law, which we committed for a friend."

"Understood, but I think Emmet knows. He plays a cop, and he knows what it's all about. How can he not know what it's all about playing a cop five shooting days a week, twenty-six episodes a year?" Jackson turned back to Tillman and smiled briefly. "In order to maintain your anonymity while explaining a silver six thirty-three . . ."

"Six thirty-five," Tillman said.

"Six thirty-five . . . you want to lay the letters on me again?"

"CSi."

"BMW, that's right, we had to put it in the impound as an abandoned vehicle. You understand what this means?"

Tillman shook his head.

"This means . . . You want another drink?"

"No, I'm okay."

"This means the car will stay in impound while the stolen car register is searched. It'll stay there for ninety days if there's no claim made upon it. Now, if you go down there to the police impound and claim your vehicle, somebody's going to want to know why you didn't come asking about a forty-thousand-dollar machine the minute you see it's missing."

"And who knows where that question will lead?" said Lubbock. "Begging your pardon, Marty, are you through?"

"I was through, Ernie. And your point is well taken."

"I mean, we're keeping your involvement in this fatal accident quiet. But these things get bandied . . ." He looked at his partner.

Jackson nodded sagely and said, "Bandied."

"Get bandied around. I mean, forget that asshole Willy Zabadno for a minute. What we're talking about is a body without a fucking head. A minority body, you understand what I'm saying? All of a sudden—who knows?—we got equal-opportunity lawyers fucking around. We got the Civil Liberties Union. We got some fucking old country family *society*."

"There could be ramifications," Jackson said solemnly.

"So what should I do?" Tillman said.

"What you can do is sign the pink slip over to one of us, see? Any fucker down there at the police impound asks us what we're doing picking up a car like that, we tell him to mind his own fucking business if he don't want his balls crushed. You know what I'm saying?"

"I turn the pink slip over to you. You get the car out of impound. Then what?"

"Then we take it to a garage. What do you think it's going to cost fixing the radiator and front end?"

"I'm not a mechanic."

"Neither am I."

"Me, neither," Jackson chimed in.

"The mechanic down at the police impound garage says six thousand minimum, give or take a twenty-dollar bill."

"Needs new fenders. Maybe a new axle."

"If . . ." Lubbock said, tossing a look at his partner. "If the frame ain't bent."

"Frame on a vehicle like that gets bent, it's never the same," Jackson said.

For a second it looked like he was going to take off his hat and hold it over his heart.

"Good for nothing but junk, the frame's bent," Jackson said.

"It's something to think about," Tillman said.

"It's a fucking headache. But we have a suggestion."

Tillman arranged his face to be grateful for what was coming.

"You got insurance on the vehicle?"

"Of course I have insurance."

"Does he look like the kind of fool wouldn't have insurance on a vehicle like that, being as famous as he is?" Jackson scolded. "Of course he's got insurance."

"So, you report the car stolen. We write up the report for you and give you a copy for your broker. We put a copy in the files in case the adjuster wants a look. You understand what I'm saying?"

"My rates go up."

"So what the fuck's that? Piss in a bucket."

"What happens to the car?"

"It's a beautiful car. I'd love to own such a beautiful car."

"Me too," said Jackson.

"But where would a couple of working stiffs like us get the money for a car like that?"

"Nowhere is where," said Jackson.

"So the best thing we can do is make a deal with the mechanic down to this dealership we know. He does the job for us half price after hours. He can use the tools, garage, heat, and light, you understand? No overhead. The boss does us that favor. Mechanic works the job in his spare time. Even gives it a new paint job. I like silver, but Jackson here says it should be black. It costs Jackson and me maybe three thousand."

"Unless the frame's bent."

"That goes without saying. We take the chance. We already got the pink. Then we maybe drive it around for a week. Have a little fun. Imagine what it would be like to really own a car like that. Then we wholesale it out to a dealer we know. Maybe we make a few thousand. Why not? You don't begrudge us?"

"No, I don't begrudge you."

"Because we're taking the chance, you see? We've been taking a lot of chances to help you out. Not that we begrudge it. After all, what are friends for except to do them a favor now and then . . . fuck the chances you got to take . . . and give yourself a good feeling."

Tillman handed over the registration and the pink slip.

"You want another drink?" Jackson asked.

"No, I've got a date," Tillman said, reaching for the tab.

"Hey, hey!" Lubbock said loudly and heartily, grabbing Tillman's wrist with one hand and the check with the other. "Your money's no good here."

Auburn could see Harry Schoonover out of the corner of his eye as they drove through the night streets. He thought about what makes a cop partnership. The trouble it was. Worse than a marriage in many ways. Harder to make work.

First there'd been the fact that he was black and Schoonover white. Harry was no redneck, but he'd been raised not wanting much to do with niggers, just like he, Auburn, had been raised not much trusting honkies. How the hell could it have been any other way? Blacks pushing into white neighborhoods where they weren't wanted just so they could escape ghettos that were so bad, even the rats were looking to move. And where the hell were the working-class whites supposed to go?

Then there was the fact that Auburn was thin, almost skinny, a runner, once an all-state forward on his high-school basketball team. And good-looking to boot, even if he did say so himself. Harry was going to fat, and there was a bald spot growing on the back of his head. He had a nose like a turkey's ass and teeth no two of which grew in the same direction. They were also going to hell from the candy bars he ate. Harry had toothaches all the time.

Auburn's own marriage was hopeful, sex life hearty, future bright. Harry's marriage was a mess, he got no fucking at home anymore.

Schoonover told Auburn that his wife, Shirley, had cut off his water because she'd said five kids were enough.

"There's IUDs and the pill," Harry'd told her.

"You want to kill me with uterine infections and cancer?"

"I could wear a rubber."

"Don't talk dirty!"

"It don't seem to bother her when the several assholes she fucks outside the home wear condoms, which they must do, otherwise she'd get knocked up again just as easy from them as me," Harry had told Auburn.

"For Christ's sake, you don't want to go talking about your wife that way," Auburn had said.

He thought Harry's wife, Shirley, was self-destructive. He and Alicia, his own sweetheart wife, often talked about it and said how lucky they were, while poor Harry's life was going down the toilet at a fearful rate.

Not to mention money.

Alicia worked and went to school too. He worked an extra job tending bar. They were saving. They were looking at houses together out in Woodland Hills.

Schoonover's wife stayed at home when she wasn't out screwing other men. Harry was always buying her useless things to soothe her. And five kids ate up money like Crackerjacks.

It was so hard making a partnership. They'd finally made one.

"You got a toothache?" Auburn said.

"You mean, have I got *another* toothache?" Schoonover said, as snappish as a junkyard dog.

"No, I mean have you got a toothache now," Auburn said calmly.

"No, I ain't got a toothache."

"How about a wild hair up your ass? You got a wild pussy whisker up your ass?" Auburn said in the same tone of voice.

Schoonover couldn't help it. He snorted through his nose with laughter.

"That son of a bitch Whistler?" he said. "He came to see me even after you told him I saw what you saw over to Hollywood and Vine."

"You mean that rascal didn't believe me?" Auburn said, half sarcastic, half amused.

"From the way he talked, it's a bet he was at the scene and left it."

"Nothing strange about that. Most people don't want to get involved."

"If this Whistler don't want to get involved, what the fuck's he doing running around asking you and me questions?" Schoonover shrugged heavily. He didn't want to think about another man's motives for doing whatever.

"You don't think the son of a bitch is Internal Affairs?" Jackson said.

"You mean those cocksuckers could be laying a trap?"

"Them bastards, they got nothing to do, they go make themselves something to do."

"Oh, Christ, I don't think so. I think I seen that schmuck hanging around Gentry's for a couple of years already."

"I think I have too. And I think I've seen him head-to-head with that kiddie vice cop, Canaan, on more than one occasion."

"You know about Canaan?"

"I heard about him, yes. I don't know if it's good for a cop to hate as bad as he does. Destroys his perspective. Makes it hard to work the deals you've got to work to make it happen out there on the streets."

"I think my brother's kid was snatched off the playground and done like that little girl was done, I'd be hating pretty good too."

"How long ago was that?"

"Two years. About two years, I think."

"They say the poor sucker hardly ever sleeps."

They drove on in silence for a while, listening to the hissing of the tires on the wet road, listening to the measured beat of the wipers as they smeared fog and road shit across the windshield.

After a while Auburn said, "I wouldn't worry. I don't think that Whistler's any cop. I think he was hanging out in Gentry's and saw the accident. I think he sees the chance for a hustle and is willing to spend a little to get a lot. How much did he give you?"

"A hundred bucks," Schoonover lied, not wanting to admit he was bought for cheap.

"That's more than he offered me."

"Did you take it?"

Auburn hesitated half a second and then said, "Yeah, I took it. Then I shined him on. You tell him anything?"

"Why the fuck not? They tell us to clam up, they don't tell us why. What the fuck's that supposed to mean? We're pups? We're fuckin' pups on a leash? Lubbock and Jackson don't even bother to tell us any lies, just give us the old slap on the back, do-this-one-for-the-Gipper crap. I don't even know who the fuck we're covering up for. Somebody's getting paid off, that's for fucking sure."

"You bet your sweet ass. But it's none of our business."

"So I didn't tell that Whistler anything a half a dozen characters standing out in the rain couldn't have told him."

Auburn grunted his assent, sorry that he hadn't taken the twenty. Sorry that he hadn't gone for a hundred the way Schoonover had done. Staying honest wasn't easy, and sometimes, he was beginning to think, it didn't much matter.

Twelve

Whistler needed somebody with a memory. Eddie Deane, a reporter who worked the crime beat, owed him one.

Deane was dressed like a Hollywood bit player hoping to be discovered leaning on a bar. Red crushed-leather boots with army twill trousers bloused at the ankles when it rained. Tan work shirt. Authentic Foreign Legion jacket bought through a mail-order firm twenty years ago. Felt hat with two wooden kitchen matches stuck in the brim, although he didn't smoke because half his lungs were already gone. Glass of something amber always in his hand for effect, although he didn't drink because his liver would have killed him in protest if he had.

"It wasn't my generation to do drugs," he said. "But I gave up booze, tobacco, sugar, caffeine, red meat, fats, and will soon give up pussy. Then I'll be perfect. Then they'll make me a saint. If you launched yourself into a program of self-improvement, Whistler, you'd be reborn just like me and live to be a hundred and ten."

"Who wants to live that long if there's a chance of ending up looking like you?"

"I'm beautiful. I'm manly. I'm what the ladies crave. I hear them whispering about the savor of my buns as I walk past them, perched like darling little finches on the bar stools of the city. What do you want to know, and why should I tell you?"

"I want to know about a headless corpse. A woman. Probably Oriental. Maybe Vietnamese."

"I know nothing about headless corpses, Oriental, Vietnamese, or otherwise. And now I no longer owe you."

"Are you shining me on?"

"I've got no reason to throw dust in your face. I've not been bribed. I've not been threatened. I've not been warned."

"Well, you missed a headless body."

"Did I? How did news of such a wonder come your way?"

Whistler told him about the story of the head in *The Enquirer*. He told him about the accident and the body that almost bounced into his lap over to Gentry's. He told him about the story of the dummy and the one-car collision in the DMV files.

"Who's your client?"

"I haven't got one."

"What's your suspicion?"

"Only that there's been a snowfall."

"To cover just exactly what?"

"I haven't got the faintest."

"Could they be right about the body being a dummy?"

"I think I can tell the difference."

"You think the body here in L.A. belongs to the head in New Orleans?"

"Don't make me crazy. It figures."

"It amazes me that we've come to think there's some kind of logic to horror," Deane said, as though Whistler's statement were among the saddest he'd ever heard.

"Do you know about *any* unidentified dead Oriental women?"

Deane closed his eyes. "There was a case. There was a Vietnamese woman found murdered and mutilated two, two and a half years ago. She was living on Alpine Hill with her ten-year-old son and her sister. One day the sisters had a fight. One of them walks out of the apartment . . ."

"What was the fight about?"

Deane opened his eyes.

"I don't remember anybody ever said. Whatever it was, the sister walks out and don't come back. Two months later they found her body out to Elysian Park. She'd been tortured and mutilated.

"A month before the discovery of her body these brothers named Corvallis—ran one of these crazy cults . . . Satanists, maybe—had been picked up for a whole string of mutilation killings, along with three of their followers. The Vietnamese woman was one of the dead. Maybe the last body found. She was discovered down in Malibu after they were arrested. There were maybe a dozen killings altogether, but murder charges were brought against them on only four. The Vietnamese woman among them. The prosecutors told her family they'd need the body for evidence, because marks on the bones of the neck, made with a knife, didn't show up good enough in the photographs. They didn't want the defense stepping on doubtful evidence. They told the family they could bury the daughter, but she might have to be disinterred later on. The family were Mahayana Buddhists from the south. Their faith doesn't allow the body, once buried, to be dug up again. So the body was kept at County Morgue."

"Has the case gone to trial?"

"What with polygraph tests, psychiatric evaluations, arguments for severance, hearings of motions, and other delays, the trial opened about two months ago."

"I don't see anything in the papers about it."

"Well, you wouldn't, would you? I mean, it hits the headlines, then it fades. It's like the phases of the moon. They come and go. The public attention span is getting shorter and shorter. Even the end of the world will only rate the front page for a day." He took a sip of his soft drink and made a face as though the taste offended him.

"You said the bodies were mutilated?"

"But not decapitated. None of them was beheaded."

"You remember the name of the murdered Viet woman?" Deane closed his eyes again.

"Let me look in my memory book." He squinted hard. "As near as I can make it out, it was something like Lynn Shoe."

"That doesn't sound Vietnamese."

"Gimme a break. I'm giving it to you phonetically, the way I remember it. Go look it up in the files."

The photographic memory Deane was so proud of was months off. The beginning of the Corvallis murders started closer to twenty-four months ago, rather than thirty-six. The film reels of the *Times* at the library said that sixteen months before, at the beginning of last year's March, Carl Corvallis, age 34, had been arrested and charged with abducting Agnes Easter, a 17-year-old prostitute. He'd handcuffed her, mutilated her with knife cuts and cigarette burns, and sexually abused her before dumping her, naked and bleeding, along Pacific Coast Highway between Malibu and Port Hueneme.

Two weeks later he was released on a fifty-thousand-dollar bond, purchased for five thousand dollars by an aunt, Mabel Putnam, who had raised him from childhood.

Another prostitute, treated in the same way six months before, identified the van Corvallis drove, as did Miss Easter.

Corvallis was taken into custody again in April and held on a bond of one million dollars, which the aunt could not manage.

Then a former roommate, Eric Yount, 23, after failing a polygraph test, told the police that a body was buried in the hills above the highway in the coastal area known as Trancas. Police searched the gullies and ravines with shovels and methane detectors and uncovered the first of fourteen bodies that would be attributed to Carl Corvallis, the apparent leader of the raggedy cult, his brother Jan, 30, Eric Yount, Paul Firth, 22, and Jan's girlfriend, Charlotte Richey, who was only 18.

Shortly after Yount's revelation he implicated Firth in the rape-mutilation murders of three more young women, two of whom were known prostitutes. Two of the bodies were unearthed in the wetlands around Malibu.

Yount and Firth were arrested and charged during the first week of May.

Information gathered by the police during several interrogations of Yount brought about the arrest of Jan Corvallis and his girlfriend, Richey. Each of the accused, except Carl Corvallis, who refused to cooperate with the police, made statements implicating their fellow cult members in the murders already uncovered, and others, the bodies of which were still to be found.

Some of the accusations proved false or, at least, had not yet been proved twelve months later. Others held up under investigation. More bodies were discovered, the count rising to thirteen.

In June, the body of Lim Shu Dok, 25, a Vietnamese-American prostitute, was found buried in a place called the Mud Hole, off the highway, just as remembered by Eddie Deane. The discovery was made by chance and not because of information offered by any of the accused, though Yount finally claimed to remember Carl Corvallis boasting about what he'd done to a "yellow whore with a butterfly on her ass." The Corvallis brothers were charged with the mutilation-murder of Lim Shu Dok.

There was no special mention made of the prosecution decision to hold the body in case it was to be called into evidence during the course of a trial or trials yet to be set.

Attorneys for the accused appeared in court to enter a motion ordering the prosecuting authorities to stop pretrial information prejudicial to their clients from reaching the press. There had already been extensive coverage detailing the evidence of Satanic ceremonies uncovered in the basement apartment of Carl Corvallis. Judge Burlingame issued a gag order.

While all five of the accused were undergoing psychiatric evaluation the prosecuting attorneys moved for severance, seeking to split the defendants for separate trial. The Corvallis brothers to be tried together. Yount and Firth to be tried together. Richey to be tried alone. Their strategy was clearly one of divide and conquer, the accused having suddenly grown uncooperative and downright loyal toward one another.

Defense attorneys successfully fought against the severance. Judge Burlingame ruled that the matter should be decided by the judge named to preside over the trial if and when the grand jury sent down indictments.

Except that Charlotte Richey, having been a minor at the time of the alleged murders, was remanded to the juvenile authority, the eventual disposition of her case a matter of special administration.

On July fifteenth the grand jury brought down the indictments. On August sixth the case was called. Judge Burlingame sat on the bench, having been named to preside, after all. Motions were heard two months later. At this time Judge Burlingame ruled that the Corvallis brothers would be tried separately in the case of four of the alleged mutilation-murders, including that of Lim Shu Dok. Since neither Yount nor Firth had been implicated in any way in those deaths, they would be tried separately for two killings in which the Corvallis brothers were not thought to be actively involved. Yet another trial would deal generally with the conspiracy aspect of the complicated series of murders and specifically with the several in which all four men, and Charlotte Richey, were implicated.

Trial date was set for January. A continuance was granted until March.

The reels ran out. Whistler went to look at the copies not yet placed on film. Except for a column inch or two now and then, the trial of the Corvallis brothers faded from the pages of the *Times*, but for a small item that recorded the death of the aunt, Mabel Putnam, on July tenth of the current year.

Then, in today's paper, Carl Corvallis was back on the front page, claiming to have found Christ, ready to confess everything.

The antiseptic ruin of the morgue always reminded Whistler of the rest rooms in the subway stations back in New York City. Cold and dank. The tiled walls refusing to be imprinted with human warmth, accepting only human misery.

He went there bearing gifts in the lonely hours of the night when the attendant was apt to welcome company. He brought two pastrami sandwiches on Jewish rye and two large coffees in Styrofoam cups.

"My name's Whistler," he said when the attendant looked up from his crotch magazine, open to the centerfold in which a girl of stunning beauty opened her legs for anyone who cared to ogle her.

"My name's Charlie, and I got nothing to say."

"I brought you a pastrami sandwich."

"Who could resist an important bribe like that?" Charlie said, closing the slick and dropping his running shoes to the floor. "I got a sliding scale of prices," he said, peeling the wax paper off a sandwich. "Two dollars apiece for little questions like, 'How did you ever get into work like this?' Five bucks apiece for big questions like, 'Did anybody turn in a body of a redheaded woman with one black shoe?' Ten dollars if you want to have a look. Twenty-five if you want to touch a corpse. Fifty if you want to be left alone with one for half an hour." He held the sandwich in one hand and picked up a pencil with the other.

"You get many requests like that?" Whistler asked.

Charlie took a bite with teeth trapped in a silver cage and made a mark on the desk blotter. "A few," he managed to mumble around the chew. "You'd be surprised." He winked one eye from behind eyeglasses as thick as bottle bottoms.

"How many?"

"Now and again. How come you didn't bring a Dr. Brown's cream soda? Don't you know a Dr. Brown's cream soda is the only thing you should drink with a pastrami on rye?"

"Anybody ever take a body away for a while?"

"This ain't fast food. We don't box anything to go."

"I'm thinking of somebody running on the inside track."

"Borrow a corpse? You got a bizarre mind." Charlie put down the sandwich and moved his hand toward the phone.

"No need to get ditsy," Whistler said. "I'm not asking you to rent to me. I'm just asking if anyone ever did such a thing. Maybe not some gazoony in off the street. Maybe somebody who knew his way around this joint. Somebody like Willy Zabadno."

"I make that a question. So you owe me twenty-five bucks," Charlie said, totting up the tab as though the transaction were over.

"You didn't answer the one about Zabadno."

"He was in a wreck. That's all she wrote."

"You can do better."

"You want I should speak ill of the dead?"

Whistler took out his gambler's roll. A fifty was on top. You'd think he was carrying big money if you didn't know the rest was ones with maybe a couple of fives.

"This is not a five-dollar answer you want," Charlie said.

"I'll be the judge of that."

"You got to understand, anybody in this job has a lot of confidential information in his ear that he is supposed to keep under his hat."

"How well did you know Willy Zabadno?"

"Willy was not a sociable person. I hardly knew him."

Whistler nodded and tossed the roll from hand to hand to give Charlie encouragement.

"Rumor has it that Willy was more than a little weird. Rumor has it that Willy consorted with the dead," Charlie said. He made a little simpering movement with his lips, which gave away his own fascination for such disgusting horrors. One of these nights, Whistler surmised, Charlie would be whispering sweet nothings into the ear of some young woman fished from the river or taken from her suicide bed.

"Willy use the desk you're sitting at?"

"He had a drawer and I had a drawer."

"He keep his locked?"

"He did."

"Is it locked now?"

"No."

"He have a locker?"

"He had a locker and I got a locker."

"He keep his locked?"

"Yes."

"Is it locked now?"

"No."

"Who cleaned the locker and the desk drawer?"

"That was my job."

"What did you find?"

"The usual."

"Tell me what's the usual."

"A pair of rotten sweat socks. A three-tooth bridge. A calendar from 1981."

Whistler sighed.

For some reason Charlie read danger in it, just as he was supposed to do. He reached down, opened up the bottom drawer of the desk, took out a magazine in a brown paper mailing wrapper, and tossed it on the counter.

Whistler turned the pages, and his belly winced at the views of bodies grossly mutilated, hung up, and disemboweled like sides of beef, parts obscenely juxtaposed.

"There was a drawer full of that kind of shit," Charlie said.

"All like this?"

"Some worse. Some not so bloody. Some S and M. Some kiddie porn. Some—"

"Zabadno was a newsstand?"

"Only retail."

"Where's the rest of it?"

Charlie's eyes did a dance like two flies looking for a place to light. "I burned them."

"Why would you do that?"

"I wouldn't want Willy's mother to know what he read."

"I wouldn't want your mother to know what a liar you are. You going to service Willy's customers?"

"I told you I burned the shit."

"You fan the magazines before you burned them?"

"Now, why would I do that?"

"To see if Willy stashed change for a hundred between the pages."

"He didn't."

"But he stashed something. His customer list. The numbers of his suppliers."

Charlie made up his mind. "Okay. But I haven't put a price on it yet."

"That tells me you don't know where you might find a buyer."

"Maybe so, but it could be money in the bank."

"Show me."

"Fifty bucks for a look?"

Whistler closed his eyes, as if he were suddenly very weary with being nice.

"You've got to learn to curb your expectations. You're not going to live to be a hundred if you don't. You've told me what you charge. Now I'll tell you what I'll pay. I'll leave you a twenty-dollar bill and your teeth so you can finish the sandwiches I bought you. If I like what you show me, I'll have the kid from the deli deliver a six-pack of Dr. Brown's cream. Cold."

Charlie went into the drawer again and scrabbled around inside. He came up with a manila envelope, much soiled and written upon, and handed it over. Whistler pulled the tines and opened the flap without taking his eyes off Charlie's teeth.

There were two separate piles, each held with a large paper clip.

One was a short list of publishers and wholesalers of sex paraphernalia, with one, Manny Flowers, doing business out of an address in downtown L.A.

The other was a pile of four-by-five glossies. Four full-figure photographs of a dead Oriental girl and close-ups of her head in various positions. In one the hair was piled up away from the neck, showing terrible knife wounds and discolorations. Looking closely, he could make out what appeared to be a small mole near the fold behind the ear. In another, her eyes were slightly open, a tiny gleam from beneath one lid pretending life.

"What would Willy be doing with these?"

"How the hell would I know?"

"They're out of the files, aren't they?"

Charlie nodded.

Whistler tapped the identification number superimposed on the lower right-hand corner of the photographs. "Are these cross-filed?"

Charlie shrugged and nodded again, still pissed off over what he considered brutal treatment.

"You check the files for me?" Whistler asked.

"You want one hell of a lot for twenty bucks and two lousy sandwiches," Charlie said, but his voice quavered and had no weight.

"You forgot the cream sodas I'm going to have sent over."

"Oh, yeah?" Charlie said disdainfully. He checked the number and went to the files. Five minutes later he turned around and said, "Nothing."

"Those are morgue photos, aren't they?"

"Sure they are."

"There should be a folder in the files matching the numbers on the photos?"

"Yeah."

"And another reference to a drawer inside?"

"That's right."

"So where the hell are they?"

Charlie shrugged again.

"The woman in these photos was found off the road down in Malibu. It's been stored here ever since, waiting to be called into evidence. You should remember something about it."

"I only been working here a year. If there was any such body, it'd be listed in the file."

"Here's her goddamn pictures!" Whistler shouted, and Charlie flinched. "I want to look through the shelves."

"For Christ's sake, I can't let you do that."

"Don't kid me. You gave me your price list five minutes ago."

"There's a goddamn army in there."

"So let's get started."

They went down the rows, pulling out one drawer after another. There were bodies of all ages, sexes, colors, and sizes. Willy Zabadno was there waiting for someone to claim him. But there was no long-dead Vietnamese woman with or without a head.

"So the body that was tossed in the gutter's the same one was dug up in Malibu two years ago," Whistler said, more to himself than to Charlie. "What the hell was Willy Zabadno doing pulling her records and transporting the body through the middle of Hollywood on a rainy night?"

"Maybe he let some wacko in there alone with her, and this pervert got carried away and took the head home for a souvenir, and Willy got scared his ass was for it, so he just decided to eighty-six it because the papers are always full of it how bodies are getting lost and replaced around here, so who would blame it on Willy?"

Whistler stared at Charlie as though one of the corpses had decided to sit up and talk.

"Once she landed in the gutter, she had to be swept up again," he said. "Which means she should have landed back here again. It's the coroner's office does the sweeping. Can you give me the names of the ambulance crews on duty that night?"

Charlie checked the daybooks and wrote some names down on a sheet of paper without asking for a price.

Whistler gave Charlie the fifty so they'd be friends again.

The coroner's ambulance crew had the look of men who knew a secret about life and death and were amused about all the fuss that people made about them. They sat on two cases with another between them, playing out endless hands of hearts. They accepted Whistler as a welcome interruption to the certainties of the night.

The one called Bo looked to be sixteen, his face round and bland, his cheeks swarming with freckles. The one called

Jose was small and swarthy, with the delicate hands of a woman.

"I don't got to check," Bo said. "We got one call to Hollywood and Vine last night. A male Cauc killed in a collision with a pole."

"I'll check," Jose said, and went away to get the clipboard with the trip sheets on it. He handed it to Whistler. "See?" he said.

"You're not the only wagon on duty that shift, are you?"

"Hell, no, but that's our district. We do Hollywood," Bo said.

"I could ask the other crews, you want," Jose said, "but I swear to you they don't do Hollywood."

"We do Hollywood."

"We even do the hills," Jose said. "That's very hard, doing the hills. Sometimes we got to carry some heavyweight down stairs that go like this, straight down. Could slip and take a tumble."

"There'd be three dead bodies at the bottom of the stairs," Bo said, underlining the danger of their profession.

"Sometimes we got to pick up people chopped to pieces. I have dreams about it for a week."

"We didn't pick up nobody without a head. Just a male Cauc."

"I'd remember a body without a head," Jose said. "I'da dreamed about it for a week."

"Would a private ambulance or undertaking service ever be called to pick up?" Whistler asked.

"Only if there was a major disaster and we was over-loaded."

"Which wasn't the case," Bo said.

"Otherwise, we do the pickup. You could ask around," Jose said.

"Nobody but us would've been called out, and we never picked up no naked woman without her head," Bo said, as though that was that.

"Not ever," Jose said, as though wanting to make clear that he did not share his partner's sensational way of saying things so anybody could get the wrong idea about how serious and solemn their work was.

"Who signed the releases?" Bo asked. "The morgue should have releases. The cops too."

"Can't take a body away unless a coroner's man had had a look and signed a release," Jose added. "So here's the duplicate release on the male Cauc. Look right there. Signed by Dr. Shelley. But nothing on a lady without her head. Dr. Shelley would never have missed something like that."

"That's right, Dr. Shelley's young, but she'd never miss anything like that."

"There's no release on the woman at the morgue," Whistler said.

"Well, there you go," Bo said, looking at Whistler levelly. "No release, how could we pick up a body? And we didn't pick up no body without a head at Hollywood and Vine that night."

"Not ever," Jose said, and smiled softly, as though he hoped that would put Whistler's heart to rest.

"What if the police swept it up?"

"Well, that could be different," Bo said, as though the idea in no way startled or offended him. He spread his hand of cards out on the packing case and grinned. A clear winner.

Thirteen

THERE'S AN ancient tale from somewhere that says if everybody were to close their eyes at the same moment, the world would disappear. It was three A.M., and Bosco, Canaan, and Whistler, the resident insomniacs, were saving the world from winking out.

They huddled in a booth together, their faces pale moons in the sickly fluorescent light, working on blue tans.

"Billy Durban's passed away," Bosco said.

"Ah, Jesus," Canaan said.

"Why do you say that?" Whistler asked.

"Say what?"

"Jesus. You're a Jew."

"Yes, I'm a Jew. It's just a way of saying I feel sorry about Billy Durban."

"Wondered."

"How tall was Billy Durban?" Bosco said.

Canaan stuck his arm out, his hand hovering above the floor. "Four foot six or seven."

"Little fucker," Whistler said.

"Yes, he was. Had a schlong like a Missouri mule, though. Jimmy Schletter—"

"The producer?"

"That's him. Worked for MGM in the old days. Well, Schletter hired Billy Durban to serve table at a birthday party he gave for his sweetheart, Mary Willibald, over to the old Mocambo. . . ."

Whistler smiled. "I remember Mary Willibald. She was beautiful."

"Couldn't act worth a damn, though," Bosco said.

"But, goddamn, she was beautiful."

"Could stop your heart," Canaan agreed.

"What about the party?" Bosco said.

"Mary Willibald liked them big Polish sausages, you know? You give her a choice—lobster, filet mignon, pheasant under glass, and sausage—she takes the kielbasa every time. It was in her contract that she couldn't eat them but once or twice a year because they was afraid she'd get so fat. So it's her birthday, and Schletter has them serve these great big fat sausages arranged on beds of boiled cabbage. Somebody gets this idea, and they make up a tray of sausages with a hole in the bottom through which Billy Durban sticks his dick and lays it out there with the rest of the sausages on the cabbage. He goes over to Mary Willibald and tells her to make her selection. She don't know the joke, of course, and she's not paying much attention. She gives the tray a quick eyeball and sticks her fork into the sausage she fancies, which is Billy Durban's dick.''

They laughed, but not as long or as loud as they might have hoped. Not enough to fill the hollows in the coffee shop.

"Christ, that must have hurt a little," Bosco said.

"Billy Durban let out a yell they heard all the way down to Santa Monica."

"So did Billy Durban sue Jimmy Schletter?"

"No, but Schletter paid off. It's how Billy Durban brought his newsstand over to Sweetzer and Sunset. But that ain't all."

Bosco and Whistler waited for what was more.

"Mary Willibald was so upset about what she accidentally done to Billy Durban's pride and joy that she took him to her own doctor and nursed his joint back to health afterward. That's how come Mary Willibald, who was so beautiful that it could stop your heart, was sweethearts with Billy Durban, who was ugly besides being short, for two years or maybe more. I mean, they said, here was this big sausage, she didn't have to worry getting fat. At least that's what people who liked to tell dirty stories used to say. There were others who said Billy Durban was the sweetest man who ever lived and could sing like an angel."

After a long silence Whistler said, "Whatever happened to Mary Willibald?"

"Oh, you know. Audiences change their minds. The major studios died. She couldn't get pictures back-to-back anymore. The public forgot her. She got old like all of us."

Whistler and Bosco stared at Canaan like children waiting for the happy ending.

"She went back home. North Carolina, I think. Last I heard, she was working as a salesgirl in a five-and-dime and living on her wages."

"She should have gotten professional money management," Bosco said, ever the practical one.

"She did," Canaan said. "That's why she went broke."

"It happened to a lot of them," Whistler said.

"Especially the kids. Mothers and fathers just sent them out to work and spent what they made," Bosco added.

"No more. The courts watch," Whistler said.

"Oh, sure," Canaan said, his voice hard and quick, "the courts watch over the money. But they don't do much for a lot of kids sold for worse than acting in regular motion pictures. There's people do to kids like you wouldn't believe. There was this Episcopal priest down south ran a farm for wayward boys and filmed them in homo orgies for customers all over the country. These other two gazoonies down in New Orleans organized a Boy Scout troop so they'd have a supply of kids for themselves and rich queers from one coast to the other. You wouldn't believe. You wouldn't believe."

Bosco got up, came back with a hot pot of coffee, and poured refills all around.

"My kidneys are floatin'," Canaan said. He got up and walked down the tiles to the toilets.

"I'm going to miss Billy Durban," Bosco said.

"Last night, when the ambulance came to pick up the bodies—"

"Ambulances."

"There was more than one?"

"There was two."

"Why didn't you tell me?"

"It was no part of any conversation we were having."

"Two morgue wagons?"

"One morgue wagon and one from Khymer Mortuary."

"Which one arrived first?"

"The one from Khymer. You're not still sticking your nose in where it don't belong?"

"I've been asking around about this and that."

"Whatever it is, it's nothing to do with you."

"Is that what you think?" Whistler said in a voice meant to warn Bosco off.

"I think when a person's got nothin' to do, anything to do looks like somethin' to do."

Whistler shifted his ass in the booth. "Maybe I should go home before we have a fight."

"Maybe that's a good idea. Go home and stay there,"

Bosco growled, getting up and going over to sulk on the stool by the register, picking up his ever-present book.

Whistler didn't go. He stayed where he was, his lips moving slightly as though trying to figure out the best way to say something.

Canaan came back, pulling at the front of his pants to settle himself.

"Why don't you shake your dick dry in the bowl?" Whistler said.

"Why don't you raise fucking orchids?"

Whistler leaned over the table. "I want a favor."

Canaan picked up his newspaper, as if he didn't hear a word Whistler was saying.

Whistler tapped the picture of Carl Corvallis. "I want to talk with this gazoony."

"You crazy? Just how in the hell am I going to get you inside to talk to a fucking multiple murderer? Just who the fuck you think I am?"

Whistler didn't want to do it, but he did it. He held Canaan's glaring eyes with his eyes, keeping his own calm and reasonable and undemanding. But reminding Canaan that when the little girl, the daughter of his brother, the apple of Isaac Canaan's eye and the owner of his heart, was plucked up from the playground and . . .

"I can't thank you over and over again for the rest of my life, Whistler. I already told you a hundred times, if it wasn't for you and all you done, my brother and me would maybe never know what happened to . . ."

"I'm not using a thing like that," Whistler said softly. "Look what it says there." He reached over the top of the paper and tapped the photograph of Carl Corvallis. "This fucking monster killer has been reborn in Christ. He is ready to confess his sins. All his sins and all his brother's sins and all the sins of those three asshole members of his crummy little cult who used to say prayers in front of Jesus hung upside down."

"Ready to drop the others in the pot to save his own ass from execution is more like it," Canaan said.

"Oh, sure, we know that. Everybody knows that."

"How could I possibly get you in?"

"His aunt died a week ago. The only person who maybe ever cared about him. She put up five grand to bail him the first time he was arrested. So now she's dead and he's got nobody to bring him cigarettes and candy. I'll be one of these people who go around comforting prisoners. I'll bring the son of a bitch a carton of butts—he should get cancer. And a couple bars of candy—he should have diabetes and die of sugar shock."

"What the hell is all this by way of proving?"

"I just can't help wondering why anybody would've cut off a dead woman's head. I just can't help wondering why so many people are covering it up."

Canaan looked for a minute like he was going to cry, staring into Whistler's eyes and remembering how Whistler had hunted for his niece without pause or rest.

"I'll see what I can do. Stay close to a phone. It could be some crazy hour."

"I'll be at home," Whistler said. "What's crazy hours to men like us?"

Whistler stared at the barren ceiling of his bedroom in his rickety house above Cahuenga and watched the patterns of the raindrops streaming down the window and casting shadows above his head. He listened to the night sounds of the house and the dialogue of the city. It breathed in and out with the sound of bells, whistles, sirens, horns, squealing tires, gunned engines, cat cries, screams, and the distant, muted murmur of restless dreamers.

It was hot and wet. The whole world was under water. He wondered if the way he felt was the way he felt before he was born, floating around in his mother's belly. He closed his eyes and tried to get there, but it wouldn't work. The years were too long and his feet were too big. A creature swam up out of the wet dark.

A phantom lady twined her long legs, wet with rain, around his thighs and belly. Her sweet-smelling hair caressed his neck, threatening to smother him. Her lips were damp in the hollow of his neck.

He reached out for the three-way lamp pinned to the wall and turned on forty watts, then got up from the mattress on the floor, useful remnant of his days of gypsy habits, spare furnishings, and youthful wine and roses, and went to the chest of drawers. Ducking an empty cage that had lost the tenth in a long line of singing feathered tenants just two months before. Never replaced. Having somehow lost the heart for bird song.

He riffled the pages of the telephone directory and found S. Andes listed there as promised. There was only one. Out of all the people in Los Angeles, there was only one S. Andes in the telephone book. Things like that never ceased to amaze him. How could there only be one person of a name in a place as big as La-La Land? It boggled the mind.

He reached for the telephone. It felt cold to the touch, reminding him of the hour. If he called her, she'd have to come swimming up out of sleep to answer. It would take a minute for her to understand that it was a man she had just met calling because he missed her.

He opened the top drawer and took out a little green leatherette address book, sorting it out from others, red and blue and black. It was nearly the oldest of several, saved for numbers no longer useful day to day, preserved for emergency and disaster. It was filled with the names and numbers of old loves, some still in place, still waiting. Not for him. For anybody good and kind enough to take them to Oz or drown them in a garden pool.

Joyce and Teetsa and Lenore and June and Ann and Maggie. No, not Maggie. She was gone. Dead of cancer. Forty-two. Luana and Cynthia and Pat and Elizabeth and . . .

There was a time when he could call at two o'clock in the morning, pleading sleeplessness, pleading loneliness, pleading the trials of his struggles with hope, art, and aspiration. "Oh, you didn't wake me. I was only just dozing off. I don't mind coming over. Give me twenty minutes," one or another would say. And—for the practical yet romantic in it— pleading poverty. "Anything I should bring?" they'd say. "I have a bottle of wine. Twenty minutes. Give me twenty minutes. Don't fall asleep before I get there."

But that game's a game for the young. Poverty and frustrated ambitions are not becoming after thirty. The part gets stale, the plot threadbare.

Whistler tossed the little book back in the drawer with the other dead leaves. He went into the tiny bathroom and relieved himself, listening to his water in the bowl, staring at his face in the mirror above the toilet as if a stranger, meaning to murder him, had finally shown up.

It didn't seem to him that he had slept at all when the telephone rang. When he picked it up, it was Canaan telling him to meet him over at the Rampart jail in twenty minutes.

Fourteen

THE RAIN wouldn't let up. It shot across the freeway in sheets of varying thickness and intensity. The big semis thundered along, throwing up clouds of spray, but there was hardly another car all the way downtown to the Pasadena-Harbor interchange where Whistler peeled off and drove along Temple to the Rampart area jailhouse. It had been built as a pre-arraignment facility but never had been put into service. Every once in a great while it was used for some special purpose. Like keeping Carl Corvallis safe after his offer to roll over on his brother and friends.

Even though it had stood empty for so long, the crowded admittance area still smelled like an old man's crotch.

There were blues and county khakis and detectives and DA's men all over. A few glanced his way when Whistler came through the door, but he was just another cop from yet another jurisdiction as far as most of them were concerned.

One or two gave him the leery eye, but he looked sure enough and tired enough to be a cop, so they went back to telling jokes and lies.

Canaan was way in the back, trying to wring another drop out of the empty coffee urn. He looked at the paper bag under Whistler's arm.

"I stopped at an all-nighter," Whistler said.

"You didn't bring a container of coffee with you, by any chance?"

Whistler put his hands out to his sides, showing them empty, and made a face of apology.

"You should know enough to always bring a couple coffees along when you got an early-morning meeting with a friend."

"Why the hour?"

Canaan stared at him as though he'd like to tear his throat out. "You wanted to see a man, I got right on it. I don't fuck around, a friend asks me for a favor."

"For Christ's sake, don't make me feel bad, Isaac. I asked a favor. I didn't hold a gun to your head."

"Ah, fuck it," Canaan said, patting Whistler's sleeve. "I'm just getting sick and tired of keeping the fucking books straight."

"I can go on home. I didn't mind the drive."

"No, no. Let's walk."

Canaan put down the stained mug and sidled away along the wall toward the door that led to the booking area. Whistler went along. They took it slow and easy, working their way through the mob so nobody would notice them. Just two cops in the crowd.

"Why the convention?" Whistler murmured.

"This crazy asshole, Corvallis, decides to turn state's evidence against his brother and them other three, all of a sudden we got half the agencies in the state claiming a piece of the interrogation. They're even coming in from other counties hoping maybe he'll clear up some of their murdered and missing. Also we got crank calls pouring in, some from gazoonies threatening to blow his fucking head off for bending over, the other half threatening to blow his fucking head off now that he's admitting to some of what he done. So they lay on plenty of protection. Also, everybody's got a suggestion. Put him in a cell by himself down to County, move him around from jail to jail every two hours, send him the fuck down to San Diego for a vacation. Shit! You listen to some of these gazoonies, they're so dumb, you wonder the thieves don't steal Civic Center and the murderers don't walk in and do the city council. Finally somebody shows some sense. They bring the asshole here to Rampart and stick him in the last cell in the old block, which isn't used much anymore."

"Who's running the interrogation?"

"The assistant district attorney's the top dog, but everybody's getting a crack at him. They question him a couple of hours, then let him have a piss and a lay-down. He's on his cot having a kip right this minute."

They were inside the booking area. The holding cage was on one side, the property counter on the other. A deputy on temporary assignment was behind the wire. He glanced up at Canaan and then looked around. Nobody else was there. Canaan tapped Whistler's elbow.

"Pay the man. If you got it, give him fifty."

"I'm getting fiftied to death."

"Get into some other business, or curb your curiosity."

Whistler handed over the fifty, and the deputy let them through.

They walked down one corridor after another, through one chain-link door after another. There was another officer at the door to the cell block. Canaan just gave that one a handshake.

The whole march had given Whistler the blues. It reminded him of the first jail experience he'd had at the Venice area jail a long time ago. Which had looked just like Rampart, except it hadn't been empty. It had seemed like nothing at first. He'd been picked up because a description of a mugger had just been called in and fit him almost like a glove. When the identification didn't hold up, they decided to book and jail him on drunk and disorderly charges, anyway, just so he wouldn't get ideas about unlawful arrest. He'd had a couple of drinks, but he wasn't drunk.

It was a Friday night, and the court wasn't sitting until Monday. He couldn't bail himself out. He was new to town and didn't have friends he could call upon for money. So he was just going to have to wait the two days. Chances were, an old drunk told him, they'd give him two days on the D and D and credit for time served. They worked it neat, so nobody could claim you were too much put upon.

It had seemed to Whistler that he'd just keep his eyes and ears open and chalk it up to experience. Maybe he could use it someday, if ever he should decide to write a film or got a chance to act in a prison picture.

The jail was crowded, mostly drunks and traffic violators, but a fair share of thieves and rapists too. He noticed that the hard types served as trustees in number-one cell. That seemed logical enough. They'd be there longest, they knew the ropes. What difference did it make, anyway? It wasn't prison. Nothing heavy would go down among the population of just a city jail.

The cells were crowded. Each one was supposed to sleep two, but most had a mattress rolled out on the floor for a third, and at night there were even some prisoners sleeping in the corridor inside the outer bars.

He was in a cell with a black thief and a white mugger from Canada being held for extradition. Another black prisoner, a man with a pink scar from eye to chin along one side of his face and small, red-veined eyes that seemed to be without humanity, spent the day sitting on Whistler's rolled-up mattress talking to the others and eyeing Whistler. Who was praying for constipation.

There was one lidless toilet for common use in each cell. Prisoners even washed their handkerchiefs in it and plastered them on the concrete walls to dry. Finally Whistler couldn't take it anymore and had to drop his pants.

The black prisoner, whose name, Whistler remembered with some surprise, had been Jeffers, looked at Whistler's thigh all the while he was at his business. Looked at Whistler's thigh and asked the white mugger if he liked "gibs," which the mugger said he liked all right when there was nothing else available. It didn't take much to figure out that *gibs* was the word they used for a man's ass, and what they had agreed upon was that in the absence of women they would take a man to relieve themselves anytime they could.

That night, as his cell mates, the white mugger and the black thief, settled themselves on their bunks, and he settled himself on the floor, the scarred man called softly from the next cell.

"Hey, Montgomery. You awake, Montgomery?"

The black thief grumbled but finally responded. "What you want?"

"I'll give you a quarter tomorrow night."

"No."

"I'll give you fifty cents."

Whistler had lain there thinking that the one black was soliciting the other. Then the scarred man said, "I'll give you a dollar," and the thief said, "I don't want your money. I want to sleep right where I is," and Whistler understood, with a rush of fear, that the cruel-eyed bastard meant to switch cells and get to him in the night. And he knew that, with the Canadian helping the black, he'd have a hard time fighting them off. And he knew that no matter how much he yelled, no help would come. The guard would be elsewhere, because he'd seen the guard take money from the prisoners for this and that, and he was a prisoner, no better in the guard's eyes than the rest of the animals. A drunk and maybe worse, getting what he deserved for getting thrown into jail. And he'd realized, with a terrible sense of loss, that nobody really gave a rat's ass and that he was alone.

"You're a cold man, Montgomery," the scarred man said, and if he hadn't been so scared and grateful, Whistler would have laughed because it sounded so funny said that way, like a lover cheated of his sweetheart.

"You're white as a sheet," Canaan said, bringing Whistler back.

"I think I'm dead on my feet."

They reached the last cell. Carl Corvallis was lying on his side, curled up around his belly, his folded hands locked between his knees.

"Carl?" Canaan said softly.

Corvallis rolled over on his back, unclasped his hands, and held them over his head, staring up at them, clenching and unclenching them as if they didn't belong to him.

"How long has it been?" he said. His voice was light and uninflected, almost colorless.

"This won't take long."

Corvallis put his hands behind his neck and sat straight up, like a bodybuilder doing sit-ups. "How long have I been asleep?"

He was a broad-shouldered man going to fat. There was a womanly softness about his neck and hands. His skin reminded Whistler of the fat beneath the skin of a slaughtered steer. His eyes were oddly shaped, irregular ovals. The pupils were large from sleep, leaving only a thin rim of green.

"Why can't I have a watch?"

"You could break the crystal and cut your wrists. You could swallow it and choke yourself to death."

"I could bite my veins." He grinned. "I could swallow my dick."

Canaan looked at Whistler and stepped back a pace, as though turning over the proceedings. Corvallis looked sharply at one and then the other, adding them up. Whistler handed him the cigarettes and candy.

"What's this?"

"A few questions."

"What do you mean, a few questions? They take me out of here to another room for questions. They ask me if I want some coffee, something to eat before they start. They do that every time. Now, why didn't you do that?"

"You don't want to eat so much. You don't want to get fat," Whistler said.

Corvallis looked at Whistler carefully. "You're not a cop."

"How do you know I'm not a cop?"

Corvallis shook his head and smiled knowingly, pleased to have put one over, refusing to explain, making a minor mystery of it. He looked at Canaan again. "You're a cop."

"How many corpses are you laying off on your brother and the others? How many are you taking for yourself?" Whistler said.

"Who are you? You the father of somebody?"

Whistler shook his head.

"You a brother, a husband, maybe a sweetheart?"

"They'd never let anybody with a reason to care that much get this close to you," Whistler said.

"I would," Canaan said conversationally. "I'd like to leave you alone with maybe half a dozen relatives of the victims. See what they could do to you with nothing but their hands and teeth."

Corvallis stared at Canaan flat-eyed. "I don't like you."

"That's a compliment."

"What can I do for you?" Corvallis said, turning to Whistler, closing Canaan out.

"Have you cut a deal?"

"Just about. I'm taking diminished capacity on four of them."

"Did you do them all?"

"Who gives a shit? What difference does it make?"

"No difference."

"They'll send me to Vaccaville and bore holes in my head for one, two, three, or four. I'm crazy. I need help. I'm not responsible."

"You don't believe that."

Corvallis smiled.

"I just wondered . . ." Whistler said, then paused.

"What do you wonder?"

"If you hate all women or just prostitutes."

"Read your bible. That'll tell you all you need to know about women. Women and whores, it's the same word."

"All colors?"

"All shapes, sizes, ages, and colors. They've all got the mark on them."

"What mark? You mean, like a flower? Like a butterfly?"

Corvallis smiled. He couldn't figure out what was going on. He couldn't see Whistler's purpose.

"No flower. No butterfly. What the hell are you talking about? The mark they bear is the mark of Baal, who is the first king of Hell, whose domain is in the east and who commands sixty-six legions. One of his three heads is shaped like a toad, another like a man, and the third like a cat." He smiled. "No butterflies."

"Did you do the Vietnamese woman?"

"What would you like me to say?"

"I'd like you to tell me the truth."

"Does it mean a lot to you?"

"It means something. Did you pay somebody to take her head from the morgue?"

Corvallis stared into Whistler's face, hunching himself on his rump along the cot to get closer to the bars.

"O Oualbpaga! O Kammara! O Kamalo! O Karhenmon! O Amagaaa!" he said. Then he fell back on the cot and turned over on his side.

"That gazoony just jacked us off," Canaan said as they walked away.

"He never had anything to do with the Saigon whore. He doesn't know anything about a tattoo. The cops saw how she was carved up, and it looked the same as the others, so they dumped her into the crowd. Why not? Clear the books."

"Was finding that out worth a fifty and a night's sleep?"

"Well, at least I know that what happened to Lim Shu Dok had nothing to do with Corvallis."

"And what does that tell you?"

"It tells me somebody did what they did to her, and Willy Zabadno isn't around to tell us why. It tells me that somebody very important is out there covering up something very bad. I saw the body in the street and I know."

"But nobody knows you know."

"Somebody knows that Shiela Andes saw it too."

William Burchard reached out of his car window and punched the button on the post by the gates. They slowly and silently swung wide, like the opening shot of *Citizen Kane*, the wrought-iron tracery looming so high above the hood of his car that it shredded the midnight fog.

A smell filled the Chrysler like the sharp smell of battery acid or onion fields. The smog never seemed to blow away anymore these days, as it used to do even ten years ago. When the Air Pollution Control Board couldn't bring down the level of emissions, they raised the limits. People kept on breathing thicker and thicker poison and fooled themselves that the air was getting cleaner.

He smiled wryly. A sour taste rose up out of his belly and stung his throat. A testament to old compromises.

He remembered years ago, when he'd been on plainclothes detail, one of the captain's men responsible for enforcement of the city's liquor, narcotics, gambling, and prostitution laws. They were always pushed for numbers. Arrests for the statistics to prove they were doing the job. A few more each and every year. Every year a few more arrests for this and that than the year before.

Generating the vice numbers created a problem. Gambling and prostitution were protected by politically powerful people, and, then as now, the police were discouraged from going after the sharks and barracudas.

Besides, it was the big mamas and papas who gave birth to the petty pimps, hookers, ass smashers, juice squeezers, child buyers, twangy boys, and street gonifs that, in their numbers, made it possible to score a little better on vice activity each and every year.

Every now and then, of course, some important asshole went too far and stepped into the shit up to his neck. The rest of the pack turned away from the stink and let the cops have him. On those rare occasions sergeants became lieutenants, and lieutenants captains, and captains commanders, and commanders deputy chiefs. If they didn't put a foot wrong and end up with their necks under the knife.

Burchard touched a button, and the electric motor whined as the window rose to shut out the atmosphere that would be delivering slow death with the morning newspaper when the citizens got up and walked outdoors.

There seemed to be no one in the gate house, but he checked the rearview mirror and caught a glimpse of an armed man stepping back through the doorway into the darker dark.

Mushroom lamps illuminated the path, clicking on and off in sequence as needed along the curving route to a private entrance like the way into an underground bunker, the earth bermed up and landscaped on three sides.

Cape himself opened the door.

"Come on in, Bill. What brings you?"

"Just thought I'd sit down for a cup of coffee with you, Walter."

"Well, I'm glad of the chance of thanking you in person for this favor you're doing for me and my friend, Tillman."

"It's no big thing, Walter, but it's not the sort of business I'd want to leave in anybody else's hands."

Cape preceded Burchard along corridors of glass with plants growing on both sides, giving the effect of walking through a twilight garden. Except Burchard felt there was something definitely unreal, otherworldly, about it. Burchard coveted Cape's house even while hating it. He always felt, as he passed from room to room, that he was leaving one stage set and entering another.

"Do you want anything to eat?" Cape said. His voice had the hollow ring of sleeplessness.

"Just coffee. You sound tired, Walter."

They passed through a doorway into a small breakfast room large enough to accommodate four people. Great fleshy, brightly colored blooms swayed on stalks like the limbs of sea creatures in the conditioned air on the other side of the curved glass. Cape gestured to one of the pastel-colored wrought-iron chairs. Burchard sat down heavily as Cape poured two cups of coffee from a silver urn.

The cream was cold and fresh. The sugar bowl filled with colored castor sugar. Burchard wondered who provided such delicate amenities at such ungodly hours.

"You look tired, too, Bill," Cape said.

"I've been running this headless body down since you brought it to my attention. I get a line on her, as you know. Then the man who's been charged with the woman's abduction and murder decided to turn state's evidence and roll over on his accomplices."

"Then you know who killed her."

"I know who's been charged with her murder. There's a difference. He's ready to lay claim to it, though."

"Did anyone ask him why the head was taken?"

"If I ask him that, then somebody asks me where's the head, where's the body."

"Still no idea of what that morgue attendant was doing with the body in the back of his wagon?"

"Not a clue. Aren't you interested in this cult killer charged with the woman's mutilation and murder?"

"The one who's ready to confess to it?"

"He's ready to confess to anything to cut a deal that'll get him into Vaccaville instead of the gas chamber."

"Cult?" Cape said.

"It was in the papers about a year and a half ago."

"Oh, yes. I remember reading about the body of an Oriental woman being kept for evidence. But I don't ever remember any mention that she was tattooed with a butterfly."

"It was held back. We hold back something in every murder case. Every time a body's found, the confessors come out of the woodwork. We have to have something they'd only know if they did the crime."

Burchard took a swallow of coffee and made a face. "I won't be able to sleep what with the sour stomach it's going to give me."

"We pay for our pleasures," Cape said.

"Didn't you have a Vietnamese woman staying here a couple of years ago, Walter? A Vietnamese woman who had a little boy, maybe seven or eight?"

"There may have been an Oriental servant with a child."

"She didn't happen to have a tattoo on her ass, did she?"

"I never looked."

Burchard stood up. The door opened, and a little boy in flannel pajamas ran into the room, grinning and chattering. When he saw Burchard, he became quiet but stared at the policeman boldly. He went to Cape and leaned his belly against Cape's knee.

"What are you doing out of bed?" Cape said.

"It's morning," the boy replied.

"Not yet."

"I'll find my way," Burchard said. When he turned around

at the door for a last word, he saw the boy staring into Cape's eyes and rubbing himself against his knee. Cape looked up at Burchard. His stare was challenging, but he gently pushed the child away.

"Something else, Bill?"

"Do you know anyone named Whistler?"

Cape shook his head. "Why do you ask?"

"One of my friends saw this private dick, name of Whistler, down to Rampart where they're questioning this cult killer."

"He has nothing to do with me, Bill."

"Just thought I'd ask."

Fifteen

BOUCHE LOOKED a picture in a chiffon dress with flounce sleeves and a low bodice. It was printed with huge red-and-orange poppies. The outfit had a hat, which she carried in her hand while walking or riding. It now lay like a flowery centerpiece near the water dripper on the marble-topped bar in Jimmy Flynn's on St. Peter. She sipped a frappé concocted of genuine absinthe, not the Pernod poured out for tourists.

Barcaloo sat pouting at a table nearby, mad because Bouche liked to perch on a stool at the bar, knowing she made a picture. He hated sitting on a stool because it showed the world how short his legs were.

Bouche observed him through narrowed eyes every time his attention was elsewhere. He'd taken off his light linen jacket. The hair on his chest, back, and shoulders poked through the mesh of his net shirt, making him look like one of those baskets filled with moss in which fleshy, tuberous begonias were grown. She giggled.

Barcaloo glared at her.

"Something goddamn funny?"

"It's such a nice day. Why shouldn't we have a few laughs?"

"It's maybe a nice day for you. What worries have you got?"

"I could write a book."

"Don't go gettin' drunk on that poison," he said. "When Pinole and Rojo pick up a couple of people, I'll maybe want you to do a little work."

"Oh, no," Bouche said.

"What did you say?"

"Whatsamatter? You got potatoes growing in your ears?"

"What do you mean, 'Oh, no'?"

"Just what it sounds like. I'm not jerking around with some creatures what maybe haven't washed. I ain't going down on some he or she what you picked up out of the gutter. I ain't fuckin' no *amateurs* don't know a goddamn thing about taking care of themselves."

"You're more goddamn trouble than you're worth sometimes," Barcaloo grumbled.

The phone rang behind the bar. It rang five times before the café-au-lait bartender appeared from a well of cool shadows in the back like some blinking animal conditioned to the dark of caves. He picked up the handset and waited to be told. Then he handed it Barcaloo's way.

Barcaloo went over and took it. The bartender stood there staring at him with velvet eyes.

"We're at the studio," Rojo said.

"You picked 'em up without causin' any fuss?"

"It was easy."

"I'm just leaving."

"You bringing Bouche?"

"That's none of your goddamn business," Barcaloo said, and glared at Bouche, who smiled back brightly, knowing that some little thing had just been said to make Barcaloo mad again.

Barcaloo tossed the handset underhanded to the bartender, who caught it on the fly and cradled it in one move. Barcaloo dropped a twenty on the marble counter.

"You know 'Why Don't My Dog Bark When You Come Around?'"

Without cracking a smile the bartender said, "No, but I know 'I Never Harmed an Onion, So Why Should They Make Me Cry?'"

Barcaloo hooted. "Keep the change."

"A pleasure."

"I'm going west pretty soon," Barcaloo said. "I'm going to miss the jokes."

"We'll be here when you come back, Mr. Barcaloo. Everybody comes back to New Orleans, sooner or later, even if it's just to die."

"Come on," Barcaloo said to Bouche.

"I told you," she said, sweetly stubborn, settling her ass on the stool with a little sideways rocking motion, setting her breasts in motion.

"Ah, fuck it, do what you want."

The bartender stepped away quickly, so he wouldn't have to hear what he didn't want to hear.

"Stay here and drink yourself silly," Barcaloo said.

"I got no money."

Barcaloo threw another twenty on the bar.

"Make it last," he said, and went along through the shadows toward the door.

Bouche saw the bartender glancing at her from the sides of his eyes as he busily wiped a glass.

"You don't look sad because I'm leaving town, Henry."

"I'm sad. I'm going to miss you, sweet sweetness."

"This the quiet time of day?"

"You could hear hummingbirds fuck."

"I'm glad you could come, Emmet," Cape said, but did not extend his hand. He walked off down a long corridor, clearly expecting Tillman to follow.

"I wouldn't miss having a look at your house for an Emmy, Walter."

"You show people have an extravagant way of talking."

"I mean it, Walter."

"I'm sure you think you do."

"I really do. You know, a peek at this house is the hottest ticket in town."

"Really?"

"Besides, I have nothing but the highest respect for you, Walter, and a chance to have lunch with you is something I wouldn't miss."

"Then I think you should demonstrate your regard in deeds as well as words, Emmet."

"I don't get your meaning, Walter. Have I done something to upset you?"

"Well, you asked me a favor, then you lied to me."

He opened a door and allowed Tillman to walk ahead of him into the wood-and-leather office.

Tillman's hands suddenly felt cold. He put them in his pockets, then took them out and clasped them in front of his belly as though at prayer. "I never did that, Walter. I never lied to you."

"You failed to say who took Shiela Andes home."

"Who said—"

"At that hour, after that kind of experience, you wouldn't have allowed her to go home without an escort, would you?"

It was a wing shot, but he got his bird. Tillman flinched.

"Oh, that. Well, that I can explain."

"What was the name of the man who took her home?"

"I think his name was Whistler, or something like that."

"Why didn't you tell me?"

"Well, I didn't think it was all that important. It just slipped my mind. I mean, this night owl was sitting there in the coffee shop when the accident happened. He got Shiela out of the car when she fainted. He offered to take her home. What else could I do? I couldn't take her home myself. I couldn't leave the scene. There were no cabs in the street. It was raining. For Christ's sake, I didn't—"

"You're babbling, Emmet. You shouldn't babble."

"It didn't do any harm, did it? I mean, what harm could it do?"

"It's a loose end, Emmet, and I don't like loose ends. They have a way of starting to unravel. They destroy agreements and accommodations."

"You mean like getting the cops to give me a pass?"

"Yes, like that."

"Well, there's nothing to worry about there. Those detectives, Lubbock and Jackson, already screwed a big bribe out of me, so there's nobody around to bring the charge against me anymore, no matter what that cunt or this Whistler says. Those pricks hustled me for a forty-thousand-dollar car."

"You've got to pay for services rendered, Emmet."

"I'm not complaining. I'm just saying I paid to squash an automobile accident with a forty-thousand-dollar foot."

"You forget that I had to use my foot, too, Emmet. And that's worth considerably more to me than any automobile."

"Look, if it cost you any money, I'd be happy to—"

Cape made a face of sharp offense, a kind of rage catching his eyes and mouth and making him look, for a moment, as though he would attack. Then he calmed himself.

"No, no, Emmet," he said very softly. "That's not how I conduct my affairs. In fact, I asked you here this afternoon to offer you an opportunity to *make* some money, not to spend it."

"A business deal?"

"One in which you might not only invest to turn a profit, but for which you might do a little simple casting. The sort of thing that would take up very little of your time. Something you do all the time, anyway."

Tillman was in the dark. He smiled and cocked his head. "I don't do any casting, Walter."

"Whoring," Cape said. "Isn't that what you're doing all the time?"

Tillman was offended. "I never had to pay for a piece of ass in my life."

"I didn't mean to say that you did. Not in cash. You have to understand, just being with a celebrity of your current stature is payment enough for a good many women."

"Oh, sure. Yeah. Well, I see what you mean," Tillman

said, jerking his chin up out of his collar and rotating his head a little like a parrot preening. "You want me to audition some actresses for some film you've got in mind?"

"A number of films."

"What's the concept?"

"Sex, Emmet."

"That's good. Sex is always good."

"Hard-core."

Tillman frowned. "Not so good. I couldn't have anything to do with X-rated."

"Oh, yes, you can." Tillman understood that Cape was calling in his marker.

Barcaloo liked the Lincoln. Its suspension smoothed the road and made it handle like a boat on still water, its air conditioning chilled the air, and its steering and braking systems made the tons of hurtling metal as easy to handle as a baby buggy. It closed out the city that steamed and rotted outside the machine's tinted windows. L.A. would be different. Warm days but cool nights. Sun on the beaches, fog on the hills. A few rainy days that didn't turn the land into swamp. Fuck the smog. He could live with the smog.

Barcaloo scorned the smooth and easy way out of the French Quarter, avoiding Interstate 10, which crossed the Mississippi at the Greater New Orleans Bridge, and U.S. 90, which connected up with Barataria Road over in Jefferson Parish. Instead he threaded the maze of streets with historic names inside the quarter, until he picked up St. Charles at the Lee Circle and Monument, west to Jackson, then south to the ferry.

He leaned on the rail going across the river, his throat clogging on the hot, wet breeze kicked by the ferry's passage, thinking about L.A. and the army of women that descended on the town each and every year. The green crop that was nothing but fertilizer for his fields. He chewed them up, but he didn't find much nourishment in women, not even Bouche most of the time. He felt like he was always mourning.

It was the lost sister he grieved for. Women like his sister,

Barcaloo knew, were very hard to come by. But she was dead, her sex cut out by a pimp who used up women too.

The Lincoln banged over the iron ramp leaving the ferryboat, and Barcaloo headed to Fourth where he turned west again until he hit Barataria Road. South again through the thicket of streets until they thinned out just beyond Estelle as the road cut through the Bayou des Familles.

Barcaloo shut off the air conditioner and punched the down buttons on all the windows so that the wet, hot wind, smelling of mud and rot, came in and filled the Lincoln like water in a bathtub. He leaned back, holding the wheel steady at arm's length, and half closed his eyes, admitting to himself with a surge of regret that he loved the heat and the enveloping damp, loved the silence of the bayous and the overhanging branches of the cypress fingering the still waters covered with a film of duckweed. The bayous had been as much the playground of his boyhood as the streets of the Vieux Carré. It was where he'd been able to be the animal he secretly believed himself to be, different from other men.

All at once he was not so sure he wanted to leave it all, big time or no big time. He quickly stripped his shirt off over his head and felt better for it, closer to himself.

The dirt track running along the subsidiary stream could hardly be seen, no more than a small wound in the heavy tangle of greenbrier and resurrection fern. Barcaloo could have found it with his eyes closed. Two miles down the twin ruts the road opened up into a clearing carelessly surfaced with gravel, rubble, and an amateurish pour of black asphalt giving way with small resistance to the fungi that burst through like tumors on a turtle's back. Then the palmetto and fern took over again. The Cadillac with the Bondoed fender and a red four-door with a vinyl top were parked side by side.

Barcaloo ran up the windows to keep the bugs out of the car. He put on his shirt while cursing to himself.

"Son of a bitch, why they have to bring the asshole's goddamn car along? Now we got to dump it *and* the Cadillac in the bayou. Can't keep filling up the goddamn bayou with cars and old wrecks. Pollute the goddamn streams and swamps. Rusting away, leaking oil and gas. For Christ's sake, why can't them two use their brains? What brains? They ain't got any brains. Between them, maybe they got half a brain. Maybe . . ."

The footpath chopped through the dry patch ended at a metal-sided, tin-roofed Quonset hut. An idle generator, colored yellow and rust, squatted like some huge swamp animal ten yards to the side, stacks of red gasoline cans huddled nearby like the creature's pups.

". . . a quarter of a brain. Look at that. They ain't even turned the goddamn generator on. For Christ's sake."

He went over and punched the starter button. The generator coughed and kicked over without hesitation, revving up to speed and settling down to a low roar, a piece of machinery often used. The smaller hinged door in the sliding barn door flew open, and Pinole stood there with his hand inside his jacket.

"Look at you," Barcaloo said, waving him aside. "You reaching for a gun?"

"Just scratching myself," Pinole lied.

"Some nosy sheriff comes to have a look at this building, you meet him at the door scratching yourself like that and he blows your balls off."

"I never thought," Pinole said.

"You don't got to tell me that," Barcaloo said, pushing past Pinole into the big shack. "You never think. What's that asshole's car doin' here?"

"They was very ditsy so I drove with him, and Jickie drove the girl so they'd think they could leave when they wanted." Pinole frowned. The slow birth of a thought was visible. "Hey, how come you knew it was the asshole's car?"

"Oh, for Christ's sake. How dumb can you get? Was we expectin' visitors? It's like a fuckin' oven in here. Why didn't you kick over the goddamn generator, get the cold air blower goin'? Where's them two?"

"Jickie's keeping them busy back by the dressing rooms."

"Jesus Christ, somebody's doin' something right. So introduce me."

Barcaloo put on his jacket and smoothed his wind-shagged hair with the palms of his hands, using his sweat for hair dressing, as they walked across a concrete floor scattered with snakes of cables; switch boxes; tripods for screens, shades, and filters; a thirty-five-millimeter camera on a western dolly; and all the rest of the paraphernalia needed to shoot moving pictures. He perked the collar of his shirt and flashed his teeth, intending to look amiable but managing instead to look like a piranha ready to slash and tear.

Chippy Byrd and Lacy Ohio were sitting on folding wooden chairs, white-faced and wide-eyed, staring like rabbits fixed in place by the menace in Rojo's eyes.

When Rojo said, "This is Mr. Barcaloo," Lacy Ohio wet her pants.

Sixteen

WHISTLER HAD called S. Andes, and nobody had answered. He'd called three times. The last time he'd let the phone ring in her apartment for five minutes by the clock before hanging up.

The pink stucco apartment house looked like a cake that was inhabited by hookers about to jump out of it any second. Whistler found a spot for his Chevy at the curb.

In the open entry there were banks of mailboxes flush with the wall on one side and a board of brass nameplates and bell pushes on the other. The idea was to find the apartment, push the button, identify yourself, and wait until they buzzed you past the wrought-iron gates.

Whistler pushed the button beside S. Andes's name just to give her warning that someone was on the way up. But the gate was busted and open, so he walked right through.

The smell of chlorine rose up, sharp as a runner's sweat, from the pool in the center of the three-story complex.

Whistler knew the pool was bigger than most of the apartments, bachelor affairs fit for bed, bath, and breakfast only. And maybe nights of watching television alone.

It was a commune for the hopeful and the hopeless. Young actors, actresses, bar hookers, and upwardly mobile thieves on one end of the age scale. Retired grips, failed writers, and forgotten pinball players on the other end.

On warm nights and on long weekends there'd be a lot of action around the pool.

Oiled bodies that sold for a buck a pound. Old men floating on inner tubes, sad because there were no skirts to look up. Old ladies looking cute in sundresses with desperate smiles painted scarlet. Cold metal glasses full of booze and fruit in hand. Waiting to be invited to a party. Parties going on in one single or one bedroom and another, all around the upper tiers. Sophisticated boys and girls in jeans bleached almost white, leaning one ass cheek on the railings and looking over the edge, down into the blue heaven of the pool, wondering if they had the guts to take a dive and call it quits.

But when it rained, the pool just lay there and dimpled helplessly under the beating of the raindrops. Melancholy but full of promise. Things can get better if you wait long enough. Any pool in the rain can tell you that.

Shiela's hutch was on the top floor. The doors marched around and around, distinguished only by their scars and numbers. Whistler knocked on 312. There was no answer. He stuck his face against the glass and tried to see through the curtains if there was a lamp lit. The place was gray and empty.

No one watched that he could see. The lock was easy.

The apartment had the feeling of a viewing room in a Pasadena undertaking parlor, genteel but very cold. A ceiling-washer lamp, like a giant plastic tulip stuck in a black plastic base, stood on commercial carpeting engineered to last a thousand years. A convertible couch had been pulled out so many times, one metal elbow had broken free.

The couch sat next to the doorway into the kitchenette. The sink was full of clean dishes, stacked and draining. A geranium burned on the sill of a little window above the sink that looked out twenty feet, across to the green stucco cake next door.

There was still the bathroom and the closet. Whistler didn't want to look. He was afraid of what he might find.

The closet was jammed with clothes and shoes.

The bathroom was empty. The bottom of the tub was still wet. The shower head above the tub dripped a tear. The place smelled of young woman and promises.

Whistler went back to the closet and counted sweaters, skirts, and coats. The days were warm, but nights cold, in La-La Land. He couldn't know how many of anything a woman like Shiela might have, but he was sure there would not be much surplus everyday underwear. It wasn't seen, so it wasn't stockpiled. Ladies did a lot of rinsing out of small things every night. He remembered the wet fright of nylons in his face when he'd stumbled into strange bathrooms in the dark after half a night of love.

But when they traveled, they took it all, every silky scrap. Every bra and halter. Or nearly all. There was only a pair of holed cotton briefs and two pairs of panty hose, laddered and toeless, in one drawer of the little chest.

He looked for bathing suits. The three rolled up in a bottom drawer were old and used, meant for swimming. There should have been a new one meant for show.

There was a scattering of small change, nickels and pennies, and a couple of new bills on top of the lace runner on the dresser. Whistler picked up the paper money. It wasn't real. It was play money advertising an adult movie house called the Beaver Run. Where it reads "Federal Reserve Note" on a dollar bill, it read "Fun and Fucking Frolic." There were women's legs with garters instead of the shields and lunettes at the corners. Washington had a grin on his face. Instead of the denomination printed out underneath, it was printed "Twoferone." On the green side was a bad drawing of the movie house in one circle and another bad drawing of a tangled couple in the other. The name of the movie house on top, the address on Poeyfarre Street in New Orleans on the bottom.

"If you're a cat burglar, you're lousy at it," a voice said at his back. It had the warm roughness of a bare foot scraped along a thick-piled rug.

Whistler folded the funny money and tucked it into his waistband. He turned around to face the lady that went with the voice.

She was tall, and as broad-shouldered as a man. No padding in the shoulders of the dressing gown. One heavy, shapely leg was exposed by the slit in the skirt, a foot in a pink mule planted on the floor like she was about to have her picture taken for a girlie magazine. Red hair down to her shoulders.

Whistler figured her to be vintage fifty. Bottled in bond. Cellar reserve.

"You won't make your million scratching around kitty-litter boxes like this one," she said.

"I'm a friend," Whistler said, taking an easy step forward, as though he were ready to go.

She backed up, and he saw the little gun that was nearly lost in the palm of her big hand.

"For Christ's sake," he said, "you must be kidding."

"Gimme a name," she said.

"Whistler."

"Not yours, sucker."

"The lady's name is Shiela Andes. But it's not her real name."

"So, what's her real name?"

"That I don't know. I'm a new friend."

Her eyes flickered over him, as if she were thinking of patting him down. Whistler had the thought that he might not mind.

She tucked the little automatic in her pocket and sat down on the sofa.

"You're not afraid of me anymore?" Whistler asked. "What did I do or say to convince you I was harmless?"

"Hell," she said, grinning wide enough to show white teeth too bright to be her own, "I haven't been afraid of a man since I was twelve and kicked my uncle's balls in for trying to put his hand down my pants."

"So why the gun?"

"I said I wasn't afraid. I didn't say I was stupid. You can sit."

Whistler sat down on the other end of the sofa.

"Where'd you meet Shiela?" she asked.

"In a coffee shop. I brought her home night before last."

"She was out with Emmet Tillman night before last."

"He was half in the bag."

She nodded as though she'd heard that song before.

"Old-fashioned boy. He doesn't do drugs," she said.

"That's what he told me."

"He a friend of yours?"

"New acquaintance."

She laughed, short and sharp.

"Something funny?" Whistler asked.

"I like your style. The man's an acquaintance, the woman's a friend."

"That's how it feels."

"I got you. I can see it in your face."

"What's that?"

"You like women. You really like women. Maybe that's what made me put the guy away."

She readjusted her big body on the sagging couch, swaying toward him as though unconsciously attracted, moving her legs so one knee jutted toward him, making a statement about her naked thigh.

"Did you have a date with Shiela?"

"No. I was concerned," Whistler said. "I called and nobody answered. So I came to see for myself was everything all right."

"You see anything?"

"She's out of town. Someplace hot this time of year."

"She got called to New Orleans."

"A call from who and why?"

"From some producer for a picture. They had an actress down there, he said, got dysentery. Couldn't work. They needed a replacement right away. Featured part. An opportunity."

"How'd he come to pick Shiela? He call her agent?"

"No, the producer remembered her from a party they'd

both been at six months ago. Shiela doesn't have an agent at the moment. She dumped him when he tried to peddle her ass to a visiting investor one weekend."

She put her hand on her bare thigh, up near her crotch.

"Shiela didn't like that," Whistler said.

"Hey, she's no fool. We women sell ourselves all the time. But there's sales and sales. You know? White-flower sales. Clearance sales. Year-end sales. Rainy-day sales."

Her eyes were nearly green. The color of her hair was her own and not dyed for drama. There was a spray of freckles across the tops of her sun-stained breasts. Whistler knew there'd be sprays across her hips and flanks as well. Like a strawberry roan Appaloosa mare. Just as wild and sturdy to ride.

"What's Shiela's real name?" Whistler asked, looking at the woman's cheek.

"My name's Katherine," she said, looking at his mouth.

"No, Shiela's real name."

"Shiela Ajanian."

"You think it's funny this producer remembers an unknown actress for six months after meeting her once at a party?"

"I think everything that happens in this goddamn town is funny, Whistler. What the hell can I do about it? Everybody's so goddamn hungry for something, you can't tell them anything could be poison. Anything at all."

Whistler leaned forward, ready to stand up.

"Everybody's got to take their own chances," Katherine said.

She moved her hand from her leg to his.

"It's a sad, rainy day," she said. "This couch opens up."

"Will you show me how it works when I get back from New Orleans?" Whistler said.

Seventeen

BARCALOO WAS talking Chippy Byrd and Lacy Ohio out of their clothes, scaring them out of their jeans and T-shirts; Byrd proclaiming the superior qualities of a motor oil that had more "Go!"; Ohio frankly declaring, "Make an offer."

"Lookit here, little pigeon, you got no cause to wee-wee," Barcaloo said, reaching over to lay his hand on Lacy's knee.

"I'm scared to death," she whispered.

Chippy's hand was in his crotch, preventing the same accident that happened to her from happening to him.

"Who scares you?" Barcaloo said, his smile slipping up and down across his teeth like they were coated with butter. "Nobody wants to scare you."

"They scare me," Lacy said, looking first at Pinole, then at Rojo, then back again. Back and forth, back and forth, rattling her brain. Finally landing on Rojo, who sat unsmiling next to Barcaloo, leaning forward with the terrible stillness of a snake. "He scares me," she went on, too afraid to say that it was Barcaloo who terrified her most.

"What's to be scared of?" Barcaloo said. "I know. It's the way Jickie looks at a person. That scares you. He's a cameraman. He's got the eye, you know what I mean? He even looks at me sometimes like I got a wart on my nose. I ask him what the hell he's looking at. He tells me 'eff four five with a thirty.' I ask him what the hell 'eff four five with a thirty' means."

"What does it mean?" Chippy asked, trying to convince himself that they were just a bunch of new acquaintances having an interesting conversation.

"Something about how much you got to open the camera lens. How the fuck do I know what it means?" Barcaloo said, losing control for a second, finding the part of smooth operator getting on his nerves. He grabbed hold of himself and oiled up his manner again. "It's the way cameramen talk. He talks like that, and Pinole, over there, talks like 'two hundred decibels, testing one, two' fucking 'three.' He takes care of the sound mixing. How do I know what they mean when they talk like that? I'm the producer and director. I come at the business from the creative angle. You unnerstan' that? We make adult films, you unnerstan' that?"

"Oh, yes," Lacy said, wanting to believe every word he was saying, feeling a sickness in the middle of her belly, caused by the stroking motion of Barcaloo's soft, pudgy hand. It was like the touch of one of those creatures that squatted wet and slimy on the end of a log sticking up out of the wetlands.

"So, we're all grown-ups, here, wanting to make a couple dollars, right?" Barcaloo said. "You two are celebrities. You unnerstan' that? You got your faces in the newspaper half the people in the country buy at the supermarket."

"We didn't mean nothing—" Chippy said.

"What do you mean, you 'didn't mean nothing'? That's what that guy said what fingered Willie Sutton. You know from Willie Sutton, the bank robber? Ahh, you two is probably too young to remember Willie Sutton. This schmuck fingered him for the reward . . ."

"Nobody give us no reward."

". . . but that wasn't enough for him. He wants to be famous too. So he shoots his mouth off and gets his picture in the papers. Just like you . . ."

"We didn't mean nothin'," Lacy said, adding her whining voice to Byrd's old beggar's tune.

"And some friends of Sutton's blows this asshole's fuckin' head off. You unnerstan' what I'm sayin'?"

"Oh, Jesus, Mary, and Joseph, have mercy on us," Lacy whispered.

"Hey, wait a minute," Barcaloo said heartily, grinning like a car salesman. "Don't misread my meaning. What are we talkin' about here? We're talkin' about gettin' your pictures in the *Enquirer*. What does that tell me?"

"That we talked about something we shouldn't've talked about."

"It tells me you got an eye for publicity. You know you got to have an edge, and you go out and find an edge. It's a goddamn jungle out there in this land of glitter and swank, ain't that right? Now, don't tell me, let me tell you. Both of you want to be in show business. Did I hit it on the nose? Did I score a bull's-eye?"

Lacy smiled and looked at Chippy. Here was a guy talking about show business. Nobody's even mentioned what they didn't mean to say nothing about. That they spilled the beans about who dropped the head by the lake. What he was doing was making them an offer to be in the movies.

Chippy knew she was staring at him, but he couldn't take his eyes off Barcaloo. He couldn't help himself, he had to ask the question, the answer to which would probably kick the hell out of the pile of shit Barcaloo was shoveling and land him and Lacy facedown in it.

"You ain't mad about we described the car and this cameraman and sound man of yours?"

"Why should I be mad? We was workin' out a little scenario, you unnerstan'? Workin' out this little scene for a horror film we're gonna shoot as soon as we raise the finances. You know, like that crap the kids like to scream at."

"But the head. The newspapers and television said it was a real head."

"So what do they know? Ain't they a bunch of liars? Ain't they in show business too? Nobody's mad at nobody here. No, indeed. We're just a bunch of grown-ups out to make a buck. You get people to pay attention to you, that makes you a commodity. So, unless you got some better offers, I'm ready to give you a chance to cash in." He grinned invitingly.

"What do you want us to do?" Lacy asked, quicker to succumb to his sweet poison than Chippy, who still hung back, saving his enthusiasm for the time he was out of the bayou and home again.

"We just want you to do what you already do."

"What's that?"

"Take off your clothes and fuck each other."

Whistler had no trouble getting through the studio gate. He'd laid down a story a year before, and the guards still thought he was the studio's cocaine connection. Who's going to question the credentials of a cocaine connection?

Whistler felt a little heartsick every time he visited this particular lot, lying in the sun just outside the shadow of the hills. His memories were offended by the executive tower that seemed to stare down on everything, a surveillance post that turned the reflections of white clouds black, monitoring the heartbeat of the magic-making machine, stunning the spirit with its impression of impersonal power. He hated the other building, which looked like a birthday cake, terrace on top of terrace, the hanging gardens of Babylon overgrown with fleshy succulents and cacti that lived on bone dust. He hated the commissary where the tourists crowded in, hoping to see a television favorite drinking a glass of beer.

Whistler remembered the studio when it had been a collection of soundstages and cottages scattered on green lawns. The rabbits had come down out of the hills. Deals were made and pictures put into production over a cup of coffee.

He drove to the soundstage where Tillman's cop show was shooting and parked in a no parking zone. Drug dealers took privileges nobody else would dare take.

There was a BMW parked in Tillman's reserved piece of curb. But it wasn't the car crushed in the accident. It was a brand-new one, slick and black, the interior bloody with red leather.

The red light was on over the door of the soundstage. A bell rang, and the light winked off. Whistler went through the lock into the air-conditioned soundstage and the noise of loud voices and hustle. Whistler strolled down toward the action, passing technicians running cable and shifting lights. They wore tool belts and black satin jackets with the name of the show stitched on the back. Hollywood warriors advertising the fact that they were employed.

Tillman was sitting in a canvas chair with his name on the back. A pretty girl was sitting next to him in the director's chair. Tillman's hand was high up on her thigh, casually placed there, declaring ownership, or at least deciding whether to have her on approval. A knit cap was pulled down over his hair. There was a wipe of grease on his cheek. He looked easygoing and tough. He looked real.

The skinny black actor who played Tillman's partner in the series sat in his chair, leaning forward, making a joke into Tillman's face, his eyes glancing away to the girl's breasts. Tongue flicking out to wet his lips. Sending a message. Invitation to her. Challenge to Tillman.

Tillman watched, sleepy-eyed. Amused. Sure of himself. He had the girl briefed. No dark meat at this turkey dinner if she expected to stay. He glanced over at Whistler's approach. His eyes looked worried. Whistler liked him for a minute. Tillman was, after all, just a guy who'd scrambled and fought to make it and had made it big. Found out there were burdens went with the blessings. The world changed around you, people changed around you. While you were counting your money and dropping your drawers, people learned to hate you and dreamed of your death. Lousy people.

Tillman stood up, looking annoyed. He put his hand straight out, showing Whistler the palm, telling him to back off.

"Who let you on my goddamn set?"

Whistler kept walking. He spoke in a low voice.

"I see you got yourself a new 'squeeze.' You don't want me to queer the deal for you, do you?"

"What the hell do you want?"

"I'd like to know if you called your lawyers like you said you were going to do on St. Swithen's night."

"On what?"

"July the fifteenth. The night of your accident."

"What accident?"

"Ah, Christ, now you believe you weren't even there."

"Wherever 'there' is, I wasn't. I was home in bed with a good book."

"You're a kinky son of a bitch, ain't you? If you didn't call your lawyers, who did you call?"

"Go fuck yourself."

"You decide to let Shiela put the arm on you, after all?"

"You're speaking Swahili."

"Did you get some friend of yours to offer her a job over to New Orleans?"

"What kind of job?"

"That's what I'm here asking."

"I don't know what you're talking about."

Whistler read him and believed he was telling the truth. He took a wild shot; it didn't cost him anything.

"I see you got a new car."

The worried look flickered in Tillman's eyes again. There was something about the car. What about the car?

"I get a new car whenever I want to get a new car."

"I guess."

"Get the fuck off my set or I'll have you tossed."

"You know, I think you're really a nice guy underneath all that shit."

"This ain't workin'," Barcaloo said.

Chippy stood there naked. His body was white and skinny. His penis and scrotum were darker, like the skin of his face and arms. His tool hung flaccidly between his thighs, all shriveled up like some small creature trying to find a place to hide. He had the urge to cover his groin with his hands, but something told him that a modest gesture like that would incite Barcaloo to more rage.

"I'm sorry," he mumbled.

"What's to be sorry? I thought I was dealing with a couple of professionals here, and instead I get a scared kid."

"Well, maybe it's because me and her only done it once."

"In the back of Chippy's car," Lacy said.

"You can't afford a bed? You can't afford all night?"

Lacy laughed. "I got a grandmother." She lay as naked as Chippy but more at ease, on a couch over which a paisley shawl had been thrown. She wasn't so scared anymore. She'd even been oddly excited by three men watching her as

Chippy first warmed her up with his mouth at her crotch, then tried to penetrate her with his unworkable tool. She felt almost good with the hot lights warming her body. The man with the terrible eyes was hiding them behind the camera most of the time. The lens explored her body with the impersonal eye of a phantom lover.

"So all right," Barcaloo said, as though accepting that as sufficient answer and sufficient reason. "He was friendly to your crotch, you be friendly to his crotch. You got any objection to that?"

"Jeez, I don't know. I never done none of this . . ."

"Don't kid me."

". . . in front of nobody before, except the person I was doing."

"So try it. That's all I'm askin'. Just try it."

Chippy walked over to her in his bare feet. They left damp marks on the dusty concrete floor.

My God, Lacy thought, Chippy's so scared, he's sweating from his feet. He stood there in front of her, slightly spread-legged. She got to her knees on the mattress and ducked her head, feeling all her body parts growing weak again. Thoughts she'd managed to brush away told her Chippy's instinct for danger was better than her own. She looked up along the plane of his belly and the rise of his chest, past his scrawny neck and little chin, the somewhat protruding teeth, and long, thin nose, to his eyes, big as saucers, sending messages she would rather not read.

It was important to perform well, to do what pleased the hairy man with the awful hands and the man with the funny eyes. That was the path to safety and salvation.

"You got to do it right," she whispered, her lips brushing Chippy's flesh. "You got to do good. You got to get it up."

The grease on the cheek of the man at the police impound was honest grease. Workingman's grease. When Whistler stuck out his hand to introduce himself, the man shook his head and said, "I got dirty hands."

"Okay," Whistler said, and kept his hand stuck out there. The mechanic wiped his hand off on a rag and shook.

"My name's Chester Wendt," he said.

"How do the shifts in this garage work out?"

"Monthly rotation."

"Change over on the first?"

"That's right."

"So you were working last out on July fifteenth?"

"Sure I was."

"You remember a silver BMW brought in?"

"Front-end collision? Radiator punched?"

"That's the one."

"Who are you? I think I should ask to see something," Wendt said with an average man's natural suspicion.

"I'm not official."

"Then we shouldn't be talking about police business."

"Insurance business too?"

"Oh, I gotcha."

"I mean, how bad was it?"

"The BMW?"

"Yeah, the silver BMW."

"Them things is built pretty good. The radiator was leaking and the fenders was crumpled. That's all."

"The owner come to take it out of impound?"

"Somebody else come with the pink."

"You recognize him?"

"Sure I recognized him. It was Detective Lubbock."

Well, well, well, Whistler thought, not a bad night's divvy for the cops. And, one way of looking at it, a bargain for the actor who would have been up to his nostrils in the shit.

"Lubbock drive it away?"

"He had it towed to a dealership," Wendt said.

"You know which one?"

"The one on Wilshire down in Santa Monica."

"Well, thanks."

"Maybe I shouldn'ta told you that."

"Why not? What's the big deal? Anybody tell you *not* to talk about it?"

"No," Wendt said, still doubtful about what he might have given away.

"So there you go," Whistler said. "I owe you a beer."

"Forget it." Wendt set his jaw a certain way, like he was angry but didn't know what about. "What the hell's going on with Lubbock and that BMW?" he finally blurted out.

Whistler grinned. "You want me to write it out for you?"

"Son of a bitch," Wendt said, mad as hell that he was in no position to climb aboard the gravy train.

After an hour it was still no soap. Barcaloo felt the rage building up in his belly and chest again. This goddamn Chippy Byrd wasn't useful. The girl maybe could be useful, except she had practically no tits and all kinds of pimples on her chest and ass. Besides, there was no way of keeping one around without the other. No real reason, either.

"Look, just get on top of her and fake it. You know what I mean? Just sort of jump up and down on her and we'll get the camera in close. Later on we'll cut it up. We'll make it look okay. Just do like that, you unnerstan'?"

Lacy started to cry again. That got Chippy crying too.

Barcaloo left his canvas director's chair and walked around behind Rojo and the camera. He patted Rojo under the arm and felt the gun.

"Do 'em," he mumbled. "And make sure you got her face in close-up when she finally sees that's she's gonna be snuffed."

He turned away and started to leave. Lacy let out one hell of a scream, like she was already dying.

Barcaloo came back, his face screwed up in rage.

"Well, don't fuckin' blame me. You people got to learn not to shit on my parade."

Eighteen

THE DEALERSHIP over on Wilshire was only a stop. Whistler just walked on through, looking for the silver BMW. He didn't see it. When the service manager told him he should learn to read signs that told customers they weren't allowed in the garage where the work was being done and asked Whistler what he wanted, Whistler said he was looking for a silver BMW and was told they didn't have any in the shop, but if he wanted new, they could satisfy him in the showroom.

He drove up and down the blocks around the dealership and found the car parked behind a drugstore in a nearby shopping center. It didn't take a lot of smarts to know that some mechanic would be running the car through for repairs at night. Everybody steals a buck now and then, one way or another.

Just like he really didn't expect the BMW to be out there for anybody to see, the headless body of the woman wasn't there at Khymer Mortuary, either. The pie-faced, dark-suited man with the silk rep tie and hands that kept washing one another was adept at lying.

Whistler went away wondering why he was double-checking on things he already knew. A heavy snow had fallen on the situation surrounding the body of a Vietnamese whore. Why should he give a damn? There was nothing in it for him. He might as well go home to the little house he owned above Cahuenga Boulevard and lay in bed waiting for it to fall down the hillside. Worry about something sensible for a change, instead of some woman who didn't have sense enough to pull her leg in out of the rain.

* * *

The animals were tuning up for the long night in the dusk outside the rickety soundstage. Birds were screaming and gators booming.

Pinole was sitting on one of the canvas director's chairs staring first at his hands and then at the two pitiful white bodies, tangled with one another and splashed with red, lying on the daybed.

Rojo came back from propping the side door open. Out of the wetlands came the sounds of a struggle. Two animals locked in fatal combat. The screams and thrashing came into the wood-and-metal Quonset through one of those "windows" in trees and underbrush that acts like a megaphone. It was like the killing was taking place right at Pinole's feet. A last terrified scream was cut right in half.

"I don't like doing this kind of thing," Pinole said.

"What kind of thing?"

"Doing people like they don't know why we're doin' them."

"Since when you get delicate?"

"I always been delicate. I mean, I do what I got to do, but I don't like it when we do them when they're naked and going at it."

"Well, they wasn't going at it. That's just the point, ain't it? I mean, if that asshole coulda done what he was supposed to do, he'd still be alive now, wouldn't he?"

Pinole thought about that. "But we woulda done them later just the same. With the cameras running and them without no clothes."

"That's the idea of it, ain't it?"

"Maybe we shouldn't be making such pictures."

"Christ, we don't make the market. I mean, people make the market, ain't that right? They're out there buying or we wouldn't be selling."

"Well . . ." Pinole said. He took a plastic pill container out of his pocket, opened it, and poured a small mound of cocaine on the curve of his thumb and the knuckle of his first finger. He brought it up to his right nostril and snuffed it. Then he did the same for the left.

"You want some?"

"You stop staring at your hands, I take a snort with you?" Rojo said.

"I don't like to touch them when they got no clothes on."

Rojo took the vial and did the way Pinole had done.

"We better not get too crazy," Pinole said. "Barcaloo wouldn't like it."

"Fuck him. Come on and help me push that sucker's goddamn car into the swamp," he said.

Pinole followed him out into the gathering dark. Rojo opened the door to the red four-door and released the hand brake.

"You like the color of this car?" Pinole asked.

"Yeah, I like it okay. You like it?"

"I like the red. I don't like the black vinyl top."

"Vinyl tops is no good in the heat."

"Goddamn sun cracks them up like tar paper sooner or later."

"This would be a good color for the Cadillac," Rojo said.

"Barcaloo wants we should dump the Cadillac in the goddamn bayou," Pinole said.

Rojo was on the driver's side with one hand pushing against the window frame and the other grasping the door molding. "You going to help me push this fuckin' thing?"

Pinole got in the back and leaned his considerable bulk against the sedan. It was heavy going only for a second, then they got it rolling. Rojo stopped pushing and just walked alongside, touching the steering wheel when the car needed to be kept on the track down to a dark place where mud and water met.

When the front wheels resisted, Rojo got in back with Pinole, and together they pushed it out far enough for the hood to tilt. The sedan sank down into a deep spot like a liner going under in the sea. After a minute an oily bubble burst on the surface and sent out concentric rings of shimmering iridescent color.

"Beautiful," Pinole said.

"I don't want we should dump the Cadillac," Rojo said. "I always liked that automobile. It give us good service."

"You heard what Barcaloo said."

"I don't give a fuck what Barcaloo said. We just put a new engine in it twenty thousand miles back."

"That's true," Pinole said.

They walked back to the soundstage. Night fell. One second there was still a little glow left in the sky, the next it was as black as the bottom of the bayou where the sedan now rested. The rehearsal light inside made the doorway a bright rectangle on velvet.

"Look," Rojo said, "we could take the Cadillac to that chop shop over to Steerage Avenue. They bake the color on right there. What could it take if we ask the favor? Maybe three hours. Maybe less."

"Barcaloo . . ."

"So if Nonny gets pissed off, we ditch the fucking Cadillac then! After he sees what we done to it. After he sees nobody is going to mistake a red Cadillac for a white one with a Bondoed fender."

"There's an idea," Pinole said.

"Fuck, yes."

"We better hurry we want to get over to the paint shop tonight."

"You're right. Maybe we should get over there soon as we can, get the job done."

They hurried across the floor to the daybed. Pinole rubbed his hands together. "Oh, shit," he said.

"There's some work gloves on that tripod over there," Rojo said.

Pinole went to get them. They scarcely fit, but he dragged them on over his heavy knuckles, anyway, as Rojo watched, annoyed and amused at his partner's touchiness.

"We shoulda put them in the car first before we dumped it," Pinole said.

"What the fuck's the difference?"

"We dump them in the mud, the gators and other creatures will come drag them out for supper just like that other creature did with the head."

"You got a point."

Pinole grinned happily at his friend's praise.

"We could cut 'em up," Rojo said, "and stuff the pieces into old film cans."

"That would take a lot of time," Pinole said, taking him seriously. "We wouldn't get over to that chop shop in time to have the Cadillac repainted tonight."

Rojo had his mind on saving his car. His eyes skittered with tension and impatience. They fell on the utility closet.

"We put them in there and worry about it later. Then we get the Caddie over for the new paint job."

"Red."

"That's right, red," Rojo said, going over and taking Lacy Ohio, born Loretta Oskanowsky, by her ankles. "Two coats."

Nineteen

THE RAIN was still coming down, blowing away the image of Southern California for another horde of pilgrims. Gentry's had seven lonelies, hunched over coffee cups, scattered around the booths and counter stools like mushrooms dotting a forest floor. Detective Canaan was among them, sitting in a booth, having a burger.

Whistler dropped his stuffed overnighter on the tiles in front of the cash register. Bosco looked up from *Freud's General Introduction to Psycho-Analysis*.

"That's an old number," Whistler said. "Nowadays we got transactional, we got Gestalt, we got primal screaming, we got mystiotranscendent . . ."

"Freud's got 'honor, power, fame, riches, and the love of beautiful women.' Freud's got fucking."

"I'm going to New Orleans."

"You going for the head?"

"I'm going for the lady who was in here the other night."

"What for?"

"Somebody's got enough clout to hush up a double homicide and let a drunken actor take a walk. This somebody's maybe got enough clout to offer an actress a picture and get a witness out of town, never to return."

"There was you and me. We were witnesses too."

"But we announced no plans to blow the whistle."

Bosco wrote on a piece of paper, "Anything you want to know, ask for Coxey at the all-night drug corner of Common and Rampart." He handed it over. "Don't fall in love."

"That's a joke?" Whistler asked.

"It's a disaster," Bosco replied.

Whistler went over to the booth where Canaan sat, and put his bag at his feet.

"Did I invite you?" Canaan said.

"You don't be nicer to me, people will think we're in love."

"Why don't you get going to New Orleans?"

"You heard that too? I got to learn sign language. As good as you hear, have you heard anything about the headless body?"

"You should leave police business to the police."

"You don't even care," Whistler said accusingly.

Canaan looked up from his food. There was a smear of mustard at the corner of his mouth.

"Listen," he said, "I don't work homicide, and I don't work traffic. I got my own troubles. There's this fourteen-year-old girl comes in to see me the other day. Oh, I know her a long time. About a year. I know her from when she steps off the bus down to the Greyhound station. I know her from when she turns her first Hollywood trick for the pimp who roped her in. This pimp that I warned her about, but who she tells me is the only person in her life was ever good to her. So why shouldn't she do him a few favors on the street in his time of financial distress? She gets to hate it. After she pays off his pimp wagon she tries to quit peddling her ass. He breaks her jaw. They wire it together at the hospital and give her some pills for the pain. They tell her to rest. The pimp puts her out on the streets the same night. When she tries to commit suicide by swallowing the pills, she vomits and breaks the wires. He don't even let her go to the hospital and get them fixed. He puts her out on the street again. She finally comes to me.

"Now, this girl is already an old lady, you know what I mean? Most of my time is spent with children, seven, eight, nine, ten years old, and the people, mostly men, who eat them alive. I'm not married. I got no kids of my own. I thank God for it nearly every night of my life.

"How many sexually exploited children you guess we got in this city?

"I'll tell you how many," Canaan said, when Whistler didn't answer. "Thirty thousand is how many. When do I find time to chase down headless bodies? When do I find time to worry about police cover-ups for what is probably nothing but fucking inefficiency down to the morgue, which we got plenty of everywhere. Nothing works right, or haven't you been paying attention? I did you a costly favor. . . ."

"I appreciate it."

"You appreciate it, but you say to me that I don't care. If I cared twenty-five hours a day, I couldn't even sweep out my little corner. Go find yourself a living, Whistler." A taxi pulled up outside. "Find a new hustle. There's a cab. You ought to grab it. They're hard to find in the rain."

Airports never sleep.

Whistler sat on a plastic chair and checked his pockets the way he did a hundred times every time he traveled. Ticket, clean handkerchief, candy drops to suck so his ears wouldn't clog up, very skinny money roll, wallet with credit cards . . . no gun. The gun was back home in a potted plant. Whistler had never heard of a place where the local cops didn't get very upset about private dicks coming into their territory packing heat. So no gun.

He watched an old lady picking through a trash bin. Three shopping bags squatted nearby like mangy pet dogs. He heard someone call his name and looked over to see Al Lister hustling toward him. Lister looked as old as he'd looked ten years ago, when they'd gone into the Valley to see Suzy. His hair was still as black as bottled dye could make it. His grin was like a big wrinkle among the small ones. Eyes like licorice gumdrops above. Small chin like half a rubber ball. His small body found it hard to remain still. His small feet, sporting patent leathers, were always on the move.

"Long time no see," he chirped.

"You haven't aged a day," Whistler said.

"Maybe a year or three. Wheat germ and yogurt."

"I'm not laughing."

"It keeps the bowels empty and the disposition positive. You should try it. You look sad. And sad is bad."

Whistler wondered how the bag lady had made her way into the terminal with security sweeping the homeless out like so much trash.

She popped up out of the bin every so often and grinned every time she did. Like a puppet in a Punch and Judy show, her face painted up like Judy or like Raggedy Ann. Orange yarn hair and round, rouged cheeks.

"So what do you think?"

"I think I'll try the yogurt but not the wheat germ."

"No, no, my friend. What do you think about my success?"

Whistler glanced at Lister, trying to read between the lines.

"Don't you watch the tube?" Lister asked.

"Now and then," Whistler said, looking back at the bag lady.

"You should watch the tube, find out what's going on in the world," Lister said. "Find out what's going on with your old friends. I'm a star. Well, so, not a star exactly, but a regular on a continuing series."

"Son of a bitch."

A black, uniformed security cop came around the corner of a long row of lockers, walking free and easy with his gun settled on his hip. When he saw the garbage picker, he pulled up short. Whistler speculated for a second on the kind of emergencies security cops dreamed about, had nightmares about. For sure, not old ladies picking through wastebaskets. The cop swung his head slowly from side to side, looking for some cause for the phenomenon. Looking for the Candid Camera. Looking for the gag. Then he stared at the old Raggedy Ann with a sad look on his face, as though it were his own grandmother he saw picking through the garbage. Whistler supposed it once might have been.

"Putting it mildly," Lister chirped on, "I know what everybody was thinking."

"What were they thinking?"

"Not you. I don't think you were thinking what everybody was thinking."

"I'd really like to know what you think they were thinking that you don't think I was thinking," Whistler said.

The cop's head perked up because of something off to one side. Whistler saw a plainclothesman from the security office come walking across the wide hall, heel taps calling echoes out of the vaulted ceiling. The young white man stopped before he reached the Raggedy Ann or the cop, settling his maroon jacket on his shoulders with a shrug that told the cop to get with it.

"We could be an act," Lister said. "The new fucking Abbott and Costello. What they were thinking was: What's this old fart, thinks he's an actor, doing coming out here for a career? Just who the fuck does this little old fart think he is? Well, this here actor has himself a continuing role on a continuing series. Two grand a week, twenty weeks a year on the contract. What do you think of that?"

The cop went over and caught Raggedy Ann's elbow on the rise. She didn't try to pull away, just stood there grinning into his earnest black face. He bent his head and instructed her kindly. She laughed out loud. It wasn't a witchlike cackle but a low, rich contralto, the laughter of another woman altogether. She disengaged her arm and went digging into the first of her three bags. In a minute she came up with an airline ticket folder. The cop pulled out the ticket and looked it over, then looked off to his supervisor. The young executive type walked over and examined the ticket too. Raggedy Ann patted his sleeve. The security men walked away in some confusion.

Lister was a little miffed that Whistler didn't make a big

thing out of his running part in the series. He saw that Whistler's attention had been elsewhere.

"You see that?" Lister said. "What the fuck was that all about?"

"It was entrapment," Whistler said. "That old lady set up the airport cops. She saves her pennies and buys a ticket to the next closest airport. Then she waits for them to roust her, and she shoves the ticket up their nose. Later on she cashes in the ticket."

"What the hell she do that for?"

Raggedy Ann grinned and waved at Whistler. He waved back. She remembered him, after all.

"She told me once there was the bottom, the middle, and the top. Cops, ticket takers, salesclerks, and so forth beat on the poor suckers at the bottom, sit down and break bread with the ones in the middle, and do tricks for the ones on top. She gets tired getting beat on sometimes and tries to get a little back."

"What are you doing flying this hour?" Lister said, not impressed at all by the antic gallantry displayed by the bag lady. "Got a deal?"

"No deal. Just chasing down a lead."

"Me too. My show's on hiatus. Friend of mine's shooting a picture down in Texas. Last time I saw him, he said he'd find something for me. So I'll see. What the hell, I got the money, I got the time. Maybe there's a little something for me in his picture. The big screen's where it is. I mean, it's okay, the money, the face recognition you get from the tube, but for me it's the big screen what counts. The way I figure, if I'm right there on the set, how's he going to avoid the issue? I mean, it's not like I'm a nobody anymore. You got a girlfriend?" he said without pause, as though it were all part of the same thought.

Whistler stared at Lister.

"I got me a babe," the little man said, his hands patting himself. He brought out a wallet and showed Whistler a picture of a hard-eyed bleached blonde who looked like a caricature out of the thirties. "Thirty years younger than me. Whattaya know? Loves me. Says an older man's a better

lover. More considerate. Let me tell you, I can still get it up.
So what's your babe like?"

"Well," said Whistler, "she's got long, wet legs."

"What the fuck you know about that?" Lister said.

Twenty

WHISTLER'S PLANE landed in New Orleans at
midnight. Walking from the air-conditioned cabin
into the wet night was like walking into a warm
bath. The smell of rotting vegetation clogged his nose.

He lugged his bag through the empty corridors of the
terminal, as though he were a pallbearer carrying one end of a
coffin.

The main lobby was as hollow as a drum. The rental
counters were empty except for a tenth-rater trying harder.

The girl behind the counter had the knowing look of a
woman who might turn a trick between flights.

He rented a compact and drove out of Moisant Field along
the Airline Highway. The air conditioner was busted. When
he opened the windows for the breeze, it was like standing in
the mouth of a blast furnace. The road became Tulane
Boulevard quicker than he expected. He checked the map
he'd found in the side pocket of the car, spreading it out
across his knees and glancing down at it every now and then,
reading it in the light of the dash. At Loyola he turned
southwest a couple of blocks to Perdido, then hung a right,
still heading toward the river.

He fell into the net of streets around North and South
Diamond and Calliope. It took him half an hour of jigging
and jogging before he stumbled on the all-night drugstore by
mistake. Its windows were so plastered with signs and offers

of sales that the light from inside scarcely crept out. He parked the car and crossed the street. There was a vagrant lying in the gutter, using the curb as a pillow for his head, his legs sticking out into the street.

If somebody came along half drunk, looking to buy a bottle, and pulled up at the gutter, he could smash the poor sucker's legs to a pulp, Whistler thought. He paused, wondering if it would be worth anybody's while to do the good deed and save the loser from possible injury and mutilation. He bent down and shifted the sleeping man's legs onto the sidewalk.

"You rotten son of a bitch," the bum snarled out of some instinct for self-preservation, scaring off the vultures and the hyenas.

A buzzer sounded when Whistler walked through the door into the drugstore. It looked like a warehouse, every aisle leading off the main one blocked off with little harnesses of chain. Both sides of the main aisle were lined with vending machines piled one on top of another. There might have been a hundred of them, delivering everything from plastic combs to chocolate bars to condoms for a couple of dimes or quarters.

The clerk sat behind his cash register with the fast night merchandise, wine and beer, in the cases behind him. A half a dozen mirrors checked out any thieves that tried to sneak past the barriers. His face was reflected back at him as though he were a prisoner always being watched by guards that looked exactly like him.

When he saw Whistler approaching, he stood up and put his hands on the wood, as though ready to pull a gun from underneath the counter. At the back of the store a bank of fluorescents overhead made sickly daylight around a lunch counter and a line of stools. Three painted women perched there like birds of paradise, pulling open the fronts of their dresses to catch the breeze from a floor fan. A bent blade ticked out a syncopated rhythm.

"Ba-da-da-da-dah," Whistler said. " 'Jelly Roll Blues.' "

"What's that?" the clerk said, drawing it out as though

Whistler had awakened him from a sleep from which he didn't want to be disturbed.

"I'm looking for a movie house called the—"

"Beaver Run."

The man looked at Whistler as though he were a pocket waiting to be picked. He reached into his crummy vest, pulled out a small stack of business cards, and started shuffling them, never taking his eyes from Whistler.

"You know the place?" Whistler asked.

"Outside, turn right, two blocks, turn right, one block, turn left, halfway down the street."

"Is it open now?"

"It's open all the time." His eyes flickered down to the cards. He snapped one down on the counter like he was dealing poker. "Complimentary ticket. Half price after midnight."

"There a hotel or motel close by?"

"Close by here or close by the movie house?"

"We're not talking miles, are we? Let's say anyplace between here and there."

"The Blue House is right next door to the Beaver Run." Another card fell on the counter. "Special rate. Ten bucks for a hot pillow."

"I'm not a husband or a visiting fireman."

"Forty bucks a night, sink in the room, toilet down the hall."

Whistler smiled. "Suppose I want a shower?"

Another card, fluttering softly, like a snowflake. "Across the street from the Blue House. Bee Bee Baths. Ten bucks through the left door, five bucks through the right."

"What's the difference?"

"Left door for twangy boys. That's where the action is."

"When I say a shower, I mean a shower."

"What do you want to go to the movies for? You want excitement, all you got to do is turn your head and take your pick."

Whistler looked. The three whores stared back, half hoping he would, half hoping he wouldn't. He heard the drop of another card, looked down at the growing pile, and picked up the top one. He caught the word *entertainment*.

He didn't have to ask, but he did. "You Crib Coxey?"

"That's me."

"What have I got here, another complimentary half-price special?"

"Nothing off the regular price. Just my personal guarantee. You just hand that to any girl back there—any girl on the street what takes your fancy—and she'll play you rim shots or rattle your castanets if that's your pleasure."

"This your commission card?"

"Why not?"

"Pimp pays you or the girl pays you?"

"The man in charge of the commodity, whoever he may be. No free-lance ladies in this town. Not allowed."

"All organized?"

"All safe and orderly."

Whistler threw ten dollars on the counter.

"You know who owns this Beaver Run movie house?"

Coxey's hands stopped shuffling the little pasteboards. His eyes flattened out the way a mouse does its body before skinnying its way under a door.

"What's your living?"

"I walk around with one foot in the gutter looking for dimes."

"It's no secret. Nonny Barcaloo owns the theater. If I don't tell you, the next man will."

"This Barcaloo run the girls?"

"Just the head shops and flicks. A little manufacturing. A little cinema enterprise. On the subject, you want a French tickler—drive her wild? You want a monster dildo—keep her satisfied? Inflatable doll what sucks? How about some eight millimeter or some tapes? I got VHS. I got Beta. I got *Naughty Nights with Nellie*. I got *Three Little Men in a Boat*."

"What about Vietnamese?"

"If that's your pleasure." Coxey's voice dropped through long habit. "I don't know she's from Vietnam, but I got something special with a slant-eyed girl in it. You like snuff? I got *Rosita Dies for It*."

A rustle of sick understanding brought up something sour into Whistler's mouth.

"Jokes?"

"Hell, no. The real thing. You don't got to believe me, but I even knew the girl in the movie. She used to come in here and sit back there at the lunch counter, just like them girls is doing. I ain't seen her around in over a year. I swear this flick's the straight goods. They really did her while she was coming."

"How much?"

"Two hundred and fifty."

Whistler counted his roll.

"Can I rent for the night?"

"Not this stuff. This is choice."

Whistler hesitated.

"I'll take plastic if you're short of cash," Coxey said.

Whistler took out his bank charge card. He signed the slip Coxey handed him after imprinting it on the machine.

"Telephone number?"

Whistler shook his head and pulled out the customer copy and the carbons.

"VHS or Beta?"

"What kind of machine's available?"

"Blue House has got VHS . . . if they got one working. You can rent a machine, ten bucks, from me. Same price."

"I wouldn't want your machine on my hands. I'll take my chances on the ones at the Blue House."

Coxey dropped the tape cassette into a paper bag. "You sure you don't want to take along one of the girls?"

"I'm sure. Where does this Barcaloo live?"

"Conversion over on Ursuline across the street from the rectory of St. Mary's Italian Church. I don't have the house number."

"Where does he hang out?"

"Jimmy Flynn's over to St. Peter Street. Mindy's Blue Grotto on Iberville. There's a whorehouse in the back. He has an office upstairs over the Beaver Run. Anywhere he's got a piece. You a buyer?"

"Of what?"

"The word on the street is that Barcaloo's selling up everything he's got except the Beaver Run and maybe an apartment house or two."

"Why's that?"

"Somebody give him an offer to go west."

"Las Vegas?"

"Hey, even I don't know everything," Coxey said.

Whistler started to leave. "Bosco Silverlake says hello."

"Whattaya know? You shoulda told me. I woulda give you a price."

Whistler didn't think he meant it.

Twenty-one

THE ROOM in the Blue House was surprisingly clean, although it had the milky smell of plaster that would never dry.

Whistler lay on the bedcovers in his shorts. It was dark except for the light coming from the television set.

As old as he got—knowing that things were as they were, neither good nor bad, right nor wrong, just as they were, mindless therefore thoughtless, heartless therefore cruel—he still felt a blaze of helpless rage at certain horrors. It wouldn't take much more of what he was watching for him to go to St. Louis Cemetery Number One or Two and find a tomb to hide in.

A young dark-skinned girl, probably Mexican or Puerto Rican, with a very immature body, did tricks with a slightly older Oriental woman who was beautiful in a remote sort of way. There was that crack about Orientals all looking alike, which might be true for some people, but Whistler was almost sure the woman in the picture was the one in the morgue glossies, Lim Shu Dok.

It was possible to imagine the Latino pretending to herself that what she was doing was somehow elevated on film to something like real acting. She saw herself in Hollywood. She saw herself a star. Petted and pampered. She was doing her best to act out everything the director asked of her, turning this way and that, lying on her side, getting on her knees, arching her back on command.

Lim Shu watched herself doing and being done as though she were a spectator. A mark on her hip could be seen as she rolled this way and that. She'd lost all hope of stardom of any kind.

The dark-skinned one showed an anxious concern to do exactly as she was bidden. It was in the tension of the lips and the quick glances cast at the camera lens. Seeking approval. Seeking mercy. Maybe she sensed the coming horror and was trying to save herself.

A man took over from Lim Shu. She did not appear again, but had she been called back another time to play the sacrifice?

There wasn't much plot, no attempt at dialogue that made any sense. The moans and heavy breathing had been dubbed in afterward, so it was sometimes out of synch. The lighting was bad and the match of color temperatures careless. Nothing like the slick pieces done with seasoned profession-als in Detroit and La-La Land. Gut basic. Truer to its purpose. Pure in its rotten fashion.

Whistler had once asked the editor of a string of crotch magazines published out in San Fernando Valley why a customer would spend five dollars on twenty pages of stupidly captioned black-and-white photographs of unlovely women exposing themselves awkwardly in motel rooms rented by the hour when they could buy a three-hundred-page slick, filled with articles, dirty letters, and heart-stopping beauties in full labial display for three bucks.

That was easy, the editor told him. Not many men could

imagine themselves screwing one of the Technicolor beauties, wrestling them to fur rugs, stained with spilled champagne, in front of marble fireplaces. But just about every one of them could see himself getting lucky with some hard-eyed blonde, with a mouth like a hand vacuum, met in the corner bar. Having a one-off in some hot pillow joint along the boulevard where fifty bucks bought the works.

In a while the director and crew of the snuff film ran out of tape, story, patience, and positions. The end came to the girl on the television screen so fast that Whistler felt as though he'd been punched in the belly. Her anxious eagerness gave way to dumb confusion. Then the terror burst like a bomb. It pulled her homely, painted little face into a witch's mask, eyes starting out of her head, mouth stretched back as though burned with acid, tongue skewered by her teeth. She reached out for the naked partner who'd just performed an "act of love" on her frail, small-breasted body. The camera jerked as her legs kicked out. It lash-panned across the wall behind her.

Once steadied, a different man, naked, too, a hood over his head, took two steps into the shot. He carried a machete in his left hand. He swung it at the girl's neck and the blood fountained.

Twenty-two

SLEEPING TOO long with nightmares that refuse to escape in a scream wracks the bones and dries out the juices of the body.

When Whistler slid out of the bed stenciled with the sweaty shape of a mummy three thousand years old, it was five o'clock in the morning. The air was already hot and tasted of brass.

He turned on the television set. The commentator said, in the hollow voice of early morning, that it had been very hot and humid the day before, and the city could expect more of the same. There might be a chance of a cooling rain if everybody prayed.

Whistler punched the button on the tape deck, running it back and forth with the search key until he found the place where the girl, in her panic, had kicked the camera tripod. He hit the pause button and examined the still, clicking the tape forward frame by frame.

It looked as though the snuff film had been shot on a makeshift soundstage with some basic equipment. There were some posters and signs on the wall. One of them read, "Go Fuck a Duck."

He ran the tape back some more until he found a close-up of the dark-skinned girl. He wondered in what nameless grave she was buried. He found the place where the blemish on the Vietnamese woman's hip rolled across the screen as she twisted her body and held it there. It was the tattoo. The butterfly.

There was nothing he could do so early, but he couldn't stay in the room. With no shower available, he took a whore's bath in the sink and got dressed in his stale clothes, wondering what the hell he was doing working a hot, wet city with little hope of reward. He put the tape into its box and tucked it into his jacket pocket.

Out on the street he walked three blocks looking for a place to eat before turning back and getting into the rented car. His shirt was soaked already, his underwear tore and twisted at his crotch. He put the cassette in the glove compartment and drove to the French Quarter. Parked it on Ursuline in front of St. Mary's Italian Church between reserved signs, across from the conversion in which Coxey said Barcaloo lived.

There was a red Cadillac parked in front. Its enamel glistened with the brittle sheen of a cheap, quickie repaint. It was better than a good guess that it was the white Cadillac with the Bondoed fender he'd read about in the *Enquirer*. It had been refinished just hours ago.

A black man came out of the building next door and started

sweeping the sidewalk, staring sidelong at Whistler. The janitor watched him as he walked all the way down to Decatur.

Whistler found a place for coffee and doughnuts in the French Market. He had three cups. The sugary doughnuts left a cool residue on his lips. He had a sudden image of the girl in the film biting into a doughnut, brushing the powdered sugar off the tops of her breasts and laughing. Fear rushed up into his throat. It was too easy to replace the girl's face with Shiela's. Knife coming down. Blood showering. Head rolling along a piece of carpet. Long legs forever stilled.

He went back to the all-night drugstore. Coxey was there unlocking the padlocks on the chains that kept the nighttime thieves at bay. He was working one side, and a pale man with wispy hair and steel-rimmed glasses was working the other. The morning clerk coming to relieve the guard in the shop that never slept.

Coxey saw the tape caught in Whistler's armpit.

"No refunds," he said, and walked away toward the counter at the rear where two transvestites in need of a shave mourned the wasted night by staring into the cold coffee in their cups.

"You told me this Barcaloo was into film. This some of his work?"

"Please. Don't make me crazy. I don't answer questions about my sources."

Whistler walked him back along one of the side aisles, past shelves of Pepto-Bismol and Alka Seltzer, into a section of small kitchenware. Coxey gave way until he couldn't give way any more. He had to stay very quiet to hear what Whistler had to say. That's how soft-voiced Whistler got when the rage caught hold of him. His eyes flickered one way and another. He grabbed the closest thing to hand that could do bodily harm. It was a novelty beer-can key with a sharp nose and a plastic Mickey Mouse for a handle.

"I want to tell you it wouldn't take much for me to do to you what somebody did to that girl. This thing won't make as clean a cut, but it could clean out your windpipe like reaming a squash. I don't want to play your gonif's games anymore. I don't want to haggle over price. I don't want to pay. Not with cash and not with plastic. I just want a simple answer to the simple question I asked you. It's no skin off your ass. Was that fucking snuff film shot by Barcaloo or any people attached to Barcaloo?"

"Yes."

"The dark-skinned girl was the one came in here for coffee?"

"That's right. She was a Mex."

"Was she ever with a Vietnamese whore?"

"I never saw her with one a them."

"See how easy that was? How much is this gadget?"

"Fifty-nine cents."

"I'll buy it. Let's go ring up your last sale of the night."

Whistler moved aside, and Coxey slipped past him, as though Whistler's touch could burn.

"I want some blowups made of a frame or two," Whistler said, speaking at normal volume. "You know anybody who can do it?"

Coxey turned at the smell of profit like a bird dog, forgetting the powerful fright he'd just been given. His hand dipped into the magic vest for a fistful of calling cards. He fanned them, cut them, cascaded them like a magician passing aces, and finally extracted one.

"I don't get a commission from this technician."

"You never give up, do you? You'll be sitting up in your coffin making deals with the undertaker." Whistler handed over a five-dollar bill as Coxey rang up the hardware sale. "Keep the change."

Coxey smiled. Four dollars and forty-one cents was as good as a twenty-dollar bill at six-thirty in the morning.

"This city got a Chinatown, a Little Korea, anything like that?" Whistler asked.

"Every city's got a Chinatown, even if it's only two old chinks playing mah-jong over a pot of tea."

"For Christ's sake, another early-morning philosopher."

"But we got no place like you mean in New York or L.A. There's maybe a couple of blocks."

"Where?"

"At the end of Saratoga at Felicity." Coxey plucked a city map out of a rack beside the cash register and circled half a dozen city blocks with a red marker. "One dollar for the map."

"Don't you ever spring for anything?" Whistler asked, handing over the dollar in small change.

"I'll buy you a breakfast if you want to tell me what you're doing here in town."

"Hell, Coxey, that information would make your fortune," Whistler said. He started to leave, then came back.

"Hey, Coxey," he said as softly as before. "Don't try to sell me. You're the only bigmouth knows I'm in town. If anybody comes after me, nobody'll be fast enough to stop me from letting Mickey Mouse drink your blood."

The photographer lived and worked at the top of a rickety wooden outside staircase that climbed to the third floor of a building ready to lie down. Whistler punched the bell. A dog with a heavy voice sounded a warning from somewhere inside the flat. Whistler checked his watch and pushed the bell again. He didn't expect the photographer to be happy about having a customer so early.

The woman who opened the inside door and peered through the screen, tousle-haired and beagle-eyed with sleep, wasn't happy.

"Who're you?" she said.

"I'm looking for J. Kissie."

"You're looking at her."

"You're the photographer?"

"Fastest finger in the South. What do you want?"

"I want some reproductions taken off a tape cassette."

"This is a rotten time of day to do business."

"I agree, but I'm on a schedule."

J. Kissie was small and blond, of a likely age and as homely as a mutt. She stared at Whistler as though it would be written on his forehead if he were a wandering rapist.

"Wait a second," she said.

She faded away behind the mesh of the screen as she went to the back of the parlor and opened a door.

"Easy, Beau," she said in a voice of soft command.

She came back into view behind the mesh. A bull mastiff padded silently at her side, standing as tall as her hip. She unlatched the screen door. "Come on in."

Whistler hesitated.

"Beau's all right. Just don't make any sudden moves." She held the screen door open, and Whistler went inside, keeping an eye on the dog, who was keeping an eye on him. "And whatever you do, don't touch me. Understand?"

"Oh, yes, indeed."

"Sit there," J. Kissie said. She palmed her eyes for a second, then took her hands away and blinked. "I haven't even washed my face."

"It doesn't need it."

She grinned and looked at herself in a mirror above a rack of television sets, tape recorders, and monitors. She fluffed her hair.

"You can always tell if a woman's a true beauty by the way she looks in the morning without her makeup. Am I a doll or am I a doll?"

"Yes, you are," Whistler said. She looked like a mutt, but there was something about J. Kissie that grew on you fast.

"Let me see," she said, holding out her hand.

Whistler gave her the cassette. She inserted it into a top-of-the-line front-loader. A five-headed machine designed for smooth slow-mo and rock-steady still-frame. She punched the start button.

"What's your name?" she asked.

"Whistler."

"Whistler, you shouldn't be rotting your brain with this shit."

"I'm not a fan."

She handed him the remote control.

"Show me what you want me to reproduce."

She got a heavy tripod from the corner and screwed a Polaroid instant camera to the plate after setting time and aperture. She checked the number of the shot coming up in the film pack. By the time Whistler found the best close-up frame of Lim Shu Dok, J. Kissie was ready. The shutter clicked. She pulled the tab and tossed the print on a table. He found the close shot of the butterfly tattoo, and the shutter clicked again. He found a close-up of the Latino girl and another at the spot where the knife met her neck. The shutter clicked twice. He ran it forward a frame at a time until the head left the body.

J. Kissie turned pale and backed off. Her dog smelled her fear and was rounding on Whistler when she laid a hand on his head to hold him in check.

"What the hell kind of sick stuff is this?"

"The kind of sick stuff I'd like to grind up into stink bombs and toss into the right places."

"Is that for real? I mean, did that man with the knife really—"

She choked on the rest of it.

"It could be faked. Can you tell me?"

"Oh, sweet Jesus, I suppose it could. It's a hell of a goddamn way to start the day."

She ran the entire last sequence three times, stopping it now and then, running it back and forth and freezing the frame. She leaned forward, intent, jaw rigid, hand steady on Beau's huge head. The technician had taken over from the frightened and disgusted woman. She stopped at the moment when the blade struck the woman's neck. She advanced the tape a single frame. Then another and another. Less than a second's running time of blurred action. The next frame was of a head striking the floor. It rolled across the carpet a frame at a time.

"I can't tell for sure," she said. "If it's a fake, they must of used up all the smarts they had in the one sequence because the production quality's sure not very good anywhere else. On the other hand, the blow with the knife could have stopped at the neck . . ."

Very fancy bladework, Whistler thought.

". . . and the rest would be easy. A quick pan. A dummy head. The way they make them nowadays . . ."

"They'd fool a coroner until he cut," Whistler finished.

She took a still of the knife about to decapitate the terrified girl. J. Kissie stared as Whistler looked the prints over.

"I think they really killed that girl."

"How much do I owe you?" he asked.

"You really trying to do something about stopping stuff like this?"

"I got to tell you, I don't know how far I'll get."

"As long as somebody's trying."

"How much?" Whistler asked again.

"Nothing." J. Kissie walked him to the door, Beau padding alongside, still wary, still ready to have a go at the intruder who caused his mistress to smell of fear.

"You know," she said, "you're not a bad-looking fellow. Remind me not to let fellows who are not bad-looking into the house so early in the morning. If you come back at night—tonight—that's another story."

"I won't be in town very long."

"Well, keep it in mind in case you miss your plane," J. Kissie said, and made a monkey face.

Twenty-three

WHISTLER CUT through Jackson Square to Chartres, walking all the way up St. Peter until, worn-out and panting like an old dog, he reached North Rampart. He shuffled along the sweltering pavement to St. Louis Cemetery Number One, rotting in a patch of swampy ground between Conti and St. Louis, Basin and Treme. The gates were open, an old white man in shirtsleeves and suspenders already sitting in a rickety wooden chair at his post, selling souvenir pamphlets, a cooler filled with cans of beer at his feet. He stared inquiringly at Whistler. Whistler shook his head and walked along the perimeter wall where the burial crypts, called "ovens," honeycombed the brick and plaster.

At the base the larger repositories of old tenants lay with their mouths bricked up except for one or two here and there. Whistler stooped down and bent his head almost to the ground so he could peer inside of one that had been torn open. There were bones piled inside, brown and dry like the teeth of old horses.

Whistler sat down on the steps of a marble tomb with a cottage front and an angel on the roof. He thought about what he was doing and why. He knew what he was doing but didn't really know why.

He'd come to New Orleans because of a woman's scared eyes, trembling lips, and long leg sticking out in the rain. He'd come down with the vague idea he'd just intercept her on the way to the Beaver Run Theater, kiss her, and tell her he'd changed his mind. He wanted to make love to her. Not in this shitty town where they were apt to melt but back in L.A. where you could depend upon the overcast.

Buying the snuff film had been a matter of curiosity because there was a yellow girl in it. And that had led to the stills he carried around, as he'd carried pictures around looking for missing persons before. Then there was the newly painted Cadillac in front of Barcaloo's.

A little curiosity, a little easy doing what he did, had led him deeper into the mystery of the Vietnamese whore who was almost positively the woman whose parts were scattered two thousand miles apart. How many Vietnamese whores, working New Orleans and L.A., could there be with a butterfly tattoo on her ass? He still couldn't see a paycheck, but he was in it up to his neck, and there was no getting out.

"No wonder I haven't got a bank account," he said aloud.

The angel made no comment.

Barcaloo dozed out on the front gallery. He was dressed in a fresh string shirt and white slacks with sandals on his feet. The toes were blunted. The separations could scarcely be seen except between the big toe and the rest. His feet were like cloven hooves.

Bouche, lounging in a skimpy bathing suit on a plastic-webbed chaise, stared at his feet.

"Whattaya starin' at?"

"Who's staring?"

"You were lookin' at my feet."

"You're crazy. I was a million miles away."

"Fuckin' a dinge?"

A vein started pulsing in her neck.

"Just what the hell you mean by that?"

"I got my eye on you," Barcaloo said.

"You got your eye on me, then you should know I'd never do such a thing. I won't have nothing to do with darkies."

"You want to tell me you don't go to seances over to Mama Bluess? You want to tell me you don't dance with your bare tits over to Bayou St. John when she has her heathen ceremonies?"

"I never did," she shouted, hoping he didn't have ideas about Henry. That he was just trying to scare her for the fun of it. "Once I went to watch just like any other tourist. It's all a show."

"And you danced."

"There were two hundred people dancing, for chrissake."

"With your shirt off."

"I had a goddamn bathing suit top on underneath," she screamed.

"If I ever find out you fucked a nigger, I'll do you," he said as Pinole and Rojo appeared in the doorway.

"You do like I tole you about that goddamn Cadillac?"

"Well . . ." Pinole hesitated.

"It's still got a lot of miles left on it. We had it painted. Go take a look. It's parked right out front," Rojo said.

Barcaloo was about to dump a mountain on them, but it was too damned hot. He just shrugged and let it go, not worth the trouble.

"How'd you get it painted so fast?"

"It was already primed. Only takes an hour to spray it. They got this oven what bakes the finish."

"You had time to take care of everything over at the studio?"

"Everything's great," Rojo said.

"You didn't leave no mess?"

Pinole glanced at Rojo, waiting to see what he was going to say. Barcaloo didn't seem to notice, but Bouche did.

She knew they'd fucked up again.

"We put everything left over in a closet," Rojo said.

"How many full drums of gasoline we got over there?"

"Twenty. Twenty drums and fifty jerry cans."

"After we shoot some stuff with this Hollywood actress—" He stopped and stared at Bouche. "I want you to work this one, Bouche," he said.

"Like hell."

"I'm not negotiatin' with you. You're going to work this one last scene for me."

Her heart lurched. "What?" The word sounded like a death rattle. She smelled the sharp smell of fear mixed with perfume.

Barcaloo smiled his white smile. "After we get to La-La Land you're going to be retired. Do nothing but sit around the pool, go shopping, have cocktails in the Polo Lounge, maybe grab Clint Eastwood by the ass."

Bouche tried a laugh. It came out all right, but it didn't comfort her.

"When we're finished—maybe tomorrow night—we burn the shack down," Barcaloo said.

"A thousand gallons of gas'll burn very hot," Rojo said, staring at Bouche.

"So meet me at the movie house in an hour," Barcaloo said.

Whistler walked back from St. Louis Cemetery Number One along Rampart. The police station was on the other side of the street just outside the Vieux Carré at the edge of the section once known as Storyville, where, once upon a time, sexual novelties could be witnessed for a penny and sexual horrors rented for a dime. The red-light district had been razed to the ground long ago and low-cost housing erected in its place. Now, in the eighties, it was the breeding ground for petty and violent crime alike, but there were no marauders out this early in the morning. He paused in front of the entrance. Two cops gave him the look. He went inside and up to the desk.

"Yes, sir, what can I do for you?" the uniformed sergeant said.

"Who do I see about a matter of vice or homicide?"

"Which is it, sir?" the desk sergeant said.

"A little of both."

"Are you a private citizen here to make a complaint?"

"I'm a private ticket from L.A. looking into a killing that might have started here or might have started there."

The honey left the sergeant's voice. "That's as clear as mud."

"That's why I'm here to talk to the experts."

"Take a chair."

"I'm in a little bit of a hurry. There's somebody I've got to meet."

"Well, hell, yes. Ain't we all? You sit. I'll see if Lieutenant Bellerose'll see you."

It wasn't long before Whistler was shown into an interrogation room. It was longer before the door opened and a man in an ice-cream suit waded in and sat down.

Whistler had kept a turtle once. It had had the patience of a rock and a look in the eye so weary and wise that—before he met Bosco—Whistler consulted it on important matters like love and minor wars.

That turtle had nothing on Lieutenant Bellerose when it came to heavy lids, snaky eyes, folded skin around the neck, and slow-mo gestures. He was like a man swimming in a dream. He wore the wrinkled suit like a turtle's carapace. When he shifted his weight from one hip to the other in the squeaking swivel chair, his skinny body moved around inside the suit without disturbing it very much. Whistler had the feeling that if danger threatened, Bellerose would just pull in head, ass, arms, and legs and become a stone.

Whistler put down the Polaroids and the photos from the morgue.

"Ah'm not quick. You got to spell things out for me," Bellerose said.

Whistler tapped the pictures of the Latino girl. "This girl was murdered for a snuff film, I think."

"Uh-huh."

He tapped the pictures of Lim Shu Dok.

"This one left her body back in L.A. and her head here in New Orleans."

"You think?"

"I think."

"Now let me get it clear. You come into my parish lookin' for what?"

"A head to go with the body back in L.A."

"You lose the head?"

"I only *read* about it in the *Enquirer*. A story about an Oriental lady's head and two guys driving a white Cadillac with a Bondoed fender playing kickball with it over to the lake."

"Oh, *that* lady's head."

"You got many loose heads scattered around?"

"Well, now, they's not exactly as thick on the ground as magnolia blossoms at the end of summer, but a man likes to make really sure what he's talkin' about an' . . ."

"I can understand that."

". . . who he's talkin' about what with. Was that confusin'?"

"I get your drift."

"That's big-city slang, is it? My drift. Like snow, am I right? Like somebody gettin' snowed?"

"I'm not unloading any blizzard on you. I'm thinking you know all there is to know about snow jobs."

"So, all right, what's your interest?"

"I was sitting in a shop having a cup of coffee back in Hollywood the other night, reading about the head down here in New Orleans, when there's an accident between a BMW and a station wagon outside the window. A body—a lady's body—comes flying out the wagon without a head."

"An' you come down here lookin' for a match? You just a curious bystander?"

"I'm private."

"Let me see your ticket."

Whistler took out his card case, opened it, and shoved it under Bellerose's nose.

"Stand up and fan your jacket."

Whistler opened his coat and pulled the sides away from his body.

"Turn around and lift your tail. All right, you ain' carryin'. You're no fool. We're hard on private Johnny Hams what come aroun' totin' iron."

"That's small-city slang, is it? Johnny Hams are private licenses and iron is guns?"

"You're bein' a wise guy. It ain't smart to be a wise guy with a man in his own parish."

"I take it back."

"You got a client?"

"Not really. I thought I was helping the guy driving the BMW, but it turned out he didn't need my help. He walked without even getting booked."

"What about the driver of the wagon?"

"He didn't need my help, either. He was dead."

"Vehicular manslaughter an' there was no charge?"

"The story on the books is that nothing happened on that corner that night except a one-car collision with a pole."

"Hoo-hoo. You sit right there. You want a cup? How about a glass of water? I'd offer you some white lightin', but I don' know you good enough."

Bellerose moved out of the office with surprising speed and was back within five minutes. He was grinning.

"Cop down in Hollywood didn' believe I was a police officer. Said actors was always tryin' that gag out on him. You must have good times out there in movin'-picture land. You know what he said? He said the thing what fell out of the wagon was a made-up dummy this fella was takin' over to some movie set."

"That's the story going around, all right."

"You don't believe it?"

"Do you?"

"Say I bought your goods. I'd still like to know why you stopped by. Just down here on a little vacation, is it? Just passed the station on the way to take a look at the housing projects where Storyville used to be and said to yourself, 'Why don' I just stop in and do some old boy a favor? Tell him about the body with no head back in L.A. Give the sucker a hand up.'"

"I thought it was something you'd like to know."

"I thank you kindly. Where'd you get those pictures?"

"Those are off the snuff reel. Those from the L.A. morgue."

"You got the reel with you?"

Whistler handed the cassette over. "You know a local smutter by the name of Barcaloo?" he asked.

All of a sudden Bellerose was no turtle. He leaned forward, hunching his shoulders and putting his forearms on the desk. His neck swelled and his body filled out the suit, assuming the disguise of a bull.

"I know him. Do you know him?" Bellerose asked.

"We never met, but I think I know him. He runs an X-rated movie house, some dirty bookshops, a whorehouse . . ."

". . . a filthy press and other enterprises. What's your interest?"

"I think he made this crap. A young Latino girl's beheaded in it. The Vietnamese woman, whose body disappeared from the L.A. morgue and ended up in the gutter, is on this tape doing tricks with the Latino. I think Barcaloo had something to do with that too. Either Barcaloo or somebody he knows is good with a machete. Barcaloo's got two gazoonies working for him, a big one and a little one."

"Dom Pinole and Jickie Rojo."

"They drove a Cadillac with a Bondoed fender. It's been painted red."

"We'll look into it."

There was a beat-up RCA tape player and a nineteen-inch color set on a table in the corner. Bellerose got up and went over to slam the cassette into the top loader. After pulling three or four buttons and depressing a couple of switches, the player hummed and the screen lit up. He picked up the remote and went to sit down again.

Whistler watched the sorry sex scenario unfold again. The

story seemed to have something to do with the delights of girls imported from Hong Kong or Singapore and sold into the flesh trade.

"We don't see many of them in New Orleans," Bellerose said.

"Many of what? Prostitutes?"

"Many Orientals. And no Vietnamese whores I ever heard about."

They watched the sex acts flickering on the television screen in silence.

"This kind of thing give you a hard-on?" Bellerose said.

"Only if I'm long deprived."

"Gives me a hard-on. Shitty stuff. Shouldn't be on the shelves. But I can understand some gazoony without a woman, or with the wrong woman, watching crap like this and having it off with Mary Fist."

"We don't have to watch the whole thing," Whistler said.

Bellerose tossed Whistler the remote control.

Whistler ran the tape at speed until he came to the close-up of Lim Shu Dok. "This look like the head you got on ice?"

"What we got on ice don't look like nothin' I'd want to show my granny."

"Can I have a look?"

"You can, but I'm tellin' you, it don't look human any-more."

"How about forensic's description?"

Bellerose nodded. "Trade you for copies of your pictures. We got a machine."

Whistler ran the tape ahead to the look of terror on the girl's face at the entrance of the swordsman and the upswing of the swordsman's arm. He stopped it before the blood gushed.

Whistler became aware of the sounds of the squad room going on outside the walls of the room. Phones ringing, voices talking back and forth, footsteps and slamming doors. Ordinary things.

"I seen this before," Bellerose said. "If that Mex girl was beheaded, we ain' found any part of her yet."

"You talk to Barcaloo about it?"

"Sure, we talked to him about it. He takes us over to the studio in a warehouse down by the river where he says he shoots his erotic films. He shows us the soundstage and the cameras and the laboratory where they do trick photography."

"You ask him where the Latino girl and the Asian woman might be?"

"He said how the hell should he know where wanderin' whores go. He practically dared me to prove he snuffed the girl. 'Fin' her,' he said. 'Fin' the Saigon whore,' he said. 'She'll tell you it was all a trick.'"

"Maybe he knew you'd never find either one of them. But now there's a head here in New Orleans and a body with a butterfly on the hip back in L.A."

"You say that, but the L.A.P.D. don't say that. You see the problem I got?" He took the remote out of Whistler's hand and hit the rewind. While the tape whirred back to the beginning he stared at Whistler.

"What else brings you here?" Bellerose said.

"There was an actress riding in the BMW. She saw the corpse they call a dummy. The day after the crash she gets an offer to come down here on quick notice and take over a part in a film."

"And Barcaloo's the man she was sent to see?"

"I think it's a fair bet."

"What makes you think so?"

"A chain of probabilities starting with a piece of funny money advertising his porno movie house, which I found on the lady's dressing table."

"You tellin' me this actress in L.A. gets a rush offer from a guy who's carryin' play money in his pocket from a porno house in New Orleans and she just comes traipsin' down here? Sounds to me like she knows what she's doin', but you don' know what she's doin'. Maybe you don' even know her too good."

"I'm going to ask her when I find her. And when I find her, maybe I'll need some help."

Bellerose settled back in the chair again, the swivel squeaking like a smashed rat. He seemed to shrink inside his shirt and suit again. His eyes took on the sleepy look of a sly old turtle.

"You just bring me cause."

"Like another head?"

"Don' smart-mouth me. What the hell you think, we're brain-stunned down here? You think I ain' seen this crap before? You think we don' watch? Looka hear what I'm tellin' you. This ain' your town. I fin' you someplace you shouldn't be, I'll bust your ass. I don' care you're down here lookin' for your lady love."

Twenty-four

NEW ORLEANS is an easy stakeout town. There are people of all kinds and classes loafing everywhere, on benches, stoops, and curbstones, leaning against storefronts, gates, and garden walls at all hours of the day or night.

Whistler sat in his rental car parked across the street from the Beaver Run.

It was either stake out the movie house or the apartment house on Ursuline Street where Barcaloo lived. A fifty-fifty chance that he was wrong or right. Except the only reason he could figure for the funny money he found in Shiela's apartment was because it had the address of the Beaver Run on it. They'd use the office in a half-assed attempt to make it look like business.

If he was wrong, if he missed her, if she arrived someplace where Whistler wasn't and was taken wherever they were going to shoot the picture, or do the terrible thing to her he feared they were going to do, he'd have lost her. Not just for now but forever.

On the other hand, even as he sweated, she could be sitting in some air-cooled restaurant lunching on prawns, jambalaya, and Sazerac cocktails while some legitimate, if marginal, movie producer talked to her about character motivation and the beautiful wardrobe she'd get to wear. Well, that would be all right. He'd rather be a damned fool than a mourner.

The sun was straight up overhead, burning like a klieg. He had an awful thirst. He was about to get out and go find a beer in some place where he could keep an eye out when two men, a big one and a little one—Pinole and Rojo, who else could it be?—parked the freshly painted red '81 Cadillac in front of the movie house.

They got out and disappeared inside.

Barcaloo turned around and put his hands on the wrought-iron rail and hung like a monkey, lowering his head to stare down at the street between the bars.

Bouche looked at the back of his neck and wondered if it would kill him if she hit him with all her strength right behind the ear with a heavy pot in which a camellia grew.

He looked around as if he heard her thoughts. Then he stared back down into the street again.

Barcaloo didn't think of himself as a brute, even if he did look like a hairy ape. He didn't get where he was in the skin trade just by scaring pussy to death. He had a certain smooth, a certain charm.

He'd learned how to control women from Fan-Tan Leaper, king pimp in the French Quarter twenty years before, when Barcaloo was just a growing boy. Leaper had been as skinny as a trout, weak-eyed and weak-chinned, with snaggle teeth that almost never saw a toothbrush. He chewed twelve packs of Juicy Fruit a day, just to keep his breath sweet. There was always a line of angry red pimples on his neck where his starched collar sawed at him. He wore a tie winter and summer. He had a stool permanently reserved for him at a place called Billy Wimple's, from which he ran his stable of high-assed, high-yellow girls and handed out bits of carnal and criminal wisdom.

"You go around tryin' to power a strange cunt into doin'

this or that—you grab her by the hair and knock her against the wall—what you got is a bitch yellin' rape on you. Runnin' down the avenue lookin' to throw herself into the arms of the first cop or pimp ready to defend her, you unnerstan'?" he'd say. "You got to do like with a cat. First ignore her. Let her come to you. Then you feed her sweet cream and peaches. You play like you don' even see she's got legs and tits.

"Now, when you feed her the cream, don' be stingy. Pour it on. If she got ugly ears, you say you never see such pretty seashells, how the light shines through them. She got a honker like a bugle, you tell her handsome noses was very highly prized by Roman emperors and French kings, pointin' out that Madame Bovary and the great witch queen, Marie Laveau, both had noses the prow of any ship would be proud to wear. If she got no tits, tell her she's a lady born out of her time, quality from the twenties come to grace this sorry age with her lovely figure. You hear what I'm tellin' you?"

"Suppose she knows what she's got ain't much and says you're full of shit?"

"What you expect her to say unless she's a sorry fool? So what you do, you eat it and make like it's tasty. You act shy and humble in the face of such misguided self-abnegation."

"Self what?"

"Never mind. We talkin' cunt, not vocabulary. You shake your head in shocked dismay. You cluck your tongue. You twist and turn and pour it on. Slop it in there by the pint. By the quart. By the fuckin' gallon! For it is written, 'There ain' no pussy alive that will not twitch when they is properly stroked.' Also remember, 'Excess is not to be feared so long as the eye is sincere.'"

"Suppose she ain' as ugly as a trout, but pretty enough to stop your heart."

"The opposite applies. Feed her vinegar. Mention that she's got a little droopy eyelid—too bad—but maybe it's better she shouldn't be perfect, after all. Say the little scar on her lip gives her face a certain character. Go easy here, you unnerstan'? Plenty of vinegar, but just a dab of cream to keep

her sweet. Pussy gets a sour stomach if she goes chasin'
somewhere else lookin' for her sweets."

"So why not give her candy right off?"

"Because she gets candy all the goddamn time from every
asshole tryin' to get into her silkies. After her tongue is
stingin' from what you give her, just a tiny candy drop from
you is worth more than a ten-pound box from any other dude.
You unnerstan' these tactics, or is it too much for you?"

"I'm learnin'."

"Next thing—get her out of her clothes. Every one of them
wants to get out of her clothes. All they's lookin' for is a
reason. If they get into long skirts, they got a slit up the front
almost to the flower patch, and their tits is fallin' out of the
tops of their blouses. You know what I mean? You look at the
back of their knees they stepping on a bus, they freeze you
with a haughty glance. Down on the beach they's dressed in
two dimes and a nickel."

"I'll get a camera and say I want to take their pitcher."

"Sheee-it. Don' talk foolish. If they do tricks in the buff
for your camera, and then you lay a hand on the skin, even an
old whore will say she's been tricked and betrayed."

"So what do I do?"

"Learn to give massage."

"Will you run that bus by me one more time?"

Leaper held up his hands like they belonged to a surgeon
just after washing and before getting into rubber gloves.

"These magic fingers has plucked more cherries than the
trees got apples in the state of Washington. Say she's a
secretary and tells you that evening, whilst you're havin' a
little drink at a bar, 'Oh, dear, my tailbone does hurt from so
much sittin'.' You say, 'I got just the thing for that.' Suppose
she's a salesgirl in a department store and she say, 'Lord a
mercy, how my poor feet do ache.' Up you smile and show
your hands and say, 'My dear old mother, may she rest in
peace, used to say I had magic hands when I rubbed her
sweet old feet at the end of a hard day.' Maybe she's a—"

"I think I got you. Say like she's a basketball player and
she's got this ugly on her thigh where somebody clipped her,
and she say, 'Oh my, oh my, that girl was rough and kicked

me with her knee,' and I say, 'See these hands? These is the hands what nursed my basketball-playin' brother back to health and strength after he was brought down by the worst charley horse ever known in Louisiana sports.'"

"A little gaudy, but I think you got the idea. So you stroke them a little, and then you say deep massage works better without clothes gettin' in the way. If only she would just take the tail of her blouse out of the waistband of her skirt. If only she would take off her stockings. If only . . ."

". . . she would take off her jeans."

"So you baby them, an hol' them and drip honey in their ear. So you fuck them."

"And you tell them how good it was."

"Wrong. You tell them how good it was in a way that says it weren't so very good at all. Fair, maybe. So-so. But you ain' goin' to have any trouble doin' without. So she's on her mettle now, you . . ."

"What metal?"

"Never mind. She wants to be a winner, even with poor, ungrateful you. So she practically begs you for an encore. You let her try again, and you act a little disgusted. Then you slap her one when she comes at you for more. That's the tricky part. Some run away after that. But just as many are glad for it. Glad they is gettin' punished for being such stupid, dirty, careless creatures, givin' it away to such as you when good-lookin' stockbrokers and doctors are ready to practically marry them to get it. You unnerstan' what's goin' on here? You unnerstan' the situation that you've built? Everythin'—the sweet and the bitter, the soft and the rough, the kind and the mean—comes from you. Comes from one man. They don' got to shop around different places to get it. You're like an emotional supermarket. You got everythin' she needs in stock. Cunt is lazy creatures, don' you forget. Most of them got a good deal of ambition but very little drive. Remember that and you can't go wrong."

Barcaloo turned around.

Bouche saw his face and was terrified all over again.

"Go get dressed," Barcaloo said. "I want you should come meet this actress somebody sent me from L.A."

Bouche tried not to wonder why someone would send an actress from L.A. to see Barcaloo in New Orleans when Barcaloo was going to be there in a few days.

Something terrible was about to happen. She just knew it.

The shadows were getting longer and longer, but it wasn't getting any cooler. The day just seemed to be withering up. The street was practically empty except for men stopping into the Beaver Run. The movie house was doing pretty good business. There were a lot of lonely, hungry men out there.

A taxi pulled up. Shiela Andes got out. She was dressed in a straw linen suit and carried a big flat oblong bag made of the same stuff. Her jacket was open to show off her yellow silk blouse, cut low in front. Even from across the street Whistler could see the flash of lighter skin as the cloth dipped away from the shallow valley between her widespread breasts. Her skirt was below the knee but slit high on both sides so that her thighs flashed almost to the tops of her seamed stockings. She straightened them as the cab pulled away, her long hair swaying like pale waterfalls on either side of her face.

Whistler felt a grippe in his belly and remembered when she'd kissed him.

She looked his way and he reached over, as though checking out his glove compartment. He had the rearview fixed so he could see the front of the Beaver Run. Shiela looked up at the marquee advertising the bill of fare. Her hair cascaded down her back. It was as hot as the mouth of hell, but she looked as cool as a yellow diamond. Whistler expected she'd be like a piece of hard candy with a crisp shell and a soft, sweet, creamy center.

She hesitated. For a second Whistler had the wild hope that she'd turn around and walk away or flag down a cab. She took a step toward the lobby. For a second he didn't know what to do.

He got out of the car and ran across the street. He tapped her shoulder. She spun around, her eyes frightened and angry, not recognizing him. He spoke her name. Then she knew him.

"Whistler. What the hell are you doing here?"

"I took you up on your invitation. I called your place. You weren't home."

Little lines appeared between her eyebrows. He wanted to put his thumb on them and smooth them away.

"You didn't follow me two thousand miles just to ask for a date?" she said.

"This is a queer deal. Can't you see that?"

"What are you talking about?"

"The movie offer. Getting you to come down here to New Orleans."

"Do you think I'm stupid? Do you think I'm a trout? I didn't swallow it just like that. I checked around before I took the offer."

"A meeting in a goddamn porno house. Where's your brains?"

"I've interviewed for things in an empty warehouse, on an old barge tied up in Wilmington, once in a goddamn dry culvert along the Los Angeles River bottom. Somebody send you after me?"

Whistler heard a car pull up to the curb. He heard the blare of a horn at his back. Shiela looked past his shoulder.

"Are you Mr. Barcaloo?" she said.

Whistler shifted his feet and turned around as Barcaloo got out of the Lincoln Continental and shuffled toward him with the troubled look of a puzzled bear on his face.

"You botherin' this here lady?" he said.

Whistler could see a plump, pretty blonde woman inside the Lincoln.

"For Christ's sake, Whistler, what do you think?" Shiela muttered. "You think Mr. Barcaloo brought his wife along to watch him do me harm?"

"You've got to take what I feel about this on faith."

"I hardly know you, Whistler."

Pinole and Rojo came hurrying out from under the shadow cast by the marquee. Whistler stepped away from Shiela.

"I'll be all right, Whistler. Believe me. I can take care of myself," Shiela said.

Afterward Whistler would remember that there was something wistful in the way she'd said it, as though she was hoping he would say in reply, "You just come with me, my little girl. Listen to your daddy." But he didn't say anything.

"You a goddamn pervert?" Barcaloo shouted.

Before Pinole and Rojo could reach him, Whistler turned and ran. Away from the rented car parked across the street. Around the corner, running the way a gazoony who accosted women would run.

Twenty-five

THE LITTLE office off the lobby smelled like the manager slept in it. Posters of naked women papered the walls.

"Who was that asshole?" Barcaloo said.

"A big surprise, I can tell you," Shiela said. "I knew him back in Hollywood maybe five years ago."

"What's his name?"

"Whistler. That's the only one I can remember, that's how well I knew him. Where he came off thinking——"

"It's awful how a lady ain't safe walking down a street in broad daylight anymore," Bouche simpered. She was half loaded.

Barcaloo frowned at Bouche, telling her to shut up, wondering how she'd managed it.

"It's really nice of you to come all the way from L.A. to see me. Can I call you Shiela? Call me Nonny. Have a seat. You want somethin' cold to drink? Bouche, you want to go see we got any lemonade at the refreshment stand?"

"Nothing for me, thank you," Shiela said.

"So, what did my people back in L.A. say about the picture?"

"Nothing much at all. Just an actress took ill and—"

"That's right. She came down with a flu or somethin'. We couldn't wait for her to get better. You know what they say, 'Time is money.' So, if it's okay with you, Shiela, we'll go over to the studio with Dom and Jickie here . . . make a test . . ."

"Test, Mr. Barcaloo? I came all this way on such short notice because I was told I had the part."

"You've got the part. I'm not sayin' a test like that. I mean a test like for your colorin' and like that. Give my crew a chance to get acquainted with how you photograph and how your voice sounds on tape. Just a little scene with Miss Cazebone, here . . ."

"Wardrobe. How about wardrobe? Don't we need some fittings?"

"I got to be honest with you, Shiela. There's not a lot of wardrobe changes. I mean, it's not a costume picture, you unnerstan' . . . it's not one of them epics. What you brought with you is probably going to be all you're goin' to need. You bring a bathrobe? We'll pay you for the use. If not, we can fix you up. Now, if that ain't okay with you—"

"That's all right," Shiela said quickly, hating how much she needed a job that she'd let herself be rushed here to this wet asshole of a city. Hating how her voice was singing like a goddamn flute and the way this hairy beast facing her, with his mean eyes and swollen hands—like the hands of a corpse left too long in water—was matching her trill for trill in a sorry attempt to sound refined. "When will I see a script?"

"Well, we don't exactly work with a heavy script. We do like that John Cassavetes does, you unnerstan'? We give the actors the situation and a few lines to get them started and then . . ."

"Improvisation?"

"You got it. You ever improvisate?"

"Oh, plenty." She couldn't decide what actor Barcaloo reminded her of. For some reason it seemed important to get that settled in her head . . . to put a tag on him. Otherwise the trembling in her belly would never go away. Barcaloo had the white teeth with the spaces just like Ernest Borgnine, but his face wasn't half so kind.

"So that's the way we do."

"I'd like to see something. A treatment, perhaps?"

"Well, I can unnerstan' that. What I'm going to do—we're in a hurry you unnerstan'?—we got to leave for the Coast in a couple days."

"What? I mean, if you're leaving town in the middle of production, how big's this part I flew all the way—"

"Hey, hey, hey. Listen to you, gettin' all upset. What did I say? I said I was goin' to the Coast for a little conference with the money. I'm not goin' there to set up house-keepin'. . . ."

He knew Bouche was looking at him, trying to sort out what was going on. She was already wondering what they were doing shooting footage just before making the big move west. What the hell was the reason for it? A favor for a friend, Barcaloo had said. What kind of favor? A little private smut is what she'd thought at first. Some jerkoff wanting footage of his woman getting fucked and having it off with another woman. So, all right, she could get behind that, but what was all this playacting about? And what did Barcaloo mean lying to this broad about coming back to New Orleans? Why'd he have to go to the trouble? It was crazy, like Dom and Jickie hustling back and forth between New Orleans and L.A. Days out of synch. There were things Nonny, Dom, and Jickie did that she'd heard whispered about but which she'd never believed.

". . . so I'll be right back. That's why I want to have a little somethin' in the can to take back with me. You unnerstan'?"

"You've got shaky finances," Shiela said flatly, warily.

This broad gets ditsy, Barcaloo thought, the next thing you know, she wants to cop a sneak, and somebody has to lay a hand on her, and she opens her mouth to make like a siren, and then you got to punch her out, shut her up, ruin her kisser. Make for lousy footage. Attract attention. Next thing you know, she's diving off a gallery, or if she gets the fit to run in the car on the way to the studio, she's jumping out of a moving vehicle. Shit.

"When's money not shaky in this goddamn crazy business, right?" Barcaloo said in a voice loaded with patient understanding. He stood up. "So we shoot a little scene and see how it goes."

"This is all very quick," Shiela persisted.

"I gave you a whole day to settle in and get over jet lag or whatever. I can't give you any more time to fool aroun', you unnerstan'? We do a little work today, and tonight we take you to Brennan's, Galatoire's, Arnaud's—you name it—for the best dinner you had in years. How's that sound?"

"It sounds okay," Shiela said, knowing she was grinning like a fool, feeling really very bad and scared all of a sudden. Wishing she'd taken Whistler's word about the nature of this deal. Wishing she'd gone with him. Understanding in a flash, like the climactic light shot in a Spielberg picture, that Whistler must care for her one hell of a lot to come all this way to tap her shoulder in front of a movie house. What the hell had she been thinking about, agreeing to meet a producer in a goddamn porno house in the first place? The theater owner was a businessman breaking out of the skin trade, the agent back in Hollywood had said. Here's the address on this piece of advertising money, he'd said. What a gag, right?

Thinking about it now, she admitted to herself that the calls she'd made around checking on the legitimacy of the man who'd made the deal hadn't been very reassuring. She'd heard what she'd wanted to hear. Wanting an opportunity. Wanting a beginning. So badly. Now, here she was wondering how to tell this Barcaloo she'd changed her mind. She stood up because everyone else including Bouche was standing up, and she didn't know what else to do.

"You want to drive over to the studio with Pinole and Rojo here? Talk about lighting and whatever? Or you want to drive over with Bouche and me?"

"She'll come with us," Bouche said, taking Shiela's arm. "You drive and we'll sit in the back and talk."

"That's good. That's good."

Bouche walked Shiela out of the office. Pinole and Rojo lingered behind.

"This broad is ditsy," Rojo said. "She could be a lot of trouble."

"So maybe we just shoot some footage today and that's the end of it. We don't try to get any more tomorrow or the next day. We just get a few shots today. And that's that."

Shiela was riding in the Lincoln Continental with the apeman in the white linen suit. The wedding-cake blonde, falling out of her flowered chiffon, sat in back with Shiela, holding on to her arm as though they were old school chums. The newly painted red Cadillac followed the Lincoln, and Whistler followed the Cadillac.

It was no trouble through the narrow streets of the French Quarter, but after they crossed the Greater New Orleans Bridge, it got a little harder.

Whistler fell back on 90 and stayed back along Barataria through the town of Estelle and into the Bayou des Familles. He was laying a half a mile behind, along a particularly lonely stretch, when the two cars up ahead turned off and disappeared along a side track. Whistler kicked it to forty-five and almost missed the twin ruts and the thinning of the palmetto. He backed up and turned into the side road, stopped, and set the hand brake.

The sounds of the two engines, quickly muffled in the heavy growth, faded away along the green, sweaty tunnel. He had no way of knowing how far the track led.

He got the courtesy map out of the glove compartment. They'd gone west just before the Ross Canal. There were wetlands and canals into Plaquemines Parrish and the United States Naval Air Station beyond. They might be going one mile or five along the unmarked track. Chances were it never got wider. If he started into the jungle, he might not have anyplace to hide the car or even turn around until he got to wherever they were going. If anybody started back, he'd be standing there with his pants down. If he walked in, he'd be throwing away mobility.

A frog, squatting in a patch of rotting moss, cocked a

suspicious eye and croaked. He started the car and backed up to the road, then drove it onto a solid patch surrounded by man-high reed and fern about a hundred yards beyond the turnoff.

Then he started walking into the hot, dank, dark green jungle, smelling of mud, rot, and abandoned swimming pools in the basements of old athletic clubs; smelling of dying two thousand miles from La-La Land.

Twenty-six

THE TIN Quonset hut with the generator alongside, squatting in the middle of the asphalt and gravel, looked like a swamp monster with its child. It reminded Whistler of isolated, abandoned motor depots and ammunition dumps that seemed to sprout out of the ground on every army camp he'd ever known.

The Lincoln and the Cadillac were parked there, ass-to-nose.

He hurried across the clearing into the protection of the shadow cast by the generator. He'd counted his paces coming in, as much to still his rising anxiety as to estimate the distance traveled. He reckoned it to be two miles, more or less. Forty minutes by his watch. The generator was chugging away, making electricity. The fuel to run it was piled beside it, half under a tarpaulin.

A red light, just like those on the real soundstages back in Hollywood, shone dully above the door that warned visitors away when shooting was in progress, even though nothing but gators and toads were around to interrupt.

His shirt and pants were wet clear through. Even his shoes felt soggy, and his watch strap was turning to butter.

The light went out. He expected it would be time to make a move when it went on again and they were back at work, but he had no plan. Who could have plans so far from home? Who could have plans for a danger without an identity? What he had as evidence was flimsier than circumstantial; it wouldn't have held up on a traffic-ticket bust.

But still he felt the danger in his belly and balls. Why'd Shiela have to kiss him and leave her leg out in the rain, as if she didn't know it was getting wet? Why the hell did she have to go and do that and twist his heart around and have him chasing around doing good deeds, rescuing foolish damsels in distress?

He checked out the cars. Neither one was locked. The keys to the Cadillac were in the ignition.

The red light came on again. He crossed the open space, glad that there was only the one window in the door and no face in it looking out. He pulled the handle, like the kind on big meat lockers, and pulled the heavy door, as thick as a wall to proof the studio against the steady roar of the generator, toward him. A rush of cool air made him weak. He was inside in a second, facing another door. He stood in the sound lock and looked through a window, laminated with chicken wire, into the belly of the shack.

It was all shadows and gloom in front. Nothing moved. He went inside, and it was colder still. His shirt turned to ice. He shivered against the cold and marveled about how quickly the body and mind complained when tossed from change to change. Hot one minute and complaining. Cold the next and still complaining. Always trying to get it just right. Always missing by a cat's whisker.

Cables snaked all over the dirty floor. He picked his way around and over them like a tightrope walker, his eyes straight ahead toward the place where a pool of light marked the playing area. The "Go Fuck a Duck" poster was on the wall.

Shiela stood under a white-hot spotlight, holding a trench coat around her as though willing it to change itself into armor. There were cheap shower scuffs on her bare feet. Even from the distance Whistler could see the dew of perspiration on her upper lip and the way the fine hairs clung to the shallows of her temples, damp with fear. Her eyes were showing too much white.

"Hey," she said, as though speaking from a great distance, the high notes bouncing off the tin roof in little singing echos, "I feel like you're rushing me again."

The cushy blonde came out of a wallboard dressing room. She had on pink feathered mules and a pink transparent negligee and nothing else.

"For heaven's sake, Shiela, honey, there's nothin' to be so nervous about. Look at me. It don't bother me. I been doin' this for years, and it don't bother me one little bit."

The smaller of Barcaloo's two associates had his arm draped over the top of a thirty-five-millimeter camera mounted on a tripod. The bigger one was sitting at a portable mixer about the size of a musical synthesizer on four spindly chrome legs with earphones draped around his neck. Both of them looked bored and impatient, like cats at a mouse hole, charged with anticipation but hiding it lest their auras scare the mouse away.

"I'm not that used to it," Shiela said.

"You've had your clothes off in front of a camera before, ain't you?" Barcaloo said.

Whistler worked his way nearer, staying close to the wall. Off to one side, beyond the cheapjack dressing rooms, he could see a side exit.

"In front of still cameras with a cameraman, a cameraman's assistant, a hairdresser, a makeup girl, a—"

"This ain't MGM—what do you think? This ain't *Penthouse* magazine. It's a little studio stuck down here in New Orleans. What we got here is a limited crew, you unnerstan'? Just enough to get the job done and no more. We ain't union. We keep costs—"

"Well, there it is, you see? I belong to the Screen Actors Guild, and I'm not even sure I should be working a nonunion picture," Shiela said with the breathlessness of a drowning woman grasping at straws.

"For Christ's sake!" Barcaloo bellowed.

It was like the silence that follows a clap of thunder.

Whistler stopped moving, but the scrape of his foot was as crisp and clear as the sound of bones breaking. Barcaloo turned his head sharply and posed, listening as an animal listens.

"Hey, Jickie," he said softly.

The cameraman left the camera and started toward the side of the shack and the shadows where Whistler stood. There was a built-out storage closet two steps back. Whistler took the two steps and slipped inside and closed the door behind him. He was standing on some soft, uneven surface. He didn't dare move. He just stood there like a demented juggler, holding his balance and stilling his breath. He could hear Rojo's measured footsteps pass the closet as he walked all the way to the entrance and back again.

"Swamp rat," Whistler heard him say from the stage area. "How long is this crap going on?"

The smell in the confined space of the closet was terrible. Whistler managed to snake his pencil flash out of his hip pocket without falling over. He turned it on and shone the beam down at his feet. He was standing on the tangled bodies of a naked man and woman. The woman had her face in the hollow of the man's neck as though seeking comfort. The man stared up at Whistler, his eyes glistening brilliantly, even in the dim light of the tiny flash.

The hair on the back of Whistler's neck and along his arms rose up with a terrible chill. His bladder almost gave way.

"You know what a bad couple days I've been havin', lady?" Barcaloo said, loud enough for Whistler to risk leaving the closet. "I've been havin' a very bad couple of days, you unnerstan'? So I don't want any more of your crap. Don't play the Virgin Mary with me. You cunt are all alike. You do things and make believe you didn't. Take off that goddamn bathrobe and lay down on that bed and do like I tell you."

Whistler took three deep breaths.

"Like hell I will," Shiela said right back, but her voice carried no conviction. "I'm getting out of here."

"You're not gettin' out of nowhere, you silly cunt. What's the game? You hurry your ass down here on a blind offer—"

"I'm an actress. I was offered a part—"

"Don't make like you didn't know what was the deal. You're a pussy. You're a pussy, and a pair of tits and a big ass—"

"Why're you talkin' to this lady like that?" Bouche said.

"Because Walter Cape, the man what's going to help me be somebody, wants I should teach this broad a lesson, goddammit!" Barcaloo roared.

Whistler put the pencil flash in his pocket and poked it out, wondering if he could convince three hard types that it was a gun. Never in a million years. He hurried back to the entrance.

"It's going to be all right, honey," Bouche said nervously. "Just let's do like he says. Nonny's really an all-right guy, you don't make him mad."

"You can't keep me here against my will, for God's sake."

Barcaloo started to laugh.

"What the hell you gonna do? Scream? You gonna scream an' wake up the fuckin' gators? You just fuckin' listen to me. You strip down and start doin' like I tell you or I'll throw you to Dom and Jickie here, an' when they're finished with you they'll toss you . . ."

Whistler went through the sound lock and out into the wet heat. He went to the Lincoln, opened the door, and released the hand brake, then pushed it over alongside the fuel dump. He grabbed one of the jerry cans of gasoline, ran to the generator, cracked the can, and poured gas in a puddle, then ran a stream back to the fuel store and the Lincoln.

He built a little bridge by making a circle of his belt.

It only took twenty seconds to shut down the generator, disconnect the starter leads, and place them an inch apart on the leather loop. He ran around to the side of the building and waited.

Pinole came out and went over to the generator. He pushed the starter button. The spark flashed across the leads and ignited the gas fumes. The tongue of fire ran along the ground and under the tarp. Pinole watched it run, saw that the Lincoln had been moved, and got the idea. He started to turn away when the gasoline dump went up and blew the Lincoln and him into the swamp.

Whistler was at the side door before all of Pinole landed, and through the door before the explosion stopped echoing across the wetlands. Birds were screaming. A bull gator sounded a challenge.

Inside the darkened Quonset a woman was screaming her head off and Barcaloo was cursing. Whistler snapped on the pencil flash and passed it across the room. It landed on Bouche.

"Oh, my God, Nonny, don't kill me," she screamed.

He moved the spot, found Shiela, and snapped it off.

"That you, Jickie?" Barcaloo shouted. "Shine it over here."

"I got no flash," Rojo said.

Whistler grabbed Shiela by the wrist, put his hand over her mouth and his lips right on her ear.

"The cavalry's come to get you."

"Have you got the flashlight, Bouche?" Barcaloo said.

Bouche didn't answer. She just kept on screaming that Barcaloo shouldn't kill her.

Whistler dragged Shiela through the door.

"Oh, you are one sweet-looking son of a bitch," she said.

They were out the side door in a second, with Barcaloo's startled and enraged curses chasing after them.

Whistler practically threw Shiela into the Cadillac and pushed her to the passenger's side with his hip. The engine kicked over first go. He drove around the pillar of fire, which had spread to the wooden parts of the studio and was starting to eat it up. He drove like hell down the long green tunnel pierced by the dirt road until he reached his rented car.

He got the tire iron out of the Cadillac's trunk, lifted the hood, and smashed the carburetor and distributor to scrap.

They got into his rental and sped away. Barcaloo and Rojo were two miles away without transport, and still Whistler didn't feel entirely safe.

Shiela was huddled on her side of the car as though wanting to grab Whistler but afraid that if she laid a hand on him, they would end up in a ditch where Barcaloo and Rojo would find and kill them.

"Why me?" she said. "Why'd they go to all the trouble to get me down here?"

Whistler turned his head to look at her. "I don't know," he said.

Her trench coat had fallen open. She was naked underneath except for a skinny pair of briefs. She saw where he was looking and closed the coat.

Twenty-seven

COXEY SAT behind his register in the all-night drugstore at one o'clock in the morning, shuffling his stack of calling cards, peering up the skirt of the whore perched on the lunch-counter stool.

He thought about that Yankee son of a bitch asshole Whistler—what the fuck kind of name was that?—threatening him the way he did. Who the hell did he think he was? Who the hell he think he was fucking with? Some two-bit hustler? Some garbage collector?

Probably was already out of New Orleans. Good thing for him. What did that fool think he was doing backing a man like him into an aisle with the dishcloths and dish drainers? Where'd he get that corny dialogue? "Clean out your windpipe like a squash." What kind of goddamn talk was that? Throwing him a fiver—no, not a fiver, four dollars and forty-one cents—like he was handing him a big score. Just what kind of shit was that? Nobody fast enough to keep Mickey Mouse from drinking his blood. That was the worst bullshit he'd ever heard. Worse than anything those television writers put into the mouths of all those faggot actors.

Whistler was probably a faggot too. Half the men in La-La Land were faggots. Everybody knew that. Fucker come nosing around, playing cozy, get a line on the manufacturer with the idea in mind that he could save some money, cut out the middleman. Faggot porn. Snuff. S and M. Kiddie porn. Cut out the connection. Fuck him out of a commission. Queer son of a bitch. Had his nerve trying to throw a scare into somebody like Crib Coxey.

He picked up the phone and rang around. He got Barcaloo over to Jimmy Flynn's on St. Peter Street where that coffee-colored nigger, Henry, worked a shift at the bar and fucked the white ladies in the storeroom. Fucked Nonny Barcaloo's woman, Bouche, too, so he'd been told. Told by Henry himself when he'd come in one night, half stoned on cocaine, to buy some Johnny the Conqueror root to wear around his neck so his tool would stay up and working. Coxey wondered if the high and mighty Nonny Barcaloo knew about *that*. He'd guess not; otherwise, Bouche would be buried in a bayou like so many others were rumored to be buried.

"Who are you and what do you want?" Barcaloo mumbled into the phone.

"You don't know me, Mr. Barcaloo. My name is Crib Coxey, and I work the owl shift in the all-night drugs over to Common and Rampart."

"What are you sellin'?"

"Well, I'm not really sellin' anything, Mr. Barcaloo. Something happened I thought might interest you."

"Yeah? So tell me."

"Maybe I could come over to Jimmy Flynn's." How the hell could a man get a tip over the phone? You can't shove a hundred dollar bill down the goddamn wires.

"Maybe you couldn't. We're havin' a wake for a very good friend of mine what just died, and it wouldn't look good for me to be takin' time with a stranger."

"Who was it died, you don't mind my asking?"

"Dom Pinole."

"Well, hell, I know Dom Pinole. Him and Jickie Rojo used to come in here for a little of this and a little of that every now and then."

"A little of what and a little of what?"

"You know. A little dope. A little skag. A little crank."

"You a fuckin' pusher?"

"Well, like, I do a little dealing with friends."

"You come on over," Barcaloo said.

Coxey chased out the solitary whore and locked up the store. If the owners found out there'd be hell to pay, but he figured he was making an investment in his future and he didn't intend to be a clerk in an all-night drugstore forever.

He was feeling so hopeful about the reward of gratitude he'd get from Barcaloo that he grabbed a cab to Jimmy Flynn's.

It didn't look like any wake to him when he peeked through the doors. A naked woman was dancing on the bar. There was a lot of booze splashing around and a lot of people getting wet. Barcaloo was sitting at the best table with Jickie Rojo and his woman, Bouche. The table had a dozen black candles burning on it, and there was a clock facing east. Old New Orleans funeral custom at a laying-out. But where was the body?

A hand like a ham pushed against his chest. Jimmy Flynn said he wasn't allowed. They were having a private wake. Coxey said he'd been asked. Flynn looked over to Barcaloo, and Barcaloo waved Coxey in.

Coxey walked over to the table.

"Hello, Jickie," he said. "Hello, Mr. Barcaloo. I'm very sorry to hear about Dom Pinole. Where's he going to be laid out?"

"Right here."

Coxey looked around, expecting he'd maybe missed the corpse lying on the bar under the dancer's naked feet.

"Right here," Barcaloo said, tapping the table for emphasis.

Coxey looked. There was the tip of a finger, complete with fingernail, in the center of the table surrounded by the candles.

"That's all we could find of him," Rojo said.

Coxey almost laughed, but when he took a second look at

the expression on Rojo's face, he knew he'd die where he stood if he dared it. Pinole had been blown away in the harshest way, and it was clear that Rojo intended to make someone pay for it.

"All right," Barcaloo said, "tell me."

"Some Yankee came into the store last night asking about the Beaver Run."

"Some Yankee? You mean somebody from the East?"

"I mean, not one of us. Not from the South. This jerkoff came from L.A. asking questions about who owned the Beaver Run. Who you was and what else you did. Where you lived."

"And you told him?"

"I didn't see the harm. After all, practically everybody knows about you, Mr. Barcaloo. A man like you can't hide his light."

"Last night? This happened last night?"

"That's right."

"Then why the hell didn't you call me last night?"

"It was very late."

"And you made some profit on this Yankee and thought you could make some more," Rojo said with a mean little twist to his mouth.

"Something like that, you shoulda called me," Barcaloo said. "Ought to break your fuckin' arms and legs. Ought to mash your liver."

Bouche giggled. "Oh, he don't mean it. Sit down and have a drink."

"Stand up and tell me anything else you got to tell me. And don't listen to her. She's drunk. I mean it."

"Well, if that's what a person gets for trying to do another person a favor," Bouche said, seriously outraged.

Coxey threw a pleading glance at her, asking her to shut up and not come to his defense. If she tried to help him again, she could be helping him right into the hospital or the grave. He could see that. He could also see that it hadn't been such a great idea coming down here hoping to make a score off Barcaloo.

Rojo started to get up.

"This asshole was stupid," Coxey said. "He gave me his credit card. His name is Whistler."

"What did he look like?"

When Coxey described the height, width, and breadth of Whistler, the pale, melancholy eyes, the rough hair and sad mouth, Bouche piped up and said, "That's the asshole who was trying to mess with our Shiela."

Barcaloo cast her a withering and pitying glance. He peeled off a hundred dollars from a roll and handed it to Coxey.

"You see or hear this sucker again, you call me, you hear? Now get the hell out of here."

"Hey," Bouche said, newly concerned about Barcaloo's manners. "Ain't you going to ask Dom's old friend to drink a memorial drink to Dom's finger?"

Twenty-eight

S HE'D BEEN okay on the ride out of the bayou to the airport and the first plane out for anywhere. Okay on the flight to Phoenix where they got tickets on his plastic into L.A. Okay that first night, begging only for the chance to have a bath and a long rest.

He'd called Bellerose in New Orleans as he watched her sleeping.

"This is Whistler," he'd said when Bellerose got on the phone.

"Where are you?"

"L.A."

"Wish you were still here," Bellerose drawled in his sulfur-and-molasses voice. "There's questions."

"That's why I called."

"There was a fire over to the Bayou des Familles. Seems a generator blew up its feed. A shack somebody was using for a movie studio burnt to the ground. Brand new Lincoln Continental burnt down to a shell. Motor Vehicles is checking ownership."

"Barcaloo owned it."

"I figured that sonofabitch had another studio when he showed us that one by the river. Found a little piece of somebody caught in a palmetto. I don' think we're ever going to know who that belonged to."

"Dom Pinole."

"You're a regular fountain of information. What am I supposed to think?"

"You don't have to bother. I'll tell you. I went in there on my own. I followed the woman from Hollywood I told you about and went in on my own. She was being threatened. I didn't have a gun. I did what I could with what I had."

"Oh, I could tell you was a resourceful fella. Brave, too. But what made you think they was goin' to off her?"

"Did you poke around in the ashes of the studio?"

"We may be country boys, Whistler, but we're careful. We found the remains of those two people and other things. You know those two?"

"I never met them, but I think I know who they were. I think you'll find out their names were Chippy Byrd and Lacy Ohio."

"Bucherleider and Oskanowsky."

"What?"

"Those were their real names."

"Are you going to bring Barcaloo in?"

"I would. Except Barcaloo and his woman and his boy, Jickie Rojo, has lef' town. Maybe I'll leave town, too. How's the weather out there?"

"Pissy. But you want to visit, you can always find me at Gentry's, the corner of Hollywood and Vine."

"I'll think on it," Bellerose said, and hung up.

So, that first day it had looked to Whistler like Shiela was going to be okay. A woman who might be as tough as she pretended to be.

In the morning she made a move on him, sliding across the bed until she bumped into him. Suddenly, while she was moving her thighs against his hip and nuzzling his neck, it hit her like a hammer. While he held her in his arms and she shook and kept on shaking, Whistler learned a little something new about himself. He learned he got off on somebody else's fear. The trembling of her long legs and flat belly, the soft blows of her heart against his chest, filled him with a kind of exhilaration he'd never felt in quite that way before. He wasn't actually glad she was so terrified, but he couldn't be all that unhappy about what it was that made her cling to him for safety and comfort. He was, he realized, a man like too many others, strongest when somebody else showed weak. The shakes went on for a long time. When he tried to still them with the soft violence of sex, it still took a long time for them to go away. Every time he entered her, he could feel the trembling there, too. Finally she calmed down.

They lay there in the half-light of the overcast sky, listening to the swishing rumble of the cars streaming along Cahuenga down below.

"If you close your eyes you can imagine you're in a house on the beach at Malibu and that's the surf," Whistler said.

"I'm so glad you were the one picked me up from Tillman's car and took me home."

"There's a modest look on my face," Whistler said.

She turned around and crouched above him, staring down into his eyes with a look he hadn't seen in a dozen years.

"My God, I thought I was such a tough bird," she murmured. "I thought I knew all the moves. I thought I could slip and slide my way through a forest of knives. Down there I found out I'm just a babe in the woods. There are rabbits out there could knock me down and hang me in a tree. That man. That Barcaloo. If I ever saw his face or felt his hands on my skin again, I think I'd die."

Whistler said nothing, but just stared back at her.

"What is it, Whistler?" she said.

"Barcaloo's left New Orleans. I think he's on his way or already here in L.A. You can't go home for a while, I don't think."

"Oh, no, oh, no." She was out of the bed, going to crouch, naked, in the corner of the room away from the dim light of the bed lamp, as though it were a klieg that would search her out and find her. Marking her for Barcaloo. Marking her for destruction.

Whistler was out of bed and on his knees beside her. His arms around her.

"You'll stay here with me."

"No, no. He'll find you, too."

Whistler thought of Coxey who knew his name. Shiela thought of the little story she'd laid on Barcaloo to explain her meeting with Whistler on the street in front of the Beaver Run. Both understood that Whistler was known or would be known.

"We'll get you out of town," he said.

"You, too."

"Oh, no, not me."

"You're not going to confront this Barcaloo?"

"I can't let him go running around loose."

"It's none of your business. You're not a cop."

"I've got no choice."

When he started to move away, she held him and said, "Not now. Not right this minute. Don't go right this minute."

There were white sheets over all the large pieces of furniture in Barcaloo's maisonette on Ursuline. They looked like the ghosts of the legendary horrors that had once lived there.

Bouche was dressed in a raspberry silk blouse buttoned up to her throat and a pale green linen suit that did nothing to reveal the lush overabundance of her breasts and thighs. It was as though she meant to erase her sexuality. It had finally come about that she could no longer fool herself about the kind of thing that had gone on there in the Bayou des Familles, at the studio where sad people, including herself, played out sad scenes of sexuality. And where, she now was sure, some people had died in the middle or at the end of what was called an act of love. All the whispers were true. She remembered a Latino girl who'd been around and then, suddenly, hadn't been around. She remembered an Asian woman with a child who Barcaloo said had worked the film and then had gone away, back to Los Angeles.

She was all packed and ready to take the cab to the airport with Barcaloo and Rojo. She was ready to fly to L.A. She'd think about what she could do once she got there.

She was more afraid of Barcaloo now than she'd ever been. He'd meant to kill that Shiela Andes, and she was sure he'd meant to kill her too. She'd managed a wild animal for a long time, but she'd finally lost the knack.

Every time she thought of Jickie Rojo, terror squeezed her heart and stomach. When he walked into a room, a black spirit in a room full of white ghosts, she turned her back. She was afraid to look at his face and eyes. If she did, he might strike her dead.

Barcaloo walked into the room where she waited. He was wearing a white shirt and tie with a gray summer-weight suit. It made him look different. Almost human. He smiled, and she thought it would be nice not to have to think about the things he did.

"You ready?" he said.

"Ready, willin', and rarin' to go," she said brightly.

She walked out of the apartment, down the stairs, through the courtyard, past the fountain making sounds like breaking glass, through the wrought-iron gate, and into the waiting taxicab, thinking all the way that she would make up her mind about what to do when she got to L.A.

Rojo was already in the cab, sitting in the front with the driver. She hesitated. She felt Barcaloo's hand in the middle of her back.

"Take it easy, Bouche," he said. "It won't be long before we get to La-La Land."

There were things to do, but still Whistler stayed in bed with Shiela, dozing off from time to time. He'd wake up and find her asleep next to him, making a cradle of her body around his back and hips. When he turned to see her face in the grainy light coming through the dusty curtains, when he put his face close to feel her breath on his mouth, she'd open her eyes, unsurprised, knowing he'd be there. And she'd arrange her legs so they held him between her thighs. And she'd work her legs a little, like she was running softly in the early morning, until he was strong enough to take her.

It seemed to happen every hour on the hour, going on for a long while each time.

"Open a window," she murmured.

Whistler stirred and started to get up, but she held him back with her legs and arms.

"I mean, open a window into you."

"For Christ's sake, who writes your material?" he said.

"You can't get out of it making fun," she said. "Tell me about you, Whistler, before I start to cry. I haven't been in bed with a man I really cared to know in quite a while."

"You shouldn't give yourself away like that. It's all we got."

"I never gave it away until now. I only put it out on loan. Goddamn it, tell me where and what you were when you were ten."

Whistler hated telling his life. It had always been his habit to erase it. No photographs of lost loves. No diaries or bits of things kept for memory's sake. Nothing but the little address books, hardly any of the names appearing in them more than once, twice at most.

"When I was ten, I lived in Rochester, New York, and went to a redbrick public school. I wanted to be rich and famous. I thought that was something you could learn how to do. Like riding a bike or swimming the length of a pool under water . . ."

"As long as your teeth were straight and you washed your hair twice a week and you kept your weight under a hundred and twenty if you were a girl as tall as me, everything was possible. . . ."

"I couldn't run the hundred under ten seconds with a

football under my arm, or move a ball through a crowd of arms and legs looking for the slam dunk. . . ."

"Knowing how to cook was a help, and keeping a clean house like your mother always did, and knowing which end of a baby was which. Things like that were all it would take to make everything possible. . . ."

"I was no brain. I flunked mathematics and . . ."

"And being pretty. Smiling pretty and being pretty. Because everything possible was a man, a husband. Maybe a doctor or a lawyer. Accountants were okay or . . ."

"I couldn't really do much of anything. I was so average, I hated myself until I found out I could make people pay attention when I acted out some movie I'd seen. . . ."

"My mother got me tap-dancing lessons, singing lessons. She saved pictures of movie stars in big scrapbooks. . . ."

"So, I thought I'd give it a try. . . ."

"Come out to Hollywood . . ."

"The land of glitter and swank . . ."

"Where fairy tales come true . . ."

"La-La Land. Oz was a depressed neighborhood compared to La-La Land. I started selling aluminum siding to get by."

"A photographer I knew paid me twenty-five dollars for four hours of posing in bathing suits and underwear."

"I met a private detective who offered me part-time work sitting in a car on stakeout. Easy money."

"Then another photographer offered me fifty an hour to take my clothes off. What the hell, I thought, somebody wants to look at my jugs, build dreams on my bush, what the hell. Poor, sorry sons of bitches."

"Got my license just to keep the money coming in to pay the rent."

"I never did porn, though, Whistler. I never did any sex acts."

"Just take a job here and there, now and then, until I got my break."

"I just did what I had to do while I was waiting. Oh, God, Whistler, I almost fell into it. I almost did a dirty picture."

"All of a sudden fifteen years had slipped away while I wasn't looking."

"That's the way it happens to you. When you're not really looking."

"I wonder when I stopped waiting for the big break?"

"Jesus Christ, I hate this movie, Whistler," Shiela said.

"Me too."

"I mean, I hear it a hundred times a year."

Twenty-nine

THE RAIN no longer kept the hustlers and the pimps, the circus riders and hussies off the streets. There were livings to be made, hustles to be hustled, body parts to be sold both night and day. You can't stay dry forever.

Whistler opened the door to Gentry's around one o'clock in the afternoon, standing so that he blocked the rain with his back as Shiela slipped under his arm and into the coffee-smelling warmth. Her cheeks were full of roses, and she looked, laughing as she was, like a fourteen-year-old coming to the sweetshop after the homecoming game. Whistler had the hopeful eyes of a man half his age.

Canaan was in his corner looking at the menu, which he must have known by heart.

Bosco was on his stool behind the register, reading the annotated *Alice in Wonderland*. He glanced up and read their faces.

"You ever sleep?" Whistler greeted Bosco. "Every time I walk in here—it doesn't matter what hour—you're sitting on that stool reading some book."

"Day man called in sick. If I don't pour the coffee, who's going to wire the town?" Bosco said mildly.

Whistler turned the cover of the book so he could read it. "Isn't this for kids?"

"It's for bitter men looking for sanity in a crazy world."

"Will you bring two coffees and two plates of ham and eggs to our booth?"

He looked down into Shiela's upturned face as if he'd just ordered quail and chanterelles at Maxim's in Paris and was making sure of her approval.

"White toast," Shiela murmured.

"Whole wheat's better for you," Whistler said, like he was saying, "Roll over and I'll do your back."

"I'll meet you at our booth," Shiela said, and let go of his arm, then walked down the length of the shop toward the rest rooms.

Canaan weighed and measured her as she walked past.

Bosco wrote up the order and put it on the wheel. Whistler stared at Shiela's retreating back.

"What do you think of that?" he murmured.

"I think you failed to take my advice," Bosco said.

"What's that you say?"

"I said you weren't gone long."

"I coulda been," Whistler said, finally looking at Bosco.

"Somebody died," Bosco said, looking hard into Whistler's eyes.

"You're a goddamn witch. Be glad it wasn't me."

"I'm glad."

"Be glad it wasn't Shiela."

"I'm glad." Bosco captured his book between his knees and went into his pocket, coming up with the keys to Whistler's apartment and car. "When did you get in?"

"Last night."

"Where you been staying?"

"My place. I stash a key in the flowerpot."

"What are you driving?"

"My car. I got an extra set."

"Why am I holding your keys?"

"In case I never got back from New Orleans, you're my beneficiary."

"I guess it's too late to save you."

"What the hell do you mean by that?"

"You saved the lady's life. Like the Chinese say, now you're responsible for her forever."

"Maybe I like the idea," Whistler said sharply.

Bosco held up his hand, fending off Whistler's irritation, a wry smile on his lips. "You find the head?"

"The cops have it on ice. I told them about the body I saw tossed out of the station wagon."

"That take care of your civic duty?"

Whistler hesitated and looked up the aisle to see if Shiela was coming back and within earshot. She wasn't.

"It's not over. They meant to kill her down there in New Orleans. Use her first, then kill her."

"How do you know that?"

"I know because two corpses told me. Shiela was conned down there to get snuffed. The con started here. On the night she was in the accident with Emmet Tillman."

"Tillman?"

"He hasn't got the stones. How does Walter Cape sound to you?"

"It sounds crazy to me. What the hell would a man like Cape be doing fucking around with an asshole like Tillman and a broad like . . ."

They stared at one another, old friends almost about to get busted up because of a woman.

"They missed her once, they might try again," Whistler said very softly.

"You should both get out of town."

Shiela's heels made a snappy rhythm as she came tapping back across the tiles. There was a foolish grin on Whistler's mouth.

"Oh, my," Bosco murmured, "you got the tiger by the tail and you can't let go. You've made promises to yourself. You can use my place for a safe house."

"Were you a spy?"

"No, but I see a lot of movies."

Whistler and Shiela went to the booth. Before he could sit

down, Whistler saw Canaan beckoning to him. He went over and shook his head when Canaan asked him to sit down.

"I've got a breakfast coming."

"It's lunchtime. Don't do to your stomach what I did to mine." He smiled nicely. "I see you rescued the lady," Canaan said, the smile turning a little sneaky with the disdain of a man who knew she wasn't worth it.

"That's just what I did."

"You find out anything about that other thing?"

"The woman without a head was a whore. She worked some smut flicks down there in New Orleans. She was in a snuff film too."

Canaan nodded, as though the news wasn't unexpected.

"The man who produced the shit, this Nonny Barcaloo, is here in town," Whistler added.

Canaan's eyes flickered. "You know that for a fact?"

"I'd bet on it."

"You ought to take Bosco's advice."

"What's that?"

"Leave town and take the woman with you."

Whistler turned his head and measured the distance from Canaan's booth to the cash register.

"I read lips, Whistler. I read lips."

Whistler drove Shiela back to her apartment for a change of clothes. He stood in the tacky living room as she went through the closet and the chest of drawers, making up a bundle, complaining about how little she'd been left with, running away from New Orleans the way they'd had to do.

Whistler thought it a wonder that she should be worried about no clothes when she'd almost been given a swamp to wear.

There was a knock on the door, and Katherine was standing there in another full-length robe.

"I see you're back," she said.

Shiela heard her voice and popped out of the bedroom, looking from one to the other as though suspecting things. For a minute it made Whistler feel very virile and strong, even though he knew it was a trick that women used to flatter men. Acting like they believed every woman their lovers met tore off her clothes and laid down to be serviced. The mixed signals they threw around could fill encyclopedias.

"Good time?" Katherine said, looking at Shiela.

"I got to tell you, you won't believe it."

"But not now. Not here," Whistler said.

Katherine widened her eyes but didn't ask.

"Shiela's coming with me for a while."

"Was it raining in New Orleans?" Katherine asked.

"It was hot."

"How long will she be gone?"

"I don't know yet."

"What should I say if anybody asks?"

"Why should anybody ask?"

"I've got friends, Whistler. After all," Shiela said.

"Anybody asks, you don't know where she is or when she'll be back. All you know is that she went to New Orleans to do a picture, and as far as you know, she's still there."

"Are you in trouble?" Katherine asked, still looking at Shiela.

"Yes and no," Whistler said.

"Speak English."

"She could be in trouble, but I'm taking care of her."

Katherine nodded as though that was all right then.

"Where's your bags?" she asked.

"I had to leave them behind."

"You must have one hell of a story to tell me."

"She does, but it'll have to wait."

"I'll lend you a suitcase," Katherine said, and went to get it.

After Shiela put the few things she still owned into it, she and Whistler left.

He drove her to Bosco's apartment and introduced her to Bosco's cat.

"Don't answer the phone. Don't answer the door."

She looked frightened.

"There's not a chance anybody can know about us staying

here. But, like Bosco would say, 'When you think there ain't a chance, there's always a chance that there's a chance.'"

Shiela moved in close to him.

"Be careful . . . and bring me flowers."

Thirty

IN THE mid-thirties the Chinese in L.A.'s "Old Chinatown" were moved out to make way for the Union Passenger Terminal. So they built China City just to the northwest. When that was burned out, the "New Chinatown" rose up out of the ashes. It was built to look like Peking's Forbidden City. It's a lot more than two old saffron-skinned men sitting around under the trees playing mah-jong.

It's a lichee nut. On the outside a thin, exotic-looking shell, mysterious and captivating, the tourist layer, as fragile as a scrap of burned paper. On the inside, the real goods, a little opium, a Saigon whore, stolen Korean jade, counterfeit temple dolls, paper parasols, and sticks of heady incense from Thailand. The legal and the illegal, all available for a price. Phony fragments of a culture as old as time on sale for a twenty-dollar bill. Proof of a Chinawoman's anatomy for a fifty. Ancient ceremonies in the dark for a hundred.

And not only the Chinese but the Koreans, the Thais, the Cambodians, the Laotians, and the Vietnamese, the whole damned troubled people of Southeast Asia crowding in where they're not wanted because they're not wanted even more elsewhere in the sprawling city.

Whites make jokes about not being able to tell the difference. "They all look a-fuckin'-like." The Asians can tell the difference.

The streets around Alpine and Broadway were crowded with Anglo and Chicano locals and tourists. Whistler softly bumped his way among them, imagining the crowded streets of foreign cities where he'd never been and probably would never be, getting the feel of the shell and the meat, trying to reach the stone.

The neighborhood around Spring Street is the one where the Chinese really live and other people rarely go. It was the place where he knew some answers waited. If the family of Lim Shu Dok still lived there.

The apartment house was there on the corner of New High and College. Whistler crossed the street and entered the vestibule. He looked at the stained bits of card with the names of the occupants set in the little windows of the mailboxes. He found the name Dok listed on the third floor. There was the name, Mei Hai. It had been scratched out and "Marion" printed above it.

He opened the inner door and saw that there was no elevator. He climbed the stairs.

It was just at the supper hour, and the lights were on behind the pebbled glass panes set in the doors of each flat. Small domestic sounds, like the chatter of wooden sticks and the clang of little bells, came from each one of them as pots and pans were moved from stove to table. The sound of slippered footfalls made Whistler turn around more than once, but there was no one behind him. Just the building crowded with lives and muted sounds like animals feeding.

He knocked on the glass pane set in the door of the Dok apartment. The sounds coming from behind it ceased. After a long moment a shadow appeared behind the glass. The door, still secured by a chain, was opened a crack. A wedge of pale face, black hair, and an eye like a glistening marble of jet looked him over.

"Yes?" the young woman asked, drawing out the syllable like a hiss, then cutting it off abruptly as though she'd momentarily forgotten herself and fallen back into old ways of speech.

"My name's Whistler. I've come about Lim Shu."

"What do you mean?" She frowned. "Do you mean you want to see her?"

"I know she's dead."

"Are you from the police?"

"No."

"The coroner?"

"No."

"Did you know her?"

"We never met, but I think I know her."

The eye seemed to pierce his forehead between his eyes. The eye and cheek left the crack. A curtain of shining black hair swept past as she turned her head. Then the eye was peering back at him again.

"How do you know her?"

"I know her for more than one reason, in more than one way."

Mei Hai laughed shortly. There was a bitter edge to it.

"Don't go getting Oriental on me," she said.

"Mei Hai? Should I call you Mei Hai or should I call you Marion?" he asked.

"I call myself Marion."

"I wanted to know because I don't want to make any mistakes or offend you in any way."

"Why should I talk to you? My sister . . ."

"Her body was being kept by the District Attorney's office at the morgue . . . ?"

"Yes." The word was leaden.

"It's not there anymore."

"What do you mean?"

A thin, querulous voice, speaking Vietnamese, sang along the hallway at her back. She replied with a single word, sharply, like the bark of a dog.

"I mean that her body was taken away," Whistler said.

He took out his card case and showed her his identification.

"What does that mean? You said you weren't from the police."

"I'm a private investigator. Don't you want to hear more about what happened to your sister?"

She closed the door, took the chain off the hook, then opened it and stepped back to let him in.

The earthy smell of vegetables and spices washed over him as he stepped inside. It was very hot in the hallway.

She walked in front of him down the hall toward the place where the kitchen was on one side and the dining room on the other.

"There are a lot of people in the house. I'll say you're a friend of mine from work, if anyone should ask."

She had almost no accent. Just a certain lisp and hesitation. Whistler stopped in the doorway of the kitchen. A dozen people of all ages—at least four were very old, at least three were children—sat around a table laid for supper with small eating bowls and large serving bowls, chopsticks, forks, and spoons. They all stared at him, mildly curious, except for one, an old woman who eyed Whistler with bland suspicion.

Marion chattered to her in Vietnamese. The old woman replied in the voice that had shrilled along the hall when Whistler was at the door.

Everyone smiled because Marion smiled. They nodded their heads because she nodded her head.

Except for the old woman. Her eyes were very knowing. She didn't believe the story about Whistler being a friend from work. She had a mother's instinct for disaster.

"We can talk in my room," Marion said.

Whistler followed her through a dining room that had been converted into a bedroom. There was a huge mahogany bedstead against one wall. Two salvaged cots and a crib filled up the rest of the space. The sheets and blankets were all neatly rolled up at one end of each bed. The room had the dark smell of sleeping people.

The living room had a large bay window with paper shades but no curtains. The light of a street lamp came through yellow. It was also a room for sleeping. There was a door to a small storage room in the back.

Marion had made it her room. There was a daybed in one corner, covered with a bright length of striped material. Big bright pillows were stacked against the wall. There was a little white desk and chair by a small window curtained in sheer cotton. A small circular rug made a splash of color on the wooden floor. A cardboard closet in another corner contained her wardrobe.

Unframed poster prints were hung, one to each wall, except the smallest one beside the door. There a photograph of two young Vietnamese women smiled shyly from a silver-toned frame. One was Marion. The other, Whistler was sure, was Lim Shu.

"Please sit down," Marion said, indicating the chair in front of the desk. She sat on the bed primly, her knees carefully together.

Whistler perched on it, feeling gross and clumsy.

"Tell me what you mean about Lillian. That's what I called her."

"Her body was taken from the morgue."

"Taken?"

"Stolen."

She turned pale. There was something very evil in what he was saying. "Why would anyone want to do that?"

"I can't be sure. Two reason I can think of."

Tiny pinpoints of moisture appeared along the line of her upper lip. "Yes?" she prompted Whistler, but turned her eyes away as though meaning to refuse whatever else he had to say.

"Either someone wanted to conceal the identity of the body, or someone wanted to make certain of its identity."

"I don't understand."

Whistler hesitated. Was there any easy way to say what had to be said? Was there any euphemism that could serve to describe it? He couldn't find any. "Before the body was stolen, somebody took her head," he said.

Marion's eyes were neutral, staring at him as though she'd lost all understanding of American words. She made a small noise in her throat. Her face turned even paler, her eyes blacker. They blazed with a sudden burst of terror, like an explosion of the heart. She lowered her head but still stared up at him from beneath the fringe of black hair falling across her forehead. She put her hands to her ears lightly, as though setting her appearance to rights.

Whistler told her part of what he knew.

"No," she said, then swayed forward.

Whistler went down on his knees to catch her in case she fainted. She placed her hands lightly on his shoulders. For a moment their cheeks touched. Whistler's hand brushed aside her hair on the left side. There was a small mole almost in the fold where the ear met her head. "Lim Shu," he said.

She said, "What?" and backed away.

He felt as though he'd molested her.

"The mole behind your ear. The morgue photographs of Lim Shu—"

"A family trait," she said.

He didn't say anything.

"Did you think I was Lillian pretending to be my sister?"

He felt foolish, his thoughts twisted and lost.

"Did you think I was Lillian in hiding?"

"Hiding?" he said.

"From the men who murdered her."

"You know who did it?"

"Oh, yes. The ones who killed her came from New Orleans. But the one who ordered her killed lives right here in Los Angeles."

"Do you know their names?"

"Two men, Dom Pinole and Jickie Rojo, were sent by another man. A filthy man, Nonny Barcaloo. Lillian was afraid of them. She'd run away because she knew they'd killed a Latino girl and meant to kill her and steal her son."

"I know."

"They wanted to use her child in filthy ways."

"This other man. The one who hired her killers."

She hesitated.

"What is it?"

"When the police came to tell me that my sister's body had been found, I told them the truth. They nodded their heads but didn't do anything about it. When the district attorney's man came to say that my sister could be buried but would have to be dug up again and used for evidence in the trial against these other men—"

"Corvallis?"

"Yes. They nodded and smiled and said I was mistaken. They had Lillian's murderers in jail, they said. And they'd prove it."

"But you knew otherwise."

"I knew the man who wanted her dead was a man named Walter Cape." When Whistler failed to react, she said, "You're not surprised?"

"No, I'm not surprised."

"Everyone else said it wasn't possible. Such an important man."

"Why did he want your sister dead?"

"She'd lived in his house. She thought he wanted her. But it was her son he wanted. He was the kind of man who wouldn't be denied anything he wanted. He wanted her son. He's a child lover."

She looked away, toward the picture in the silver frame.

"My sister was a whore. In old Annam she would have been called a concubine. But these are modern times. She was a whore. She lived her life among the rich and powerful. But she could never explain them to me. She could never explain a man like this Walter Cape to me. What does a man like that want? Can you tell me?"

"They think it's smart to say they want everything the world has to offer and a little more. They gorge themselves. You'd think they'd roll over and die with busted bellies. But they cry for more."

"Dogs eat their own vomit."

She walked Whistler to the door.

"Will they give my sister's body back to us?"

"I don't know."

"Thank you for coming to see me. It was very hard for you."

"I want to be honest. I didn't think it would be. Not so hard."

He stood there, having all he'd come for but still feeling that he wanted something more.

"In the newspaper stories it said that you and your sister had a quarrel and she left the house."

"That's right."

"What was the quarrel about?"

She smiled. "Would you believe it? She wanted to buy me a dress and I wouldn't have it. She thought it was because I thought her money was dirty. It was just because I hated the dress she had in mind. She was out of the house and gone before I could explain."

Thirty-one

GENTRY'S WAS crowded to overload. Steamy breaths condensed on the rain-misted plate-glass window. The coffee shop smelled of wet hair and wool sweaters.

Bosco came over to the booth where Whistler and Canaan sat and refilled their cups. He perched himself on the edge of the seat, not meaning to stay long.

"You're as busy as a one-armed paperhanger tonight," Canaan said.

"For Christ's sake," Bosco said, "Johnny Carson's a cop." He looked at Whistler. "Shiela okay? No complaints?"

"You're out of soap for the dishes."

"So, whattaya know?"

Whistler looked out the window. "There he goes again," he said.

"Goes who?"

"Shelley Pope in the Mercedes wagon."

"Scumbag," Canaan said.

"How come you let him walk the streets?"

"You mean Pope? We're talking about Walter Cape."

Canaan stared at Whistler as though he'd like to bite his nose off, crush his eyes. "I don't let him walk the streets. You let him walk the streets. Everybody who won't take the trouble lets him walk the streets. People don't want to think about child fuckers. Christ, ain't it a nasty subject? Let's not think about it, do anything about it. Maybe it'll go away."

Whistler leaned over the table, ready to claw and tear right back.

"So do something about it. Roust the bastard's ass."

"For buying dirty pictures of little boys? Be your age. For doing with them? I'd have to catch him in the act."

"For calling a hit on a Vietnamese whore."

"You've got nothing but hearsay on that. From what you said the sister never saw it, she just was told."

"So guys like Cape got no worries."

"For Christ's sake," Canaan said, half angry, half pleading, "give me a break. I'm no fucking cowboy. I can't go out, shoot these people down in the fucking street. Bring me a crime. Bring me a witness. Bring me something I can use!" He turned away and looked out into the street, calming himself down.

"Will you look at that?" he said.

A caricature in a white suit that didn't fit, carrying an old-fashioned carpetbag and an aluminum camera case, was getting out of a taxicab.

"I'll be damned," Whistler said.

"Somebody you know?"

Whistler got up and went to the door to open it for Bellerose, who winked his turtle eye and grinned his turtle grin.

"This place?" he said. "I could use a cup of coffee. How I hate to travel."

Whistler reached for the aluminum case, but Bellerose moved it back and gave Whistler the carpetbag instead. Whistler led the way over to the booth where Canaan sucked a Coke up through a straw and eyed the newcomer like he was something either silly or dangerous.

"Lieutenant Bellerose, New Orleans Police Department," Whistler said. "Sergeant Canaan, L.A.P.D."

"Hello, brother," Bellerose said, and stuck out his hand before he sat down. "You've got a wet city here."

"What do you do?" Canaan said.

"I do homicide. What do you do?"

"I do kiddie vice."

"I don' know which is more heartbreakin'."

It was as though Whistler weren't even there. As though Canaan and Bellerose were members of the same family. Long-lost brothers. They spoke the same language, suffered the same aches and pains. It was as though they'd known each other for a hundred years.

"You here on business?" Canaan said.

"I've got some evidence in my bag here. Deeds and leases for various and sundry shops, warehouses, and buildings, including two what you call soundstages. One on the river, one in the Bayou des Familles. Ain' there anymore. Burned to the ground. Got medical examiner reports on two bodies nearly, but not quite, burned up in the fire. Photographs of a red four-door sedan with a vinyl roof we drug up outta the mud with a duplicate certificate of ownership to same in the name of Chester Bucherleider. I got an inventory of various magazines, books, and films confiscated on the basis of a warrant signed by a superior court judge giving me and mine permission to look into the possessions and properties owned, stored, leased, or rented by one Nonny Barcaloo. Among these films is one of a Saigon whore with a butterfly on her ass. That's of some interest to your friend here," he said, cocking a thumb at Whistler. "There's others of little kiddies and some I ain't even got the stomach to mention. I got this chain of evidence pointing to this here Nonny Barcaloo, who, I unnerstan', is in your fair city."

"You come to extradite him?" Canaan said.

"That's the slow way, ain' it?" Bellerose said, smiling slyly.

"You got another way?"

"I don't know. I'd maybe like to push the son of a bitch a little, you know what I mean?"

"This ain't your jurisdiction."

"I mean that could be a drawback or a benefit, dependin' on how you look at it. I don't have to jump in all official right off, askin' for cooperation and like that."

"As long as you got a badge to back you up in case you break your leg."

"Somethin' like that. I just knew this here Whistler would have at least one smart cop for a friend."

"What's in it for me?" Canaan said.

"Well, if we can get the dominoes to fall, all I want is this Barcaloo and his pistoleer. You can have whatever else."

"How do we get the dominoes to fall?" Whistler said.

"How you think? You push."

He put the aluminum case on the tabletop.

Whistler put out his hand and laid it flat on the aluminum. It was damp and cold.

"Dry ice," Bellerose said.

"Jesus Christ!" Whistler said.

It was awesome how Bellerose sat there as though the aluminum case contained nothing but his lunch.

"An' that ain' the only surprise I brought with me."

Thirty-two

THE NEXT time the Mercedes station wagon passed Gentry's, Whistler was standing at the curb waiting for it and waved it down. When it pulled over, the front wheel splashed his shoe. The driver leaned across and opened the door. Whistler got in.

"Not having much luck, are you, Shelley?"

Shelley Pope was a producer. He had access to half the beautiful women in town. Actresses were ready to buy professional opportunities with daring circus acts. Young executive women were ready to outperform the actresses. Streetwalkers left their calling cards. His wife was proud and pleased that her Shelley would have no truck with any of them. She didn't know her Shelley craved young boys with runny noses.

"This goddamn rain keeps everybody inside," Shelley complained.

"Lucky children. Hey, there's one. Looks like a wet rat huddled over there in that doorway."

"Too old. Must be fourteen."

"Goddamn ancient."

"It's a girl."

"How the hell can you tell? The connoisseur's eye. My, my. You like boys ten or eleven, am I right?"

"You people got funny ideas. You think I go around abusing these kids?"

"You shove it up their little asses, Shelley. Is that a kindness?"

"For Christ's sake, the little buggers are out on the streets half starved. No homes to go to. No friends."

"Except you're a friend, right, Shelley?"

"Yes, I'm a friend. I give them clothes. I feed them. I give them money."

"And put them back on the streets three hours later, they can sell themselves again?"

"I'm no pimp."

"That's right. You don't make it or sell it, you just buy it. You ever break bread with the people who make it and sell it?"

"When was the last time you gave a thousand to the Children's Fund?"

"I never."

"So give it up. I don't need righteous. I got righteous. I was the chair for this year's fund-raising dinner. We raised fifty thousand for the Children's Shelter."

"How much you raise at that other dinner for NAMBLA?"

Pope hit the brakes, and the Mercedes fishtailed on the wet leaves along Sweetzer. Then he applied the gas, and the tires took hold again.

"Watch it there, Shelley," Whistler said. "You're going to drive us into a tree and end two distinguished careers."

"What's this NAMBLA?"

"Don't make me crazy. North American Man/Boy Love Association. You should know what it is. You're the president of the local chapter. Speaking of fund-raisers, Shelley, you got money to raise every year for your emergency defense fund?"

"What defense fund?"

"The one that hires lawyers for the needy perverts who get arrested for molesting children. Need a little money for your prisoner-support committee, too, don't you? Maybe you skim a little off the top of the Children's Fund?"

"You want me to drive you somewheres, Whistler, or what?"

"Also you're a member of the Rene Guyon Society, aren't you? Tricky motto you got there. 'Sex by year eight, or else it's too late.'"

"Don't make me mad. I'm not going to take your shit tonight, Whistler. Who the hell are you to judge? Show me where it says a busted hustler like you knows what's right and wrong?"

"We going to match bankbooks now, Shelley?"

"Don't make me fucking laugh. Why would a gazoony like you need a bankbook?"

"Maybe to save my money so I can buy some of the crap you people like to watch."

Pope looked at Whistler out of the corner of his eye.

"You getting bent, Whistler?"

"I'm looking for somebody who's already bent."

"So first you abuse me and now you want a favor, am I right?"

"It won't cost you."

"I'll be the judge of that."

"You know all the snappy comebacks. You know all the suppliers too?"

"Manny Flowers is the best."

"I heard about him. You have any secret passwords? Any special way to introduce yourselves to make a purchase?"

"Grow up. It's all on the up-and-up. It's all legal. All out in the open. What do you think, I go sneaking around back alleys?"

"Any private language?"

"We're just like you, Whistler. We put on our pants one leg at a time."

Whistler was about to tell Pope that they were nothing alike, but he looked at the producer's face in profile and saw that all the tone had left the flesh. His muscles sagged. There were little pouches everywhere. He looked like a powdered corpse all of a sudden, or a man in terrible pain.

"I like you better when you're not a person," Whistler said.

"Don't we all."

"Can you drop me down to Manny Flowers's?"

They drove in silence to La Brea, south to Santa Monica, then turned west.

After a while Pope said, "You think this rain is ever going to end?"

Thirty-three

FLOWERS'S ADULT Bookshop was between a boutique selling crotchless panties and bras with open peepholes for the nipples, and a shop that sold religious artifacts, plaster madonnas, and holy children with the swollen bellies of the starving. Across the street a nightclub advertised a show featuring half-life-size puppets that performed sex acts on stage. Where else but in La-La Land, Whistler thought, would people get so bored with live fucking that they'd sit and watch dolls go at it?

Pope pulled in at the curb.

"What the fuck's got into you, Whistler? You never talked so lousy to me before."

"I had a bad dream. When I woke up, it didn't go away."

"Whatever the fuck that means. Okay, here you are. Whatever you want, just ask for it. Like buying a book at Pickwick's. That's how easy it is, Whistler, so don't blame me."

Whistler stepped out into the rain, then turned back and bent over, thrusting himself partway back into the car.

"Is Walter Cape a member of any of your clubs, Shelley?"

Shelley moved back sharply, as though he'd been slapped.

"What the hell would I know about somebody like Walter Cape?" he said.

"You both have the same twist," Whistler said, and turned away, slamming the door of the Mercedes behind him.

He felt furtive going through the door, uncomfortably aware that someone he might know would see him and tell the story of Whistler's new taste in reading matter and viewing pleasure. Inside, an attempt had been made to make the place bright with paint and strip lighting, but water stains like dried semen on the walls turned it into the waiting room of a whorehouse run out of a trailer.

A man with shaggy hair, a rabbi's beard, horn-rimmed glasses, and the stunned air of a film director thinking sat behind a tall counter from which he could eyeball anyone trying to tuck a magazine or two into a pocket or down the front of his trousers. The cigarette stuck in the center of his mouth sent up a spiral of smoke that poked at his eye in the breeze from Whistler's entrance. The man closed the eye but didn't stop reading the book in front of him, except for a single glance to check the potential profitability of his latest customer.

There were three other men in the shop, all checking out the covers of the plastic-wrapped magazines. They stood in separate corners of the room, facing the walls, like rats afraid that other rats would try to steal their stash. They threw glances at Whistler over their shoulders, then turned quickly away when he returned them. Whistler wandered around like a man making sure there were no traps. One by one the customers left.

He jittered up to the man with the beard and glasses, taking small steps, backing off, circling around through the racks, playing a nervous ferret's part. He kissed off the counter like a billiard ball caroming off the cushions.

"You Manny Flowers?" he said in passing.

"That's who I am," Manny Flowers said.

"We got a mutual friend," Whistler said, passing by again.

"Is that so?"

"Yeah, that's so."

"Can you light somewheres?" Flowers said. "You're like a fucking bumper car. Who's the friend?"

"Willy Zabadno's the friend."

"Willy's dead. He killed himself."

"Willy's coworker, Charlie, is my friend."

"You one of the morgue freaks?"

"I've got a preference, but it ain't dead bodies."

"I'm without interest. You're free to browse."

"Crib Coxey's my friend."

"Oh, yeah? You up from New Orleans?"

"Nonny Barcaloo's my friend."

"Why the fuck didn't you say so? What's your pleasure?"

The cigarette was about to burn Flowers's beard. He snatched it out and doused it in an ashtray filled with a small mountain of butts. He leaned over the counter with his hands clasped, a preacher in a pulpit, ready to counsel the sinner.

"So, tell me, my friend."

"Chicken. I like chicken," Whistler said.

"How much you want to spend?"

Whistler took out his gambler's roll. The sight of it gave Flowers a lot of pleasure.

"Something special. You want something very special?"

He stepped down off the platform and went over to lock the door. "I want to show you something in the back. Something choice. I don't want some gonifs coming in here robbing me blind while I show you my merchandise."

Flowers reached out a hand to touch Whistler's sleeve and guide him toward the back room. Whistler moved off in a fright.

"Don't touch me."

Flowers put his hands shoulder high and walked to the back of the shop. He opened the door and showed Whistler into a room equipped with a television set and a tape player.

Whistler sat in the viewing room, hands in the pockets of his raincoat, head thrust forward.

"I've seen this one," he said. "I bought this one a year ago."

"How could you buy it a year ago? It only came in from Boston six months already."

"I saw one just like it, then. This is nothing special."

"Look at that little blonde doll, that cute little charmer. You telling me you seen one just like her?"

"Little girls are all right."

"I thought you'd like a little of this, a little of that. A little variety."

Whistler's mouth tasted of brass. "I don't like to waste my time."

"All boys. I understand."

"Boys are more like it," Whistler said, astonished at the flatness of this conversation he was having with the porno merchant. Like Pope said, it was like buying a book at Pickwick's: commonplace, matter-of-fact.

Flowers showed Whistler snatches of half a dozen tapes featuring frail boys with round stomachs and shoulder blades like the folded wings of birds. Small, naked boys doing things with grown men.

Whistler shrugged and looked impatient.

"You're hard to please," Flowers said.

"I want the newest. I want the best. I can pay."

"How much can you pay?"

Whistler looked sly. "Well, not as much as Walter Cape."

Flowers looked at Whistler for a long time. Something didn't fit. What didn't fit? Whistler patted his pocket where he kept his money. Greed struggled in Flowers and won. He got a tape out of a locked drawer. "When you say special, you mean really special, don't you?"

Young boys engaged in every manner of act. In the end a child was strangled. Unlike the Mexican girl, the child showed no special terror. Perhaps he'd believed, even with all the other horrors, that no one could want to do such a thing to him.

Whistler stood up.

"How about that?" Flowers said. "It's reserved for Mr. Cape, but I can run you a dupe. Take an hour and a half."

"I got to think about it," Whistler said.

He left the shop. After a while, when he didn't come back to buy, Flowers would begin to wonder about him. He'd call somebody, and somebody would call Walter Cape. And Walter Cape would know someone was taking his name in vain.

Whistler's stomach moved; something sour came up. He looked for a place to vomit. But in the alley all he could bring up was spit. Not even a last shred of innocence.

Thirty-four

THE TROUBLE with going somewhere without your car in La-La Land is that there is very little public transportation and you could die waiting for a taxicab. But after walking seven blocks in the direction of Hollywood and Vine, Whistler lucked out and flagged down a cruiser.

At Gentry's they caught the light at the corner. Whistler tapped the driver and handed him a bill, then got out.

There was a black BMW parked in the yellow with its parking lights on, and somebody sitting inside behind the wheel. Whistler ducked his head against the rain and started to walk around the corner when the BMW's horn beeped him from behind. He turned around with a crunching feeling in his spine and belly. Had Barcaloo and that Jickie Rojo searched him out already? Was somebody going to be standing there with a gun in his hand, ready to blow his guts out?

It was Emmet Tillman standing there, wearing a six-hundred-dollar Burberry, one hand on the top of the open door. Why, Whistler wondered in the midst of a surge of relief, couldn't he look that good in a trench coat? Tillman got back into the car and leaned across to open up the other door. Whistler slipped inside. The car smelled of the best glove leather. If anybody asked him right that minute what he'd give to be rich, Whistler didn't know what he'd say.

"Why are you hanging around out here?" Whistler asked. "You wanted to see me, you could have waited inside."

"I was doing the Durante song," Tillman said. "You know, 'Did you ever have the feeling that you wanted to go, but still you had the feeling that you wanted to stay.' "

"You're making jokes, but somehow I don't think you're having fun," Whistler said.

"I come from Newark, New Jersey, you know that?"

"Maybe I read it somewhere. In some column."

"Ninety percent of that stuff is a load of crap. Everybody knows that. But people like crap."

"So you're not from Newark?"

"Oh, I'm from Newark, all right. Born and dragged up. Old man was a drunk. My mother . . . Anyway, all that's true. What they say about how poor I was and how I lived in doorways sometimes while I was going to drama school in New York is true. But everybody probably thinks it's crap."

"Who gives a rat's ass?"

"Well, nobody wants to think people don't believe you're real."

"Are you having an identity crisis?"

"You don't like me much, do you?"

"Oh, for Christ's sake," Whistler said with a shake of his head, scolding himself, "what's not to like? I hardly know you. I suppose the bottom line is, you got to drop your drawers to take a crap. Just like me."

"There you go," Tillman said with a twist of his mouth that looked something like a wry grin.

"Go where, Tillman? Just where are we going?"

"All right. You got to admit, a person has a chance to use a little juice, pull a couple wires, keep his balls out of the wringer, he's going to do it."

"Save your ass, that's the name of the game," Whistler agreed.

"That car crash shook the shit out of me. I mean, it's bad enough you got a few in you, looking forward to a little pussy, all of a sudden there's a dead man lying on the road. That's bad enough. But when you find yourself in the middle of a fucking horror story, that's really the pits."

"Ain't it the truth?"

"Lay off me, will you? I'm trying to do the right thing here."

"I'll shut my mouth."

"After you took Shiela home I thought about calling my agent, my producer, my lawyers. You want to know what I found out? I found out I didn't really trust a damn one of them. Worse than that, I couldn't think of one friend I could count on to give me a hand without they wanted something from me. So I called the one person I knew who could maybe do me an important favor, who'd told me to ask him a favor anytime."

"Walter Cape," Whistler said.

Tillman's eyes showed some white. He was that surprised.

"How the hell . . ."

"It doesn't matter," Whistler said, pleased that he'd

scored a point, if only to make up for the two-hundred-dollar tip Tillman had practically tossed on the ground for him to pick up. No matter what, Whistler thought wryly, you got to give your ego a little pat, a little stroke. "Go on."

"Cape told me not to worry. He'd handle it. So I go out and talk to the cops. They give me a little shit. Then the detectives arrive and give me a little more."

"Lubbock and Jackson?"

"Yeah, Lubbock and Jackson. Guys I knew from the show. Guys I'd fucking worked with. Treated me like I was something you wipe off your shoe. Then, all of a sudden, just like that—well, not just like that, because this supervisor comes driving up and they have a little head-to-head—they come over and start kissing my ass. They tell me do go on home . . ."

". . . and sin no more."

"They didn't even hand me that shit. They gave me a pass. They tell me the body without a head isn't real. It looked goddamn real to me, but nowadays . . . Well, I wanted to believe it. Who wouldn't want to believe it?"

"You were home free."

"Yeah. Home free. But, you want to know, I didn't feel all that good about it. You think I'm an asshole, I'm not an asshole. I was just trying to keep my balls out of the wringer. I'm home and not feeling too good when Shiela calls and lays the arm on me. I won't call it blackmail, but I don't know what else you'd call it."

"Call it taking a career opportunity."

"Okay, that's what we'll call it."

"You told Cape about her?"

"Yes. And he says I wasn't to worry about her, either. He'd persuade her not to go around blowing any whistles."

"Did you know what he meant?"

"I didn't think about it, exactly. I don't know how a man like that operates. Maybe I thought he'd call her on the phone, have a little talk with her, show her there'd be nothing in it for her if she wanted to cause me any trouble."

"You never expected he'd send her down to a porno shop in New Orleans."

"Is that what he did? Jesus Christ."

"You mean, you don't know?"

"All he said, when I told him I ended up squashing the deal with a forty-thousand-dollar foot . . . you know about that?"

"The car? Yeah, I know about Lubbock, Jackson, and your car."

"All he said was that he had to use more than a forty-thousand-dollar foot."

"And you didn't ask him what the fuck that meant? Never mind. I don't want to hear about the wringer and your balls again."

Tillman laughed briefly. It caught in his throat and got tangled in his tongue. "Shit. They got caught in the wringer good. Cape called in his marker."

"You sound surprised. Why are you surprised?"

"I thought he was just a celebrity fucker, you know. I thought it just gave him an orgasm knowing he could do things for important people they couldn't do for themselves. I never thought there was anything a man as rich as him could want from me."

"How do you think they get so fucking rich? What did he want from you?"

"He wanted me to rope young actresses into doing fuck flicks."

"Act with them?"

"For Christ's sake, no! Just drag them in. Get them to do a little of this, a little of that, for the cameras. Set the hook. Reel them in. You know how it goes."

"That's all?"

"Later on maybe put these women on my show in a little part. Just enough so they can use it in their promos. You'd be surprised how people buy that kind of stuff if they can say there's somebody legitimate fucking in it. It's an edge."

"You sound like you're getting an education."

"I'm not so damned dumb as you think."

"Why are you telling me all this?"

"I don't want any part of it."

"So you decided you didn't want to go to anybody else; you'd come to me, and I'd be the guy who'd keep your balls out of the wringer this time."

"No. I figured maybe you could tell me what to do. I had some street smarts once, believe it or not. But they rust away; you don't have to use them. I started to think. That was no dummy in the gutter. That was a naked woman without a head. So I can understand they can write it up so a Willy Zabadno gets checked off as running his station wagon up a pole. But I can't understand how they could cover up a body with no head, or why they'd want to."

"That's what I wondered too."

"And what did you decide?"

"I decided this town is at the bottom of the rabbit hole in *Alice*. I decided that, at first, Cape was only doing you the favor. It didn't look like a hell of a lot for the muscle he's got, all things considered, and it would put you where he could use you on this deal he's making. Then, later on, he found out the headless body had something to do with him, after all."

"What could it have to do with him?"

"He had her snuffed because she wouldn't give him her little boy to cornhole."

Tillman made a face of disgust and pain.

"Say a prayer," Whistler said.

He got out of the black BMW with the blood-red leather seats and walked around the corner and into Gentry's where Bellerose and Canaan were still sitting, their heads together, probably telling cop jokes and lies. Old friends at first sight.

Whistler slid in beside Bellerose, pushing the aluminum camera case aside. It chilled his fingers. "I got something for you," he said to Canaan.

Thirty-five

A PERSON CAN read something wrong in their own house the minute they walk in the door. Even in the dark. Maybe it's something akin to the facial vision they say some blind people have. Knowing a wall is there before they touch it. The feeling of air that should be empty but is full. A smell not quite right.

A person can almost never read a strange house that way. Even when the lights are on. Strange houses always feel wrong. Bosco's felt wrong, and Whistler felt naked.

The television was going, the sound turned low, the way Shiela had told him she left it on for company when she was alone. Even during the day. Even when she went out, she left the television on low so she wouldn't come home to a silent house. It made the room look as if it were filled with moonlight. It was the only light in the place, except for the tiny night-light in the hall, just enough to find the way to the bathroom in the middle of the night.

Whistler could hear a faucet dripping. He went out into the kitchen, making a lot of noise, and snapped on the lights.

"I'm back," he called out, as though he really believed Shiela was there. Hoping desperately that she would answer.

He was so scared, he couldn't raise spit.

He ran the tap, filled the kettle, and put it on the burner to heat up. He opened and closed a couple of cabinets and the refrigerator. He sat down and took off his shoes. When the water was boiling, he filled a large mug and took it with him as he went into the living room and padded across the carpet toward the hall and bedroom. He didn't know what he'd find.

It might be Shiela, dead, hunted down by Barcaloo and Rojo. It might be one of them still lurking in the apartment. Behind a piece of furniture. Under the bed. In a closet. He had no gun. It was in the potted plant at home. What he had was a mugful of boiling water.

In the bedroom Shiela's suitcase was still on the bench at the foot of the bed. Living out of a suitcase. How she hated it, she'd said. How she hated putting her bath oils and lotions on the corner of a shelf loaded with the toilet articles of a man she didn't even know. When he was away from his house, Whistler kept his things—his toothbrush and toothpaste, nail clippers, and extra comb—in the pockets of his raincoat.

No room in the closet for her things, she'd said. It was a hint of what it would be like when she came to live with him. His stuff would be shoved aside, packed up in one corner of the closet, one drawer of the chest, one shelf of the medicine cabinet. Everything rearranged. For efficiency. For his benefit as well as hers. Men were so bad at organizing space, she'd say. Bird cage would have to go, even if he said he intended to get another canary . . . someday. Drawers cleared out and old address books thrown away. Years and years of Whistler thrown away. When she came to live with him. *If* she came to live with him. The crazy things you thought about while waiting to see if disaster had struck or was about to strike.

He put his hand on the doorknob of the closet and started to turn it. He heard a key in the front door. He hurried across the room and through the hallway. He was standing in the doorway to the living room when she opened the door. She had a brown paper grocery bag in her arm. She saw him and let out a yell. His hand jerked, and he splashed hot water all over his hand.

"Jesus Christ," he yelped.

"You scared me half to death," she said. "Why didn't you put on some lights?" She hit the wall switch beside the door, and the overhead chandelier went on. "You burn your hand?"

"Where the hell have you been?"

"Down to the all-night market. I wanted something to eat."

"There's things to eat in Bosco's pantry and refrigerator."

"I don't like canned sauerkraut and hard salami."

"Half the people in town go to the all-night market. Barcaloo could have been there."

She stared at him. "I can't live like this. I can't live cooped up."

"For Christ's sake, it's been hours. Not even days. Can't you stay put a few hours?"

"I can't live in somebody else's rooms and sleep in somebody else's bed. I've got an apartment of my own. You've got a house."

"I don't think they're safe."

"I've been thinking about that. I've been thinking about what happened in New Orleans. Somebody spotted me and wanted to use me in a dirty picture. When they offered me the deal, I wasn't as careful asking questions as I should have been. They got the wrong idea. They thought I was ready for it. I don't think they meant to kill me."

"Oh?"

"I think that was your idea. I think you overreacted."

"Maybe you're right. Maybe I overreacted then, but I'm not overreacting now. The big man died in the fire. I don't think the little one's the kind to forget."

"Well, if he's after anybody, he's after you."

Whistler thought it might be nice if the television started playing some sentimental tune. He had a feeling he was seeing the end of the shortest love affair on record.

"You better put some ice on that burn." With a strangled little cry Shiela dropped the groceries in the easy chair and just about threw herself at him.

"Smack me in the mouth, Whistler," she said. "I got it coming."

"What do you think I am, some kind of pervert?"

"Let's go in the bedroom and find out."

Thirty-six

"WELL, TALK to me, Nonny," Cape said.

Barcaloo sat near the fire in Cape's library and sweated. If he closed his eyes, he could imagine himself back in New Orleans.

"How's that, Walter?"

"There's no doubt about it. The headless body that flew out of Willy Zabadno's station wagon and landed in the gutter at the corner of Hollywood and Vine was Lim Shu's. I received a call from a friend who told me the L.A.P.D. had an inquiry about the head of an Oriental woman they found down there. Somebody told them about the accident, and a lieutenant named Bellerose wanted to know more about the body. I once asked you if there was anything outstanding that might draw unwanted attention to you. You said there wasn't."

"Well, there wasn't."

"There was a dead Vietnamese whore lying in the L.A. County Morgue who didn't stay put."

"I can explain all that."

"That's why I'm asking you to talk to me."

A flush spread across Barcaloo's neck and face.

"I got these two assholes working for me," Barcaloo said. "Well, I had two, but one got done by a fucker named Whistler, who come down to New Orleans looking for his girlfriend. This actress, Shiela Andes, you sent down for me to snuff."

"I never said that, Nonny. I said I wanted some film I could use against her. I said nothing about snuffing her. But we'll get to that. Right now I want to hear about Lim Shu and why she lost her head."

"A year ago, when you told me to do her, she must of smelled a rat and started running before we got the chance. She run back here. I sent Pinole and Rojo to do the job."

"You never told me she'd come back here."

"Why would I bother you with details? You gave me a contract to do her, so I done her. What's the difference if it's a Monday or a Friday? What's the difference if it's New Orleans or L.A.?"

"It made a difference."

"Because when you make me the offer to take over this new production organization, you ask me is there anything outstanding could embarrass you. I say no because I know it's no. But then I start to worrying about if Pinole and Rojo did the right whore. You know how these things can start buzzin' around your head? I mean, there wasn't no reason for me to have any doubts. Except, sometimes, Pinole and Rojo are a little slow, you unnerstan'?"

"I hired you, not Pinole and Rojo."

"You didn' expect me to do the job with my own hands?"

"I expected you to see it was done right."

"This is exactly what I was tryin' to do. I sent Pinole and Rojo here to bring back proof that they did the right whore. I tell them to take some of them instant pictures. How am I supposed to know these two assholes is going to get high on some crank? How am I supposed to know they're goin' to have a party with this morgue attendant, this Willy Zabadno, and get foolish? How the hell am I supposed to know they can't get the fuckin' camera to work right? How the hell is anybody supposed to know they go and saw off her goddamn head and bring it back to show me, I should see with my own eyes they got the right whore a year ago?"

Barcaloo was in a rage.

Cape shook his head slowly from side to side, a strange smile on his mouth.

"I agree," Barcaloo said. "If it wasn't such a serious thing, I woulda fell down laughin' when they showed up with that fuckin' head, myself."

"I hope I'm not giving you the idea that I'm amused."

"Me, neither. I raised particular hell with them two. I told them to get rid of that fuckin' head the minute I see it's Lim Shu. So how am I supposed to know, after I ream their assholes out the way I done, that these two lamebrains is gonna play football with it?"

Something in Cape's expression made Barcaloo run down, but he couldn't sit through the silence that followed very long.

"When you asked me the question, I knew the answer," Barcaloo said. "It was only after I got to worryin' about it that I sent Pinole and Rojo back here. Besides, how was I to know this goddamn Willy Zabadno was going to panic when he sees the broad without her head and run off in the middle of the night with the body in the back of his wagon?"

"How, indeed," Cape said. "Now we come to the matter of Shiela Andes and this man, Whistler."

"Don't worry about them two another minute. Me and Jickie got Whistler and that cunt on the top of the list of things to do. They're as good as done."

Whistler drove his old Chevy. Bellerose sat in the passenger seat with the aluminum camera case on his lap. There was a manila envelope on top of that.

"You're sure this Bouche, this Cazebone, is in her room at the hotel?" Bellerose asked.

"That's what the desk clerk told me. She's in the room she and Barcaloo are sharing. He's not."

"I know he's not. He's not there, and neither is that other one, Jickie Rojo."

"Suppose they come back while we're talking to Bouche?"

"Your frien' Isaac Canaan's right on their asses. They start back to the hotel, he calls the room an' lets us know."

"You two got friendly awful fast."

"Professional courtesy, you know what I mean? The fuckin' brotherhood of law-enforcement officers."

Whistler pulled up in front of the hotel and parked. The

doorman stepped over and said, "You can't leave that there."
Bellerose opened his wallet and showed his shield. "You take
care of it for us." They stopped at the desk and made sure
Bouche hadn't taken a walk in the time it took them to drive
over. As far as the clerk knew, she was still in her room. He
reached for the phone to double-check. Bellerose flashed his
shield again. "Don't do that. Just keep it under your hat."

Whistler and Bellerose walked over to the elevator bank.

"Why the hell is it they look at your tin and let you do
whatever you want? That shield doesn't even look like any
used by a local agency," Whistler said.

"Who would want to try me? What the hell for?"

They stepped into the elevator car and punched the floor.

"You ever thought of bein' a cop?" Bellerose asked.

"It's not my line of work."

"Oh? What's your line of work?"

"The motion picture business. I just carry a ticket for times
when things get thin."

"I unnerstan'."

"You do?"

Bellerose grinned. "Oh, yes. I'm a brain surgeon when I
ain' a cop."

The doors opened, and they walked down the corridor to
Barcaloo's room. Bellerose rapped on the door. Bouche
opened the door without even asking who it was. When she
saw two men standing there, she took a step back, pulling her
robe around her at the waist.

"You shouldn't open your door without askin' who it is,"
Bellerose said in a kindly voice.

"I thought it was room service. So who are you?"

Bellerose flashed the badge yet another time, but she didn't
notice it. Her eyes had popped open along with her mouth
when she got a better look at Whistler. "You're the fuckin'
gazoony what kidnapped Shiela." She started to close the
door, but Bellerose stuck his foot in the door.

Whistler pushed past and into the room, backing Bouche
off. "Well, no," he said, "I didn't kidnap her."

"You're the one blew Dom all to hell. All we could find
was his fuckin' finger."

She was startled but didn't seem that afraid of them. The pupils of her eyes were very large and black. She was high on something besides alcohol. "You don't get the fuck out of here," she said, "I'll scream this place down."

"Will you please look at this, ma'am?" Bellerose said, slightly irritated. "I'm a police officer all the way up from New Orleans, and I mean to ask you a few questions."

"You know this man here blew Dom Pinole's ass off the face of the earth?"

"Indeed I do know that, but right now I've got a lot of interest in Nonny Barcaloo and Jickie Rojo, who are both surviving."

"I don't know nothin' about them."

There was a knock on the door. Whistler took a step and opened it. The room-service waiter was there with a bowl of salad, a little loaf of bread and a knife to cut it, a plate of butter, two bottles of vodka, a bucket of ice, and some mixers on a rolling cart.

"Well, here's my lunch," Bouche said. "Look at the size of that salad. I'm sure it's enough for three."

"What kind of dressing?" Bellerose asked.

"Blue cheese."

He went to sit on the couch, putting the aluminum case down beside his foot. "My favorite."

The waiter wheeled the cart over in front of him. Bouche signed the tab with a flourish and went to sit beside Bellerose. Whistler stood there, wondering what it was all about.

Bellerose served all three of them, though Whistler said he'd rather not have any salad. Bellerose made a little face that said Whistler should not refuse and offend their hostess, and then asked Whistler to make three vodkas with tonic.

"I prefer absinthe," Bouche said, "but I doubt they got the real stuff here."

"I doubt it too," Bellerose said. He took a bite of salad and declared it good. Bouche sat there, half falling out of her dressing gown, nibbling lettuce off her fork like a white rabbit. Bellerose opened the manila envelope and laid out all the horror pictures, one by one.

Bouche stared. She leaned forward to get a better look. The fork fell out of her hand and the food out of her mouth.

"Don' get sick," Bellerose said in the calmest possible voice.

"Why are you doin' this to me?" Bouche asked piteously.

"Nobody's doin' anythin' to you. Whatever doin' done was done to these two poor women. One's no more than a girl. You ever see this little dark-skinned girl before?"

Bouche nodded.

"When did you see her?"

"About two years ago."

"An' where did you see her?"

"In New Orleans."

"Whereabouts in New Orleans?"

"At the studio in the bayou."

"And what was she doin' there?"

"Actin' in films."

"Fuck films?"

"Love films."

"Is that what Barcaloo calls 'em?"

"No, it's what I call 'em."

"Why's that?"

"Well, sounds nicer than what you said, doesn't it?"

"Were you there when somebody chopped her head off?"

"Oh, no. Oh, no." Bouche started to cry. "Barcaloo's goin' to be comin' back."

"Where's he been?" Whistler asked very softly. Like a disembodied voice. Like the voice inside a person's head.

"Over to see Mr. Cape. He's a very important man. They're goin' to be partners, you know."

"In what?"

Her eyes focused and grew crafty. "Oh, no, you don't."

"Oh, yes, we do," Bellerose said in a certain voice, and gave it back to Whistler.

"In what?"

"Well, you know. What we're talkin' about. That's all I know. Nonny don't discuss his business with me."

"How about the Vietnamese woman?"

"They didn't chop her head off in front of the camera, too, did they?" Bouche asked, wide-eyed.

"Too? So, even though you weren't there when it happened, you know for sure that they killed the Mexican girl that way?"

"I don't know that for sure. I don't know that at all. I never said that. I heard that's what happened. But I always heard all kinds of things about Nonny, and Dom and Jickie. All kinds of terrible things."

"Didn't it bother you enough to make you want to get away?" Whistler asked.

Bouche looked at him as though he were asking a very foolish question. "I been hearing terrible stories all my life," she said.

"All right, now," Bellerose said, starting fresh, "this Vietnamese woman. You knew her?"

Bouche nodded.

"What was her name?"

"She had lots of names."

"Like what?"

"She called herself Connie Woo or Sally Saigon or Doris Quim. Cute, huh? She told me to call her Lillian. I called her Lillian."

"Did you know her real name?"

"I don't know. What's it matter? Who's got a real name?"

"You ever hear Barcaloo talking to his friends about killing these women?"

She shook her head.

"Or killing anybody else?"

She shook her head more vigorously.

"How about a couple of people called Chippy Byrd or Lacy Ohio?"

"No, no, no, no."

"How about Chester Bucherleider or Loretta Oskanowsky?"

"No, no, no, no! I'm going to be sick."

Bellerose shook his head as he gathered up the photos and put them in the envelope. "Anything else you can tell us?"

"Nonny would kill me, he knew I was talkin' to you two."

"You've been livin' with a fuckin' monster, you know that?"

"Nonny'll kill me."

"If you hear Barcaloo talkin' to Rojo about doin' anybody else, killin' anybody else, like maybe Mr. Whistler here, I want you to call one of us at this number." He took out one of his cards and handed it to Whistler. "Gentry's?" Whistler wrote the number on the card and handed it back to Bellerose, who folded it up until it was no bigger than a quarter. He handed it to Bouche, but she hugged herself and turned away, pouting like a child. Bellerose tucked it into the front of Bouche's nightgown, between her white breasts. She looked up at him as though she thought he was caressing her and wanted him to know that she didn't mind.

"I'm gonna burn that the minute you two fuckers get out of here," she said. "Nonny'll kill me."

Bellerose put the aluminum case up on the coffee table. "Maybe Nonny didn't have that Saigon whore's head chopped off, but somebody chopped it off and sent it down to New Orleans. Lef' the body here in Los Angeles."

"What?" Bouche said, as though he were no longer speaking English.

"That's another story maybe we'll go into another time." He snapped the catches and flipped them open. "Point is, I thought it a very cruel thing to let that woman's head stay on ice in one city and her body in another." He cracked the case. The steam of dry ice seeped out all the way around.

Bouche started to draw away, getting an idea about what Bellerose had in mind.

"Jesus, Mary, and Joseph, you haven't got her . . ." Bouche couldn't say any more. Her voice was drowned in bubbles bursting in her throat. Water streamed out of her eyes. She bent over as though her stomach ached, staring at the case as the lid came up an inch at a time, lifted by Bellerose's freckled hands.

"You call now, ya'll hear?" he said.

* * *

Barcaloo stood up. "I'm already on it. Them two better be havin' some fun because, for them, it's as good as it'll ever get."

"You're not thinking it out," Cape said. "This Whistler is running around using my name in places where my name is never to be used."

"I just said you don't have to worry anymore."

"You don't understand. If something happens to either one of them now, I doubt if I have enough influence to prevent my name coming into the investigation. I want you to let it lie. For a while. Until he gets discouraged. Until he has to make the rent. Until it all dies down."

"Well, now, Walter, I don't know if I can do that."

Cape frowned but said nothing.

"This Whistler killed Dom Pinole. Now maybe you and me can let that pass, but Jickie Rojo can't. Won't. He's out lookin' for that asshole right now."

Thirty-seven

IT FELT almost domestic, going out to get the paper together. Walking arm in arm down to the newspaper vending machines on the corner. It was as though they'd been married for at least a year or three. Except Whistler was thinking about a gun. The gun he hadn't carried with him down to New Orleans just in case a cop frisked him. The gun that was still back at his house where it would be no use at all in case those two gazoonies, Barcaloo and Rojo, or maybe some other gunsels hired by Walter Cape to stop Whistler from taking his name in vain all over town, came looking for him.

The gun that was tucked away, wrapped in plastic, in the sphagnum moss surrounding the one sad and sorry house-plant, a ficus benjamina, sitting in a plastic pot beside the table in front of the living-room window overlooking the balcony.

People keep guns in drawers in night tables beside beds, between springs and mattresses, on the top shelves of closets behind Christmas tree ornaments, under kitchen sinks, and even in waterproof bags hung by hooks in toilet tanks. All places that people looking for guns will look. On the other hand, only house keys are kept in flowerpots, and since whoever was looking for whatever would not be looking for a house key since they'd already be inside the house, chances were very good that they wouldn't be looking for a key in a pot and therefore wouldn't find the gun. At least that's the way Whistler had worked it out one night.

He scarcely ever carried the goddamn gun. No matter where he wore it, in a holster clipped to the back of his belt, tucked into his waistband pointing at his cock, or under his armpit, the thing that started weighing twelve ounces started to feel like it weighed twelve pounds, dragging on his pants so he worried they'd drop right down to his knees. Or giving him a boil in his armpit. But right at the moment he would welcome the uncomfortable piece. Right at the moment he wanted and needed it. He thought about padding around in his stockinged feet with a cup of hot water in his hand when he thought he might not have been alone in Bosco's place. Hot water was no kind of weapon.

There were tremors out there. Killers were on the move. He'd been long enough in the trade to feel that much. He wanted the comfort of the gun.

So when they got back to Bosco's apartment house, he went past the entrance to the alley that led to the parking spaces in the back.

"Where we going?" Shiela said.

"I've got to get a change of socks and underwear. I feel silly as hell washing them out every night like a chorus girl."

"That's good. After we get yours we can go over to my place and get some more of mine."

It was a nice ride over to Cahuenga Pass and up the winding road to his shack hanging over the edge of the hill. The rain had let up a little again, and the air was sweet and clean for a change. There was a spot along the road where they passed almost directly underneath his balcony off the living room. On bad days, when he worried about mud slides instead of other things, he thought about standing on the balcony when the house fell and landing on the roof of some car with a messenger in it coming up the road to hand him first prize in a million dollar lottery. Killing himself and everybody in the car.

As usual, the street in front of his house, all the way up to the top and almost all the way down to the last turn, was crowded with cars on both sides. There were a lot more cars than there could be people living in the houses, unless half the neighborhood was renting out rooms, which they probably were in order to make enough to live in La-La Land. But for a change, nobody had blocked his driveway. He poked the Chevy between the front of a Mercedes and the ass end of a BMW, set the brake, and killed the engine.

"You want to wait here? I'll only be five minutes."

"What are you going to do, Whistler, pick some messages off your answering machine? Afraid I'll learn about the rest of your women?"

"Unnumbered," he said. "Women unnumbered."

He got out of the car and went around to help Shiela out, but she was already out. He walked up to the door first, reading the path, the azaleas beside the path, the bougainvillaea over the door, the panes of glass in the windows, the shingles on the roof. Something was wrong, at least not quite right. He didn't want to jump at shadows. He didn't want to get Shiela jumping at every passing breeze. He put his key in the lock. Shiela was right at his shoulder, touching him with her body. He pushed the door open and started to step inside.

"Oh, for Christ's sake," he said, "the porch light's on." He half turned, pushing against Shiela, who was crowding in behind him. The blade of the machete made a sound of rustling silk in the air near his head. It just missed his outstretched hand and thudded into the wooden door.

Whistler put his hand against Shiela's chest and shoved as hard as he could. She went careening back along the path, caught her heels on the uneven brick, and went down hard in the azaleas. Whistler ducked under an arm and hand heaving the machete out of the door, shouldering a body back and away. The blade came free, and Whistler slammed the door closed as he skidded across the floor toward the sliding doors and out to the balcony and the potted plant standing in front of them. In the brief moment before the closing door shut out the porch light, which he never left on when he expected to be away for more than overnight, he had the chance to catch a glimpse of Jickie Rojo struggling with the machete.

Now it was as dark as the inside of a magician's hat. He was on his knees pulling out the sphagnum moss by the handful, scrabbling for the plastic wrap and the gun that should be in it.

"You silly son of a bitch," Rojo said. "That's the first place I looked."

Whistler started to stand up, his right hand wrapped around the skinny trunk of the ficus benjamina. "How the fuck did you ever come to do that?"

Rojo didn't answer. He was too busy running headlong toward Whistler, the machete held off to the side so it would be very hard to block the next blow without losing a hand.

First the hand and then my fucking head, Whistler thought as he swung the potted plant at the full length of trunk and arm and caught Rojo right across the knees.

Rojo let out an awful howl of pain, stumbled, half fell, regained his feet but not his stride, windmilled like a dervish trying to check his headlong charge, failed to do so, and went crashing through drapes, glass door, and railing. Over the side.

Whistler was too slow to see him falling, but he saw him lying smashed flat on the road below in the lights of an oncoming car. The driver slammed on his brakes. They sounded like a woman screaming.

Thirty-eight

CANAAN AND Lieutenant Muncie lifted Barcaloo right out of the lobby of his hotel when he came back from Cape's mansion.

Bellerose and Canaan had talked to Muncie and made their case, then gave him a chance to retrieve the mistaken favor he'd done for somebody—they didn't ask who—that night when a headless body had been tossed out the back of Willy Zabadno's station wagon. They pointed out that a gunsel by the name of Jickie Rojo, up from New Orleans, up from Bellerose's parish, had tried to kill a citizen of Los Angeles and had swan-dived off a balcony onto Iris Terrace just above Cahuenga Boulevard instead. The investigation of that matter was going to lead to an investigation of the headless body that was missing from the county morgue, removed by Willy Zabadno for reasons ultimately known only to himself, since he was dead and couldn't testify to anything anymore.

But one thing was very clear: A favor had been done. There was a good chance it was about to have repercussions. If Muncie wanted to continue being loyal to whomever he was being loyal to, that was his business, naturally, but it was better than even money that when they brought down whomever, Muncie was going to be trampled underfoot.

That was all it took to convince Muncie that he should protect his wife, kiddies, and pension. Not to mention the fact that Muncie was actually an honest cop and that the favor done for Burchard hadn't seemed like such a great distortion of the law at the time.

Barcaloo went along with them very quietly, being, as he

told them, a respecter of uniforms and asshole detectives with bags under their eyes.

"Take me downtown and show me your telephone," Barcaloo said.

"I thought you were from out of town, Mr. Barcaloo," Canaan said. "Don't tell me you've provided yourself with a lawyer already?"

"I wouldn't come to your asshole of a city if I didn't have some friends."

"Influential friends?" Muncie asked mildly.

"With enough juice to fry your balls," Barcaloo said.

On that friendly note they drove in silence to Temple Street and the Rampart area jail, which was no longer the home of the confessed cult murderer, Carl Corvallis, but was as empty as a tomb.

They walked Barcaloo through the front door into the echoing, empty building. Muncie hit the switch, and Barcaloo saw Bellerose sitting on a straight-backed chair in the middle of the tile floor with an aluminum camera case beside his feet.

"What the fuck is this?"

"I come to visit you, Nonny. I come to tell you of a little bit of misfortune that has befell you. I don' suppose you know that your movin' pitcher studio has burned down?"

"That's okay, it's insured."

"Oh, not the one down by the riverfront. The one out to the Bayou des Familles."

"I ain't got no—"

"Don' fuck with me, Barcaloo. There ain' no percentage in it for you."

Muncie brought over a nearby chair just like the one Bellerose was sitting in. "Take a load off your feet, Mr. Barcaloo," he said.

"You see how polite these L.A. cops are, Nonny? I don' have to be so goddamn polite. This ain' my jurisdiction. I got no authority over here. I'm just a private citizen. I could break your arms an' legs, an' there wouldn't be any of this police brutality shit you could lay on me."

Barcaloo sat down and showed his white teeth.

"So thanks for tellin' me about my misfortune. How'd it happen?"

"The gasoline for the generator blew up. Totaled a Lincoln Continental. Blew some fuckin' fool all to hell."

"Who might that have been?"

"Your faithful employee, Dom Pinole."

Barcaloo made a noise with his lips, kissing Pinole good-bye.

"You don' seem surprised."

"Well, now, I'm not surprised. Dom wasn't very bright. I always tole him he'd be killin' himself one of these fine days."

"Other bodies in the rubble, Nonny."

Barcaloo sat there, calm and easy.

"Man named Chester Bucherleider. Young woman named Loretta Oskanowsky."

"Don't know them. Was they vandals?"

"Chippy Byrd and Lacy Ohio. Maybe you knew them?"

Barcaloo shook his head. "They got caught in the fire, huh? What do you think they were doin' on private property?"

"They were dead before the fire got 'em. Bare-assed and dead. You think your assholes was takin' their pitchers?"

"That could be."

"Maybe you was there takin' their pitchers?"

"No. No, I wasn't there."

"A frien' a mine, name of Whistler, says you was. In fact, he was standin' on their bodies in a closet while you were tryin' to get a lady named Shiela Andes to do a little fuckin' for the cameras too."

"I don't know anybody name of Whistler."

"Sure you do," Whistler said, stepping out from the shadows behind the charge desk.

If they'd thought that Whistler's sudden appearance was going to send Barcaloo into a dither, they were dead-ass wrong. He stared at Whistler like he was just another citizen waiting at a bus stop.

"No, I fuckin' don't," he said, emphasizing each and every word.

"I'm the guy in front of the Beaver Run down in New Orleans."

"Oh, sure. Now I remember your face."

"Aren't you surprised to see me?"

"Why should I be surprised to see you?"

"Didn't you expect Jickie Rojo to do me?"

"I didn't know Jickie was lookin' for you." Barcaloo swiveled his head and looked up at Muncie. "Officer, you should arrest this man. I got reason to believe he caused the death of my friend, Dom Pinole."

"That's a case for New Orleans," Muncie said.

Barcaloo turned back to Bellerose.

"I just tole you, I got no authority to arrest over here."

"Son of a bitch," Barcaloo said, without anger, looking at Whistler. "Looks like you got yourself a pass on a fuckin' technicality."

"Now, in your case, we'll go through the paperwork and the trouble to get your ass for those two dead bodies we found in the closet," Bellerose said.

"Well, you'll just have to talk to Pinole and Rojo about that, won't you?"

They sat around in a pool of quiet, nobody moving, nobody hardly breathing, everybody waiting for something to snap. Whistler had the definite impression that Barcaloo already knew that Rojo had taken a header onto the concrete. Why not? If the cop who'd done the favor for Cape had gotten the word of Rojo's death, he would have passed it on to Cape. And Cape would have passed it on to Barcaloo.

"Rojo's dead," Whistler said.

Barcaloo paused a beat. "It looks like I'm going to have to put an ad in the paper for some new employees. Now, who the fuck's goin' to drive me back to my hotel?"

He started to stand up, but Bellerose reached forward and shoved him in the chest, and Canaan clapped a hand on his shoulder.

"There's still the murder of a Vietnamese prostitute by the name of Lim Shu Dok."

"Prove it."

"And there's still a young Mexican whore by the name of Rita Sastre."

"Don' know her."

"You had her head cut off."

"I tole you once before about these two cunts. I never done nothin' to 'em except to take their pictures fuckin' and suckin'. That's my livin'. There's no law against it. You don't like what I do, go make a law."

"You had Rita Sastre's head cut off while the cameras were rollin'. You sell it on movies and cassettes."

"I told you that was a trick."

"No trick, Nonny. We didn' only find the pieces of Dom Pinole and the charred bodies of Chester Bucherleider and Loretta Oskanowsky. We found Rita Sastre's bones. Her head was in one place and her body was in another. Under the floor of the stage, Nonny."

Barcaloo's eyes flickered. He was trying to focus in on information he hadn't had before. Those stupid assholes, Dom and Jickie, he thought. Couldn't they fucking *ever* do something right?

Bellerose stood up. "All right, then."

"All right, what?" Barcaloo said.

"Let's go book you in."

"Don't jerk my chain. You were going to book me, you'd have took me down to city or county jail, not this pisshole. This was to scare the shit out of me and make me cry. Because you know, and I know, you can't prove a fuckin' thing."

"We can prove a little, Nonny. Just wait and see."

Barcaloo stood up. He tucked his shirt into the waistband of his trousers and adjusted the lapels of his jacket.

"Maybe we don't book you," Muncie said. "Maybe we just hold you forty-eight."

"All legal," Canaan said.

"Hold you forty-eight. Your friend . . ."

"Walter Cape," Whistler said.

"Walter Cape thinks you're cutting a deal. Maybe you can tell us if he hired you to murder Lim Shu Dok?"

"Up your ass," Barcaloo said.

"Don't answer right away. Think about it," Bellerose said. He reached into his pocket and took out a coin. "Flip you to see who drives this asshole back to his hotel." He spun the coin. Muncie called heads. It was tails. Bellerose looked at Whistler. "Fuck, we lose."

After they dropped Barcaloo off, Whistler drove Bellerose back to Gentry's. Bellerose still had the aluminum case on the floor between his feet.

"Why didn't you give him a look at that?" Whistler asked.

"You saw that man. You think the rottin' head of a woman he killed, or had killed, would stir him any?"

"So what do we do about him?"

"We just keep on pushin'. We just keep on pushin'."

Thirty-nine

BARCALOO WALKED into the hotel suite feeling mean. Like a bull gator. The loss of Pinole, and now Rojo, was a territorial threat, not a cause for sadness.

Bouche was on the couch, a bowl of lettuce and tomatoes wilting in a bowl, slices of egg and avocado turning color. A bottle of vodka was gone and another started. There were stains of a spilled drink on the carpet.

She had her head thrown back, her mouth open, showing the gold teeth in the back he'd paid a bundle for, maintaining his property.

Her dressing gown was open, and her nightgown gaped in front, exposing her heavy white breasts. Her skirts were up, exposing her thighs almost to her bush. Thighs spread wide. As pale as slabs of suet. He felt nothing. He was through with her.

Pinole and Rojo were dead. The big deal with Cape had turned to shit. He didn't want to fuck Bouche anymore. He'd leave her here in La-La Land and go back to New Orleans where he belonged, where he was a little king.

Look at the sloppy broad, he thought. He reached over to cover her ugliness. His fingers touched the sharp edge of the folded calling card. He read the name of Lieutenant Bellerose and saw Whistler and a number written on it.

She opened her eyes sleepily.

"Hullo, there, Nonny, honey."

The rage boiled up out of his belly. He knew, without doubt, that he was going to kill her. It would be better if it could be cold-blooded, but the fury was running all through his blood and bones like an electric flood. It numbed his hands and made the veins in his neck beat on drums inside his head with terrible power. It filled his gut and swelled his balls. It gave him an erection like he hadn't had in twenty years. He'd kill her, but first he'd crush her. He'd use his cock to punish her. Punish her mouth and her cunt and her asshole. He'd stab her with it and tear her apart.

Bouche was grinning at him with an oddly knowing look, as though she knew for certain what he had in mind and didn't care. "Hey, nonny nonny, and a hot cha-cha," she said mockingly.

He tore open his belt and dropped his pants. He'd take her first like she was a whore doing it for a dollar in a doorway. A utility fuck taken on the run.

"Hey, for Christ's sake, Nonny, let's use the bed. You're payin' three hundred dollars a day for the room, so let's use the bed."

He landed on her, not caring that his weight was almost crushing her. She tried to squirm away, but he clutched at her like a beast holding its prey for the fatal stroke.

Oh, dear God, she thought. *This ain't the fucking pig in heat. This is the day he means to kill me.*

He grunted and thrashed his head from side to side as he fought her legs wider. His spittle sprayed on her cheek and neck. It seemed to burn like acid and sent her into a frenzy. She managed to roll him off long enough to get out from under. But he attacked again and knocked her to the floor. She didn't scream. Neither of them spoke another word. Her arms were raised above his back, hands waving desperately in the air. She felt him enter her and instinctively adjusted to make it less painful for her, which seemed to make it easier for him. Her groping hand touched the table. The bottle fell over and the dishes clattered. Her fingers closed on the bread knife. She looked along Barcaloo's heaving back. She raised the knife and plunged it into his body just above the kidneys.

Just like she'd said once not long before, Barcaloo was alive going up and dead coming down.

Forty

BOSCO WAS at the register reading Plato's *Earlier Dialectic* in the second edition. It was still raining, and business was once more on the ebb.

Bellerose and Canaan sat on one side of the booth, the aluminum case between them. Shiela and Whistler sat on the other. The three men were glum to one degree or another; she was not. So far as she was concerned, everything had turned out just right. Every threat against her had been taken care of. She'd never really believed that a man like Walter Cape would have bothered arranging for her to be sent down to New Orleans and filmed in a fuck flick just to shut her mouth about the accident and Tillman. But even if he had, there'd be no reason to stir the cesspool another time. What they had was a pack of sleeping dogs, and anybody would be smart enough to let them lie. She could get on with her life and her career. She could feel Whistler's thigh warm against her thigh.

"This rain is never going to stop," Whistler said. "It's going to keep on raining until every house on every hill slides down into the canyons and the valleys. Then the rising water's going to wash it all down Wilshire and Sunset to the sea. When the sun finally comes out again, there'll be nothing but a lake where L.A. once was."

"You want wet, we got wet down to where I live," Bellerose said. "If ever you want wet, you come down an' visit me." He looked at his watch.

"When's your plane?"

"I got a couple hours before I grab a cab to the airport."

"I'll give you a lift," Canaan said.

Bellerose looked at Canaan. "City car, city gas?"

"That's right."

"Thank you kindly."

Whistler looked from one to the other and then at the case. "What are you planning to do with that?"

"It's a hell of a piece of inventory to be carryin' aroun', ain't it?"

"You can turn it over to me. I'll see it gets to the right people," Canaan said.

Shiela shuddered and stared briefly at the case but didn't say anything.

Little pools of silence lay around their conversation like the oily, trash-fouled puddles in the gutters and on the parking lots.

"Son of a bitch," Whistler finally said in a low voice that sounded like it wanted to be a yell. "We didn't do a fucking bit of good."

"Hey, hey, hey," Bellerose said, "look again. We took three assholes—beggin' your pardon, ma'am—off the streets, one way or another."

"Cape's still up on the hill, buying and selling children."

"Someday we'll do him too," Canaan said. "We sent him a message. The level of shit'll be down for a while."

"For Christ's sake," Whistler said, "what are we, just a bunch of sewer workers?"

Canaan nodded his head like a wise old bird. "That's what we are, Whistler. Didn't you know that?"

"If one of you says, 'It's a dirty job, but somebody's got to do it,' I'm going the fuck home . . . begging nobody's pardon," Shiela said.

The three men didn't think she was funny. They stared at her as though they wondered about her good intentions.

"I got to wade in the shit, it's only fair Cape should wade in the shit," Whistler said. "Tillman called me. Wanted to whine. Wanted to ask me how he could get out from under this deal Cape's boxed him into. Cape's called a meeting of the stockholders for tonight. I told him not to fret, Cape would probably dissolve the company, at least for a while. I figure they should be sitting down to dinner right about now."

Canaan picked up the aluminum case and slid out of the booth. Bellerose followed. They said good-bye to Shiela and went to wait at the door.

He handed her the keys to the Chevy. "You want to go back and pack your things at Bosco's? I'll have Canaan drop me off there."

"I want to go home, Whistler."

"Okay, I'll have him drop me at the house."

"My home, Whistler. Back to my apartment. You understand? I want to sleep in my own bed."

He handed her the keys. "Your apartment, then."

"I want to sleep alone. Please? Tomorrow. I'll bring your car back tomorrow. Is that okay? Maybe we'll have breakfast here tomorrow."

"In the morning maybe it won't be raining anymore."

Forty-one

WHEN CANAAN drove up with Bellerose sitting beside him and Whistler in back, the guard came out of the gate house with a shotgun cradled in his elbow. He was wearing a felt hat with a wide brim and was squinting through the rain, which was pierced by the headlights. Canaan got half out of the car, fumbling around in his pockets.

"Excuse me," he said. "I seem to be lost."

The guard didn't answer, just stood there, heavy with suspicion, paid to be professionally suspicious of everyone.

Canaan got all the way out, then stuck his head and shoulders back into the car, saying loudly, "Hey, Carl, you got those directions your sister-in-law gave us?"

Bellerose got out of the car and walked over toward the guard, taking a piece of paper from his pocket. Canaan walked up the other side. They were ten feet apart when they closed in. The guard's eyes flicked back and forth between the two. He started hefting the shotgun. Canaan pulled his piece and shoved it into the guard's ribs as Bellerose reached out and grabbed the barrel of the gun so it couldn't be raised any farther. He got his own gun out.

"Take it from me frien', what they pay you ain' worth dyin' for."

The guard gave up the shotgun. Canaan tapped him on the elbow, and he put his hands behind him. Canaan backed him up to the wrought-iron gate and cuffed his wrists around a bar. Whistler got in behind the wheel. He drove the car slowly up to the gate, then fed it gas. The mechanism resisted at first, then slowly gave way as the engine roared and the tires whined, making dry patches on the drive. The guard walked backward as the gate opened enough for Bellerose to slip through and go into the gate house. He threw the switch. The gates opened faster. Canaan helped the guard so he wouldn't fall and get dragged.

Whistler carried the shotgun as they walked up the long, sloping drive. At the main entrance he glanced at Canaan and Bellerose, who stood on either side of him.

"Don' bother ringin' the bell," Bellerose said.

Whistler gave the lock both barrels. The doors flew open. They stepped inside as a butler came running down the hallway. He stopped when he saw their guns.

"Show us," Whistler said as he threw the shotgun over on a bench upholstered in Bayeux tapestry. The servant walked in front of them down to the double doors that led to the dining room.

Canaan flashed his shield and said, "Step aside and don't bother calling the police." He handed Whistler the aluminum case. "I think Whistler should do the honors."

There was a babble of voices coming from the dining room. It came at them in a rush when they opened the doors and went into the room.

"Sit the fuck down," Bellerose said, his gun held out to his side, pointed at the floor, but there for all to see.

May Tuckerman, Monsignor Moynihan, Shirley Quon, Frank Menifee, Ralph Parker, Henry Warsaw, and Emmet Tillman all sat down. Walter Cape was already seated up at the head of the table. Apparently he'd never even moved at the sound of the shotgun blasts.

There was nobody sitting at the foot of the table. Whistler put the case down and snapped open the catches.

"You people would sell your own mothers, sons, and daughters to make a dollar. Some of you would even want to watch what assholes like Walter Cape would do to them."

"Be careful," Cape said.

"Another time, another place, you'd be creeping up to tourists on the street selling them dirty postcards. What the hell, that's not so bad. Isn't that what you'd say? But that's not the worst. You sell pictures of women being mutilated, humiliated, even killed. Not only women but also little children. You're a child fucker and a child killer."

He lifted the lid, and the steam from the dry ice came out in a stinking cloud.

"I want you people to see the sort of thing he does."

He took out the bloated, battered, rotting head by the thick, coarse, shining, black hair and rolled it down the table. Bits of flesh and corruption spattered the linen tablecloth, gowns, and shirtfronts. When it reached Cape, he threw out his hands to keep it from falling into his lap.

Nobody screamed or fainted. Nobody got sick into the mousse. They just got up, one by one, walking past Bellerose, Canaan, and Whistler and out the door. Out of the room, out through the shattered front doors, stumbling to their cars and leaving Walter Cape sitting at the head of his table, staring into the dead eyes of Lim Shu Dok.

Forty-two

BOSCO SAT down at the table with Whistler. The rain had stopped. The night air was so clear, you could bottle it and sell it to Vermont. The four corners were crawling with chickens, chicken hawks, whores, twangy boys, grifters, drifters, and undercover cops with ear-to-ear grins wiped across their faces like jelly smears.

Whistler was adding up his assets.

"That was a terrible thing you did," Bosco said in a neutral voice.

Whistler took Bosco's gaze head-on and nodded. "It was,

Bosco. I admit it. But in a funny way it gave Lim Shu a chance to get something back. She'll be buried, with nothing missing, in the morning."

Bosco pointed to Whistler's calculations with his chin. "Doing your bookkeeping?"

"I got two hundred bucks from Tillman for driving Shiela home. I spent fifty on Officer Schoonover, seven bucks on the sandwiches for the gazoony at the morgue. Also I gave that Charlie fifty. It costs me fifteen bucks for the cab to LAX and a hundred twenty-nine bucks on my plastic to New Orleans. Then there was two hundred fifty for that cassette, forty bucks for the hotel room, and ten bucks for rental on the video machine. Ten and five to bribe Crib Coxey."

"You got the Mickey Mouse can opener," Bosco said, his eyes on the paper, following Whistler's calculations with great care.

"Credit, fifty-nine cents. Car rental, thirty-eight bucks a day, two days. Oh, for Christ's sake. Two times one hundred seventy-eight dollars, two airfares from New Orleans to L.A."

"How come a hundred twenty-nine going, a hundred seventy-eight coming back?"

"We were in a hurry and couldn't get a direct flight. Taxi back from LAX."

"You figure in gasoline for your own car, meals out of town, and so forth?"

"I got it here under incidentals. I figure a hundred."

"You should get out of the business, Whistler. You're not doing very good."

"I don't count the meals Shiela and me had together," Whistler said, finishing his thought.

"They were like dates?"

"That's right."

"How is Shiela? You don't come in together anymore."

Whistler hesitated for just a breath. Then he said, "She got an offer for a picture shooting in New York City. Six weeks and some billing."

"There's a lot of runaway production nowadays."

"No more major studios like the old days." Whistler sighed. "So, whattaya know, Bosco? I'm on my own again."

"I never like to say I told you so."

"What are you talking about? You say it all the time. What did you tell me that you think I should remember?"

"I said iron rusts. And I said you should never try to eat the holes in Swiss cheese."

MORE MYSTERIOUS PLEASURES

HAROLD ADAMS
MURDER
Carl Wilcox debuts in a story of triple murder which exposes the underbelly of corruption in the town of Corden, shattering the respectability of its most dignified citizens.   #501 $3.50

THE NAKED LIAR
When a sexy young widow is framed for the murder of her husband, Carl Wilcox comes through to help her fight off cops and big-city goons.
#420 $3.95

THE FOURTH WIDOW
Ex-con/private eye Carl Wilcox is back, investigating the death of a "popular" widow in the Depression-era town of Corden, S.D.
#502 $3.50

EARL DERR BIGGERS
THE HOUSE WITHOUT A KEY
Charlie Chan debuts in the Honolulu investigation of an expatriate Bostonian's murder.   #421 $3.95

THE CHINESE PARROT
Charlie Chan works to find the key to murders seemingly without victims—but which have left a multitude of clues.   #503 $3.95

BEHIND THAT CURTAIN
Two murders sixteen years apart, one in London, one in San Francisco, each share a major clue in a pair of velvet Chinese slippers. Chan seeks the connection.   #504 $3.95

THE BLACK CAMEL
When movie goddess Sheila Fane is murdered in her Hawaiian pavilion, Chan discovers an interrelated crime in a murky Hollywood mystery from the past.   #505 $3.95

CHARLIE CHAN CARRIES ON
An elusive transcontinental killer dogs the heels of the Lofton Round the World Cruise. When the touring party reaches Honolulu, the murderer finally meets his match.   #506 $3.95

JAMES M. CAIN
THE ENCHANTED ISLE
A beautiful runaway is involved in a deadly bank robbery in this posthumously published novel. #415 $3.95

CLOUD NINE
Two brothers—one good, one evil—battle over a million-dollar land deal and a luscious 16-year-old in this posthumously published novel.
#507 $3.95

ROBERT CAMPBELL
IN LA-LA LAND WE TRUST
Child porn, snuff films, and drunken TV stars in fast cars—that's what makes the L.A. world go 'round. Whistler, a luckless P.I., finds that it's not good to know too much about the porn trade in the City of Angels.
#508 $3.95

GEORGE C. CHESBRO
VEIL
Clairvoyant artist Veil Kendry volunteers to be tested at the Institute for Human Studies and finds that his life is in deadly peril; is he threatened by the Institute, the Army, or the CIA? #509 $3.95

WILLIAM L. DeANDREA
THE LUNATIC FRINGE
Police Commissioner Teddy Roosevelt and Officer Dennis Muldoon comb 1896 New York for a missing exotic dancer who holds the key to the murder of a prominent political cartoonist. #306 $3.95.

SNARK
Espionage agent Bellman must locate the missing director of British Intelligence—and elude a master terrorist who has sworn to kill him.
#510 $3.50

KILLED IN THE ACT
Brash, witty Matt Cobb, TV network troubleshooter, must contend with bizarre crimes connected with a TV spectacular—one of which is a murder committed before 40 million witnesses. #511 $3.50

KILLED WITH A PASSION
In seeking to clear an old college friend of murder, Matt Cobb must deal with the Mad Karate Killer and the Organic Hit Man, among other eccentric criminals. #512 $3.50

KILLED ON THE ICE
When a famous psychiatrist is stabbed in a Manhattan skating rink, Matt Cobb finds it necessary to protect a beautiful Olympic skater who appears to be the next victim. #513 $3.50

JAMES ELLROY
SUICIDE HILL
Brilliant L.A. Police sergeant Lloyd Hopkins teams up with the FBI to solve a series of inside bank robberies—but is he working with or against them? #514 $3.95

PAUL ENGLEMAN
CATCH A FALLEN ANGEL
Private eye Mark Renzler becomes involved in publishing mayhem and murder when two slick mens' magazines battle for control of the lucrative market. #515 $3.50

LOREN D. ESTLEMAN
ROSES ARE DEAD
Someone's put a contract out on freelance hit man Peter Macklin. Is he as good as the killers on his trail? #516 $3.95

ANY MAN'S DEATH
Hit man Peter Macklin is engaged to keep a famous television evangelist *alive*—quite a switch from his normal line. #517 $3.95

DICK FRANCIS
THE SPORT OF QUEENS
The autobiography of the celebrated race jockey/crime novelist.
#410 $3.95

JOHN GARDNER
THE GARDEN OF WEAPONS
Big Herbie Kruger returns to East Berlin to uncover a double agent. He confronts his own past and life's only certainty—death.
#103 $4.50

BRIAN GARFIELD
DEATH WISH
Paul Benjamin is a modern-day New York vigilante, stalking the rapist-killers who victimized his wife and daughter. The basis for the Charles Bronson movie. #301 $3.95

DEATH SENTENCE
A riveting sequel to *Death Wish*. The action moves to Chicago as Paul Benjamin continues his heroic (or is it psychotic?) mission to make city streets safe. #302 $3.95

TRIPWIRE
A crime novel set in the American West of the late 1800s. Boag, a black outlaw, seeks revenge on the white cohorts who left him for dead. "One of the most compelling characters in recent fiction."—Robert Ludlum. #303 $3.95

FEAR IN A HANDFUL OF DUST
Four psychiatrists, three men and a woman, struggle across the blazing Arizona desert—pursued by a fanatic killer they themselves have judged insane. "Unique and disturbing."—Alfred Coppel. #304 $3.95

JOE GORES
A TIME OF PREDATORS
When Paula Halstead kills herself after witnessing a horrid crime, her husband vows to avenge her death. Winner of the Edgar Allan Poe Award. #215 $3.95

COME MORNING
Two million in diamonds are at stake, and the ex-con who knows their whereabouts may have trouble staying alive if he turns them up at the wrong moment. #518 $3.95

NAT HENTOFF
BLUES FOR CHARLIE DARWIN
Gritty, colorful Greenwich Village sets the scene for Noah Green and Sam McKibbon, two street-wise New York cops who are as at home in jazz clubs as they are at a homicide scene. #208 $3.95

THE MAN FROM INTERNAL AFFAIRS
Detective Noah Green wants to know who's stuffing corpses into East Village garbage cans . . . and who's lying about him to the Internal Affairs Division. #409 $3.95

PATRICIA HIGHSMITH
THE BLUNDERER
An unhappy husband attempts to kill his wife by applying the murderous methods of another man. When things go wrong, he pays a visit to the more successful killer—a dreadful error. #305 $3.95

DOUG HORNIG
THE DARK SIDE
Insurance detective Loren Swift is called to a rural commune to investigate a carbon-monoxide murder. Are the commune inhabitants as gentle as they seem? #519 $3.95

P.D. JAMES/T.A. CRITCHLEY
THE MAUL AND THE PEAR TREE
The noted mystery novelist teams up with a police historian to create a fascinating factual account of the 1811 Ratcliffe Highway murders. #520 $3.95

STUART KAMINSKY'S "TOBY PETERS" SERIES
NEVER CROSS A VAMPIRE
When Bela Lugosi receives a dead bat in the mail, Toby tries to catch the prankster. But Toby's time is at a premium because he's also trying to clear William Faulkner of a murder charge! #107 $3.95

HIGH MIDNIGHT
When Gary Cooper and Ernest Hemingway come to Toby for protection, he tries to save them from vicious blackmailers.   #106 $3.95

HE DONE HER WRONG
Someone has stolen Mae West's autobiography, and when she asks Toby to come up and see her sometime, he doesn't know how deadly a visit it could be.   #105 $3.95

BULLET FOR A STAR
Warner Brothers hires Toby Peters to clear the name of Errol Flynn, a blackmail victim with a penchant for young girls. The first novel in the acclaimed Hollywood-based private eye series.   #308 $3.95

THE FALA FACTOR
Toby comes to the rescue of lady-in-distress Eleanor Roosevelt, and must match wits with a right-wing fanatic who is scheming to overthrow the U.S. Government.   #309 $3.95

JOSEPH KOENIG
FLOATER
Florida Everglades sheriff Buck White matches wits with a Miami murder-and-larceny team who just may have hidden his ex-wife's corpse in a remote bayou.   #521 $3.50

ELMORE LEONARD
THE HUNTED
Long out of print, this 1974 novel by the author of *Glitz* details the attempts of a man to escape killers from his past.   #401 $3.95

MR. MAJESTYK
Sometimes bad guys can push a good man too far, and when that good guy is a Special Forces veteran, everyone had better duck.
     #402 $3.95

THE BIG BOUNCE
Suspense and black comedy are cleverly combined in this tale of a dangerous drifter's affair with a beautiful woman out for kicks.
     #403 $3.95

ELSA LEWIN
I, ANNA
A recently divorced woman commits murder to avenge her degradation at the hands of a sleazy lothario.   #522 $3.50

THOMAS MAXWELL
KISS ME ONCE
An epic *roman noir* which explores the romantic but seamy underworld of New York during the WWII years. When the good guys are off fighting in Europe, the bad guys run amok in America.
     #523 $3.95

ED McBAIN
ANOTHER PART OF THE CITY
The master of the police procedural moves from the fictional 87th precinct to the gritty reality of Manhattan. "McBain's best in several years."—*San Francisco Chronicle*.   #524 $3.95

SNOW WHITE AND ROSE RED
A beautiful heiress confined to a sanitarium engages Matthew Hope to free her—and her $650,000.   #414 $3.95

CINDERELLA
A dead detective and a hot young hooker lead Matthew Hope into a multi-layered plot among Miami cocaine dealers. "A gem of sting and countersting."—*Time*.   #525 $3.95

PETER O'DONNELL
MODESTY BLAISE
Modesty and Willie Garvin must protect a shipment of diamonds from a gentleman about to murder his lover and an *un*civilized sheik.   #216 $3.95

SABRE TOOTH
Modesty faces Willie's apparent betrayal and a modern-day Genghis Khan who wants her for his mercenary army.   #217 $3.95

A TASTE FOR DEATH
Modesty and Willie are pitted against a giant enemy in the Sahara, where their only hope of escape is a blind girl whose time is running out.   #218 $3.95

I, LUCIFER
Some people carry a nickname too far . . . like the maniac calling himself Lucifer. He's targeted 120 souls, and Modesty and Willie find they have a personal stake in stopping him.   #219 $3.95

THE IMPOSSIBLE VIRGIN
Modesty fights for her soul when she and Willie attempt to rescue an albino girl from the evil Brunel, who lusts after the secret power of an idol called the Impossible Virgin.   #220 $3.95

DEAD MAN'S HANDLE
Modesty Blaise must deal with a brainwashed—and deadly—Willie Garvin as well as with a host of outré religion-crazed villains.
                    #526 $3.95

ELIZABETH PETERS
CROCODILE ON THE SANDBANK
Amelia Peabody's trip to Egypt brings her face to face with an ancient mystery. With the help of Radcliffe Emerson, she uncovers a tomb and the solution to a deadly threat.   #209 $3.95

THE CURSE OF THE PHAROAHS
Amelia and Radcliffe Emerson head for Egypt to excavate a cursed tomb but must confront the burial ground's evil history before it claims them both. #210 $3.95

THE SEVENTH SINNER
Murder in an ancient subterranean Roman temple sparks Jacqueline Kirby's first recorded case. #411 $3.95

THE MURDERS OF RICHARD III
Death by archaic means haunts the costumed weekend get-together of a group of eccentric Ricardians. #412 $3.95

ANTHONY PRICE
THE LABYRINTH MAKERS
Dr. David Audley does his job too well in his first documented case, embarrassing British Intelligence, the CIA, and the KGB in one swoop.
#404 $3.95

THE ALAMUT AMBUSH
Alamut, in Northern Persia, is considered by many to be the original home of terrorism. Audley moves to the Mideast to put the cap on an explosive threat. #405 $3.95

COLONEL BUTLER'S WOLF
The Soviets are recruiting spies from among Oxford's best and brightest; it's up to Dr. Audley to identify the Russian wolf in don's clothing.
#527 $3.95

OCTOBER MEN
Dr. Audley's "holiday" in Rome stirs up old Intelligence feuds and echoes of partisan warfare during World War II—and leads him into new danger. #529 $3.95

OTHER PATHS TO GLORY
What can a World War I battlefield in France have in common with a deadly secret of the present? A modern assault on Bouillet Wood leads to the answers. #530 $3.95

SION CROSSING
What does the chairman of a new NATO-like committee have to do with the American Civil War? Audley travels to Georgia in this espionage thriller. #406 $3.95

HERE BE MONSTERS
The assassination of an American veteran forces Dr. David Audley into a confrontation with undercover KGB agents. #528 $3.95

BILL PRONZINI AND JOHN LUTZ
THE EYE
A lunatic watches over the residents of West 98th Street with a powerful telescope. When his "children" displease him, he is swift to mete out deadly punishment. #408 $3.95

PATRICK RUELL
RED CHRISTMAS
Murderers and political terrorists come down the chimney during an old-fashioned Dickensian Christmas at a British country inn.

#531 $3.50

DEATH TAKES THE LOW ROAD
William Hazlitt, a universtiy administrator who moonlights as a Soviet mole, is on the run from both Russian and British agents who want him to assassinate an African general. #532 $3.50

DELL SHANNON
CASE PENDING
In the first novel in the best-selling series, Lt. Luis Mendoza must solve a series of horrifying Los Angeles mutilation murders. #211 $3.95

THE ACE OF SPADES
When the police find an overdosed junkie, they're ready to write off the case—until the autopsy reveals that this junkie *wasn't* a junkie. #212 $3.95

EXTRA KILL
In "The Temple of Mystic Truth," Mendoza discovers idol worship, pornography, murder, and the clue to the death of a Los Angeles patrolman. #213 $3.95

KNAVE OF HEARTS
Mendoza must clear the name of the L.A.P.D. when it's discovered that an innocent man has been executed and the real killer is still on the loose. #214 $3.95

DEATH OF A BUSYBODY
When the West Coast's most industrious gossip and meddler turns up dead in a freight yard, Mendoza must work without clues to find the killer of a woman who had offended nearly everyone in Los Angeles. #315 $3.95

DOUBLE BLUFF
Mendoza goes against the evidence to dissect what looks like an air-tight case against suspected wife-killer Francis Ingram—a man the lieutenant insists is too nice to be a murderer. #316 $3.95

MARK OF MURDER
Mendoza investigates the near-fatal attack on an old friend as well as trying to track down an insane serial killer. #417 $3.95

ROOT OF ALL EVIL
The murder of a "nice" girl leads Mendoza to team up with the FBI in the search for her not-so-nice boyfriend—a Soviet agent. #418 $3.95

JULIE SMITH

TRUE-LIFE ADVENTURE
Paul McDonald earned a meager living ghosting reports for a San Francisco private eye until the gumshoe turned up dead . . . now the killers are after him.   #407 $3.95

TOURIST TRAP
A lunatic is out to destroy San Francisco's tourism industry; can feisty lawyer/sleuth Rebecca Schwartz stop him while clearing an innocent man of a murder charge?   #533 $3.95

ROSS H. SPENCER

THE MISSING BISHOP
Chicago P.I. Buzz Deckard has a missing person to find. Unfortunately his client has disappeared as well, and no one else seems to be who or what they claim.   #416 $3.50

MONASTERY NIGHTMARE
Chicago P.I. Luke Lassiter tries his hand at writing novels, and encounters murder in an abandoned monastery.   #534 $3.50

REX STOUT

UNDER THE ANDES
A long-lost 1914 fantasy novel from the creator of the immortal Nero Wolfe series. "The most exciting yarn we have read since *Tarzan of the Apes.*"—*All-Story Magazine*.   #419 $3.50

ROSS THOMAS

CAST A YELLOW SHADOW
McCorkle's wife is kidnapped by agents of the South African government. The ransom—his cohort Padillo must assassinate their prime minister.   #535 $3.95

THE SINGAPORE WINK
Ex-Hollywood stunt man Ed Cauthorne is offered $25,000 to search for colleague Angelo Sacchetti—a man he thought he'd killed in Singapore two years earlier.   #536 $3.95

THE FOOLS IN TOWN ARE ON OUR SIDE
Lucifer Dye, just resigned from a top secret U.S. Intelligence post, accepts a princely fee to undertake the corruption of an entire American city.   #537 $3.95

JIM THOMPSON

THE KILL-OFF
Luanne Devore was loathed by everyone in her small New England town. Her plots and designs threatened to destroy them—unless they destroyed her first.   #538 $3.95

DONALD E. WESTLAKE
THE HOT ROCK
The unlucky master thief John Dortmunder debuts in this spectacular caper novel. How many times do you have to steal an emerald to make sure it *stays* stolen? #539 $3.95

BANK SHOT
Dortmunder and company return. A bank is temporarily housed in a trailer, so why not just hook it up and make off with the whole shebang? Too bad nothing is ever that simple. #540 $3.95

THE BUSY BODY
Aloysius Engel is a gangster, the Big Man's right hand. So when he's ordered to dig a suit loaded with drugs out of a fresh grave, how come the corpse it's wrapped around won't lie still? #541 $3.95

THE SPY IN THE OINTMENT
Pacifist agitator J. Eugene Raxford is mistakenly listed as a terrorist by the FBI, which leads to his enforced recruitment to a group bent on world domination. Will very good Good triumph over absolutely villainous Evil? #542 $3.95

GOD SAVE THE MARK
Fred Fitch is the sucker's sucker—con men line up to bilk him. But when he inherits $300,000 from a murdered uncle, he finds it necessary to dodge killers as well as hustlers. #543 $3.95

TERI WHITE
TIGHTROPE
This second novel featuring L.A. cops Blue Maguire and Spaceman Kowalski takes them into the nooks and crannies of the city's Little Saigon. #544 $3.95

COLLIN WILCOX
VICTIMS
Lt. Frank Hastings investigates the murder of a police colleague in the home of a powerful—and nasty—San Francisco attorney. #413 $3.95

NIGHT GAMES
Lt. Frank Hastings of the San Francisco Police returns to investigate the at-home death of an unfaithful husband—whose affairs have led to his murder. #545 $3.95

DAVID WILLIAMS' "MARK TREASURE" SERIES

UNHOLY WRIT
London financier Mark Treasure helps a friend reaquire some property. He stays to unravel the mystery when a Shakespeare manuscript is discovered and foul murder done.   #112 $3.95

TREASURE BY DEGREES
Mark Treasure discovers there's nothing funny about a board game called "Funny Farms." When he becomes involved in the takeover struggle for a small university, he also finds there's nothing funny about murder.   #113 $3.95

■ ■